HARDROCK
Crazy Jake's Fish Bomb

L. Bracken — *Author*

New Flight Books — *Publisher*

HARDROCK
Crazy Jake's Fish Bomb
Publisher: New Flight Books | www.hardrockbooks.com | V5120311
Copyright © 2009 by Lisa Bracken
All rights reserved.

ISBN 978-0-615-33706-7
Paperback: 5.5" x 8.5" - print-on-demand (POD)
Adult fiction / humor

Library of Congress Control Number: 2009913933

Cover notes: Photographs of rough-tooled, wood-burned leather together with a fictitious portrayal of Quartz Creek Inn comprise the cover's original graphic design. Tooled segments portray seven species of flora common to the Colorado high country: blue spruce, oak, mushroom, fern, sunflower, columbine and wild rose. The photograph of the Inn is anchored at each corner with a photograph of a handmade rivet taken from the leather holster Dad made to carry his .44 magnum revolver, a Ruger Super Blackhawk. HARDROCK title font is in Open Type Zebrawood. Book text font is Times New Roman.

Trademark information is listed on the following page.

Trademarks and Trademark Registrants

HARDROCK (stylized series title); *HARDROCK Crazy Jake's Fish Bomb* and *End of the road. Beginning of hilarious adventure*... are trademarks of Lisa Bracken

All other trademark references used in this publication are used for purposes of description only and are used without permission from the trademark owner. The use of any trademark does not imply endorsement, sponsorship or association of any kind between the owner of the trademark and the author or publisher. All trademarks are owned by their registrants, not by the author or publisher. Trademarks used in this book together with their registrants follow: (Note: The registrants of the following registered trademarks are believed to be accurate as of December, 2009. Any omissions or incorrect references are a regretted oversight with apologies from the publisher. Further trademark information may be found at www.uspto.gov)

Trademark(s)	Registrant
Looney Tunes	Warner Bros. Entertainment, Inc.
Celica and *Land Cruiser*	Toyota Motor Corporation
Chrysler and *Plymouth*	Chrysler Group LLC
Rand McNally	Rand McNally & Company
Stanley	Pacific Market International, LLC
Birkenstock	Birkenstock Orthopaedie GmbH & Co.
Lord & Taylor	Lord & Taylor LLC
Ruger and *Blackhawk*	Sturm, Ruger & Company, Inc.
Budweiser	Anheuser-Busch, Inc.
Miller High Life	MillerCoors LLC
Kansas State University	Kansas State University
Froot Loops	Kellogg Company
M&M's	Mars, Inc.
Ladies' Home Journal	Meredith Corporation
Wile E. Coyote and *Road Runner*	Warner Bros. Entertainment, Inc.
Barbie	Mattel, Inc.
Scrabble	Hasbro, Inc.
Ford and *Bronco* and *Fairlane*	Ford Motor Company
Muppets and *Kermit*	The Muppets Studio, LLC
Lil' Abner	Capp Enterprises, Inc.
Rolling Stones	Musidor B.V. LLC.
Eagles	Eagles, Ltd.
The Doobie Brothers	The Doobie Brothers Corp.
Lynyrd Skynyrd	Lynyrd Skynyrd Productions, Inc.
The Allman Brothers Band	The ABB Merchandising Co., Inc.
Gunne Sax	Jessica McClintock, Inc,
The Flintstones	Hanna Barbera Productions, Inc.

A Grateful Measure of Thanks

To My Family ~ This book is dedicated to my family with great appreciation for their enduring encouragement. Thank you for the countless reading sessions and your insightful suggestions. Your giggles, laughter and even perplexed expressions aided immeasurably in crafting this book's final form. The spontaneous, public eruptions of laughter at recounting a particularly descriptive scene has been a social side-effect of this work for which I apologize. Mom, thanks for allowing me to exploit and exaggerate some of your most endearing qualities for the benefit of readers' joy. I know you now cannot collect turkeys or reach for a canned good without passersby speculating as to your seemingly uninspired chuckling. Dad, thanks for staying on my ass to get this done, shepherding it through to fruition and most of all, for our long ago journey into the mountains.

To my best friend, daughter and guiding inspiration behind countless adventures. Here's to life's greatest gifts and everlasting goofiness!

To Tuck-Tuck and Dacalackus. There are no words to express the gratitude I feel for your eternal, quiet patience and devotion as I wrote and endlessly edited this book. Waiting quietly beside me just for a few minutes to sit together in a chair or play ball. My lovies, tuna and steak could never fully reward such gifts of singular loyalty.

Unfortunately, this project outlasted a number of family members and friends who, over the past twenty years, had been patiently awaiting its release. Thankfully, shared stories over the phone seemed to aid one person's house-bound condition, though not without falling out of her chair from time to time due to uncontrollable giggle fits. Sorry about that... you, alone, are the reason for the sub-title.

L. Bracken | HARDROCK - *Crazy Jake's Fish Bomb*

For those of you who remain, have patiently awaited the release of this book, quietly encouraged and sometimes politely if not effectively demanded my haste, well... the larger font is just for you. Hopefully you aren't yet past the point of bifocals.

Carol, a very special thank you for catching the glaring errors in this book's initial release. Your skilled eye saved me from a good deal of my own embarrassing dumb-assery. And, Bev - my good friend and great librarian, thanks for that useful word!

To My Readers ~ Thank you for your purchase of this book. Your purchase will help facilitate future printings, a second book in this series now awaiting edits, and a new coat of paint and wheel hub on Big Red. Profits will also help replenish the trees used in this book's physical production.

Like the most entertaining fiction, life is a composite of experiences distilled into a unique, personal perspective. I hope this book contributes in some meaningful way to the design of your joy, the wealth of your life.

As you close the back cover, I hope you will have had as much fun reading these stories as I have had writing them.

Until the second in the series... please enjoy!

HARDROCK
Crazy Jake's Fish Bomb
Table of Contents

Rocky Mountain Bound - 7

Quartz Creek Inn - 21

The Hardrock Welcoming Committee… as it were - 32

The Gamblers - 44

Coyote Blind - 58

Cooking With Joe and Al - 84

Myth or Mystery… - 97

Crazy Jake's Fish Bomb - 109

The Legend of the Rat Man - 124

The Ladies' Society of Diamond Hills Luncheon - 142

Amy Wilson's Pool Party - 162

Peevil's Revenge - 174

Bear Feet and Bare Ass - 187

Turkey Run - 206

A Tale of Two Deer - 221

A Hardrock Thanksgiving - 231

Tic's Addiction - 282

Christmas Eve Miracle at the Church of Hardrock - 294

Sadie Hawkin's Dance - 311

Winter Hazards - 339

Rocky Mountain Bound

Mother and I stood in our suburban driveway waiting for Dad to silence the deep rumbling engine of the "Water Buffalo" motorcycle he'd borrowed from John, our neighbor. John's sixteen-year-old son, Wes, was pulling off his helmet and lifting off of his smaller street bike.

The pair wore the gritty, ruddy faces of time and miles remnant of their journey back from the Colorado Rockies where they'd gone two weeks before in search of mountain frontier or what might be left of it.

Hungry for clues that would communicate the story of what they might have found, I visually devoured Dad's bike, his bedroll and saddlebags, the bugs on the windshield. The road-cobbled ensemble exuded a scent of acrid tailpipe, worn leather, sweet grass and wind. I stood breathing it in, awaiting the venerating truth to roll from Dad's cracked lips.

He was our questing hero who had gone in defiant search of a different reality — someplace far from the smoggy, crowded, cookie-cutter lifestyle we had come to quietly begrudge for half a decade in the oil-boom south Texas metropolis that was 1979 Houston.

"Well," Dad grinned at Mother and me, his brown eyes dancing in the low angle of the afternoon sun, "how long will it take you two to pack?"

For most people, such a statement would amuse and

inspire a light line of interested questioning.

But, I knew Dad.

The new, three-bedroom, two-bath house in Memorial Glen subdivision, complete with its azure-blue carpeting, white walls and chrome fixtures, was the fifth house I remembered living in since I was seven. Dad had a habit of rolling in and out of professions, few of which captivated his attention longer than a year or two and many of which he engaged in simultaneously.

A mid-century renaissance man, I'd known Dad as an artist, welder, photographer, diver, cowboy and saddle-maker. He'd been a building contractor, candle-maker, jeweler, arts director, sporting goods salesman, street cop and federal investigator. Together, he and Mother had established and sold several businesses like a steak house, drive-in, and a diesel gas station. For the past year, he'd been an executive with the phone company. Extraordinarily capable, more than anything, Dad was easily bored and perpetually attuned to life's next adventure.

That glint in his eye. That grin. It was all I needed to see.

Wordlessly, I ran into the house, upturned drawers out of my dresser and dumped their contents onto the bed. Soon, we'd be on an exciting new adventure, off to the mountains of Colorado.

Events from a couple of weeks previous had set everything in motion when Dad walked in the front door on a Friday evening following a two-hour commute. Mother had come home an hour earlier. I'd been home since four, miserably hammering on long division and noun modifiers in between episodes of *Bewitched* and *Gilligan's Island.*

Mother had come home exhausted and frustrated, unable to buy gas for her car due to the fuel shortage. She shouted into my room on her way down the hall, "Tomorrow morning, you'll need to get up at five, so we can get in line for gas. I'm packing a cooler, so we shouldn't get thirsty like last time."

'Last time' was three hours in ninety-four degree heat without anything to eat or drink. Unable to run the air conditioner because it gobbled gas, Mother and I had bickered like rats while waiting impatiently in a gas line extending for blocks. When we'd finally inched our way to the pumps, it was only to find the station had run out of gas twenty minutes earlier. A few days before, someone had been shot while waiting in a similar line. Probably brought on by bickering in a hot car.

"But I'll miss *Looney Tunes!*" I protested.

Mother was in no mood to argue and snapped impatiently from down the hall, "I have to find that blue fabric for your school uniform, and getting to the mall means getting gas. You have to come with me because you have to try on shoes…" her voice trailed away as she presumably walked into the master bathroom or maybe the walk-in closet. As accounting manager of the southern division of the largest home builder in the country, she was at the back end of a long week of confrontations with her new supervisor.

I heard Dad's car drive up an hour later and I walked out of my bedroom to find Mother standing in a pair of cut-offs and a halter top, barefoot on the patio, pouring water onto the skirt belonging to her new pastel, polyester suit. It lie in a heap at her feet, and she stood over it with a watering can just as if she were watering one of the house plants.

"How come you're watering your skirt?" I asked

She sighed, "The zipper broke." Long pause. "I had to cut myself out of it."

"Oh…" I absorbed the scene. "So, why are you pouring water on it?"

"I don't know," she sighed. "It just… it just seems like the thing to do."

"Dad's home."

"Okay."

Dad walked in, gave me a kiss hello and walked out to greet Mother on the patio. He stood watching her a minute then put his arm around her shoulder and asked gently, "Whatcha doin', hon?"

Mother was now stepping lightly onto the skirt, watching the water squish between her toes and run off the edge of the concrete.

"Drying my skirt."

"Huh..." Long pause. "Is there any dinner?"

Mother looked at him. "I forgot to turn on the slow cooker. So, unless you want raw chicken and potatoes, no."

Dad looked at the skirt. "You okay?"

"I'm just tired. It seems like no matter how hard we try to get ahead, we just get further and further behind. I'm just tired."

Dad drew Mother closer. Quietly, he gazed beyond our backyard into the swampy woods that would soon fall in the next phase of the subdivision she signed corporate checks to support.

He looked up at the sky then back into the woods. "I was standing at my office window today when the V.P. came in and asked me what I was doing. I told him I was considering captivity. He said, 'What do you mean?' I told him to look out over the city, and I asked him what he saw. He said, 'One-point-three million people who need phone service.' I said, what's out there is a world of possibilities. And every day, you, I and everyone else in this high rise live our lives in one of a thousand little gray boxes. We're never out there. We live in a cage. Of course, he tried to convince me that being handed an executive position off the street with the phone company was the chance of a lifetime and I just needed to give it more time. But, I told him I won't live in a cage, even if it's one of my own making. So, I handed him my briefcase and walked out."

"You resigned?"

"I chewed through the bars."

Mother studied Dad's face, frantic flickers playing about her eyes.

"Forget about dinner," Dad hugged Mother close. "Let's just go get a pizza."

Mother looked up. "Can't. We can't afford it."

"What do you mean we can't afford it? We pull down a hundred-thirty thousand between us, and we can't go out for a pizza?"

"That's what I mean. There's the mortgage, insurance, car lease, credit cards, groceries — I mean, every paycheck is a string of payments going right back out the door."

"We can't even afford a damn pizza?"

"Nope. I can make us some peanut butter and jelly sandwiches."

"Okay. Throw 'em in a cooler, and we'll drive up to Conroe. Watch the moon come up over the lake."

"We can't do that either. No gas."

At around noon the next day, when Mother and I returned from filling the tank on her little yellow Celica, we found Dad in the garage tightening the rope on a bedroll fastened to the back of our neighbor's motorcycle.

"Whatcha doin', hon?" Mother asked in a tone similar to Dad's the night before. She shut the driver's side door, and I grabbed the shopping bags out of the car as we walked into the garage.

Dad pulled down on a knot and adjusted the pack he'd tied on top of the bedroll. "Wes and I are heading to Colorado. Nose around, see what we can find."

She paused, considering what he might mean. "What are you looking for?"

Dad leaned over and gave Mother a peck. "Well, after I find the siphon to get some gas out of your tank… possibilities, darlin', possibilities."

So, here we were two weeks later. Dad and Wes had returned, and I could hardly wait to hear what possibilities Dad had uncovered.

During the animated conversation which ran late that evening around our coffee table strewn with kippers, garlic, mustard and saltines, Dad sketched a map to a place called Hardrock.

"It's up in the mountains," he said, tapping the paper

with his pencil. "Remote as hell. Wilderness." He looked at Mother. "We need to get out of this city, get to know each other again. We never see each other anymore. Hardrock's a damn sight better place to raise a family. You've got maybe a dozen year-round residents. Clean air. No traffic. No crime." He arched an eyebrow in reference to law enforcement, his longest running career and the one which had kept Mother up nights worrying.

"But, what about work?" Mother looked mildly concerned.

"That's the best part. There's a little place up there called the Quartz Creek Inn. Martin, the real estate broker, is on the board of directors. He introduced me around and they offered me the job of general manager." Dad popped a whole cracker, loaded with kippers and garlic into his mouth then grinned at Mother and I, his cheeks protruding comically.

Despite her best efforts to hedge against his infectious enthusiasm, Mother grinned back. But only a little.

"It's a neat little place," Dad continued, "only maybe an hour or so drive from Granite — that's the little town down the mountain where Lisa will go to school."

"What's in Granite?" Mother asked. "I mean, is there a grocery store?"

"Oh, yeah," Dad nodded. "It's not the Woodglen Mall, but there's a place you can get some grub."

"The mall isn't exactly my favorite place. Last year, Lisa and I were almost run down by a herd of chunky chickens stampeding for discounted candy the day after Valentine's."

"There you go. Too many people. And, let's see, there's

a bank, a library, a ranch supply store — most everyone in the area is a rancher or a potato farmer. Or a coal miner… there's a coal mine up in Bituminous just down the mountain from Hardrock. Let's see, what else is in Granite? There's a high school for Wes."

"Wes is coming too?" Mother and I asked together.

Even before Dad's work as the first juvenile officer in Oklahoma had made our home a safe haven, he and Mother were always extending our couch and kitchen table to someone in need of a place to stay. So, it wasn't surprising that Wes would be coming with us into the mountains — only news. Wes had a happy home, but his Mother, Joannie, had become concerned for his habit of frequenting late night parking lots, running with a questionable crowd and tying up their phone line with a revolving roster of amorous teenage girls.

"Yeah," Dad nodded, "he's coming, if Joannie can convince John to let him go. I think they're working on that now. He's got a year and a half left till graduation. He can help out up there until he heads to boot camp. Come home for a month or so next summer, maybe."

"So, tell me about this inn," Mother shook a cigarette out of her pack and lit it, marking the transition to the middle stage of serious discussion between her and Dad. "How in the world can a dozen people generate enough business to keep the doors open?"

"Summer tourism," Dad brightened. "There's a bunch of little lakes in the area, and, like I said, it's surrounded by wilderness, so hunters come up in the fall. Folks come up and camp at the campground by Muskrat Lake or hike up to the old abandoned rock quarry. There's a famous old generating station up there on the creek. They come up and take pictures when the aspens turn color. Oh, and there's an old mansion up in Bituminous built by the town's founder. That place is also famous, draws lots of folks. Plus, Hardrock's only maybe an hour's drive from Diamond Hills, a pretty renown celebrity hang-out, so folks from all over the world head there for ski season and drive back to Hardrock just to see what's there."

"What *is* there?" Mother peered at the small dot representing Hardrock which Dad had drawn on the sketched map and labeled *"End of the Road"*.

"Wilderness, baby, lots and lots of wilderness!"

She looked up. "Is there a house for us to live in?"

"What, you think I'm going to have you girls living in a tent up in the boonies?"

"Well?"

He rolled his eyes, "Yes, there's a house."

"And? Is it nice?"

"I don't know, I didn't go in. It looks okay, though. It's got a nice little barn, shop-type thing attached."

"It figures you'd check that out."

"Yep," Dad munched another cracker. "You'd have to walk thirty yards to work."

"How high is this place? What's the altitude?" It was a loaded question, the answer to which could make or break the whole deal. Mother feared heights and detested mountain driving.

"About eight-thousand feet, I think," he answered nonchalantly, "but, listen, hon... I know you're worried about snowy roads and all. We'll just stock up on supplies in the summer and hole up over winter," Dad winked at me and sipped his iced tea.

He continued, "Just think, no more comptrollers. No more late nights at the office. No more working holidays and weekends, well, at least not in an office. We'll bust ass four or five months out of the year during the summer tourist season," he went on, enhancing his optimistic tone, "and then, come winter, you'll be able to work on that recipe book you've always wanted to write. It'll be fun, hon."

Mother had grown silent which meant she was seriously mulling the possibilities... and possible consequences... of such a move. She was also probably considering how Dad might define 'fun'.

Dad leaned back on the couch, "There's a café and a saloon and a few hotel rooms. We'll build a trading post. We can do trail rides and jeep tours in the summer. We'll find some folks to manage the café, saloon, and the trading post, and we'll oversee the whole outfit. The place needs a little TLC, but there's a lot of opportunity up there. It's basically a resort, honey. Tourists love it. Martin says the place is overrun from May through September." He paused again, knowing that financial security was, for my mother, a perennial garden which required constant planning and tending.

I piped up, figuring my enthusiasm might win her over should Dad's prove insufficient, "So, what's the wilderness like?" I smiled, reflecting on *Jeremiah Johnson*, a favorite movie for both Dad and me.

"Oh, man," he sighed, "tall pines as far as you can see.

Snow capped peaks on the mountains... Quartz Creek, cold and crystal clear, tumbling down the mountains through the woods right behind the inn. Wes even saw a white wolf up there one morning when we were getting water out of the creek."

"No *way!*" I was beside myself with his mere description.

"Yep, and elk wander around right outside the living room windows." He reached for Mother's hand. "We can even stay open through hunting season to bring in a little extra cash if we need to. Honey, it's not like it's off someplace at the end of the world. And if things get tight, I can always find work in Bituminous or Granite."

Mother quietly listened, but her silence was about to make me hyperventilate. Good grief, I thought, what was she thinking? She hadn't even been smoking her cigarette. It just rested in the ashtray wisping away in long tendrils of blue smoke. We had transitioned to the third and final stage.

Dad's pitch was over, and I waited to hear the verdict from the Chairwoman who remained silent an inordinate amount of time. I couldn't swallow around the lump in my throat. Cripes, would she let us go? I contemplated my wretched fate should she decline.

I pictured the following Monday, returning to a school that corralled six-thousand students within its sterile concrete walls. Each weekday, I ran my trail to and from seventh grade classes and kept my head so full of rules associated with the management of such a hoard that real education was otherworldly. I craved the kind of freedom Dad spoke of, and regardless of its potential economic peril, it lured me with its promise of isolation, rugged wild terrain and unimagined adventure like a moth to flame.

Mother, of course, was wiser having seen many a moth disintegrate from its own ambition. She had grown up on the post-depression side of a farm in north-eastern Oklahoma — the eldest and therefore surrogate mother to five younger sisters and two brothers. She had lived hard times enough to hear them coming like a freight train. Like her grandmother before her, who had single-handedly defended the family from a band of rustlers, Mother was four feet, eleven-and-a-half inches of fierce, Irish determination leveraged with a steeled measure of Cherokee resilience. And it was that mix of no-nonsense fortitude that had secured her the well-paid position of accounting manger at a time and in a profession dominated by men.

Dad was proposing she not only leave the hard-fought familiar behind, but relocate to a place she had only known clouds to dwell. I knew it would only take a look from her, and it would all be over.

She reached for her cigarette and inhaled deeply, her gaze never leaving the coffee table. Dad and I looked at one another as she slowly exhaled and absently examined the glowing ash before returning the cigarette to the ashtray.

She turned and studied Dad with a look that suggested she was recounting the lyrics to a favorite Waylon Jennings song... something about not marrying a ramblin' man or a cowboy or some other thing pretty much along the lines of what she had already done.

Then she spoke, "Thirty yards to work?"

"Thirty yards."

She grinned, "Then let's sell this house and get the show on the road."

I sprang instantly from the floor and galloped toward the front door, eager to tell Wes the news. I flung open the door and met him standing on the porch wearing his broad, signature grin.

"We're *going!*" I breathed.

"Me too! Suitcase is already packed."

The cars were the first to go. Dad sold his suped-up Chrysler and settled Mother's lease. The house went on the market and sold within two weeks for enough to pay off the credit cards, secure a vehicle suitable for mountain driving and fill up the gas tanks.

By the time the thermometer nailed to the garage dipped to sixty-five, we were leading a caravan out of the west Texas hills with a red, '71 Land Cruiser, Wes' beat-up Plymouth Duster and a twenty-six foot moving van snaking into the distant mountains of Colorado, heading toward someplace called Hardrock.

*A vague but sufficient notion of a special place
in the Colorado Rockies*

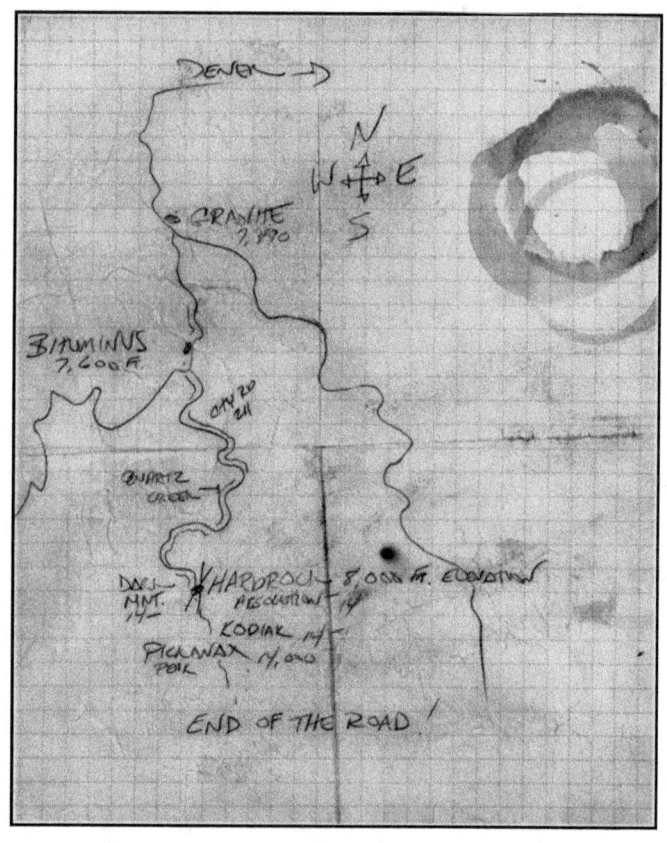

L. Bracken | HARDROCK - Crazy Jake's Fish Bomb

Quartz Creek Inn

The long, dark highway beckoned beyond Amarillo's red sunrise, and even before we'd cleared the Texas state line my eyes were straining to be the first to glimpse the Rocky Mountains looming off the high plains the way Dad said they would.

He'd said over the C.B., "You keep watching, and all of a sudden there they are — chiseled and deep blue, rising up to the sky, filling up the horizon."

Mother drove Wes' "Green Rag", as Dad referred to it, Wes drove the Land Cruiser which Dad had named "Big Red", and Dad commanded the moving van which he not so fondly referred to as the "Gas Hog".

Black coffee, a Rand McNally *Road Atlas of the United States* and the dark expanse of an open road at two in the morning gripped me in a romantic embrace yet to abate.

Linked by C.B. radios and a common destination, we crossed the plains headed west. And, suddenly, just like Dad had said, there they were.

The Rockies loomed.

At first, the range stretched long and jagged across the horizon. Then the crescent of rugged mountain peaks grew and grew until they filled the windshield. Before I could examine the details of each magnificent contour, we were rolling over the foothills.

The air had become dry, cool and crisp. Easing through low passes, the mountains gradually closed in behind us, wrapped around us and finally engulfed us in their high, rocky, spruce-clad slopes.

Periodically, we'd stop at a scenic overlook to reaffirm our grand pursuit and pry Mother's grip from the steering wheel so she might better enjoy the view from under the dash.

Mother's anxiety over roads which seemed to rise rapidly, disappear suddenly around hairpin turns or top pinnacles that dropped into gaping space culminated in an eventful episode as our caravan approached the top of the Continental Divide.

Mother had begun the trip singing giddily along with me and Jimmy Buffet on the 8-track, but, as we rose in altitude from the broad four-lane and switched to a winding two-lane highway at three-thousand feet, her enthusiastic vocals were gradually displaced with demure, tentative humming.

By the time we reached seven-thousand feet, her humming had grown much livelier.

Finally, we ascended the paved route to one of the loftiest domes on the Divide, the top of which was newly bore through with twin tubes known as the Eisenhower Tunnels. Here, her loud humming was finally displaced altogether with unusual, sporadic outbursts of decidedly non-melodic grunting.

A light snow was swirling about the snow-packed roads, and soft, four-foot mounds of fluffy, white drift lined either side of the pass. I pointed out the loveliness of the scenery to Mother who seemed intent on spoiling my enjoyment by now grunting continually and wrenching the wheel toward her in a manner which caused the 8-track to skip. Curious about this behavior, I sought advice from Dad.

Me on the C.B.: "Break one-nine. Dad, Dad? Come in, over."

Dad on C.B.: "Yeah? Over."

Me on C.B.: "Something's wrong with Mom. Over."

Dad on C.B.: "What do you mean? Do we need to pull over?"

Mother (trying to wrestle C.B. from me): "NO, NO, NO!"

Me, regaining C.B. control while scuffling with Mother over the steering wheel: "Mom doesn't want to pull over. She says there's no shoulder. But, I think we should stop or something, she's breathing weird."

Dad on C.B.: "Okay, look, you're going to have to talk her through this. Keep your voice calm and reassure her that everything is okay. All she needs to do is keep the wheel steady and keep going slow. Got that? Over."

Me on CB: "Okay, I'll give it a try. Over."

I thought it was odd that Dad had begun to refer to Mother as though she were not present and privy to the conversation. I was, however, unaware that it had once taken Dad three hours to talk Mother — six months pregnant — down out of a hundred-foot observation tower. It had been the episode that triggered her fear of heights and likely had something to do with her reluctance to appreciate sweeping vistas from an eagle's vantage point.

Here she and I were together again, this time eleven-thousand feet up.

"But, Mother," I soothed, ignorant of the tower episode, "this is beautiful! You're missing out on all the snow. And look at that creek way down there… man, does it look *tiny!*"

"grunt… grunt… grunt…"

I later learned this type of response to be a self-soothing mechanism which, when employed by persons possessed of desperate and loosely organized thoughts, should not at all be discouraged. Considering the alternative.

Dad's words echoed in my head as I recalled him briefing Mother and I on winter, mountain driving. We three sat in Wes' car, parked in his parents' Houston driveway. It had been a sunny eighty-five degrees, and there she sat in her cut-offs and Birkenstock sandals with a happy smile and twinkling eyes. Lightly, her hands rested on Wes' steering wheel. Seeming to easily contemplate slick roads, steep climbs and perilous drops, she responded calmly to Dad's gentle coaching.

"First of all, go slow in snowy and icy conditions and allow plenty of room between you and the next driver. You don't want to brake or accelerate suddenly, or you could spin out." Dad instructed. "Just gently pump your brakes. And don't ride your brakes. If you do, you could burn them out. Okay, try it. Try pumping your brakes, nice and easy."

Mother tapped the brakes, pumping them lightly. She looked over at Dad who offered positive encouragement.

"Okay, good," he continued, "and don't turn your wheel too sharp, you could spin out. Just ease into it. If you lose front-end control, just let off the gas and gently rewind your steering. If you panic and over-correct, you could really spin out.

Never hit the brakes in that situation, okay? Okay. Try that."

Mother gently realigned the steering wheel, and Dad offered a scenario, "Okay, now you're driving along, and the road looks fine, nice and clear then, *bam*, you hit a patch of black ice. Remember that? That's the ice you can't see, because it blends in with the asphalt. But it's slick, and you want to be ready for it. Okay, black ice. This time your *back* end starts to spin out and drifts a little to the right, what do you do?"

Mother let off the gas, eased the wheel to the right and started to hit the brakes.

"Good job on the gas and steering. Just gently steer into the direction of a rear spin, but remember," Dad corrected, "no hard brakes on ice. Just ease into the spin until you regain traction, and, if you get in a bind, try to aim for a snowbank. Let's try it again, black ice, left spin... what do you do?"

We spent several hours over the next four days perfecting our techniques on dry concrete, even driving to the Woodglen Mall under imagined extreme winter conditions. This didn't go over well with other Texans, who, among the most impatient drivers in the country, were accustomed to whizzing through a parking lot at eighty miles an hour while hunting a parking spot in front of Lord & Taylor.

On the plus side, their hysterical gestures and disgruntled expressions probably immeasurably aided Mother's ability to concentrate.

Now, however, near the top of the Great Divide, Mother's carefree manner had vanished. With only the top of her head peeking out from beneath a billowing, down parka, Mother clutched the steering wheel with her hands at eleven and one. Lifting three inches off the seat and craning over the dash, her wide eyes frantically swept the road ahead.

Unsure, it seemed, of what to do with her braking foot, she periodically stomped at the floorboard. Reluctant to steer too far left or right, her response was to yank the wheel toward her.

Realizing she now appeared to be having difficulty recalling Dad's important instructions, I helpfully reminded her of Dad's training.

"Be careful not to accidently hit the brakes, or we could spin out and go over a cliff."

STOMP, "grunt... grunt..."

"Remember what Dad said about hitting the brakes too quick."

STOMP, STOMP, STOMP

"Or too much."

She yanked the wheel dramatically toward her.

"Careful the steering. Remember how easy he said it was to over-correct and spin out?"

YANK, "grunt... grunt..." YANK, YANK

Quietly I sought a firmer grip on the door handle.

Finally, we entered the tunnel and Mother seemed overcome by a sense of calm, perhaps reassured by the fact it was not technically possible to slip over the side while driving inside a cylinder.

She slowed to a creeping pace, as if reluctant to exit the long portal. She fixed her gaze ahead then startled me by suddenly glancing my way and muttering, "S-s-see, we're f-fine. We're fine. I s-said we'd be fine, and now we're f-fine."

Lightning quick she jammed her hand into her purse, wrenched out a pack of cigarettes, shook one out and tossed it to her mouth where she snapped it out of the air like a bass going after a black gnat. Clenching it in her trembling lips, she flipped her lighter out of the pack's cellophane and spun the striker like a flywheel.

Were we fine? Mother didn't seem fine at all. And, now, I'd begun to wonder whether *I* was fine.

Dad's voice crackled over the C.B.: "Breaker one-nine, Lisa? What's going on? How's Mom? Over."

Silence.

Dad on C.B.: "Lisa? What the hell is going on? Answer me. *Over.*"

Me on C.B.: "grunt… grunt… grunt…"

We slowly descended into valleys then rose again, winding through Vail Pass. For most of the morning, we curled our way along a state highway that seemed to squeeze us through narrow valley passages, each one little more than a path of erosion in the grander scheme and not much more improved for vehicular transport.

Every route was flanked by a tiny, frigid-looking stream at the bottom of a cliff on one side and the sheer mammoth face of a raw-hewn mountain on the other.

Around mid-afternoon, we finally turned onto County Road 211 which was to be part of our new address. We were now approaching the dot on Dad's map.

Hardrock.

Seven slow miles later, the tight, dark fringe of towering blue spruce and clutches of bare-branched aspen yielded suddenly to a tiny haven nestled on a gently descending slope above Quartz Creek.

The house and inn seemed to each possess an initial, nearly angelic quality… as if each building were sitting quietly reserved and festooned with improvements awaiting our perfectly timed arrival.

Wes and I encouraged Mother to partake of the extraordinary setting. For such a petite woman, she was quite persistent, and it took some dexterous persuasion and leverage to first loosen her from the upholstery then dislodge her from the vehicle.

Parallel to Quartz Creek, Dark Mountain rose several thousand feet almost immediately behind the inn. It was a mirror image of Absolution Mountain which loomed as high, several hundred yards in front. Down the road a couple of miles, at the southern end of Hardrock, rested the twin pinnacles of Kodiak Mountain and Pickanaxe Peak. Beyond that, endless wilderness. We were cradled at eight-thousand feet in the rugged, stony heights of fourteen-thousand foot giants.

Within a few minutes, the inn revealed itself through my fog of euphoria.

Did I use the word "improvements" in a preceding paragraph? I apologize for the misleading description. Improvement technically suggests some manner of betterment through the application of effort.

The only evidence of such an effort was what appeared to be a gaping hole in the south end of the building, indicating a half-hearted attempt at leveling the 260-foot long, two-storied, lumpy-roofed structure languishing in the snow. Apparently, the bulldozer operator had been overcome by depression at gazing upon it and left with the improvement project incomplete.

As we stood pondering the scene, a crest of snow slid from the roof of the inn into the interior of what must have once been a motel room.

"This is utterly righteous!" Wes exclaimed as he loped off on lanky legs to explore more of the inn and its surroundings than his first trip had allowed.

"Dad, this is *so* cool," I said, in awe of the grandeur, the beauty, the exhilarating, enveloping sense of complete liberation. The air smelled exceptionally clean — a crisp, thin atmospheric cocktail of sunshine, chlorophyll and moldering pine forest floor. Pristine wilderness extended as far as you could imagine in all directions.

It took Mother and Dad another ten minutes or so to expel the refinery-induced smog which had long occupied their lungs. At least that was to what I attributed their sudden lack of conversation.

Judging by the signs affixed about its various entrances, the inn appeared possessed of a saloon, a restaurant and ten motel rooms we later found to be inhabited by marmots and raccoons — notoriously non-compatible neighbors who nightly engaged in raucous competition for control of the remaining, rotting inventory left behind by the former management.

Former management had, according to Dad, consisted of a continually propagating family of eleven who had subsisted through several winters by supplementing their income with a nearby sheepdog breeding facility.

The doors of the inn swung back and forth, banging in

the sporadically gusting October wind, dispossessed of their anchor and loudly announcing their lonely state of disregard.

The main sign, chipped, faded and scrawled in large block letters reading, *Quartz Creek Inn,* sat perched atop the roof. Hanging from a single corner post, it creaked with every breeze like a snapped arthritic limb. Newspapers, aluminum cans and beer bottles lie wind-swept against dark, icy alcoves of the building which had been abandoned nearly two months. It was imminently depressing and silently begged its deliverance.

Mother still had not uttered a word, and Dad and I exchanged nervous glances, both relieved that the house, at least, appeared in good condition.

"It'll just take a few weeks to get the inn lined out, hon. It just needs a little TLC. Let's go look at the house…" Dad offered, leading Mother gently up the drive to the enormous windows which looked out upon the county road winding through Hardrock toward the snowy mountains beyond. "Just look at that view, honey!"

More interested in the view on the inside than what threatened from beyond, Mother cupped her hands around her eyes and tentatively peered through one of the windows.

Observing, with Mother, the interior of what would be our new home, I blurted out my first impression, "Holy cannoli, Dad, look at the snow! Part of the roof must be off the house. There's snow all over the living room."

Mother made a weird sound, but at least it wasn't a grunt.

"That's not snow!" Wes said, crunching along as he burst around the corner of the house.

I heard Mother and Dad utter a long, collective sigh.

"It's dog hair! *Ha!* Can you believe that? *Dog* hair!" and, he was off again.

It appeared we had located not only our new home, but also the sheepdog breeding facility.

The Hardrock Welcoming Committee...
as it were

In a most calm and deliberate manner, much as one might expect of four flatlanders suddenly thrust into the frigid fingers of oxygen-starved outer space, the next three hours found us fairly charging up and down the ramp of the moving van, skirting one another like ants milling about the entrance of an anthill. Well, we moved more like slugs, but our minds and lungs believed we were charging.

We lugged furniture and boxes into the house through the front door which opened into a country kitchen. It was nearing mid-afternoon, and our determined excavation of the truck had made little more than a dent in what amounted to a wheeled time capsule yet containing two-thirds the story of our lives recorded in artifact.

Dad, Mother and Wes had detained themselves within the grotto that defined the house, doubtless intrigued by some shocking new find. I paused to take in the grand scene before once again carting a load to what would be my new bedroom opposite Wes' at the back of the long, narrow house.

That's when I thought I heard shuffling some distance behind me. The sound grew, and with my finely tuned receiver, I was sure I detected the unmistakable sound of heavy, rushing footfalls in the snow. A bear! A rampaging bear!

Before I could choke out the words, a girl about my age

tore around the side of the house, breathing in long rasps, "I think... I lost him... in the woods!"

"Who?" I asked, searching her reddened face.

She furiously brushed away her hair and scanned the nearby trees in a resolved, expert manner suggesting routine, "My brother!" Her breathing calmed quickly, "He's got the gun again."

"Holy cripes!" I exclaimed.

"He's coming, I hear his bike!" she instinctively crouched and began scouting for a hide-out.

"Here," I said, "get in the truck! Hide behind that dresser!"

Like a pro hurdler, she sailed over the ramp into the back of the truck and was out of sight.

The beast bellowing and snorting hot on her trail was even more alarming than I had imagined. As her brother rounded the side of the house, he skidded his bicycle brakes on the packed snow and leaned back, resting one hand on a handle bar and a long, fat, steel tube across his thigh. He was short, stocky and looked to be about ten. Oblivious to our moving in, he scanned the area, eyeballing under the porch.

"You seen anyone hangin' around here?" he growled, scowling darkly and squinting his right eye. Except for a swath of tortured scalp about three inches wide running across the top of his head and phasing out with random hairs at the crown, his beady eyes shone beneath a shock of longish hair matted to his pulsing, red face. I later learned both the swath and the squint were the combined result of an unfortunate accelerant accident with the homemade gun-like device he now gripped against his thigh. He viciously chewed a plug of tobacco and spat toward the tire of the truck.

"No," I said, unable to appear casual.

"Huh," he took a last look around, expertly flipped the tube over his left shoulder, lurched forward and pumped furiously down the road toward town.

"Good grief!" I said, signaling to my new friend that the coast was clear. "That was your *brother?*"

"Yeah, Mark. The jerk. I hate him. He's always throwing knives around the house, and now he's got this stupid potato gun the Peevil boys showed him how to build."

I was speechless. In our five year association, Wes and I had developed sophisticated means of aggravating one another to near madness, but this was a type of guerilla warfare I'd never seen among immediate family members.

She continued, "I was coming down to see if the new managers had any kids. He saw me on the road and started after me. I took off through the woods, but he's pretty good at jumping logs and stuff, even in the snow." She stifled a giggle, "I call him Skidmark. He thinks it's because he's a hot shot on his bike."

Hee hee. The nickname seemed not only imaginative, but wildly appropriate.

"You guys want some help moving in?" she offered.

"Sure!" I said. "What's your name?"

"Al," she replied. "Well, Alex — that's actually my middle name. Everyone just calls me Al. What's your name?"

"Lisa. My middle name is Joe."

"Lead the way, Joe," Al smiled and grabbed a box,

nodding ahead of us.

This couldn't be better, I thought. We'd just arrived and already I had met a partner in crime and acquired an alias, not to mention a shared nemesis... Skidmark.

It turned out Al was from a large family of siblings, many of whom had already left home. Her sister, Georgia, was sixteen and Al was next to the youngest. Miraculously, the entire beneficial selection of Hubert family genetic material appeared to have been bestowed upon Al, alone, leaving her younger brother in particular to clamor through life in what we could only hope were the throws of evolutionary progress, however unkind.

Within days of our arrival, Al and I had claimed one another as best friends and worked covertly to successfully relocate her to my house two grocery bags at a time roped to the handlebars of our bikes and wholly unbeknownst to either of our sets of parents.

As Al and I stood staring at the thick layer of white dog hair which adhered spectacularly to the dark-green, deep-pile shag spanning the vast living room, Al looked up through the huge naked windows and noticed two people approaching the house.

"Who are they?" I asked, interested in their primitive, mountain folk appearance.

She was a tall, slouching woman in her mid-thirties wearing a homemade muslin shirt and carrying a heavy coat over her arm. As she trudged along the drive, leather boots kicked away the hem of an ankle-length, woolen skirt. An exaggerated expression of happiness punctuated her plain, elongated face much like one might see on a mask portraying the theatrical arts. Her hair was pulled fiercely into a pony tail, but most shocking was her rejection of upper-body concealment which she flouted with free-wheeling abandon.

Her escort was a smallish man, his long wavy locks loosely bound beneath a leather cowboy hat. He had a mellow, friendly face with optimistic eyes. Dressed in a flannel shirt, faded jeans and softly worn work boots, his most notable feature consisted of red suspenders emblazoned with large, bright-green marijuana leaves.

"It's Willy and Gert. They're pretty nice," Al mused, shooting me a sideways glance. "Potheads."

Holy cannoli, I thought. We had an insider.

Since our front door was still standing open, Willy knocked on the door frame and peered tentatively inside the house.

Dad was busy loading green aspen logs into the fireplace, intending to de-stinkify the house over the next three days by flushing it with smoke while we found relative refuge in the inn. Mother was on the phone, haggling with the electric company to turn on the power but enjoying limited results given the eight-hundred dollar balance the previous managers had left unresolved. Wes was fighting off an avalanche in the back of the moving van.

I met our neighbors at the threshold with Al beside me.

"Hi Al," Willy paused, "are you guys the new managers?" He smiled and nodded toward Mother as she banged the receiver several times on the kitchen table.

"Dad?" I yelled into the living room.

"Just a minute," he yelled back, "I've got to get this damn grate out of this fireplace. I don't think anyone's ever cleaned this piece of..." — *CRASH* — *"Son of a ..."*

"We have company!" I shouted.

Dad stormed into the kitchen covered in grey soot which dignified his riotous, Comanche-French, black hair and accentuated his flashing eyes. Fine ash puffed around him each time he stomped a foot or swung his arms. He was upon Willy and Gert before they had a chance to dismount the porch or release Gert's skirt which had snagged a nail as she vaulted over the railing.

"CAN," Dad cleared his throat loudly, "I *help* you?" Evidenced by his restraint, all those executive management training seminars were paying off.

"Um, yes... I'm Willy, and this is my wife, Gertrude... er, *Gert*. We live up the road a piece, and, uh," he seemed distracted by Dad's appearance and exhibited difficulty concentrating on his speech let alone meeting Dad's wild stare, "well, we, uh... thought maybe we could, um, you know, run the café for you." Willy released a shuddering sigh of obvious relief.

I whispered to Al from our vantage point near the hall, "Hey, that's great!"

"Yeah," Al remarked, "but they think you guys are rich Texans. The whole town does. Just wait till they start talking about money." She gave me a look like she knew how the whole scene was going to play out.

Dad introduced himself, "I'm Ike. This is my wife, Jessie." He gestured toward Mother and brushed a torrent of ash from his right sleeve. "Do you know anything about the restaurant business?"

"Oh yeah!" Willy's eyes brightened. "Gert ran a little café back in Idaho. We owned a little silkscreen shop, too, but Gert mainly managed the café. We've got the menu worked out and everything. We figured we'd call it the *Pan Handle*. We'll show you what we've got planned if you want to sit down and talk about it." Willy beamed, boldly snapping his suspenders then looking immediately concerned for having done so.

"What do you need a month, salary-wise?" Dad asked, raising his voice over the periodic banging of the receiver and Mother's loud, quavering voice.

"Well, we were thinking in the three or four-thousand range," Willy nodded affirmatively.

"Uh huh… how about forty-percent gross. You take care of stock. We take care of utilities, printing and advertising." It wasn't exactly a question, but Dad awaited a reply nonetheless.

Willy and Gert looked at one another, calculating their response in a split-second, as only long-married couples can do, "We'll take it! When can we start?"

"When you hang the open sign in the window."

Dad and Willy vigorously shook hands, cementing the deal between Dad's sooty ash and Willy's sweaty palms.

Al and I watched Willy and Gert hurry down the road, scarcely making thirty yards before Willy stopped and frantically mined his pocket. The pair paused and exchanged something then were off again at a markedly slower pace, their arms around one another, slight wisps of smoke escaping over their heads.

Mother sat at the kitchen table which was comprised of a varnished pine picnic table with bench seats. Holding her head in her hands and puffing furiously on the cigarette clammed tightly in her lips, she stared out the window at the moving van.

Dad dropped down opposite her and poured another cup of coffee from the old, green Stanley vacuum bottle he'd used on a hundred stake-outs. "What's the deal on the electric?" he asked.

"They're going to turn it on. We'll have to get them verbal authorization from the board that they'll get payment then they'll send a guy up."

"Good," Dad nodded.

Mother appeared irritated, "By the way… I don't think we have private phone service up here. I think we've got a party line." She was referring to the practice of providing several rural households shared phone service. Unfortunately, shared lines meant unintentionally shared conversations across an entire neighborhood.

"How do you know we've got a party line?"

"Because, when I was arguing with the electric company, I heard a click then someone else talking. Then I heard dialing. Then everything got quiet except for on my end. After I finished, I said 'bye' and waited a minute. I heard two phones hang up," she sighed and tapped the ash off her cigarette. "A party line. Isn't that just wonderful?"

"Well, we'll just have to be careful. Could be *exciting…*" Dad grinned, exaggerating his wide-eyed effect, "depending on who lives up here. Gossip makes the world go 'round for some folks, don't-cha know."

Mother rolled her eyes, "I could do with a little less excitement."

"Okay, here's some good news. We've already got a manager for the café."

"Really?" Mother asked, disbelieving.

"Yep. Listen, don't worry. I've been thinking…" Dad reached over and took Mother's hand, "we'll tear out what's left of the motel rooms down on the south end and turn them into a trading post. We can outfit it with a few groceries, film, pop, ice-cream in the summer… I'll put in a woodstove and a little place to sit and have coffee."

Mother listened, appearing to see beyond the moving van which blocked our view of the inn from the kitchen window.

"We'll turn the other four motel rooms on the north end of the boardwalk into a couple of apartments, that way we'll have a steady income stream. That will still leave us four motel rooms upstairs to rent out. We'll get the café open — let Willy and Gert run that. We'll get the saloon open, and I'll bartend until we can find a manager. We'll have the basics rolling within a month, and the rest we can work on through the winter. Everything will be ready before next summer's tourist season. It'll have an old western ambiance. What do you think?" he winked at her, borrowing a long drag from the stubby cigarette butt left on the scrounged aluminum can sufficing as an ash tray.

Al and I beamed at one another. Dad was such a visionary.

"I think we'd better figure out how to get the dog hair

out of the carpet and that weird smell out of the house. We can't keep the doors open all winter."

"I'm working on that," Dad said, scowling over his shoulder in the direction of the fireplace.

Al nudged my ribs, "I am so glad you guys moved here!"

"Me, too! Think you can spend the night?" I asked, hopefully.

"Well," she shrugged, "they haven't come looking for me yet."

Wes lumbered through the front door with a box of books threatening to disembowel its self.

KA-BOOOOM! A huge concussion rattled the windows, which left Wes standing in the doorway holding an empty box, buried up to his knees in encyclopedias.

Shocked immobile mere seconds, everyone quickly scrambled over the heap to get outside and see what had happened.

Once outside, we looked collectively down the road toward town and the presumed direction of the sound.

"What the hell was that?" Dad asked no one in particular.

A few rocks and clattering gravel tumbled from the ridges of Dark Mountain and splashed into Quartz Creek, behind the inn.

A cloud of debris and white smoke began rising about a quarter-mile away.

Momentarily, what appeared to be a man came staggering toward us.

We met him at the end of the drive. He was tall and thin, wearing a worn-out, smoldering denim jacket. He carried a cowboy hat which looked like an exhumed Civil War relic, the brim of which gave off a steady fog of smoke. A trick hip had him skittering oddly along... long filaments of red hair waving haltingly above his head. His look of shock was enhanced by comically expressive eyebrows, a long, scraggly mustache and a free-ranging gotee which he beat at with his hat when it flared. His eyes, wide and shadowed with fatigue, appeared kind and good natured.

"I knew it had to be Jake," Al said, shaking her head. "He's always blowing something up."

Jake beat at his beard again, as if running a herd of cattle through it, then smoothed back his hair and replaced his hat, the edge of which had not yet burnt out. Staggering, he caught himself.

"When's the saloon going to be open?" he asked, eyeballing Dad and steadying his stance. "I need whiskey. *Fast.*"

"It's going to be a while, friend," Dad said. "What's the hurry?"

"Well, first, to steady my nerves. Second, to keep the blaze goin'."

Al and I exchanged looks of jubilant expectation. Three hours in, and the adventure had already begun…

Tour a larger, full-color map of Hardrock at
www.hardrockbooks.com/hardrockmap.htm

The Gamblers

We'd only been settled a few days when tensions between Dad and Wes began mounting. With so much to be done in preparation for winter, cleaning the house and opening the inn, we were lucky to finally sit around the table for a late dinner around nine o'clock.

Quietly eating our bowls of canned chili, no one commented on the broken tire iron which conspicuously rested on the kitchen table still illuminated with only a kerosene lantern.

While Mother cleared the table, Dad handed me a flashlight and gave me and Al a look that suggested a one-on-one was in order between him and Wes.

"Goodnight, girls," Dad said, as Al and I pretended to wander off toward my bedroom. Halfway down the hall, we whirled around, tip-toed back and crowded up against the door frame so we could hear the conversation about to unfold.

"Is he in trouble?" Al whispered, trying to peek around the corner without being caught.

"I don't know," I whispered back, "but Dad's sure not happy."

"Look, Wes," Dad's deep voice boomed softly across the kitchen table, "your mother trusted me to look after you when she agreed to let you come up here and live with us. I never would have even suggested it if I didn't think I could trust you. But, so far, you've only let me down. I stuck my neck out for you, kid."

"I'm almost seventeen, Ike. I think I can handle myself."

"I'll tell you when you can handle yourself," Dad's tone was even and sure.

"You don't know me, man. How can you say that?"

"Because you've made it clear you've got a lot to learn. Smoking. Not showing up when you say you will. Not doing what I ask you to do. Every time I ask you to take care of something, you break a tool. How in the hell did you break a steel tire iron?"

"I don't know," Wes was defiant.

"Wes, I need to see some discipline. If you don't learn it here, the Marines will damn sure teach you."

"Are you saying I'm not Marine material?"

"What do *you* think?"

"I think I don't need this crap, man."

"Tell you what, son, you think about it tonight. Tomorrow, you decide whether you want to shape up and stay here or whether you want to keep acting like a know-it-all little kid and head home. Because, I'll tell you something, you screw up here in these mountains, and it isn't just me you'll have to worry about. You won't even make it into the Marines. These mountains are a hell of a lot more unforgiving than I am. In the morning, you get that wood chopped and air up the spare tire in your trunk like I asked you to do three days ago."

"Fine."

Al and I crashed into one another trying to outrun the abrupt end of their conversation, but Wes didn't seem to see either of us standing in the hallway as he stormed by on the way to his bedroom.

Al and I wandered off to bed wondering if Wes would decide to stay or go back and live with his parents in Houston.

"You'd have your own room," I said, quietly reflecting on the ceiling. "And, we wouldn't have to deal with his disgusting black fingerprints on the cheese." I turned toward Al, "plus, he wouldn't be tormenting me all the time."

"Yeah, but then Georgia wouldn't have Wes to hang around with, and *she'd* be tormenting me." Georgia, Al's older sister had made Wes' immediate acquaintance once Al shared news of our moving in with her family.

"True," I acknowledged.

Wes shut his door, and Al and I dozed off to Mother and Dad's low toned conversation drifting down the hall.

I was sure they were discussing Wes' future. Dad and Mother were always adopting kids short and long-term. Young men in particular seemed to somehow find our doorstep, like lost dogs looking for a home. As a father figure, Dad had an allure some other fathers didn't. He was one of those guys that other guys looked up to. And, when young men got off track, it was often Dad their mothers turned to in hopes he could somehow reverse their sons' destructive courses.

Having spent much of his own youth searching for self and freedom, Dad's philosophy was that most young men only needed a good friend to talk to, a little discipline and a lot of direction. He could also tell the sometimes subtle difference between ornery and irresponsible, and meted punishment accordingly. It was a formula that had worked many times, and

Wes was the latest adoptee.

Dad saw a lot of himself in Wes. Dad could always see the core of a person and knew Wes was smart, driven and had the potential to achieve anything he set his mind to, which was why he got upset when Wes failed to measure up to his expectations. But, even when hard language had to be used to lay out hard choices, Dad always spoke as a friend, and that intent seemed to forge bonds of respect that lasted a lifetime.

I'd heard Dad say a hundred times over the years, "They may be pissed off at me now, but that's okay as long as they can stand on their own two feet, down the road."

Despite his disgusting fingerprints, I kind of hoped Wes would choose to stay. He got assigned most of the heavy or scary chores, I loved listening to him play his guitar and he knew all kinds of neat magic tricks. All in all, he made a pretty tolerable brother. At least he never came after me with a potato gun.

Later that night, some time around two in the morning, Dad got up and walked into the kitchen. Passing in front of the large window that overlooked the inn from the kitchen table, he noticed a dim light glowing from a window in the café. Willy and Gert hadn't yet opened or even stocked the restaurant, so he wondered who might be in the building.

He watched for a while and saw no shadows moving inside.

Pulling on his boots and fastening his gun belt, he grabbed his coat and stepped out into the biting cold of an early winter.

The vapor of his breath blew back into his face as he

walked slowly toward the café. Stopping outside the door, he stood on the boardwalk, listening.

The low voices of several men could be heard inside.

"Ante."

"Too rich for my blood."

"He's bluffing."

"Call."

"Son-of-a-*bitch!* That's the third damn time tonight you've had a full house!"

"You callin' me a cheater?"

"Yeah, I'm callin' you a cheater."

"Drop the money."

Hearing the hammer of a pistol click, Dad withdrew his own revolver, turned the doorknob and let himself into the café.

Seated around a table were Crazy Jake's friend and neighbor, Boris, who had a gun pulled on Doorite, who had a gun pulled on Crazy Jake, who had a skinning knife in one hand and a bottle of beer in the other. Wes sat with a stunned expression and what was left of his coin collection in front of him on the table, beside a half-empty bottle of whiskey, a nearly empty bottle of vodka and four of about fifteen empty beer bottles.

As Dad walked through the door, none of the men wavered, continuing to train their weapons on one another.

"What the hell is going on here?" Dad asked. "And, how the hell did you all get in here?"

Wes spoke first, jumping up from his chair and tipping it over, "We-re jusss playin' a-game-a poker."

Dad holstered his weapon.

"But this sorry bastard can't play without cheating," said Doorite, his right arm extended with his gun pointed at Jake, "so, I'm going to shoot him."

"You shoot *him*, and I'll shoot *you*." Boris grunted, wobbling his pistol at Doorite and taking a swig from a bottle of vodka while keeping an eye squinted at his adversary.

Dad stood behind Wes, his thumbs hooked in his gun belt, "You asswipes put your weapons down. No one's going to shoot anyone in here. Wes, did these guys take any of your money?"

Steadying himself by placing a hand on Jake's head, Wes cautiously considered the rangy, beady-eyed crew around the table, "Umm... *nope*. They won it. They won it... um... square an' fair."

"Uh huh," Dad looked dubiously at the fat piles of cash and coin in front of each of the men. "Wes, you get your ass back up to the house. We'll discuss this in the morning. You three fools get your money, pay for your liquor and get the hell out of here. I'll remind you, *once*, that he's a kid. I'd better not catch any of you trying this crap again. If anyone's going to pull a gun around here, it's going to be me, and I don't pull a gun unless I intend to use it. Understand?"

Doorite and Jake nodded and reluctantly put away their weapons.

Steady as steel, Boris, a tall, coal-mining Cossack with a chest nearly as wide as a door, held his weapon on Doorite and looked at Dad with cold, dark eyes.

Challenged by no one, Boris was a man used to getting

his way.

There were three things Dad couldn't tolerate: liars, thieves and bullies. And every town had its assortment. As an officer with a small police department in northern Oklahoma, he'd gained notoriety by putting a seven foot Osage up against a wall in a restaurant for harassing a waitress. In a classic, "We own this town." type of confrontation, he'd been tagged "Godzilla" after a scuffle with a barrel of a man and his two sons in a bar.

Dad was a man who didn't like to repeat himself.

Boris continued his menacing gaze.

Dad returned it and lowered his right hand over the butt of his holstered .44, "You want to try me, friend?"

Though few people knew, Dad held the U.S. western regional quick draw title, a fact that contributed little comfort to Mother's restless nights when he was off chasing bad guys, since he continually reminded anyone who might forget that there was always someone faster.

Tense seconds passed as Boris shifted his attention to his vodka bottle and mulled the weight of the question.

Dad offered more encouragement for Boris to call it a night, "It'll be the last mistake you ever make."

No one moved, or blinked, or even breathed as time seemed to stand still.

"Is that a threat?" Boris spoke slowly with ominous intent as he lifted his eyes to Dad whose steady gaze never wavered.

"That's a promise."

The two men continued to study one another. Half a

minute ticked by, during which time Jake eased his chair away from the table, stood up and pulled Wes out of the line of fire.

Doorite pressed backward into his chair, surprised by the sudden escalation.

Boris finally rested his weapon in the middle of the table and stood to put his money in his pocket.

Waiting with Wes for the men to leave the café and begin walking back to their homes, Dad asked, "How'd you all get in here?"

"Troo... th'... door," Wes carefully sounded out each word.

Dad walked over to the split partition door dividing the café from the saloon. He shut the door and latched it, "How'd you get it open?" He was losing his patience.

Wes concentrated, listing heavily to the left, "I turned th' door knob..."

Dad blew out the flame in the kerosene lantern and picked it up to return it to the house. "Was the door locked?" he asked.

"Mmmm. Yep."

"Where did you get the keys to unlock it? Never mind. Wes, do I need to tell you what could've happened here tonight?"

"Nossir."

The pair walked up the embankment to the house.

"Drinking? Gambling? With your coin collection? With *those* guys? Guns? Knives?"

"I... urp...ugh... I know."

"How many coins did you lose?"

"I kept the Edgit... the Egypt...kon... all the good ones."

"You're in a pretty damn big hurry to grow up and get yourself into trouble aren't you, son?"

Wes said nothing.

The two stopped on the front porch as Dad asked, "Am I going to have to put a boot in your ass or are you going to straighten up?"

"Straighten up... s-sir."

Dad considered Wes thoughtfully, "Good. Then, you can start right now." He walked into the barn, started the generator and hooked up the air compressor. "Get that spare tire aired up and put back in the car. And stack some firewood on the porch." Dad picked up the maul and axe from the porch and took them inside, "You can have these and chop the rest when you sober up. And that better be by six bells."

"Yessir."

Dad reached around the door frame in the kitchen and pulled his watch cap off a hook. "Here," he said, stepping off the porch, "you'd better cover your head, so your ears don't freeze and fall off. You already have a hard enough time listening."

Wes pulled the hat onto his head and stared blankly at the open doorway were Dad had just been standing.

"And, you might want this," Dad tossed Wes a flashlight from the kitchen table.

Wes grabbed for the light two seconds after it hit the snow.

"Don't break it." Dad leveled a finger, recalling the tire

iron.

Sitting at the kitchen table while drinking a cup of coffee, Dad supervised through the window as an oblivious Wes labored to carry out the simplest function under the heavy influence of beer and whiskey.

Mother, hearing the commotion, had meanwhile gotten out of bed to share a cup of coffee with Dad at the table.

Having relayed the night's events, Dad watched Wes stagger into the barn with the spare tire.

"So, do you think he'll make it up here?" Mother asked.

Dad shook his head, "I have to wonder sometimes."

"You know, he looks up to you. You're the reason he joined the Marines."

"I know. They managed to make a man out of me."

"After they beat your head against a wall for three hours."

Dad looked at Mother, recalling those days, "I didn't say it wasn't without brain damage."

Wes returned with the tire and, balancing it on the trunk of the Green Rag, went back into the barn. He emerged, dragging the long, air compressor hose behind him.

Dad scraped out the bowl of his pipe, emptying it into the ashtray. "Boot camp has changed some since then."

Wes took the valve cap off the tire and positioned the air hose over the tiny intake stem. He jiggled the compressor hose head, squeezed the air trigger once or twice and examined the end of it.

"Yes, it has. But it's still the Marines. Do you think he'll survive it?"

Peering into the compressor head's tiny air hole, Wes squeezed the trigger shooting high pressure air into his eye. He stumbled backward, fell over and spent the next minute blinking and feeling around his eye socket.

Dad sighed and lit the fresh tobacco in his pipe, "If I can keep him alive long enough to report for duty." He drew several times on the pipe stem, pulling the flame from a wooden match into the bowl.

Finally, Wes got the air hose positioned on the tire valve where he continued to fuss with the trigger and examine the hose.

"Do you think it's safe for him to be out there airing that tire up after he's been drinking? We can't even turn on the porch light," Mother looked doubtful, frustrated by a lingering lack of electricity.

"Well," Dad puffed his pipe and glanced out the window, "I didn't think he could hurt himself with a damn air hose, but he may prove me wrong. He's got enough moonlight… but it sure is taking him a long time to…"

POW! The tire blew apart.

Dad stopped in mid-puff, "What the *hell?*"

Mother gasped, "Good grief! I've never seen that happen."

Stunned, Wes stood looking at the ribbons of tire dangling off the rim resting on the trunk of his car.

Mother began to rise from her seat, "I hope he's okay."

"Sit down, he's fine. Look at him. He's just standing there."

Mother sat back on the bench, "Now, what's he looking

for?"

"There's no telling," Dad chuckled. "Just give him a minute and I'm sure he'll surprise us."

"What could he be looking for?" Mother wondered aloud. "He's all over the place..."

"You're not going to believe this..." Dad peered lower to avoid the glare on the window. "Look what he's doing."

"What?" Mother squinted to see in the dim moonlight.

Dad cracked up, "He was looking for the *valve cap*. The damn tire blew apart, and he just screwed the valve cap back on. Oh man," Dad wiped away a tear, "this is better than a movie. Look at him. He's putting the damn thing back in the trunk..." Dad hooted as he relit his pipe, "Well, it probably needed to be replaced anyway."

"He just threw up in his trunk," Mother grimaced.

"Good, he'll sober up faster," Dad looked at the clock. "Two hours until he'll be splitting that cord of wood for the inn."

"You're going to give him an axe?"

Dad looked out the window at Wes doubled over in his trunk. "Maybe I'll give it till seven."

The next afternoon, Wes had split and stacked the wood for the inn and was busy scrubbing the trunk of his car when I stuck my head out the front door. "Hey, Wes, Dad's teaching me and Al how to play 5-card draw. You want to learn?" I turned to hear what Dad was saying in the living room, "Dad says you need the lesson."

"Yeah... I'll be in there in a minute. Let me finish stacking the wood on the porch."

That night after dinner, we were all sitting in the living room. Dad was smoking a pipe in his recliner, Mother was putting spilled photos back into a photo album, and Wes, Al and I were gathered around the carpeted cable spool used as a game table gambling our pennies away using the skills Dad had taught us that afternoon.

Wes shuffled and bridged the cards, eyeballing us girls, "You girls want me to show you the best magic card trick ever invented?"

"*Yeah!*" we said in excited unison.

Wes grinned, dealing out the cards to a complicated trick that ran five full minutes in duration. We were riveted as he had us select a card that we had to continually and secretly re-identify from piles of cards he re-distributed several times. Finally, he turned the cards face down and through the process of elimination, narrowed the piles down to only one card.

He looked at the remaining card and asked us, wryly, "What do you want to bet that's your card?"

Al and I looked at one another. No way, we thought. Feeling bold, we decided to bet half our winnings. We shoved the pile of pennies toward the middle of the table and smiled expectantly.

He flipped over the ace of hearts — our card of choice.

"Whoa!" Al leaned in to verify the card. "Do it again!"

I was mesmerized as he began dealing out the trick again.

Wes winked at us, "This is how I'm going to get my coins back."

Dad looked over at Mother who was also watching with

fascination. "Yeah," Dad said with a slight grin, thoughtfully puffing his pipe, "I think he'll survive."

Coyote Blind

By the end of our first week, someone from the electric company pulled a truck up in front of the saloon. Mother was inside, behind the bar, quietly humming and busily setting out glasses beneath a sparkling tower of freshly stocked liquor bottles. Each uniquely shaped bottle was displayed with its label forward on shelves arranged like a glass staircase. The shelves were backed and flanked with a long, tarnished mirror which created a spectacular combined effect.

The driver of the truck, a scrappy-looking man in his late twenties with shoulder-length hair and a longish scraggly beard, walked through the front door and surveyed the dim interior. Spotting Mother arranging glasses, he walked over and took a seat on a stool at the bar.

Looking around the darkly paneled tavern, his eye was drawn to the old branding irons, pelts and trappers' fare displayed randomly throughout the room. A neon Budweiser and Miller High Life sign hung either side of an old stag's head. Clad in faded jeans, a worn denim jacket and a cowboy hat, the man looked as much a relic of the bar as any other decorative addition.

He took in the enormous rock-faced fireplace tucked inside a cozy alcove near the low stage, behind which hung another wide band of tarnished mirror. A dusty and fully racked pool table commanded an adjoining room.

His gaze fell upon the heavy wooden chairs and small tables then finally the bar where he sat. The top of the bar was sixteen feet of four-inch thick local spruce. Its gnarled face was stained dark and studded with a collection of antique coins, scrub oak leaves and a few items from ages-old newspapers — all of it blanketed beneath thick coats of varnish softly dulled by thousands of scraping glasses.

He glanced around the room once more, drinking in the ambiance. Running his hands along the edge of the bar, he quietly sighed in admiration, *"Damn..."*

"Ack!" Mother croaked, whirling around and crashing several glasses into one another on the counter.

Her sudden reaction sent the startled driver scrambling off his stool, "Geeze, sorry about that, ma'am, you surprised me..."

"That makes *two* of us," Mother said, catching her breath. "I know the door was unlocked, but we won't be open for another week."

"Well," he grinned, "I could come back later... but I'd have to reschedule your electric hook up." He sniggered in an ornery, boyish way while twisting the end of his beard, "I hear you've been waitin' on it." He extended his hand across the bar, "I'm Ty."

Mother reached across the bar and shook his hand, "Jessie, and that's the understatement of the century."

"I'm not the electrician," he said, "but they sent me up to check out your service before they kick it back on."

"Well, good grief," Mother sighed. "As far as I know, it hasn't changed in two months."

Ty shrugged, "You should put in solar. I probably put in sixty or seventy systems in Reno before I moved up here. Everybody's gettin' off the grid."

Mother looked at Ty like he'd lost his mind, "Did you see the sky coming up here? It's as thick as pea soup. Believe me, after the conversation my husband and I had a week ago with the electric company, we talked about it. In fact, we were ready to put in a darned *water wheel*. We'd love to have solar, but, one, it's expensive and, two, it doesn't have the battery storage capacity... especially for the inn."

"It doesn't have to be expensive. I can put in a small system from leftover parts off other jobs. I got a whole pile of stuff in storage," he beamed. "I'm thinking about setting up my own company."

Mother glanced at the glasses left to stock then motioned for Ty to follow her out onto the boardwalk, "My husband, Ike, is down there working on a remodel. He can show you the electric service and you two can talk about the solar thing. I'd take you down and introduce you, but I've got a bar to open."

Ty looked at the outside of the building and studied the bark-on, lodgepole pine railing off the boardwalk, "Man, this is some *cool* place."

"You think so?" Mother asked, scanning the front of the inn and trying to muster an appreciation for his optimistic perspective.

"Heck yeah! How long you all been up here?"

"Oh, about a week."

He pulled back with an animated look, "A week?

Where'd you come from?"

Mother gave him the short version, and Ty's face radiated upon learning Dad was in the process of converting two motel rooms into an apartment — the same two rooms we'd lived in while smoking out the house and running it through a post-sheepdog cleaning.

Following the sound of hammering, Ty walked along the elevated boardwalk which ran the length of the inn. He introduced himself when Dad emerged from a motel room to toss a chunk of drywall into the parking lot.

A couple of hours later, on nightly furlough from our torturous sentence of school, Al and I were heading down the driveway toward home.

Ty pulled out of the darkening parking lot and waved to Mother who was making her way up to the house. "See you tonight!" he shouted with a broad grin.

"Who was that?" I asked Mother, following her into the house.

"That was Ty. He and his wife, Abbey, will be moving into the inn tonight."

"Who's his wife? Have you met her? What does she do?"

Mother cast a glance which suggested my normal attempt at twenty questions had already run its course.

Al and I were overjoyed at the prospect of who we hoped would be a friendly young wife willing to drive us into Granite with her own set of wheels. We hoped for a potential ally as we begged Mother for trips into town, continuous sleepovers, late nights of extended game playing and extra pots of hot chocolate. Though mild-seeming, to be successful these plots required careful planning and flawless execution aided immeasurably by an adult co-conspirator close enough in age to sympathize and sometimes participate in our plans.

"Do you think she'll be pretty?" Al asked.

Poor Al. Her half-dozen years in Hardrock had largely starved her of aesthetically pleasing models of the feminine form. It appeared that after only a couple months in the mountains, most Hardrock women took on the appearance and manner of genteel men, at best. Life in Hardrock was a difficult existence comprised of battling elements through a pronounced lack of amenities and near total absence of financial opportunity.

Hardrock women considered feminine peripherals, like hot rollers and makeup, nonsensical. And, Hardrock defined no-nonsense. Wood chopping, snow shoveling and wild game cleaning left little time for lipstick application.

Coming from Houston, I was familiar with high-haired, heavily made-up women who dressed to the nines for a jaunt to the mall. I, myself, had begun wearing makeup (subtly and known only to my mother) when I was ten. Makeup helped mark a southern woman's rite of passage, much like hairspray. In Hardrock, womanhood began when you could swing an axe and lay in a cord of firewood without supervision. Clad in flannel shirts, jeans and heavy boots while sporting bare complexions, ultra-practical hair arrangements and usually a knife or sidearm, mountain women tended to be a direct and fearsome breed.

Since Mother had already begun to take on that

hardened cast, I suspected that within that first week she had burned her hot rollers, makeup case, high heels and every one of her pastel polyester pantsuits. I had happily reverted to the wild immediately outside Houston city limits.

"I don't know," I pondered. "Maybe she'll let us play with her makeup and stuff."

"Fun!" Al grinned.

Al and I waited at the kitchen table, hunched over our social studies assignments and impatiently watching out the kitchen window for any sign of approaching headlights. Finally, at eight o'clock that evening, an old pickup pulled into the driveway in front of the motel room where Dad was still working.

The room was located off the north end of the inn and enjoyed easy access off the boardwalk to a large balcony overlooking a small open area over the septic field and surrounding woods.

The door to the passenger side of the pickup opened and someone stepped out.

By moonlight shifting under a mantle of cloud cover, we could see only a golden reflection off her short, wavy hair. Her remaining features remained silhouetted – backlit from the kerosene lantern Dad burned inside the room.

"I can't tell! Can you?" I asked Al, who was squinting through the darkness.

"No... too dark."

We jumped up from the kitchen table and headed for the door.

"Just a minute, you two," Mother halted our progress as

she prepared to put a pan of biscuits in the oven. "She doesn't need to be mobbed by two hoodlums the second she pulls into the driveway. Give her a minute to at least see where she is." Mother was likely recalling her less than gracious introduction to the inn only a week or so earlier.

Frustrated, we fidgeted absently with our pencils while Ty's wife approached the room.

The night was cold, and I wondered what she was thinking as Ty led her toward the warm, amber light spilling from a window where sounds of hammering, sawing and muted music from a transistor radio could be heard echoing off the silent wilderness surrounding us.

Finally, after three minutes, we could stand it no longer and harangued Mother for the nodding go-ahead to invade Abbeys' world.

We tore to the inn and, pulling up short of the doorway, peeked tentatively inside. She was being shown plans for the kitchen and turned to look at us when Dad invited us in. Attentive to every detail, Abbey's quick, bright smile accented warm, friendly eyes which appeared only a little weary. She wore tailored jeans, a sky blue sweater and exuded natural radiance. If Al and I could have placed a custom order for a big sister, she was exactly what we would have asked for. Surprising to Al and I, she seemed strangely relieved to see us and patiently indulged our hovering.

During the conversation between Dad, Ty and Abbey, we gathered insight into their lives. She had once been Sugar Beet Queen of Bellville, Kansas, her hometown. She'd been working through her second year at Kansas State University as a bookkeeper when she met Ty and quit school. Ty was from New York and had worked his way west as a truck driver, roughneck, farrier, brick layer and, most recently, a solar system installer. He and Abbey met at a bar in Reno and were married two days later. Within a week, they had found themselves in Granite where they'd been living for the past couple of months with her fat black and white cat, Finneas.

"I have a cat too!" I said, excitedly. "A Siamese. Her name is Pedo."

Dad rolled his eyes. "See these fang marks?" He paused from stooping over a two-by-four long enough to curl in his lower lip, jut out his chin and point to the recent attack. "Cat..."

Ty nodded knowingly and held up the back of his forearm while frowning at a meowing cardboard box resting on the floor near Abbey.

"You tried to make her eat raw garlic." I defended my pet, for the umpteenth time, who had long ago gained disfavor from an incident involving unplanned transport on a camping trip. His allegations unproven, Dad's so-called 'bites' and 'lacerations' had likely been the result of raking thorns as he too vigorously 'coaxed' Pedo from a thicket of river brambles.

"Damn cat was wormy," Dad muttered, scribbling a note on the board. He straightened and continued his explanation of the remodel to Abbey, "What I'm doing here is combining two rooms into a single apartment. Over here, you'll have a living room and a kitchenette. And over here, where the bed is, this will be the bedroom and bath area."

Abbey smiled appreciatively and asked a few questions about the kitchen as Ty brought in a suitcase and the last box from their truck.

Setting the box on the bed, which had been covered with a sheet of plastic and a stack of plywood, Ty beamed at Abbey and lit a cigarette. "Well," he ventured, walking over and putting his arm around her waist, "what do you think?"

"It's wonderful," she said, "and, this apartment is bigger than our other place by a long shot."

Their possessions appeared few, and Abbey guarded from fugitive sawdust her hooded rabbit-fur jacket resting on the bed. "Ty gave it to me for a wedding present," she explained to Al and me as we fawned over its supple warmth. "And, watch your ash." She furrowed her brows at Ty then snatched the jacket out from under the cigarette dangling in his hand.

"How about I watch *your* ash?" he said, grinning. Eyes glittering, he patted her behind and winked at Al and me.

Abbey, smiling, half-heartedly pawed him away.

This was interesting, and Al and I observed closely.

Once settled into their new home, Abbey continued to endure several weeks of drywall dust in her hair and two-by-four splinters in her feet as she, Ty and Dad worked to complete the remodel. When the last nail was hammered in and the last bit of sawdust was vacuumed from the floor, Abbey celebrated by buying a brand new set of white sheets for their bed.

With its little kitchen and living room, Al and I considered their new tiny home a grade-A fort, and, for the next couple of months, endeavored to spend as much time in it as possible. Desperate for a gin rummy and backgammon partner, Abbey was only too happy to oblige, teaching Al and me the nuances of both games.

For a short while, all was bliss, but by December, I could see from the stressed look on Abbey's face things weren't going well.

One Sunday, Al and I traipsed through the snowy drive toward Abbey's apartment, looking forward to a crochet lesson. Sitting on the couch, Al fed yarn from a large skein and intently watched Abbey deftly wrap and hook her way through a six-foot-long row of stitching. Happily, I occupied Finneas with a loose string.

"This is going to be so cool," Al observed, complimenting Abbey on the patterned weave and her choice of colors for the intended bedspread.

"I guess," she said, pausing for a sip of soda and a drag on her cigarette, "but I don't know if I'll be able to finish it anytime soon. We're pretty broke."

Such a confession came as no surprise, since Al had informed me that any substantial income generated by Hardrock residents had to be earned during the three-month summer tourist season. Their meager savings extinguished, by mid-winter most folks were destitute and picked up jobs in Granite or worked as ski or hotel staff in the nearby resort town of Diamond Hills until summer.

After trading six months rent in exchange for helping with the remodel and installing a small solar system to serve our home's hot water heater, Ty had decided to quit his job with the electric company in Granite and launch his own solar installation company — a decision which had immediately drained their savings.

"We've got over a thousand dollars tied up in panels, a

truck that barely runs and one job lined up in three weeks... maybe," Abbey twirled a length of yarn around her crochet hook, pulling it away from Finneas when he reached for it.

"Yeah," I said, "but aren't Dad and Ty bringing horses over from Barrow's Stage next summer to do trail rides? I thought that was going to be Ty's thing."

"Yes," she nodded, "but summer's a long way off. And instead of finding customers, Ty needs to help build the tack shed and corrals over winter. It's just getting tough to eat regular, you know. And I hate mooching off Ike and Jessie."

I smiled, "Me and Al mooch off 'em all the time." I pulled a long length of yarn from another skein and tied a small loop in it to begin the process of crocheting a chain.

Since money was scarce for everyone, every Sunday through winter Mother and Dad put on what Dad called a 'big feed' in the café for the five of us, plus Abbey, Ty, Willy and Gert.

Once word of Mother's fried chicken, biscuits and cherry pie got around, it seemed more and more folks began wandering in around dinner time.

Abbey stroked Finneas as he sat in her lap observing the yarn twitch inch by inch into the bedspread, "I went into Granite to see about working as a bookkeeper, but no one's hiring. We don't need much, but a few dollars to get by on would help out a lot. Singing in the saloon, helping out... it's barely enough."

Al and I had learned that in addition to cigarettes, Abbey, like Willy and Gert, also supported an expensive herbal habit.

Abbey reached to assist Al with her second row of stitching when Ty came bounding through the door, shouting, "I got it! Crazy Jake just told me down in the saloon, the Division of Wildlife is paying fifteen bucks apiece for coyote pelts!"

"So?" Abbey looked at once alarmed, hopeful and irritated.

"So? So, I'm going to get us some!"

"Ty, what are you talking about?" Abbey lowered her work into her lap.

"I'm talking about blastin' coyotes, Abbey! I figure, I can get ten a night, and that'd be…"

"A hundred and fifty," she offered.

"Right! This place is crawlin' with 'em. You can hear 'em almost every night outside our window. *Every night,* man, it'll be like picking cash up off the ground!"

Despite Ty's accounts, the place wasn't exactly crawling with coyotes. Once or twice a month, a few would sound off in the wee hours of the night in the woods around our house. There were a few, however, that indeed frequented the thick brambles under Ty and Abbey's back window, probably due to the small wire basket of food Ty had suspended off the sill, nine feet or so above the ground.

The basket served as a convenient mini, winter freezer. It was cheap on electricity but extolled a high price when it came to marital accord. Each night, the high-whining wails and yips of excited canine carnivores looking for a meal triggered a tense chain reaction that began by driving Finneas under the blanket, led to Ty activating his long skinny kickers, and ended with an annoyed Abbey shoving Ty off the bed.

I knew Abbey's thoughtful silence meant she was pondering the advantages of a few less coyotes. She sighed and wrapped a short length of yarn around her crochet hook, "I like coyotes. I don't want you killing any coyotes."

"You like to eat don't you? You like to put gas in the truck? You like to.... *shop?*" Ty wiggled his thumb and forefinger, inhaling from an imaginary cigarette.

Distressed, Abbey looked at Al and me which launched both of us into a chorus much like the coyotes we lobbied to protect. *"Not the coyotes!"* we protested in unison.

Ty thought a minute and looked at Abbey, "You know... if your cat gets out. By *accident,* I mean. Those coyotes will have him for lunch."

Abbey looked down at Finneas and scratched his chin, "Fine. Kill coyotes if you want to. Just don't let them suffer."

"I won't, I won't. They won't know what hit 'em. Have you seen my shotgun shells? All I could find were four boxes in the truck."

Later that afternoon, Mother, Abbey, Al, Gert and I were in the café preparing the week's big feed. In the dining area, tables had been pushed together where Dad, Ty and Wes sat discussing the coyote venture.

"Fifteen bucks a hide! Damn, that's good gravy!" Ty's eyes were as wild as his beard which he kept ferociously scrubbing up and down between outbursts.

Ty erupted again, "Hey! Right off the balcony. I'll pick 'em off right off the balcony. *Brilliant!* I'm a friggin' genius. I'll shovel off a little snow and use the old sofa or picnic table for a coyote blind. There's probably three feet of snow out there. They'll never even see us. I can shoot right down on the little buggers and pick 'em off — one, two, three. Probably get a half dozen before they know what's going on."

"First of all," Dad advised, temperately, "it's better to wait until a full moon, so you can see what you're shooting at. That's only in a few days. Second of all, a shotgun will tear the hell out of any coyote you *do* manage to shoot. I've got a .22 rifle you can use, or a .30-30, whichever you want."

"I'll use the .30-30." Ty grinned at Wes, "More power."

"Uh huh," Dad lifted his cup of coffee.

Wes was all ears and eager to get in on any action, "I've got a coyote call."

Though Wes grew up in a Houston suburb, he was a woods rat and constantly hunted anything that could manage a patch of grass and fished anything bigger than a puddle. Stuffed in a bulging backpack was his small but impressive collection of woods and lake gear scrounged, bought, makeshift and borrowed.

"Yeah!" Ty exclaimed. "We'll call 'em in! Wes, you hold the light, and I'll blast 'em."

"What you need is some bait," Dad said.

"Oh, yeah!" Ty's eyes widened as he began absently twisting the end of his beard. "We'll get some bait and lure 'em in with something… something so good, they can't resist."

"Old nasty chicken skins ought to do the trick," Dad offered.

"Hot *damn!*" Ty banged the table. "That'll bring 'em in for *sure!*"

Bolting for the kitchen, Ty promptly began collecting

slimy skins from the counter where Mother was preparing a meal of fried chicken.

Wes, Ty's ready accomplice, emptied a coffee can from the café storeroom, piled the smelly skins inside and lidded it with the intent of ripening the ghastly contents until the night of the full moon.

For the next several days, Ty and Wes worked out their plan, impatiently checking and re-checking their can of nastiness which could only have elicited such an enthusiastic response from coyotes or those who planned to catch them with it.

The more Ty and Wes discussed their dark proposal, the more blood-thirsty they became, causing Al and I to protest the whole affair. We'd considered sabotaging their efforts by discretely disposing of the bait-can kept warm by the fireplace in our living room, but, the toxic brew was too heinous to go near let alone handle, which led Al and me to pray for divine intervention. According to Dad, we were likely to receive it.

"I wouldn't worry about it, girls," Dad said, having a cup of coffee at the kitchen table while watching Ty slam his finger in his truck door across the parking lot. Wes met Ty on the boardwalk and the two of them hurried over to the balcony to check out the intended hunting blind. "Remember who we're talking about here. Those two can inflict some serious damage to themselves without anyone's help."

Each day leading up to the 'big night' added to Ty's anticipation. He could almost smell the cash he had already spent in his mind. Each night, a small pack of coyotes gathered beneath Ty and Abbey's window, howling, scraping and carrying on, driving Finneas to seek shelter deep under the covers.

Each night, Ty imagined more and more coyotes — thirty, forty, a hundred-and-eighty. He sweated under the itchy wool blanket, lashing out at poor Finneas and growing more restless.

"Aughiieee!" Finneas raked Ty's leg.

Ty thrashed under the covers, aiming his heel where he imagined Finneas might be.

"Auggh!" Raked again.

"What is the *matter* with you?" Abbey asked, annoyed.

"Your damn cat's attacking me!" Ty grabbed his pillow and swatted blindly among the lumps.

"Well, knock it off, he's only scared," Abbey beat at Ty with her own pillow and pushed him out of bed. Finneas peeked out over the covers, and Abbey snuggled him in her arms as Ty hurried to the window where the coyotes had gathered. "Besides," Abbey continued, "if you didn't insist on hanging meat out that darned window those coyotes probably wouldn't even be down there."

Ty wrenched the pane up and flicked on the flashlight, jabbing the darkness with shafts of light and probing the dense woods for signs of the beasts. "Tomorrow night!" he laughed evilly. "You're mine tomorrow night, you miserable, rotten bastards!"

Ty switched off the flashlight and performed a little dance on his way back to the bed, making up words to a song as he went, "Shoot me a coyote, sell his hide for fifteen clams, use Finneas as the bait... maybe shoot him too..."

"Shut up and get in bed," Abbey threw her pillow into the darkness.

Finally the day arrived, and Wes and Ty tromped a narrow path through the snow leading from the covered boardwalk onto the exposed balcony.

Careful not to disturb the mounds of snow cloaking their would-be blind, they pushed the couch to within a couple of feet of the railing. Next, they tipped the picnic table over on its side and shoved it up against the couch.

Snatching up the rifle and crouching low, Ty settled the barrel on the upturned edge of the table and sighted it in.

Wes trundled down the slope beside the balcony to check the bait station which consisted of a designated spot on the ground in the middle of the field. He quickly scuffed up the area with his boot and eyeballed the woods, as if a coyote spy might have been sent ahead to scout enemy positions.

"Looks good…" Wes whispered up to Ty who sat thirty yards away fiddling with the trigger mechanism on Dad's rifle.

"Good, good… c'mon back up here."

The two spent the next twenty minutes jumping up and hunkering around various places on the balcony in an effort to pick the best spot for their ambush.

"Hey — you know what we need?" Ty glanced at Wes.

"What?" Wes wondered, thinking they had thought of everything.

"A *decoy*."

"Right, a decoy."

The two sat looking at one another as if a decoy would manifest itself with mere nods of mutual agreement.

"What are we going to use?" Wes finally asked.

"I'm thinking." Ty twisted his beard. *"Hey,* I got it. Be right back." Ty hustled off to his apartment where he emerged five minutes later with a handful of yarn he'd unraveled from Abbey's bedspread. He shouted around the corner to Wes, "I'll be back in a minute. I'm going to see if I can find anything in the motel storeroom."

Ty came into the saloon where Dad was splitting kindling for the fireplace. "Hey, Ike," he asked, "can I check around in the storeroom?"

"What for?" Dad asked.

Abbey looked up from helping Mother stock beer bottles in the coolers behind the bar. "Hi hon," she smiled.

"Sweetie pie..." Ty winked, spying an object on a nearby table. He slyly reached for it and discretely stuffed it down the back of his pants.

"What do you need from the storeroom?" Dad asked, resituating a small chiseled log on the uneven stone hearth. "Jessie's heading that way in a minute…"

"Never mind. I got it," Ty blew Abbey a kiss as he backed out the door.

Back on the balcony, Ty untangled the thirty feet of yarn and wadded a small furry object.

"What's that?" Wes asked.

"Nothing," Ty said. "Just something I scrounged up. Ought to make a good decoy." He tied one end of the yarn around the furry wad and wound the long remainder into a ball the size of a grapefruit. "What we'll do, see, is put this decoy down next to the bait. We'll put a stick in the ground next to it and put the decoy on one side of the stick. Then I'll run the string around the other side of the stick, so when I pull on it from up here, the decoy will wiggle."

"*Wicked*, man! And look at that thing. It looks just like a rabbit," Wes observed.

Abbey, returning from the saloon, wandered toward the two finalizing their strategy. Studying Ty's contraption, she suddenly demanded, "Is that my coat?"

Taken by surprise, Ty stammered, "Wha — no, honey, no. I wouldn't use your coat to rig up a decoy."

She turned to go into their apartment then paused, "Promise?"

Ty nodded reassuringly and winked at her.

After she was through the door, Ty looked at his handiwork, "It's the *hood,* and friggin' brilliant, if I do say so myself."

"Man, didn't you see her face when she asked if that was her coat?" asked Wes.

"Yeah, but it's just the hood — snaps off, see? She'll get it back after tonight none the worse for wear. Meanwhile, we got us a decoy."

Ty and Wes had decided that ten o'clock was to be the hunting hour, so Al and I set up our own observation blind up at the house, on the kitchen table. We had binoculars on hand and figured we could see everything either by moonlight or the mercury light in the parking lot, if the forecasted snow storm rolled in.

By nine o'clock that night, a light snow had begun to fall, but the moon still beamed through the drifting clouds, illuminating the balcony and septic field like a spotlight.

At nine-thirty, Wes tore up to the house from the café where he and Ty had been drinking coffee. Al and I were testing our spy equipment when he bolted through the door and beat feet for the living room.

"Where's the can?" Wes asked redundantly, as if to punctuate his mission. Before racing back out the door with his prize, he paused by the table, lifted the lid and stuck his nose inside. "*Uuggh!*" he gasped, dropping the can and causing it to wobble on its rim, sloshing some of its contents onto the table. "Oh, *man!*" he said, wiping his hands on his jeans and re-lidding the brew.

"Hey, dufus, clean that up," I commanded from my perch while focusing in the binoculars. "It'll probably burn a hole right through the table."

"No time... got to get this bait down by the station."

"*Wes!*" I shouted after him.

"No time!" And he was out the door, loping for the septic field.

Al and I looked at the reeking puddle on the table.

"Gross," Al observed.

"Disgusting," I contributed my appraisal. "We ought to clean it up with his pillow."

We looked at one another.

"Nah," we said together. Not that it was too cruel. We just didn't want to spend unnecessary time contemplating retribution. Wes was, after all, skilled in the sport, and we were more interested in spying on the hunting operation and learning whether and how our prayers might be answered.

At 9:45 that night, Ty and Wes took up their positions on the balcony. The night had grown dark and densely silent as a result of heavier snow clouds moving in over the valley.

Suddenly, we heard the weird, squally squeal of the small wooden coyote call which was supposed to emulate an injured rabbit.

Reaat reaat reaat reeeeaaaat. The sound echoed off the mountains and heavily blanketed sky.

Silence.

Reeat reeaat reeeaaaat.

Silence.

Suddenly, Ty leapt up and ran into his apartment. He came out thirty seconds later gripping a white bed sheet over his head, its bulk billowing behind him.

Al and I watched him slip on the ice near the balcony and go down in an adjacent snowbank. Almost instantly, he was vertical again swiveling his head left and right. He stood motionless a couple of seconds then lurched over to the picnic table and shoved a second sheet toward Wes.

After a good deal of banging into one another, the pair hobbled with great animation around the table and hunkered down between the couch and the railing. There, they squatted perfectly still, concealed against the snow excepting their dark eyes peering out under the railing.

Reeat reeaat

Reeat reeaat reeeaaat

"My ass is froze," Ty grabbed his hind end, now wet with melted snow from his spill on the balcony. "You sure you heard something out there?"

"Yeah, I heard it," Wes assured. "I heard rustling. *Shhh... shhh.*"

"Man, you *stink*," Ty grimaced, scanning Wes for the cause.

"*Shhh*," Wes put the call to his lips again. *Reaat reeat.*

"Let me do it," Ty reached for the call and blew on it.

Rrrrrrrr Rrrrrrrr Rrrrreeeeeeeeeeaat

"Try short, harder blows, then a long, high one," Wes instructed.

"*Shhh, shh...* I think I hear 'em!" Ty motioned for Wes to be quiet and jiggled the string which led to the decoy. He tugged it lightly then gave it two small, quick jerks.

The two sat in silence a moment, scanning the woods surrounding the bait station which stunk of rancid chicken skins sharing space with Abbey's hood.

"*Eyes, man, eyes!*" Ty whispered, excitedly. "Do you see those eyes over there? Keep blowin', keep blowin'!"

Wes took the call and blew a couple more times while Ty grappled with the rifle, keeping his sheet tight around him and rising higher onto his haunches. "Damn it," Ty cursed, "I forgot I busted my trigger finger."

Ty awkwardly rested the rifle across the railing, contorting in the cramped quarters to sight it in.

"You want the light?" Wes whispered, still scanning the fringe of woodland.

"No, no — not yet! There's more eyes comin'! Look, man, they're comin' in, they're comin' *in!*"

Six sets of eyes descended on the bait station and appeared to be settling in for dinner.

"Hit the light, man, *hit the light!*" Ty shouted.

The six pairs of eyes looked up just as Wes hit the light and flooded the field.

"*Skunks!*" Ty exclaimed, startled. He jumped and dropped the rifle off the balcony into the snow some nine feet below, "*Damn!*"

"Wow, look..." Wes commented, shining the light around on the small herd. Shooting skunks and tacking pelts onto the back of his parents' house had been one of Wes' favorite suburban pastimes.

Startled, the skunks dashed for the light, humping hurriedly up the trail toward the balcony.

Ty's eyes widened, "What the *hell?* They're rushin' us! *They're rushin' us!* Get out! *Get out!*" Restrained by the clinging, wet sheet, Ty pushed Wes ahead of him through the tiny corridor and over the couch.

Floundering ahead of Ty and grappling with his own wet sheet, Wes shone the wavering light on several skunks near the railing. Attracted by the stench of Wes' pants, the furry troupe had worked their way up the trail in the dark, preparing to claim the feast they thought awaited them while the rest of their clan dined in the field below.

"They're up here *too!*" Wes shouted, putting one hand on the railing and one hand on the edge of the overturned picnic table. Tucking his legs, he vaulted over the skunks and landed on the boardwalk, adding some distance between himself and the waddling herd advancing on Ty.

Seeing the skunks, Ty launched a panicked retreat back over the couch.

Swiping at the sheet hanging over his face, Ty fought to turn around. He scaled the top of the couch but was stopped short when the sheet wedged in the joint of the couch frame. Wrapped tight and unable to free his arms to regain balance, Ty flailed helplessly backward over the railing where he thrashed upside down two feet above the trail, *"Aaaauuggh! Wes, Wes! Get the rifle!"*

The frightened skunk family made a hasty retreat themselves back down the trail. As they trundled past Ty, he wrenched an arm free and instinctively waved them away.

"Hold still, man, hold still!" Wes shouted advice from the edge of the parking lot.

Heedlessly, Ty clipped the tail of a passing skunk with a waving hand. The terrorized beast jacked up its tail for a quick defense — *ppppsssssssssttt*

"Aauugghh! Aaugh!" Ty waved the air and swiped at his face receiving another shot by a passing relative of the first — *pppsssssssssstt*

"AAUUGGGHHHHHH!" Yanking his other arm free and propelling both wildly, Ty bucked and gyrated like Houdini trying to escape from a straight jacket.

A third skunk, overwrought by the threatening spectacle of Ty spinning, twisting and screaming above, attacked Ty's cowboy hat where it had fallen on the trail. It bit through the brim twice then turned and unleashed a full dose of spray, soaking it through.

Rrrrrrriiiiiiippp—thunk, the sheet gave way.

Ty hit the ground and rolled into the septic field, scattering the remaining skunks into the woods and frightening away a lone coyote engaged in chomping up the decoy. The coyote jostled the largest remaining piece of hood and clamped down for a more toothy grip before trotting off for the woods.

Ty lie in the snow, stinking from his disastrous encounter, hopelessly tangled in the sheet, finger throbbing, hind end frozen numb. Defeated.

The commotion had brought Al and me outside. Abbey, rushing through their apartment door, led the parade to the septic field.

She hurried to the bait station and stopped short, waving off the rank odor of skunk juice and rotten chicken skins which seemed to concentrate around Ty, *"Auugh..."* She pinched her nose and grimaced, kneeling to check on him, "What happened?"

"Oh, *man... gack,"* Ty gasped for breath, "you wouldn't believe—"

"Is that my *coat?"* Abbey bent to retrieve a demolished fragment of hood still sporting two snaps. "This *is* my coat, you jerk!"

"Oh, sorry about that, hon, *hack*, here..." Ty raised a feeble hand for assistance, "I can explain if you'll help me out of this... *gag...*"

"Are *those* my *sheets?* Those *are* my sheets! *Arrrgrgg!"* Abbey reared back and kicked Ty's backside, spun around, stomped back up the trail into the apartment and slammed the door.

Clearing everyone out of the saloon when he staggered in to thaw his hind quarters at ten till eleven, Ty dropped his jeans and backed up to the fireplace, steam engulfing his battered form.

It took a dousing in two quarts of tomato juice and an hour of begging at the door before Abbey finally let him back into their apartment.

No amount of begging would open the door for Ty's hat, however, which, never to make a full recovery, was banished to a hook outside their front door till summer.

Cooking With Joe and Al

"Hey, let's make some brownies!" I said brightly.

"No way, not again," Al recoiled.

"Oh, c'mon, just some brownies..." I pleaded, knowing that Al could be swayed with the slightest provocation. "It'll be fun."

"Okay," she grinned, knowing that it would, of course, be fun. The 'Joe Style' of cookery was always fun and adventurous and a little bit dangerous.

This was because as a child I was never allowed to accompany my mother into the kitchen on her cooking excursions and, therefore, had been left to my own devises when home alone and struck with the creative desire to express myself via the edible arts.

"Kindest mother," I had implored hundreds of times, "why will you not allow your very own loving child to accompany you in the kitchen on your numerous and exciting cooking excursions?"

She would always then turn and look sharply at me, "Maybe because of the biscuit incident or the cookie affair or how about Grit-Gate? Pick one."

"*First* of all," I defended myself yet again, "anyone can mistake flour for shortening. Second of all, if you can't *press* cookies through a cookie press, then why do they call it a cookie '*press*'? And, last of all, the box never said to put water in the pan before you boil the grits."

Mother indulged a rare pause while rushing around the kitchen with a towel and an armload of plates, "*First* of all, that's what *recipes* are for. *Second* of all, cookie presses aren't designed to handle chocolate chips, Froot Loops, M&M's and whatever else you crammed into that dough. And, *third* of all, 'boil' *implies* the use of water. Plus..." she held up her fingers and ticked off five other reasons from sliced thumbs and hot pans to flaming hand towels. Inhaling deeply, she continued her barrage, "Do you remember how long it took me to scrub the half inch of baked-on carbon out of my..."

"*Twenty dollar pan...*" I lodged my eyeballs into the upper right quadrant of their sockets. Everything she mentioned had been the unintended consequence of being left alone two hours after school every day to absorb the inspiring kitchen adventures of Julia Child and *The Frugal Gourmet*. Mother hadn't found it the least bit amusing that, ransacking our suburban super market, I could only *visually* identify weird and sought after ingredients such as artichokes, and wholly forgot to remove their thorns before serving them in my first ever gourmet salad.

My mother. She sorely lacked in humor and felt strongly that cooking should be reckoned only as a very serious means to an end, not a means of inventive design. What she lacked in humor she made up for by possessing an unhealthy affection for her cooking utensils, pots, pans, supplies and entire kitchen space itself.

This time, knowing that Mother could be provoked with sufficient persistence, I would not be dissuaded — which is why I prepared to duck and cover by grabbing the pizza pan.

"C'mon, please..." I assumed the prayer stance hunched over and boinging on the balls of my feet, "Plea-he-heeeese..."

"No."

"But, Mom... I just want to make cookies or a cake or pudding or something... *please*..." I followed at her earlobe into the pantry, around the kitchen, along the counter to the stove.

"No... get away from me."

I resorted to the tactical ploy known rarely to fail, "But, Mom, you *never* let me cook, and what am I going to do when you're not around anymore?"

Ah *ha*, the very same reverse psychology unwittingly taught by my own parents. To this, I added a pinch of guilt, "What do you want me to do, eat cold cereal for the rest of my life? What will my children and husband eat? What kind of a mother will I be if I can't prepare my own child a nourishing meal?"

"Fine," she crammed a wooden spoon into a basket bristling with brethren and turned with her hands on her hips, "You do it, you're on your own. You make a mess, you clean it up. You burn the house down, you live with it." And this was the usual way between Mother and I, which is why I did most of my cooking when she was working down at the inn, away in town, or otherwise out of eye-shot, ear-shot and short reach of my latest endeavor.

Such was the convenient case this day.

Al seemed uneasy, "Joe, what if we get caught?"

"What? What are you so worried about?"

"Everybody's gone, that's what!"

"So? That's a *good* thing," I gazed under the stove. "Do you know how to light this thing?"

Al, more prudent than I, possessed the uncanny ability to foresee certain consequences wholly beyond my reckoning until I found myself actually reckoning with them. The inn was closed and everyone had gone into town for supplies. It was a rare chance to be alone *and* in the kitchen at the same time. I would not be thwarted by some unfounded fear of failure. Although, I had to admit, on the several other occasions when Al and I had attempted brownies, it had always ended in some inexplicable fiasco.

One time, the whole batch seemed to propagate itself into a colossal, pulsating hulk which thankfully had been killed when Al slammed the oven door on it. Another time, it had shriveled in the pan, resembling the gaskets I'd seen Dad use on engines. And once, the batter had baked to surprising perfection, yet was chock-full of giant flour-filled tumors. But this time things would be different. This time, experience had made us wise and an iron will made us invincible. We would conquer the odds and create a masterpiece of cuisine.

"Where's the recipe?" Al asked, looking in the cupboard. "I can't find the book."

"Mom probably hid it again. We don't need one anyway. I can remember the ingredients."

"Yeah, but how much of each thing?"

"Oh, I pretty much remember."

Al looked at me with dread in her eyes.

"It's okay, Al, we can remember it."

For some reason, the fates blessed me with a desire to

create but cursed me without the means to materialize a vision. At least, that has always been the way with culinary-type mediums. In fact, now that I reflect, it has been a rather constant theme throughout my life.

I pulled a huge mixing bowl from the shelf. "Brownies are the easiest thing in the world to make."

"So how come they never come out right?"

"Probably the barometer." I had learned through distant observation of my mother that the barometer was an inexhaustible excuse for any failed attempt at baking.

Al rummaged in the pantry. "I can't find the cocoa."

"Then get the hot chocolate stuff. That'll work."

Mother endlessly arranged and rearranged her pantry, obsessing over new locations and means of camouflaging key ingredients while intending to discourage my forays into the kitchen realm. It was her territory, and she never tired of defending it.

Before adding the hot chocolate mix, we gobbled giant spoonfuls and tried to look at one another's bulging cheeks without laughing. I gave Al the 'don't smile' look. Predictably, she would be the first to crack, stifling a grin while knowing full well the worst thing you can do under such circumstances is suppress a laugh. Such an act could easily result in severe sinus burns or even brain damage. Overcome by one another's convulsive expressions, the powder inevitably found its way up our noses, into our eyes and hovering in the atmosphere.

We washed down our three-minute hacking fits with tall glasses of cold chocolate milk and resumed our task, time being of the essence.

"How much baking powder?" Al held the spoon above the can which had finally been located behind several jars of noodles and dried beans on the very top shelf.

"Oh, a couple tablespoons I guess. But toss in a couple more of baking soda, because I can't remember which we use."

"We'd better only put in one tablespoon of each then, huh?" suggested Al, mathematical genius that she was.

"Right," I agreed utterly without question, as math was not a strong subject with me.

I stopped to ponder. "Okay..." I said, "what should we use for a secret ingredient?" Somehow, years earlier I had gotten the notion that anything delicious was surely possessed of a secret ingredient.

"Joe, we don't need a secret ingredient. These ingredients are weird enough."

"What about black pepper? I wonder how that would go with chocolate."

"Forget it. Now hurry up and mix these in." Al handed me an egg carton and flopped down on the bench at the table.

I picked up an egg and, with Al as my audience, adopted my Julia Child instructive mode, complete with voice impersonation: *"Here, is an egg. What you'll want to do... is... crack it into the bowl, like so..."* I poised the egg over the rim of the mixing bowl intending to execute the one-handed method of egg crackery which I'd seen so many others perfect — even Willy.

"Now," I continued, *"don't fear the egg... it cannot harm you... all you have to do is tap it..."* I tapped the egg, caving in the side of it, *"...lightly..."* I craned the seeping mass

over the center of the bowl, *"and simply separate the two halves... one from the other... artfully using a couple of fingers to..."* bits of egg shell began oozing with the broken yolk down into the bowl, *"...to pick out any shells..."*

Al piped in with her rendition, *"This method is best used by people who are not Joe..."*

In no time, we had amassed and mixed reasonably appropriate ingredients into the bowl.

"Taste the batter." I held it out to Al.

Had these been Mother's brownies, we would have been overjoyed to sample the batter as well as lick the spoons, bowls, beaters and counter spills. But, since this particular concoction had begun to fester and swell like some dark, seething incarnate, we were more inclined to recall our polite upbringing and control our initial impulses.

"No way, *you* eat it."

So I did. And something was missing. "It tastes weird," I commented to Al who acted as though she anticipated such an appraisal. "Wait a second..." I sucked the tarry substance off my front teeth, *"sugar!* We forgot the sugar."

"Well *duh!"* Al seemed immensely relieved that the weirdness was easily corrected.

And so it was, that after searching high, low and in-between, we resigned ourselves to the fact that all our efforts were for naught.

Having separated and hidden each key ingredient, including the cookbook, Mother had successfully, even in her absence, foiled our grand plan. As far as Al and I were concerned, there was no known substitute for sugar.

"Ah, but w*ait!*" I held up a finger. "What about the café, huh, huh?"

"*Yeah!*" Al brightened.

And we were off.

Grabbing the ring of master keys off the hook by the door, we hurried to the café where we began scouring cupboards in search of the single one ingredient that would instantly turn our fermenting brew from dismal failure into sweet success.

Sadly, we could locate neither canister nor bag.

"How can there be no sugar in a restaurant?" Al looked around irritated.

"Oh, there is sugar. But they've hidden it. They think they can stop us from baking, but I *will* find a way."

"Joe," Al searched my eyes and seemed more concerned than usual, "maybe this is a sign."

Slowly, a grin spread across my face, "Oh, they are tricky… tricky, tricky, tricky. But they have forgotten one thing."

"Forgotten what?" Al looked dubious.

"The sugar packs on the tables."

Al and I loaded a hundred-and-fifty sugar packs into our up-turned T-shirt bottoms, pilfered the booty back to the house and began ripping madly away. Afterward, we hid the evidence in a rumpled brown bag stashed under my bed, which led to a later situation there is no time to discuss here.

With the mountain of gooey dishes quickly washed and put away, and all bottles, cans and jars returned to their secret locations in the pantry, the time had come to bake the readied confection.

Despite Mother's attempts at confusing ingredients by constantly switching labels... despite her rearranging pots, pans and key utensils into cupboards, drawers and upon unfamiliar hooks... despite her every sly tactic at foiling my ability to assemble a near-edible manifestation, Mother had gravely miscalculated our persistence and ingenuity in her absence.

However, to her crafty credit she had undermined our remaining chance at marginal victory by deviously reserving the greatest barrier for the last step in the baking process. I am speaking of our relic gas stove which had been decommissioned from safe use sometime just after the Bronze Age.

The beast, roughly the size of a battle cruiser, had been rightly abandoned by the house's former occupants. Made of enameled cast iron, its top was tunneled through with orifices grown over with black claw-like fingers fond of grasping at shirt cuffs and potholders. It lurked in the corner of the kitchen, silently threatening any but her who might dare come near it.

I had been taught to fear it. Taught that it was complicated and dangerous. And there was good reason for this.

I had only known electric ranges which were easy to operate... friendly. But this oven was different. There was no electric anything. It did not even possess numeric dials for adjusting heat. It had only two settings: flame, no flame. I was allowed to know three things about the stove.

1: It consumed explosive gas through a vaguely suggested network of copper tubing.

2: It would only come alive through a specific and

difficult series of maneuvers. And,

3: In Dad's words, "Never light this damn thing, or — *look at me* — never light this damn thing, or you could blow you *and* the house up."

Only Mother was privy to the nuances of its secret means of ignition. Observing casually from the living room, however, I had been able to discern the more obvious steps involved in her complicated and highly orchestrated set of maneuvers.

First, she would drop the broiler door and peer into the depths of the beast. Then, she would twist around, practically dislocating her hips and shoulder blades while leveraging a foot beneath a nearby drawer handle. Flattening herself into the broiler compartment and using her chin as an inverse fulcrum, she would then — lit match in hand — reach underneath all the way up to her shoulder while simultaneously grasping for and turning the big, red flame/no flame knob.

Somehow, following this procedure, the stove would miraculously growl to life.

She constantly reminded me the lighting ritual had something to do with safety and pilot lights and gas leaks, but I knew her real reason for keeping the beast was simply to employ yet another complicated obstacle along my path to gastronomical independence.

Though I lacked detailed information on lighting the beast and further lacked her ability to simultaneously unhinge, stretch and flatten myself, making the most of her technique, I guessed a pretty fair imitation was probably within my grasp and would certainly be necessary to complete our masterwork.

Match in hand, I looked up at Al from my position on the floor beside the stove, "Okay, so when I say *go*, you turn the red knob there to the right, but not too much or we'll get blown across the parking lot."

"Joe... I don't think this is a good idea."

"C'mon, it's no big deal. I've seen Mom do this a hundred times." Such was the force to bake brownies within me.

"Yeah, but *you've* never done it."

"Just turn it. Okay, ready? Ready? Al?"

"I can't do it Joe, I'm scared. What if it blows up?"

"I'm not going to light the match until you turn the knob, I think that's how Mom does it. It'll be okay. Ready....? Go! Turn it, turn it!"

"Okay, Okay! It's *ON* — Oh my *GOD*! You're going to kill us!" Al ran for the front door.

"Al, get back here and turn it off! I can't light it! It might blow up! Hurry and turn it off! *Turn it off!*" Now it was my turn to freak-out.

"No, I can't, I'm scared!" she screamed from the corner of the kitchen.

I re-hinged my dislocated bones, clamored to my feet and whipped the knob to the 'off' position.

"Okay, look, we'll wait a minute or so and try again." I repositioned myself on the floor in front of the opened broiler door and fanned away the gas, trying desperately to catch the breath that seemed to have fled my lungs.

"No way, you are totally crazy. Let's just forget it," Al urged.

L. Bracken | HARDROCK - Crazy Jake's Fish Bomb

"Oh yeah, right, and if Mom and Dad find out we made up all this batter..." Ever the repressed optimist, my kitchen adventures were so rare, I always triple-batched anything in case it turned out to be really good.

"Okay," Al sobered instantly. Anything was less fearsome than the consequences that awaited us '*if Mom and Dad found out*'.

She steadied her hand on the red knob as I positioned my upper torso, match in hand, under the broiler. There, I squinted beneath the darkened labyrinth of steel grates watching and waiting for some signal I'd never seen.

"Okay, ready? *GO!* But *SLOW!*" I commanded, squinting even harder.

As Al slowly turned the knob, smelly, noxious fumes began enveloping my head. Naturally, I hesitated then thought of the gases accumulating as I hesitated, so hesitated even longer gripped in a perpetually disabling panic and visualizing cumulus clouds of explosive particles mounting within the room, sufficient to level the top of a mountain...

"Oh my God! They're *home!*" Al shrieked.

In a frenzy of tornadic motion, Al turned off the gas and snatched up all three pans of bubbling goo. Racing down the hall into my bedroom, we leapt onto the bed and began devouring raw globs of batter with our spatulas.

Halfway through the second pan, Al slowed to three rotations per second. "I think I'm going to up-chuck."

In the spirit of camaraderie, I seized the pan and vacuumed the remainder.

Two minutes later, we emerged bloated, our minds

numbly imperceptive to the reality walking through the doorway.

"What's that smell?" Mother set two bags of groceries on the kitchen table and sniffed at the lingering odor of propane drifting about the house.

"Al farted," I said, surprising myself at the flash of quick wit under the circumstances.

Mother rolled her eyes and looked doubtfully around the kitchen.

She left for Big Red as I hurriedly pulled one of the baking dishes, wiped clean by a dirty shirt, from behind my back and returned it to its shelf.

Reappearing, Mother lifted a red box from a grocery sack.

"Here, I thought you two might appreciate this..." she handed me the box, pausing to study Al who had suddenly taken on a greenish cast. "What's the matter?" she asked. "It's just instant brownie mix."

Myth or Mystery...

You will probably find this hard to believe, but I was not a model student. For instance, during seventh-grade English, I was content to fritter away innumerable hours staring at the giant shuffling blue spruce happily languishing a few feet from the window which I had claimed early on as my portal of virtual freedom.

During Mr. Fillmore's discussions of modifiers intended to introduce brilliant depth to thin topics, I often turned my attentions to the infinitely more interesting resident squirrels who riotously squabbled over pinecones alternately in one another's possession. I suppose my preference for wildlife observations over the rules of language explains quite a lot about my writing style.

Despite the challenges I surely posed, Mr. Fillmore was a dedicated teacher and sought to commend my "gifted sense of perception" while simultaneously covering my writing assignments with so much red ink he could have saved himself a good deal of time and effort by simply dipping them into a can of red paint.

"Pay *attention*," he would say. But, it was spring, and after the long winter, attention was too high a price. The tree, the sky, the squirrels claimed it all.

This day, Mr. Fillmore had a gleam in his eye. And it was possibly related to having unexpectedly run into Al and me at the Mort Mart procuring refreshment in lieu of education the previous glorious morning on our way to the soft, grassy banks of the pond in Granite's town park.

Mr. Fillmore stood in front of the class, looked directly at Al and me and, grinning, announced a trip to the library for the unusual purpose of watching a movie.

A movie! Al and I shot a look at one another suggestive of activities suitable for darkened environments. Napping. Note passing. Escape.

Our lives were pinched miserably within the confines of a regimented schedule consuming five-sevenths of our burgeoning existence, so, naturally, we *lived* to sneak out and run vacated halls, forage our lockers, dash beyond the chain link fence for quiet parks and riverfronts, and, if Abbey was in town, maybe even catch a ride back home. This was a tendency I had wholly inherited from my father who spent the majority of his youth outrunning truant officers in the Allegheny forest of Pennsylvania.

A trip to the library, wandering among a throng toward a dark room possessing a distracting focal point was the long awaited lapse in judgment we knew would eventually befall even the most jaded and wily faculty member. A movie. In the library. What luck! Darkness *and* mobility. We could hardly believe our fortune and grabbed all our possessions in preparation for a long sojourn abroad.

As we took up our positions in the rear of the marching line, ever alerted to the opportunity to detach from the herd, we found every possible passage blocked by one inconvenience or another: locked doors, bandy-legged social-studies teachers, stoolies assigned lengthy respites in the hall and looking for ways to rat their way back into temporary good graces.

Finally, we found ourselves at the threshold of the school library which, most times, offered nearly as much sanctuary as the bathroom, cafeteria, or small space under the second-floor stairs.

Neither television nor radio reception reliably pierced the mountainous barrier around Hardrock, so even though our institutional escape had been thwarted, the next best thing was passive entertainment. We shed our baggage and secured forward seats around the television. Even if we were about to view a troupe of cartoon fruits and vegetables extolling the benefits of fiber, we were thrilled at the prospect of moving, color pictures.

With maddening and mounting anticipation, we endured the ceremonious positioning of the audio/visual cart; the cajoling of cables; the fussing with buttons, dials and switches; Mr. Fillmore's muttered curses who, without the assistance of the visual aid department, was left to his own minor devices. At last, the television popped, buzzed and flickered to life. The sound was finessed as the horizontal adjustment settled into place.

Slowly, a title focused into view. What was it? We strained to see. Would it be *Gilligan's Island? Tubers and the Innovative Gardener? You, Too, Can Love Modifiers?* I hoped it wouldn't be *You, Too, Can Love Modifiers.*

Then, there it was, looming large upon the gleaming screen accompanied by eerie, lingering music: *Myth or Mystery.*

Hmm... Al and I looked at one another wondering, is

what a myth or a mystery? We looked back at the screen.

Moments later, the *what* became apparent as a hunched, hairy creature lumbered across the foreground gazing back at our wide, wondering eyes.

In a deep, authoritative voice, the announcer broke over the visual specter and announced, "What *is* this lumbering beast? Some call him ape. Some call him man. Some call him... *sasquatch*..." Ominous music rose, its deep base vibrating the plastic housing of the television set as I stared silently gaping at the screen, craving more footage of this wild, horrifying creature I had never before seen.

The narrator broke in again... "In this episode, we investigate the myth... the mystery of bigfoot..."

Mr. Fillmore had definitely gotten my attention. Without any truant officers of his own, he had resorted to the old Native American trick of frightening children back to camp through tales of terrifying beasts wandering nearby woodlands.

Consumed with fascination, I scuffed my chair closer to the screen and watched, spellbound, as the hulking man-beast lurked at the outer edge of a campsite, thundered through woods and loudly menaced a cabin full of miners by flinging boulders down upon their sagging tin roof as the men slumbered in their bunks.

Wow, I thought. This particular show was my first introduction to any creature outside the limits of recognizable society, other than my own father to which I noted a significant resemblance.

I had not been a child unnaturally attracted to swampthings and the like. In fact, even brief exposure to movies like *Jaws* and *Empire of the Ants* deeply triggered my instinct to avoid bodily injury. Believing such creatures were indeed real or at least plausible, *Jaws* kept me out of the community pool and bathtub (unbeknownst to my mother) for days after its showing. *Empire of the Ants* somehow manifest the subconscious notion that colonies of man-eating insects were streaming beneath our carpeting, the only avoidance was to navigate the house by leaping from chair to couch to coffee table and so on. Giant rabbits, the Blob, all these creepy otherworldly entities drove me under the covers, on top of tables and toward any means of securing even minimal refuge.

Al, on the other hand, examining the hem of her shirt, seemed oblivious to such skin-crawling, hair-raising, spine-shrinking horrors. On reflection, I suppose it was within a comfortable arena of familiarity that she watched a boulder smash through the miners' roof while another beast from the ravaging sasquatch pack crashed an arm through a window and grabbed one fellow's head. She, after all, shared a precarious existence with her younger brother, Skidmark, compared to which, the relatively lighthearted antics of frolicking man-beasts must have seemed almost humorous.

For me, however, the existence of sasquatch was a serious matter and one which evoked detached fascination on-screen, until it became apparent through a series of re-enactments that the creature was known to reside in remote, inhospitable, heavily wooded mountainous areas possessing few human inhabitants.

Wait a second. What did the narrator say? Did he say "wooded, mountainous areas possessing few human inhabitants?"

It took approximately four seconds for the meaning of his words to sink in and lodge in the pit of my stomach where they remain the grist of ulcerated anxiety to this day.

Hardrock!

Riding the bus home, I began to consider the folly of accompanying Al to her house, two miles from the inn. On the rare occasion she was required to make a formal showing of her occupancy, such an arrangement typically left both of us without our familiar mode of bicycle transportation.

Al's house was out near Muskrat Lake. Out where the road became a trail on its way to the remote wilderness of Pickanaxe Peak, Kodiak Mountain and Obsidian Basin. In the recent past and without a single thought for my personal safety, I had accompanied Al to her house only to make the seemingly ever distant five-mile or so return trip alone even in the company of slowly descending darkness.

Bears, wolves, Boris... nothing had posed so great a concern as the predicament of pedestrian travel in the remote, inhospitable, heavily wooded, sparsely populated, mountainous village of Hardrock. Why, it was little more than a miners' camp, really, and Al and I dwelling so far from one another... what was it, ten miles?

I realized such a trek could prove increasingly hazardous to my health.

Although the plan that morning had been to get off the bus at Al's house after school and walk home that evening, I resolved to disembark at my house. Yes, that's what I would do. If Al wanted to hang out later, she would have to walk to my house by herself. It was a shorter distance for her to travel to my house than it was for me to travel to hers.

Plus, I reasoned, Al was more equipped psychologically and physically in these matters. In her ten years with Skidmark, she had developed both steeled nerves and sinewy muscles adapted to rapid retreat.

As I contemplated these complexities, I noticed my fingernails had pierced small holes in the back of the seat in front of me and my eyeballs, intensely searching the forest, had fogged the window.

Al, fiddling with the zipper on her backpack, glanced up to see me staring at her and caught my uneasy expression. "What the heck is the matter with you? Freak."

"Nothing," I stammered. "I just… well, I just remembered… I, uh… I have to feed the dog right after school, so I won't be able to go home with you tonight."

"You don't even have a dog," she mumbled, rummaging for something in her pack.

"Right," I said, straining to see around the person's head in front of me as the bus began to squeal to a stop.

"Still…" I began to grow frantic, shouting, "I have to do something right after school!" Wild eyed, I burst into the aisle and lunged for the doors as Al swung her knees out of the way.

Accustomed to extreme behavior and unconcerned with my weirdness, she peered casually inside her backpack. "Okay, I'll see if I can walk over later, then," she mused absentmindedly without realizing I'd already hit the muddy ground, intensely alerted to bigfoot. In my zeal to avoid walking home from Al's house, I slowly realized I had disembarked one stop early.

As the doors to the bus slammed and the engine idled down, I looked around hoping something would inspire a sense of comfort and calm. But, of course, there was nothing but woods.

Wait! A half-mile up the hill ahead, the newly built corral off the back of our house was barely in sight.

Should I turn and dash back to the bus or should I make a break for it? Would I make it? *Could* I make it? I heard shuffling in the bushes. A twig cracked. I jerked my head in the direction of the sound. My respiration tripled as my heart revved like a jet engine winding for take off. I felt eyes all over me, hot breath on my neck, a hand grabbed my shoulder!

"Aaaieee!" I whirled around.

"Here, you dropped this." The bus driver handed me a text book.

Through the haze of terror, the driver suddenly seemed unrecognizable. I vaguely remember my hand fluttering to block an attack before I turned and sprinted madly for home.

Even April's slick mud could not stall my determined acceleration. Slipping and spinning, my sneakers relentlessly chewed through to permafrost.

Fumbling suddenly onto all fours, I scrambled to my feet and leaned into the steep grade of Deadman's Hill. A hard lurch left helped me regain a near-vertical stance as, hitting a patch of dry gravel, I kicked in the turbo jets.

Speeding toward the top of the hill, blood roared in my ears. Eyes ricocheting left and right, I happened to notice the bus' front bumper aligned with my pumping knees, its grinding engine drowned out by peals of squealing laughter unleashed by the bus' unfeeling occupants, all of whom were now hanging out their windows and beating on the side of the bus, as if whipping it onward.

Yard by yard, I pulled away from the yellow behemoth climbing the hill. Staring straight ahead and curling a vapor trail, I disappeared around the bend, down our driveway and toward the safety of our beloved dwelling.

Finally, I was in sight of the porch and woodpile, the shop and Big Red. Decelerating in time to inflict minimal damage to the screen door before bolting through the kitchen and into the living room, I came to a halt on the back of the couch.

Reserving household funds for things like flour, gasoline and .30-30 shells, a night-light didn't rank high up on the "family" list of essentials. Late that night while lying in bed, I yelled down the hall, "Why can't I have a gun in here?"

Dad: "Go to sleep."

Me: "They could crash right through my window. I have this big window looking out over the woods."

Dad: "Go to sleep."

Me: "That's when they broke into that cabin... when those miners were sleeping."

Dad: "Lisa, what are you so afraid of? Sasquatches just want to be left alone like anyone else."

Me: "So you're saying they *do* exist!"

A muffled chuckle and snort from down the hall...

Mother: "Go to sleep."

Fine, I thought bitterly. Parents would never appreciate the unspeakable, life-threatening horrors of the night. The hypocrisy of two grown adults double bunking — one to hit the light, one to get the shotgun — did not escape me.

Fortunately, I was familiar with a number of styles of subterfuge. I had worn thin my album of Bill Cosby's *Wonderfulness,* so knew how to thwart the advance of a sinister chicken heart. As such, smearing slippery desserts on the floor sprang quickly to mind as a ready and affordable means of defense. However, our home was carpeted in all but the kitchen and bathroom, and frankly my bedroom was of immediate concern. Besides, I certainly didn't care to consider the consequences of Dad skittering across my battlefield on his way to a midnight snack.

Wary of the darkness which often accompanies night, and poignantly aware of the prime sasquatch habitat created in the eight inches under my bed, I considered my options.

I had long ago abandoned the normal, that is, the *expected* method of getting into bed. From the age of seven, it had become clear in my mind that all manner of insidious creatures lurked patiently under my bed awaiting any opportunity to thrust out a slimy, boney hand, seize my ankle, drag me under the bed and devour me whole. The standard, one-legged approach to climbing onto a mattress seemed like a clear invitation.

Now I had to worry about sasquatches sharing space with or even edging out the familiar, nightmarish hellions that normally dwelled in that dark space.

My usual technique of streaking to the bed from the hallway and knocking the light off with a hurled shoe now seemed risky under these new, high-pressure circumstances.

Anyone could see that, with sasquatches, one should not leave a shoe or any other external device which could be employed against one loose in the vicinity of their bed.

The following night, seeking an alternate means of defense, I enlisted the newly devised, acrobatic lunge-fly. How it worked was, the instant I flipped off the light switch on the wall by the door, I leapt four-and-a-half feet to the bed in a high-loft, peddling, flailing array, dashing my target with great velocity and weight.

I was comforted by my theory that should a sasquatch attempt to seize me upon boarding the mattress or even during sleep, the impact from such a maneuver would compress the beast sufficiently that it would have to spend the night hours re-hinging its limbs in preparation for the next night's ambush.

Also, I knew the sagging and protruding springs beneath the mattress caused by this technique added deadly snags and increasingly cramped conditions.

Not long after enlisting my new technique, Mother was under constant suspicion that large rodents were gnawing at the box springs under my bed, prompting her to set rat traps around the house. It was a notion I didn't bother to refute. A snapped sasquatch toe would surely elicit a howl of forewarning.

I deemed Al's willingness to continue walking to or from my house, alone in the dark, to be the result of ignorance not bravery. Within days of my repeated urgings, tales of chilling scenarios and reminders of televised horrors, Al, at last and for her own benefit and protection, was convinced that sasquatches were no trifling matter.

No longer did she happily stroll along the dark road, joyful thoughts fluttering about her idle mind. Now, thanks to my efforts and training, she walked a few paces then spun around and walked a few feet backwards, never the same number of steps, never developing a pattern. She cautiously searched the woods, training her eyes to detect subtle movements, her ears to perceive the slightest sound. Ever-present in her mind was the image of a snarling, slathering, hairy, glowering-eyed beast inches from her back.

Over time, our resistance to solo foot-travel proved impractical, so we decided to divide the distance. Al still walked a mile alone, as did I, but only during daylight hours and always armed with a large, forked stick.

While some may argue the unlikely odds of a sasquatch attack — Dad among them — my keen sense of perception, recognized and encouraged by Mr. Fillmore, gifted me with a deep and indelible sense of paranoia which I felt obligated to share and I am certain contributed immeasurably to Al's many safe returns home.

Crazy Jake's Fish Bomb

At the start of every summer, Lloyd Lars, a game warden for the Department of Wildlife (D.O.W.), drove a truck full of trout from the fish hatchery in Granite up to Muskrat Lake. Accustomed to a comfortable life in open, fresh-water stock tanks where they were hand-fed buckets of food pellets and worried only of the occasional passing crane, the fish partook of the thirty-mile trip into the mountains where, usually numbering two or three-hundred, they were pumped from a round holding tank on the back of the delivery truck through a fat hose right into the lake.

D.O.W. calls this "stocking", and it's done several times a year throughout the state so tourists trying for a six-pound lunker can have an enhanced angling experience without depleting natural lake stocks.

This is a great conservation practice in theory. However, stunned from the transfer, many of the fish remain close to the surface, disoriented and loopy from the ride. Some turn belly-up and others linger around the shoreline, slow to move and seemingly uncertain of where in the comparatively vast body of water they ought to be.

Most fish go on to make a full recovery and within half an hour are making wake for the ledges and deep pools at the roadless, reedy, densely wooded end of Muskrat Lake. But, the slow-to-recover types often fall prey to natural predators always ready to make short work of the unfortunate. The D.O.W., of course, accounts annually for this phenomenon and realizes that resident otters, eagles, hawks and bears will all partake of the easy feast.

Unfortunately, there was another predator, more elusive and crafty, the D.O.W. perpetually failed to consider and whose diligent persistence quickly trimmed their conservation efforts.

Crazy Jake.

Spring was winding down in the high country, and Jake, carefully noting increased cartons of fishing worms in the cooler at the trading post, had taken to continually peeking through various knotholes in the plywood which covered the street-facing windows of the abandoned house he'd claimed as a squatter. Here, he listened for the deep rumble of the D.O.W. truck easing through town on its way to the lake.

Jake knew preying upon the dozens of disoriented fish gave him an unfair and illegal advantage over licensed tourists, so he made every effort to get to the lake right away, before the fish recovered from their transfer-induced daze.

Once snowmelt started in earnest, Jake began carrying a large plastic trash bag in his pants pocket, figuring to improve his chances for a bigger haul of fishes in the event the truck rolled through town while he was in the saloon or other less than convenient location.

Preparing to dehydrate most of his anticipated catch, Jake had even repaired the web of bailing wire which suspended the chimney pipe of his wood-burning stove throughout his living room.

Bearing no sense of guilt or remorse for the illegality of

his actions, Jake considered himself among society's accountable members only when convenient. When it came to snagging stocked fish from the lake, Jake regarded himself equal in stealth, ability and special need to Hardrock's bear population. For these intents and purposes, on the morning of May 20th, between the hours of seven and eight, sitting in his outhouse while reading a nine-year-old copy of the *Ladies' Home Journal*, Jake was basically a bear.

Thinking he heard the familiar, distant grind of an engine, Jake slowly lifted his eyes from a weathered page and stared vaguely, hopefully into the dim light of his outhouse.

He listened, sniffed the air, then quickly waved the crinkly pages in front of his nose and jerked his head toward the peek hole above the latch in the door.

He pressed his eyeball further into the portal, scanning left and right along the road, peering hard through the trees. Suddenly, he detected a slight vibration in the floor boards. Accidentally dropping the magazine down the hole while grabbing up his britches, Jake rushed out the door.

Hopping and hobbling as he struggled to keep hold of his pants while scurrying into the woods across the road, Jake crouched behind a bush just as the D.O.W. truck rumbled by.

Making his way down the trail through the woods to the lake a mile distant, Jake came to the usual place of transfer.

He hung back in the thickly tangled woods, watching in rapture as a dark, pulsing stream of fish flesh poured into the lake. Now and then, whirling to check behind him, Jake kept the game warden in view and counted the minutes till the truck ground into gear and made its way back into town.

Checking the sun through the branchy canopy, Jake estimated thirty minutes had gone by. Hurriedly, he scanned the early-morning light for witnesses then dashed to the shoreline and waded in.

Surrounded by the shimmer of glistening dark scales flipping and splashing in the shallows and bumping into his legs, Jake plucked a dazed trout from the water and furiously dug into his pants pocket for his trash bag.

Wrong pocket.

He shuttled the fish to the other hand and dug into his other pocket.

No bag.

He checked his shirt pockets. Nothing. He'd left his jacket back at the house. Maybe the bag had fallen out along the road.

Damn! he thought, looking up to see a hawk observing him from a bare branch in an old pine. "You ain't gettin' my fish, bird. *Forget it.*"

Jake looked around at the bounty of fish floating on their sides and others trailing slowly between his legs, just beneath the water's surface. One suddenly launched out of the water, dove back into the swirling brew and streaked out of sight.

"Damn hell!" Jake began grabbing at the slippery fish and stacking them like cord-wood into his upturned shirt tail, squirting two out from under his arms. Bending to grab those, he lost three others through a gap between his snaps. "Cripes! I'm losin' my catch!" Jake cursed as the hawk flew in a few feet from shore and looked into the water. Kicking water at the huge

bird, Jake slipped in the mud and went down, losing all his fish. The bird hopped a few feet to the right, then back again. Jake floundered to his knees and chased five floating trout into his make-shift net.

Clamoring out of the cold muck and hunching over the fish scooped in his shirt tail, Jake made his way back into the woods, now with three fish cradled in his shirt and one under each arm. By the time he got to the house he was down to two fish.

His trash bag lie on the floor of the outhouse.

"There you are, you good-fer-nuthin…" Jake grabbed the bag and, again, dashed through the woods toward the lake. Over an hour had passed by this time, and Jake returned to a placid lake surface. No fish could be seen, except for the reflection of one in the talons of the hawk as it gracefully rose back to its perch in the pine.

I was working the counter at the trading post when Jake sloshed in, his cowboy boots squishing with water.

"Good grief, Jake, you stink like fish. Have you been in the lake?"

"Maybe," he said, his red, rangy eyebrows shadowing his deeply frowning face.

Removing his cowboy hat, long hair poofed off the top of his head and waved around like an orange feather boa. He dragged a chair over to the woodstove blazing with a fire Dad had started earlier, and began the arduous task of removing his soggy boots.

Hoisting a long, skinny leg in the air, with the other splayed out to the side braced against the wall, Jake grunted and tugged, scraping the chair along with every pull. Finally, the boot popped off, lobbing a shower of hissing water droplets onto the hot stove.

He commenced upon the other boot, crossing one leg over the other and pulling. Twisting his body to such a degree that he lifted himself off his chair and danced into an aisle, he hopped and spun his way across the store.

Finally, the boot released and flew across the room, whizzing by my head as Jake crashed into the fishing rod display. Muttering and untangling himself from yards of line, Jake repositioned the ten or so rods and resumed an annoyed seat by the fire.

"Here's your boot," I arced it over the canned goods aisle, and Jake intercepted it.

He sat there staring at the woodstove, head in his long gnarled hands, crooked fingers accented by graceful filaments of static-roving hair charged by sudden furious outbursts of head rubbing.

"What's the matter, Jake?" I asked from the counter where I had been assigned the task of hand-writing tiny price labels for two new cases of corned beef hash.

Jake looked around with suspicious eyes, as if he should be careful of his reply. We had learned from Jake he was wanted in Arizona for an offense he contested had been manufactured by a hostile ex-wife. Something to do with the unauthorized presence of a backhoe in his front yard. Jake, was, therefore, highly attuned to all manner of law men, D.O.W. or otherwise. It was why he strictly confined himself to the relative limits of Hardrock, or what Dad referred to as our 'Hole in the

Wall'.

"Lost all my damn fish," he muttered.

"What do you mean?"

"Lost my fish. *Lost* 'em."

"Did your line break?"

He took a long time formulating his response, "Yeah..."

"That's why Al and I conk-fish."

Jake sat quietly, then rotated his head, peering an eye through a notch between his fingers, "What's conk fishin'?"

"You know..." I paused to add a dollar sign to a label, "where you just tie on a great big sinker and cast it out into the riffles on the creek trying to conk a fish on the head." I looked up to see him gazing beyond me in reflection. "Beat's baiting up a line. I don't know if you'll catch much, but it sure is fun. If you get one, you'll have to run out and catch it before it heads down river. We've never caught one like that, but we keep trying."

Jake shifted his gaze to the window behind me. "Huh..." he grunted.

Jake conjugated by the fire for another thirty minutes or so. I thought he had drifted off to sleep, which is why a box of candy bars scattered to the floor when he suddenly leapt out of his chair and clapped his hands together.

"Hot damn, that's it!"

I stuffed the candy bars back into their box and scrambled from kneeling on the floor, "*What's* it?"

"I need a pipe." Jake grabbed a boot and, hopping around while gripping the pulls, crammed in his foot. "Prob'ly got one of them." He stopped struggling halfway to the heel and grabbed the other boot, jamming it on in similar fashion. "Might need some more matches though." He mashed his hat on his head and wobbled to the door, half the length of each wet boot mangled under his heels. "Lemme get back to th' house and check out what I got on hand. I'll be back." *squish, squash, squish, squash.*

And that was the last I saw of Jake... until after the explosion.

The rest of the story came to me from Al, who heard it from Skidmark, who heard it from his young associate, Stretch Peevil, who had been enlisted in the scheme. While worth the wait, it took some detailed investigative work and a good bit of patience while Al and I coaxed the remainder of the tale from Jake.

According to Al, Jake approached Stretch to trade for some old dynamite his dad had used to blast a rock slide off the quarry road some years back. No one knows how either Jake or Stretch came to know about its existence or whereabouts, but evidently, the exchange was made, and Jake procured four sticks of dynamite and a long coil of fuse. In the trade, Stretch procured an axe head, half a can of tar and a box of broken light bulbs.

Next, Jake secured a twenty-foot length of inch-and-a-half steel water pipe relieved from the bone yard behind the inn. Then he raided his stash of scrounged fishing gear.

Every summer, careless tourists left miles of line, hooks, sinkers and bobbers tangled in brush, trees and underwater snags. Competing with Skidmark, Stretch and his brother, Stomp, for the best of the lot, Jake stashed his booty deep in the kindling box by his woodstove.

Tying several shorter pieces of fishing line together and ferreting out a large red and white bobber, Jake sat on his living room floor with a length of pipe and all the fixins for what would become his infamous fish bomb.

Before the tourists could cast a line, Jake worked feverishly for three days and nights, engineering, re-engineering and tinkering with the bomb until all seemed perfect.

On one end of the long, open pipe, Jake filed a small notch. He then melted a little candle wax around the width of the bobber, tied on a thirty-foot length of fishing line and gently wedged the waxed bobber into the end of the pipe. He ran the fishing line along the outside of the pipe clear to the top and secured it in four or five places along the way with tiny dots of melted wax.

Jake's idea was to attach a long fuse to a stick of dynamite and drop it down into the pipe until it rested on top of the bobber. While leaving a little fuse hanging out the open top, Jake figured that while standing-knee deep in the water, he could submerge the pipe about fifteen-feet off a rock ledge at the far end of the lake. From there, he'd light the fuse, and once it burned down near the explosive, he'd yank the fishing line, pulling out the bobber and releasing the dynamite into the water at precisely the right moment to create an underwater concussion to a small surrounding area. Using this method, he figured he could stun enough fish to the surface that he could easily bag fifty or sixty.

He counted on a deep, soundless detonation and the cover of pre-dawn darkness to carry out his plan.

Those readers familiar with the oft-despoiled Wile E. Coyote vs. Road Runner plots can probably guess what happened next.

Early the next morning, while the frigid chill of a late mountain spring clung to the ground, Jake hurried with his bomb to the lake, scattering deer and small woodland creatures for cover as he dragged the heavy, twenty-foot pipe behind him through the underbrush.

At last, Jake made his way to the thickly wooded far end of the lake. Carefully, he secured his plastic trash bag in a nearby tree, lest he drop it into the lake in his excitement to gather in his catch.

Wading into the shallow water of the submerged ledge, Jake wrestled the bomb into the water where, for a flicker of a second, he questioned the soundness of his pending deed.

"Genius," he muttered, checking the tension of the line.

Casting squinty glances about for potential witnesses and peering into the deep water, he pulled a wooden match out of his jacket pocket and lit the fuse.

For a moment, Jake considered that from this point forward, there was no return, no slowing down, no stopping what he had begun.

He tilted the pipe and looked down the shaft. Good… he thought, still burning.

He had previously tested a length of fuse and knew it should take exactly sixteen seconds for the burning wick to reach the stick of dynamite waiting to spark twenty feet down.

He lowered the pipe farther into the water and counted the seconds, tasting the fish which would hang suspended throughout his living room by the end of the evening.

Fourteen one-thousand, fifteen one-thousand… Jake tugged the line attached to the bottom of the pipe. His effort met with great tension, and he realized he hadn't accounted for the pressure at that depth of water. He worried instantly that he might not be able to loosen the bobber.

"Eeeeeee," he squeaked in wild-eyed panic, making tiny jumps on the ledge while pulling and wiggling the line so it could work its magic loosening the stubborn stopper at the bottom. With not a moment to spare, the line released and the bobber gently floated toward the surface, sending the explosive into the water as planned.

At least, that's what Jake visualized occurring twenty feet under the water.

What actually happened is something of speculation, but those of us involved in the investigation (Jake, Al and myself) suspected that the rotted line actually severed in the notch, though not before loosening the wax seal and freeing the small air-filled plastic bubble to race up the shaft under pressure, pushing with great enthusiasm, the festively flickering stick of dynamite ahead of it.

As Jake stood, holding a slack fishing line and waiting for the bobber to float gently to the surface, he was surprised by the hollow-sounding pop just to his right.

As the bobber spurted out the top of the pipe, Jake looked up to see the stick of dynamite launch into the sky like a tiny, sparkling flare.

Unable to utter a sound, any rational thoughts Crazy Jake might have possessed at that moment unexpectedly fled his mind as his whole body fell instantaneously limp.

His hand involuntarily dropped the pipe into the water while his legs collapsed like thin ribbons, leaving gravity, alone, to lead Jake though a graceless half gainer over the ledge into the water.

Arms outstretched, mouth agape and legs sprawled overhead, Jake splashed into the lake just as the dynamite — KABOOOOOM — detonated overhead, illuminating the scene in a thunderous blaze of light and shower of sparks.

Luckily for Jake, he only clipped the rock ledge with his jaw and was thrashing well under water by the time the concussion hit, so was spared any further brain damage.

Temporarily deafened by the explosion, Jake hadn't heard the rumble of the D.O.W. truck approach. Just as he began to climb out onto the ledge, he caught sight of the huge white tank and Lloyd, the game warden, getting out to hook up the transfer hose.

Immediately sinking back into the cold water and hoping the warden wouldn't look up and notice his hat floating in the middle of the lake, Jake's eyes peered just above the surface.

"Cripes, I'm *f-freeeeezing* to death!" Jake chattered as he slowly made his way toward shallower water. Finally, the transfer was finished, and the warden packed up the truck and headed back into town.

Scrambling out of the water, Jake slogged as quickly as he could toward the dumping area and waded out to the pool of stunned fishes loitering about the surface. Shivering madly, Jake grabbed a fish only to have it vibrate out of his hands.

Then he remembered his bag hanging in the tree across the lake.

"D-d-d-dang it all..." With numb fingers, Jake jammed his shirt into his pants and furiously stuffed listless trout down its front.

Hurrying down the road toward home with his sides, back and belly bulging with violently flipping fish, Jake wriggled through the woods, trying to avoid the business end of needle-sharp dorsal fins.

"Quit your squirmin' around, d-d-d-dang it. *Yeeeeee heeeeheeehee,* d-d-damn fish, *YEEhee YOW!"*

Jake had nearly made it to his front door when he looked up and saw the game warden standing on his porch.

Stunned by Jake's approach, appearance and gyrating antics, the warden jumped back and instinctively reached for his pistol then paused, "Geez, I'm sorry, sir, you caught me off guard there. You, uh, you all right, mister?"

Jake, hunkering over and holding his sides, breathlessly replied, "Hooo, oh… yeah, yeah… I'm alright, just f-f-fell in the lake back there t-t-trying to, uh… get my hat."

"Well, good gosh almighty, that water's cold this time of year, you'll catch your death of cold!"

"Yep, yep, it's c-c-cold alright! Heh heeeeeee heee*yee-Oow."*

"Why, you look like you're getting hypothermia, there, you ought to let me help you into the house — this your house?"

"No, no, no I'm all right. Actually, no, this ain't my house. I'm headin' b-b-back that way, through th-th-the woods — only came up here to, uh, see if my b-b-buddy here might have a p–p-pole to get my hat with. Heck, I'll get that later, though. I'm gonna get on b-b-back to my place and change out of these s-s-smelly wet clothes. Warm up by the f-f-fire."

"Well, do you have a phone I can borrow? I'm having some trouble with my truck. Need to call the office."

"Nope, don't have no phone... but, uh... there's a ph-ph-phone back at the inn. Up the road a piece. *Heeeaauggg augghh!*" Jake doubled over and backed quickly into the woods.

"You sure you don't need some help?"

"N-n-nope, I'm f-f-fine, cold water just got my arthritis agg-g-g-gravated. Back s-s-spasms, is all... *whhhooooeeee ah ah ahhooooowww*. Th-th-that's all it is."

"Well, okay. I'll head on up to the inn, then. Be seein' ya." The warden, who had begun walking toward the inn, waved to Jake who continued wheedling his way vigorously into a thicket.

Safely out of sight, Jake tore his shirt out of his pants and ripped it open unleashing twenty-eight slimy, smelly fish. Looking like a victim of some weird massacre, Jake collapsed among the fish on the ground, his whole torso crisscrossed with long, thin, bleeding lacerations.

I was taking a cup of coffee to the warden who sat in the trading post warming his hands by the fire, when Jake squish-squashed through the door.

Grabbing a fishing pole, Jake slammed it on the counter, "Put this on my tab, will ya?" He glanced around and saw the warden sitting by the woodstove. "...and a license. Put a license on there too, heh heh."

"Decide to do a little fishing this morning?" The warden glanced over at Jake. "I just stocked the lake — ought to catch your limit in no time, pretty easy."

"Easier than a dang fish bomb that's for sure…" Jake muttered, rubbing his jaw as he grabbed his pole and headed toward the door.

"What's that?"

"Said, yep, been waitin' all winter long, that's for sure…" *squish, squash, squish, squash.*

The Legend of the Rat Man

Sent by my Mother's sister, Aunt Ruby, in a possible effort to evade his apprehension, my juvenile delinquent and slightly older cousin, Ricky, had arrived by express bus service from Kansas and moved into Wes' room while Wes spent a month over the summer with his folks back in Texas.

Apparently, Aunt Ruby harbored some hope that in the span of only four weeks, Dad would somehow turn Ricky away from petty theft, vagrancy and vandalism and onto the straight and narrow path. Having once shared a nap room with him as a toddler, I personally doubted a habitual crap-flinger could ever be rehabilitated.

Less than three days into his stay, Ricky was seriously beginning to get on my and Al's nerves. Already he had claimed everything as his own, popped off two dozen sarcastic comments and connected with every juvenile delinquent in town, namely Skidmark, Stretch and Stomp.

In our effort to reclaim turf, Al and I attempted to terrorize Ricky with stories of sasquatches and, of course — always whispering — the legendary *Rat Man.* When evoking the name of the Rat Man, whispering was an unspoken rule, as if leavening some potential curse with an appreciative degree of dread.

While Ricky foolishly shrugged off bigfoot, the Rat Man was a living, local legend which immediately drew not only Ricky's attention but boasts of bravery and threats of hostile harassment.

The Rat Man was a thin, balding man in his late forties who nested in a tool shed behind an aging Victorian house near the outskirts of town. Al told me the story late one November night while on a sleep-over.

"In the winter," she whispered, scooting back against a wall and glancing to either side, "he nests in his mother's basement next to the coal stove."

"*Nests?*" I quietly asked, eyebrows furrowed.

"He's the *Rat* Man," she stressed.

"Right." And suddenly it all made sense.

I never would have thought to go anywhere near the Rat Man, except that, now and then, Mother would bake two extra loaves of bread or an extra tray of cinnamon rolls and deliver them to the Rat Man's elderly mother, Cleo.

Standing on Cleo's porch one such afternoon, I leaned into the rickety railing to see if I could detect movement out behind their house. Nothing. Branches swayed lightly in the breeze and birds chirped… as if nothing odd were going on and a grown man weren't busily doing rat things in the dim light of the tool shed out back.

Mother and Cleo finished chatting about the weather, and we drove back to the inn.

Drawing on my experiences with Ralph, the hamster living on my dresser, I theorized aloud, "He must be nocturnal, I wonder if he has a wheel…"

Mother gave me a sideways look, "You know, he only thinks he's a rat because he had a really high fever one time."

"It's still weird," I said.

"Well sometimes you are, too. How do you think it looks to people who don't know us, when you and Al hide out in that stupid two-story cat fort you made out of cardboard boxes in the living room and spy on company?"

"That's true."

"It's no wonder no one ever just stops by to say hi."

Once, at dusk, Al and I were riding our bikes over from Al's house when we decided to detour through the woods near the Rat Man's.

We paused a good distance away and scanned the yard from behind the thick branches of a low-hanging spruce. Movement caught our eye, so, hoping to spy on him, we tip-toed astride our bikes to a vantage point behind some sparse bushes. We watched the Rat Man with electrified apprehension, as, hunched over, he clamored around on the ground sorting and stroking the long, gleaming white bones stacked three feet high around the walls of his shed.

Mother had assured us that every summer the Rat Man simply scouted the nearby forest for winter-kill and added new deer and elk thigh bones to his collection. But, every kid in town was sure where the bones *really* came from. And few dared say.

It was said that most nights, especially on moonlit nights, the Rat Man slipped out of his shed and rattled around in his bones or in the cans scattered around behind the house. Al and I now knew it to be true.

A couple of weeks after our discovery, Dad had taken Mother, us girls and Wes night-fishing out at Muskrat Lake.

Emboldened by our successful spy encounter and bored of waiting for a trout to bite, Al and I studied the night sky, reeled in our lines and said we were going for a short ride around the lake. Our eyes glinting with mischief, we pedaled off to Cleo's house — less than a half mile distant and, more importantly, close enough that Dad could hear us shouting should the Rat Man attempt an attack.

We eased into our spot behind the bushes where we could easily observe the Rat Man rummaging through a bag of garbage on Cleo's porch.

Beneath the dim mercury light in their yard some thirty yards distant, his grayed form blended softly with vague shadows around the old house.

Intently consumed with his task, he rifled through newspapers, shredded them into fluffy piles then hauled them off the porch into his shed. A minute later, he came out again, pulled out more papers and shredded some more.

Thinking again about my hamster, I nudged Al and whispered, "Look, it's just like watching Ralph."

"*Shhh!*" Al admonished, keeping her eyes locked on the specter before us.

The Rat Man hauled several apple cores and a milk carton from the trash then trundled across the yard toward the shed. Unexpectedly, he stopped and turned, looking directly at us.

Lifting his chin, he cautiously sniffed the air.

Al and I froze, unable to breathe and hoping desperately his eyesight had not permanently adapted to dark conditions. A few long seconds later, he turned and eagerly resumed his task.

Without a word, nod or look behind us, we peeled out as fast as our legs could pump.

Rounding the bend to the lake an eternity later, we sped toward Mother and Dad, skidded to a stop, grabbed a pole and, without even baiting up, flung our lines in the water on either side of Dad.

Everyone talked about the Rat Man's stash. Purportedly he had stolen some antique silverware from Gert and a few wrenches from Sol, up on the hill. Anytime something came up missing, especially something shiny, most everyone's first unspoken thought was... *the Rat Man.*

The thought of the Rat Man creeping around in the woods near his own home was unsettling enough. The thought of him sneaking into barns and houses and garages while everyone lie sleeping was more than Al or I could even contemplate. But, in an effort to try and scare Ricky, we told him about it nonetheless.

One morning, Al, Ricky and I were scouting the parking lot of the inn for bottle caps and cigarette butts — a tedious, unpleasant job which paid a nickel per unit. *Plip plip*, four butts went into an empty coffee can. I looked over at Ricky. He was shoving two long butts into his shirt pocket.

"No bottle caps all week," I muttered to Al, initiating our skit scripted the night previous.

"I noticed that," Al said, tossing another butt into her can. "Rat Man."

"You think he was HERE?!" I straightened and looked at her, eyes wide. The truth was, in preparation for our little ruse, Al and I had collected all the bottle caps the day before.

"Probably," she said. "It's almost a full moon. You know how he runs the riverbanks at night looking for bones... or fishermen... or whatever."

Ricky looked mildly alarmed but even more intrigued. You could tell the cogs were turning, though none too smoothly.

"He probably gathered them up for his stash," Al noted, stooping to pick up another butt.

"Yeah, or to gnaw on. That's how he keeps his teeth sharp," I almost sniggered at the last comment which Al and I had invented for the sake of keeping Rotten Ricky in line over the coming weeks.

Ricky's eyes widened. "He's got a stash? What kind of stash?"

"All kinds of stuff," I said, impatient to get back on the subject of bottle caps. "Shiny stuff, like silverware and tools. Stuff like that. Plus," I continued, bringing the subject back on track, "he chews on bottle caps."

"Silverware? What about coins? Or jewelry?" Ricky's beady eyes narrowed.

"Who knows?" I said, irritated.

"Well," Ricky snorted, "I ain't afraid of no dude collecting bottle caps."

"I don't know..." I looked at Al, trying to think of something scarier than a bottle cap eater, "remember that fat kid?"

Al had no idea what I was talking about but nodded knowingly, adding raised eyebrows for effect.

"Cripes," I went on, "that kid lost his little brass

telescope down by the creek, and later on, he saw it when he and his parents drove by along the road near the Rat Man's. And, remember…?" I looked at Al again who nodded somberly. "He jumped out of the car to get it, but the Rat Man ran him down. He came into the trading post all full of rat bites."

That story was only partially true. A fat kid did lose his telescope along the river and he did see it from the road near the Rat Man's, but standing at the ice cream counter in the trading post, I easily talked him out of trying to retrieve it.

Ricky seemed a little shaken by the story, at least deep down, but he smirked and took a long, dramatic drag off a cold butt. Then he turned toward town and sneered, "I ain't afraid of no Rat Man."

That afternoon, after stacking a pile of two-by-fours out behind the inn and mowing the back yard, Ricky was let off chores two hours before dinner to "go fishing at the lake" with his gang of miscreants.

Missing dinner, he snuck in the back door at eight o'clock that night, lugged his backpack across the hall and scanned the kitchen.

Dad was out in the shop tinkering and thinking up a miserable punishment for Ricky, while Mother was down at the inn helping Abbey refinish a table in her and Ty's apartment. Al and I were standing at the sink washing dinner dishes when Ricky snuck up behind us.

"Check this out!" he said excitedly, hoisting his backpack.

"*Aaiieee!*" I screeched amid an explosion of soap suds as Al snapped a wooden spoon in half and whirled to skewer anyone behind us.

"What do you want, weed?" I asked, sucking in a gulp of air and pushing Ricky back with my foot.

"You are *not* going to believe what I got! You're not gonna believe it, man!"

"What is it?" I demanded, figuring it was probably some kind of road kill and surprised he hadn't already tossed it in the dish water.

"Check *this* out!" He unzipped the pack and uncovered a trove of shiny treasures: coins, tin foil, keys, nuts and bolts, wrenches, cans... and bottle caps.

I stared.

Al stared.

"It's the Rat Man's *stash*, man! Skid stood guard, and I ripped it off while the Rat Man was crawling into the basement of that old house! Can you believe it?!"

Believe it? It was stunning. Rotten Ricky had actually been bold enough to tempt the notorious and legendary Rat Man. With an accomplice, of course.

Al muttered under her breath, "Skidmark..."

As shocking as it was to look into the backpack at the infamous stash, Ricky's theft had now deflated some of the Rat Man's mystic. I mean, now the Rat Man just seemed like some poor messed-up guy whose stuff got stolen. By a rotten punk. *Our* rotten punk.

Even worse than any of that was the admiration that was sure to be heaped upon Ricky and Skidmark once word spread throughout town and even down-valley into Bituminous. His dark deed would be twisted into a tall tale of bravado, and for the remainder of his stay he would be regarded by every kid in the valley as a living legend, himself. His inflated self-importance would be impossible to tolerate. Skidmark might be too cowardly to boast of the deed himself, but Rotten Ricky was a braggart.

Somehow, Al and I had to prevent news from spreading or otherwise thwart Ricky's assured rise to infamous glory.

Fourteen games of backgammon later, at two in the morning, Al and I quietly sawed a chunk of hamburger off a larger block of meat in the freezer, ripped a piece of butcher wrap off the roll in the pantry and finalized our elaborate plan.

A plan nearly ruined over breakfast at sunrise.

Dad swiped a piece of bacon around in his syrup, forked another pancake onto his plate and reached for his coffee. "What are you kids so quiet about this morning?"

"Nothing..." I looked up and reached for my orange juice.

Dad met my gaze — his deep brown eyes lifting the hidden truth from my very soul. To not have looked at him would have been worse, so I concealed my eyes behind the upturned glass. Dad's gaze never wavered.

We could have ratted Ricky out right there, but then we would have been robbed of the delicious revenge of our master plan. No. It all had to be kept secret.

Al quietly snapped off bits of bacon from the strip on her plate and nibbled them demurely.

Ricky grunted and shrugged while shoveling in wads of pancakes stacked five high on his fork.

Dad sipped his coffee and bent toward a bite of fried

egg. Raising his gaze beneath a slightly furrowed brow he said, "Nothing, huh? How come I don't believe that?"

Without looking up, Ricky wiped his mouth on his sleeve and pushed away from the table. He had been assigned the task of mucking out horse stalls.

Since winter, Dad and Ty had brought over a string of leased trail horses from Barrow's Stage, and Ty was now offering guided trail rides to tourists. From the regular stock, Dad had bought Mother an Arabian and himself a tall Dunn too unpredictable for the rodeo circuit and too wild for the trail. Ty bought a stallion. Half of our garage had been converted to a barn with a couple of stalls leading to the corral out behind the house, and already, according to Dad, they needed cleaning.

Ricky grabbed his gloves off the phone table by the front door and lifted his baseball cap off the peg on the wall. "Uncle Ike, I'm heading out to get started cleaning the stalls in the barn. Sorry I forgot about dinner last night."

"Uh huh," Dad replied, casting a dubious glace toward Mother who had only just sat down to a plate of pancakes, herself.

Al and I attempted to quell further inquiry by making as much noise as possible doing up the morning dishes and loudly singing ad jingles over the clatter.

Finally, the kitchen cleared out. Walking outside to check on Ricky's progress, Al and I commenced upon our plan.

He was only a third of the way through the smelly task. With plenty of time to lay the groundwork, Al and I lingered long enough to plant the seed.

"Man," Al said fawningly, "I can't believe you stole the

Rat Man's stash."

Ricky looked up, proudly grinning. *Shovel, shovel, scrape, scrape...*

"Yeah," I chimed in, eyes wide, "that was *way* brave. Are you sure he didn't see you?"

Ricky grinned wider and shook his head side to side, "Nope." *Shovel, shovel, scrape, scrape.*

"I hope he isn't able to follow your scent," Al said, barely able to contain a full-on smile.

Shovel, shovel... "What do you mean?" Ricky looked suddenly alarmed.

Al had to look away for a minute, pretending to refit the lid on a feed bin. "I mean, he can smell like crazy. He had some kind of radiation poisoning that made him whacko and think he's a rat, but it also gave him really sharp eyesight and a super-human nose. That's how he finds all those bones."

Ricky swallowed. He was taking the bait.

"Don't worry about it," I said. "He lives a mile and a half away. How can he smell that far? Plus, if he's going to trail something, it'll probably be Skidmark's stinky feet."

Al wrinkled her nose.

Ricky blurted, "Skid waited by the house in the bushes. He wasn't even in the shed. *I* was!" A look of panic began to overtake his face.

I affected a look of concern and turned to look at Al who did likewise. "Oh my God, Ricky," I said, "I hope you didn't lure him *here!* He loves that stash! He guards it! He might come after it!"

"No." Ricky gripped the shovel handle. "He won't. Like

you said, he won't be able to trail me that far. Plus, I hid the stash, anyway. He won't be able to find it."

"I just hope Skidmark doesn't go bragging about it. I mean, once word gets out who stole it..." Al shook her head slowly.

Ricky swallowed again.

Dad walked into the barn and surveyed we three who had suddenly fallen silent.

"Ricky, what are you doing standing around talking to these girls? Didn't I tell you to get this mess squared away before ten?"

"Yeah..."

"What?"

"Yes sir." Ricky looked at his feet. "But, I was going to go over to Skid's hou..."

"*What* are you going to do?" Dad leaned in, eyeballing Ricky.

"I'm going to finish cleaning the barn."

"That's what I thought you said. You girls leave him alone, so he can finish his work."

Al and I left the barn knowing one of two things would happen: either Ricky would keep shoveling or the minute Dad left, he'd tear out for Al's house in an effort to silence Skidmark. Either way, he'd be preoccupied with fearful thoughts far from his bedroom.

Al kept watch in the hall while I looked under Ricky's bed for the Rat Man's stash. Sure enough — there it was, still in the backpack.

Next, I opened Ricky's sock drawer and seized his

prized fishing lure collection. It had taken him four years to amass a wide and impressive selection of fifty-seven gold and silver, striped and spotted, twisted, dangling bits of sparkling metal. It was the first thing he flaunted when he arrived, bragging he'd catch a hundred fish his first week in town.

"Perfect!" I said, stuffing the leather case into the backpack. "Quick," I shouted to Al, "give me the note!"

Al shoved the crumpled note she'd written into my hand, and I carefully placed it where the lure case had been. The note was a wrinkled piece of butcher wrap with jagged letters scrawled in hamburger blood. It said: *I know what you did... I'm watching you.* She had signed it, *Rat Man,* and added an extra measure of spilled blood streaked claw-like across the bottom half of the torn paper. I stifled a snort as I slid the drawer back in place.

"Hurry up, darn it," Al ran in and looked out the bedroom window.

Suddenly, we heard the front door open, and Al and I made a dash for the back door, through the living room. Something fell from the pack, bounced twice and rolled down the hall, weaving from wall to wall toward the kitchen and gaining in momentum.

"Cripes, Al, a marble! Grab it, hurry!" I flew out the back door with the backpack and, cramming it into a brown paper sack, tied it to the handlebars then waited nervously for Al. She appeared in seconds and, with the marble still in her fist, we grabbed our bikes and peeled out of the yard.

"Give me the marble..." I panted, as we pedaled down the road.

Al held out her fist, and I took it into my palm. For some reason, I opened my fist to look at it, and it looked back.

"Cripes, Al, look! It's Earl's eye!" I was referring to One Eyed Earl, the man who lived out by the highway and plowed the county road every winter.

"*Gross!*" Al rubbed her palm on her pants.

The glass eye was cracked throughout, and had a big chip near the iris, but I shoved it into my pocket to give to Earl next time he plowed snow past the house. I figured glass eyes probably cost about ten-thousand dollars, and even if he couldn't wear it any more, he could mount it or something, recounting to his grandchildren how it had once been in the possession of the Rat Man.

Al and I made it to the Rat Man's in less than five minutes and eased our bikes boldly up beside the shed. We listened and thought we heard muffled rustling inside.

"Get away from there!" A shrill, crackly voice rose on the wind and flew up our shirts along a trail of goose bumps. The Rat Man's mother was leaning out an upstairs window, waving a newspaper, "Go on, you damn kids, get out of here!"

I tore the bag loose of the rope and tossed it in front of the shed door, knocking a tower of bones to the ground. Two bones clattered against my bike tire. With screams still bursting in our throats and adrenaline pumping, we wrenched our front wheels toward the county road and sped toward home.

We were riding up the driveway as Ricky, filthy and covered in sweat, carted the last wheelbarrow-load of horse manure to the woods out behind the house.

"Hey, Ricky," I shouted, "we're going to get a

sandwich, want one?" Our unlikely invitation was all a part of our plan which was, so far, neatly unfolding.

"Does a bear fart in the woods?" he shouted, attempting a sanitized version of one of Dad's frequent retorts. Tiring of Rotten Ricky's constant profanity, Dad had imposed a one-dollar cursing fine within thirty minutes of his arrival.

Al and I made up a stack of peanut butter and jelly sandwiches and were cutting them in triangular halves when Ricky walked into the kitchen. Leaving the door open, he snatched two halves off the plate. Inhaling one, he crushed the other in his hand as he leaned against the counter.

"Aren't you even going to wash your hands?" I asked, grimacing at the green filth that ran the length of his body.

"Nope." He wadded the rest of his sandwich into a ball and ate it in one bite, licking globs of grape jelly out from between his fingers.

At that moment, it became clear that Al and I had done the right thing. Rotten Ricky easily lived up to his moniker, and, regrettably, it had become our task to try and redeem him. We had carefully arranged the penance for his cruel misdeed upon the Rat Man, though he had yet to find out.

It was time for Phase II.

Curbing my impulse to up-chuck just looking at him, I munched my sandwich over by the sink. "You know what, Ricky? No one's going to believe you actually got the stash. You'll have to prove you stole it."

"Yeah," Al said. "What good is having it if no one knows? You'll probably have to show everyone something from the stash, or even the whole thing."

"But then," I threw in the wrench, "if you tell, it will get around, and then the Rat Man will know who stole it."

"You don't want that," Al said.

"Yeah…" Ricky reflected, working a dirty fingernail between his front teeth. "Maybe I'll just sneak it back into his shed. There ain't nothin' good in it anyway."

Ricky turned and ambled off purposely down the hall.

Al and I grinned the broad grin of the knowing.

We heard the door to his room open. Something shuffled. Something shuffled louder. Something slammed. "Where the hell *is* it?" Ricky fumed. "Damn it, somebody stole it!"

Al and I ran down the hall and stood in his doorway, looking dismayed.

Assuming an annoyed tone, I asked, "What are you yelling about?" Al hit me in the ribs. I shoved her back. Ricky tore through the closet and looked under the bed.

"Somebody stole the damned stash!" Ricky was assuming his macho mode, in which he employed foul language and physically destroyed his surroundings appearing to be more in command than he actually was. He unleashed a streak of profanity as Al cast a knowing glance my way. We knew, given our undivided attention, he would be unable to resist pulling open dresser drawers, if only for effect.

We waited.

More cursing, then he flung open the comic book drawer. A dramatic flourish, another curse then he ripped open both his underwear and sock drawers simultaneously. He glanced down and froze. Turning ashen, he appeared to wobble.

"What is it?" I asked. "Ricky... what's wrong?"

Al and I walked over to him and looked into the drawer.

"Oh, my God! What *is* that?" I whispered, as if leavening some curse with an appreciative degree of dread.

Al shrieked and ran from the room.

Ricky hesitantly retrieved the note and, hands trembling, quickly scanned the bloody words.

"He got m-my lure c-coll-collec..." Ricky couldn't even finish his sentence.

"Oh my God..." I repeated. "Oh, my *God,* Ricky, he was in the house! He was in *your room!"*

Al, who had been standing by the door frame, screamed and covered her mouth with her hand.

"Stop it! Just stop it!" Ricky commanded. "Don't tell anyone about this!"

I cast a terrorized look at Al, "I won't, I won't. But what about Skidmark? Maybe the Rat Man got Skidmark and he squealed!"

Wordlessly, Ricky crumpled the note, shoved it in his pocket, ran outside, jumped on his bike and took off into town.

I picked up the phone and called Sol's son, Bucky, a town kid superior in intellect but junior in age to Skidmark. "Have you heard anything about the Rat Man?" I asked Bucky when he picked up he phone.

"Are you kidding, it's all over town! Skid's telling everyone! I'm coming over to see."

"Yeah? Well, I think it's a bunch of bull. I haven't seen any stash." I glanced over at Al and grinned. "I don't think they were even *there.* I'd make Ricky show you the stash to prove he has it. Well, gotta go, talk to ya later..."

I waited for the second click, indicating our habitual eavesdropper had been on the party-line listening in. I hung up, and Al and I did the high-five, low-five, in-the-middle-five, gottcha-bad boogie.

Next day, Al and I heard that Ricky had denied stealing anything from anyone, and in the absence of proof or confession, there was little for either Skidmark or Ricky to do but bicker viciously over slanderous accusations and alleged truths, all with the effect of revitalizing and even elevating the mythic dimension of the Rat Man.

The Ladies' Society of Diamond Hills Luncheon

"You and Al, all four hours. Plus, you'll get a free gourmet lunch and a bonus twenty bucks at the end of the day."

"Apiece?" I asked, shrewdly eyeing Willy.

Al and I were in the midst of negotiating compensation for our work as the set-up, break-down and service crew for a special event Willy and Gert were hosting that day at the Pan Handle.

"Yeah, yeah, apiece," Willy said. He and Gert had been slicing, dicing and sautéing since one o'clock that morning, so were anxious to get home and catch a nap before the big event.

Given what we knew about the special menu, we were definitely more interested in the cash than the food.

The event was to be a luncheon for the Ladies' Society of Diamond Hills. Diamond Hills was an international resort community located thirty or so miles away and comprised of wealthy business tycoons and Hollywood celebrities. Willy had landed the gig when a member of the Society dropped by the café with her husband one afternoon a few weeks earlier.

Willy's offer of a twenty dollar bonus was minimal. I knew too well the level of maintenance the wealthier set could sometimes demand, since I was the one who catered to Her Majesty's every whim the day she first graced the café.

Observing through a window, I'd seen her pour herself from a silver sedan and totter across the graveled parking lot on four-inch spike heels. I guessed her high, wide, hair-sprayed platinum-blonde locks easily outweighed her by thirty pounds. Grappling for the door frame in a sudden stiff breeze, her abundant jewelry appeared to be the only thing keeping her ground-bound. She entered ahead of her suit-clad husband and, together, they took one of only three available tables in the middle of the busy dining room.

I set two glasses of chilled water and two menus in front of them.

"Oh, heavens *no, no, no*, I need *iced* water!" She shooed away the glass with one hand as she delicately smoothed her hair with the other.

Stopping with a pot of coffee to top off a diner along the way, I dashed through the short, swinging doors into the kitchen.

During the summer, three days out of the week, Al and I worked at the café. One of us would work the fourteen-table dining room and cash register while the other washed dishes. Next day, we'd switch. Willy was always on the grill, and Gert shuttled parts or plates or handled whatever else needed immediate attention.

From the dining room, you could look over a partition wall into part of the kitchen, which was basically a sixteen-foot run with the dishwashing station and freezer at one end, and the grill, refrigerators and pantry located at the other. The narrow passage could barely accommodate two people side-by-side let alone the violently flung ice-chest or loaf of Texas toast prone to going airborne by either Willy or Gert at the height of the lunch rush.

Willy and Gert, weaned temporarily from the calming effect of their herbal indulgences, commonly hurled insults and implements at one another proportionate to the number of cars parked off the boardwalk. It was predictably at the peak of such a rush that Willy would bolt through the kitchen's back door and make for a nearby tree where he'd sit on a low branch, look around and swing his feet. Occasionally, if Dad were no where around, Willy might even partake of a 'smoke' break.

The day of Her Majesty's first visit, we still had two tables to fill before I figured Willy would cut and run.

"How's this?" I asked, returning to the woman's table and delivering, along with my sincerest smile, the requested glass of ice water full of tinkling cubes.

"Have these been washed?" she asked, peering dubiously at the glass.

"Of course," I said with certainty, since either I or Al had washed it.

"Really?" She appeared less than convinced. "You say these ice cubes are washed?"

For a moment I stood processing the question. Somehow, the pieces of information didn't add up... "washed", "ice cubes". I mentally calculated that ice-cubes floating in water might qualify as washed, so ventured a question of my own, "What exactly do you mean by *washed* ice cubes?"

Assuming a haughty tone, she glanced at her husband then back at the poorly compensated, obviously under-educated help, "My dear. I mean, have these ice cubes been washed *before* they were added to the glass of water?"

Oh. *That* clarified the whole issue. Now, I understood.

"No," came the flat reply.

Her husband, elbows on the table, tucked his chin behind his intertwined fingers and briefly glanced up at me. Appearing slightly entertained, his eyes seemed to apologize.

"*Well,* I cannot drink this water without the proper ice cubes. Bring me a dish of washed ice cubes and a glass of cold water."

I nodded affirmatively and hustled back to the kitchen where I was waved down in mid-stride by a diner asking, again, for his tardy side of bacon.

"Willy, table seven needs his bacon side," I said, busting through the swinging door and filling a new glass with water. Pulling a bowl off a shelf, I hurried to the freezer.

As the ice cubes clinked into the bowl, Willy leaned away from the grill with furrowed brows. "What are you doing?"

"Putting ice cubes in a bowl."

"Why?"

"So I can wash them."

Not a picture of patience, I knew he was trying to process the information just as I had.

"What the hell are you talking about?"

"The lady out front asked me to wash these stupid ice cubes. Don't ask *me*." I barely had time to conjure a confounded expression before Gert set two plates on the partition, ready for delivery to table four.

Al leaned away from the sink as I quickly rinsed the

cubes, drained the water from the bottom of the bowl and slipped a spoon inside. Delivering the items as requested, I was eyeballed en route by the bacon man.

Back by Her Majesty's side, the woman lifted the bowl of ice and closely examined its contents. "For heaven's *sake,*" she sighed, "do you have something I can dry these on? They should have been set out to drain separately then added to a *dry* bowl. Otherwise, they stick together, and that *simply* will not do."

Despite the hugely annoying woman and her demanding manner, I began to appreciate what her husband had formerly found so amusing. She really was too absurd to be taken seriously, and I began to perversely enjoy my central role in the ten-minute drama she had manifest over a glass of water. In fact, something of this ability was probably to be admired. "Right," I said, feigning enlightenment. "I'll get you something *right* away."

"Well, I hope so," she stated flatly. "These may be ruined. I may have to order new ice cubes."

I hurried through the kitchen and opened the back door, dragging in the huge, filthy utility towel used to dry muddy shoes.

"Where are you going with that?" Willy asked, as I began dragging it through the swinging door into the dining room.

"Customer request." And off I slogged.

She stopped complaining to her husband and gazed with clear disgust as I approached.

"This is all I could find. Want me to rinse you a new

set?"

Amazingly, though I anticipated the drama to escalate, she merely cast a peevish look my way and proceeded to order.

Without looking at the menu she rotated a huge diamond ring around her finger, "I'd like to have the veal."

"We don't have any veal." I actually had no idea what veal was, but since I'd never heard of it, I was pretty sure it wasn't on the menu.

Her husband interjected, "Why don't you just bring us a couple of hamburgers with fries. Is that all right with you, honey?" He looked at his wife now busy examining her diamond-studded bracelet.

"Fine, *whatever...*" She rose from her seat. "I'm going to the ladies' room." Two steps from the table, she whirled and added, "I don't want any meat on my hamburger. Also, no bun... no sauce... two slices of tomato... no onion. Extra lettuce."

I nodded, trying to keep everything straight in my head while fumbling for the order pad in my apron pocket. "Do you just want a salad?" I asked.

"Of *course* not. If I had wanted a salad, I would have ordered a salad. And, for heaven's sake, hold the *fries.* Bring me a glass of grapefruit juice instead."

The man at table seven suddenly shouted toward the kitchen partition and pointed at his plate, "*BACON?*"

Willy appeared instantly above the partition, clutching two raw strips of bacon in his raised fist. "If you don't pipe down, I'm gonna wipe your ass with these. How's that grab ya?"

Gert flew past, ripped the bacon out of his hand and threw the strips onto the grill.

The hungry hordes of tourists kept me too busy during the afternoon lunch rush to think much more about the annoying couple until her husband and I were standing at the register.

"May I please speak with the owner of this establishment," he said politely, handing me a credit card.

"Sure," I said. "He's out back in the tree. I'll show you the way."

Strangely, the man seemed quite adaptable and took up a comfortable position beneath the tree on a crate, where I later learned he negotiated with Willy to host the ladies' annual luncheon at the café.

According to Willy, the man was evidently enchanted by the rapturous views and rustic charm of our humble inn. As a financial contributor to the Society, he apparently was cashing in on his influence. Doubtless, his wife would be displeased with his selection, which seemed to be his intent. A deal was struck beneath the tree, and for this, a small sum was advanced and a few details were arranged.

The remainder of the couple's visit was uneventful — other than inspiring the euphoric dance which possessed my feet when I discovered he had left a twenty dollar tip under the sugar bowl.

I thought I had been rid of her, but now she was to return with what I imagined to be a clan of those just like her. I could only imagine the tirade which followed her husband's announcement that the venue for her annual event was to be the

Pan Handle Café.

Thrilled for the opportunity to, in their words, "put the Pan Handle on the map", Willy and Gert were geared for high-society all around. Willy bought a new pair of jeans, and Gert put on a bra.

"So, what do we have to do?" Al asked Willy.

"Get the linens on the tables, make sure all the place settings, center pieces and markers are in place according to the seating list. Set out the flowers. And decorate the windows, the counters and the walls with the crepe garlands. Oh, and change the menu." He fished in his pocket and handed us the seating and menu lists.

Leaving the cosmetic preparations to Al and me, Willy double checked that the sign on the door read "closed", made a last minute visit to the kitchen then was out the back door headed for his cabin.

Implementing the credo of the flat-fee wage earner, Al and I worked furiously in an effort to squander for ourselves the second of the two hours set aside for dining room preparation.

After close to an hour, nearly all had been accomplished. The room, now filled with tables draped in white linens and bedecked in white dishes and white vases with white flowers, seemed to glow. Gobblets of sparkling water sporting lemon wedges reflected the sun shining brightly through the window, and the room was adorned with long strands of white garland draped gracefully from center ceiling to walls. The dining room had been transformed from a rustic café into a sophisticated and elegant rustic café.

By this time, Al and I had worked up a powerful thirst

and headed for the refrigerator for some hard-earned refreshment. Dad had established rules early on about Willy and Gert's herbal cigarettes, and both of them were given orders not to bring them onto the property. Al and I knew Willy snuck a puff now and then, but we never ratted anyone out. We liked the mellow Willy a lot better than the ice-chest flinging Willy. Unbeknownst to any of us, however, Willy kept a second vice around to calm his nerves in the event Dad was nearby.

Besides fluffy omelets and juicy burgers, Gert and Willy had an apparent knack for brewing homemade apple jack. For those readers unfamiliar with the elixir, it's an alcoholic concoction a lot like apple juice — in fact, looking and tasting very similar but possessing a significant kick when consumed in large quantities.

Large quantities were exactly what Al and I were looking for.

"Hey," Al shouted from the kitchen, "you want some apple juice? Doesn't that sound really good?"

"Yeah!" I seconded. "That sounds great."

Al brought over a brimming gallon jug. "Smell this... it smells weird to me. It was in the back of the fridge on the bottom shelf."

I took a sniff. "It's okay. I think it's cider. I've heard cider smells weird. Let's taste it."

Looking around for a small glass, I suggested we use two shot glasses from the saloon which was closed for the morning and resided adjacent to the café, behind a split-partition door.

I ran over to the saloon, grabbed two of the tiny glasses,

hurried back over and plopped them onto the kitchen counter. Al poured our shots.

I sniffed again and ventured a small taste. "It's pretty good. I don't think apple cider goes bad anyway."

"Are you sure?"

"No. Here, taste some."

Al ventured an actual sip. "Yeah, that's good stuff. Let's get a big glass."

"But this looks neat — this looks just like whiskey!" I threw back the shot swallowing the whole thing in one gulp, wiped my mouth with my sleeve and slid the glass down the counter to Al. "Another shot, bar keep!"

Sniggering, Al complied then passed the jug to me, so I could play bartender and she could play outlaw.

Oh, the irony.

Al downed her shot, sucked her teeth and sighed greatly before unleashing a cascade of giggles.

We sat at a table in the dining room and passed the jug and shot glasses back and forth snorting and chortling as we made believe we were rancid outlaws at some old western tavern, imitating those we had seen at the saloon every night all winter long.

Half a jug and twenty minutes later, Al leaned back in her chair in an exaggerated display and did her best John Wayne impression, "Whall arrr you callin' my horse a *liar*, strrranger?"

I leaned in, eyes unusually wide, and fired right back, "Whall I'm sayin'... hay bales ain't on th' menu, an I don think your-horze izzn't gonna like baked 'laska."

Al sat thinking for a minute.

"Heyyy," she drawled, "aren't we sss'pposed ta do th' menu? We beterrrr git th' hay on th' menuu."

We both collapsed in a fit of mirth, somehow realizing we were supposed to change the menu but possessing no faculties to suggest we ought not include hay bales on it. In fact, it was to have read like the lunch menu of a fine French bistro replete with an expensive and complicated array of delectable edibles.

"You go git th' letters for th' thing, an I'll... I'll git th' thing..." I directed.

Al stumbled over to the register. From the cupboard beneath it, she snatched the bag of tiny, blue plastic letters designed to fit neatly into the grooved surface of a massive board unchanged since the opening of the Pan Handle.

She returned to her chair where she sat sprawled, clutching the bag of letters and watching me scale a table in an ungainly attempt to unhook the board from its tenacious grasp on the wall in an unassuming corner of the room.

I lumbered over to the table with the board on my head and unintentionally slammed it on the table as I fell into my seat. A thousand tiny blue letters popped out of their housing and vibrated in disarray all over the board.

Al looked up at me, shocked into some notion that what had occurred was a bad thing. I looked at the board then up at Al, speechless, but nonetheless interested in the board's ability to entertain us to so great a degree. Suddenly, we both broke with raucous laughter and began grabbing letters and placing them in earnest.

"Hey. Howwwd-ya spell intestines?" I asked Al.

"I dunno. In... in... test... I dunno. Jusspell *guts,*" she said, spurring another riotous round of laughter.

"Hee hee, fly gut *ssssurpizzze!* Howzzat fer dinnnner?" I asked, rearing back to focus my eyes on my handiwork.

"Thasss-GREAT!" shouted Al. "But howzisss? Termite an frog-lips a'la mmmmode! *Ah ha ha"* Al cracked herself up and slapped the surface of the board popping all our letters out of their slots. Silence. Then more laughter as I heartily joined in.

Together we brainstormed all kinds of weirdly grotesque soups, desserts, entrées and even a beverage list. The limits of our wild and quite drunken imaginations were boundless.

Poo pile stew and maggot loaf boldly stood in for anchovy canapés and miniature spinach quiches which, with our advanced palates, we considered closely related anyway.

I wobbled back over to the wall and climbed onto the table as Al handed me the menu board.

"Cerfulll nnnow," Al assumed a low tone, steadying herself against the wall and looking serious as her eyes crossed and uncrossed, competing with one another for the best view of her nose. "You don-wanna drop it an ruin our wwwurk."

We spent an excruciatingly long time getting the menu positioned exactly right, during which time we completely forgot the nature of our task and became quite enraptured with the seriousness of squaring the board with the ceiling.

"*Whew.* I think, issss boootif.. boootifffule. Iss great, Al," I leaned back and somberly stated.

"Yeah... iss perrfack. Perfick," Al sniffed and wiped a

misty eye with her sleeve.

A furious pounding on the café door recaptured our attentions, and Al cast me a concerned look. "Somebodeezz trapped *inside!*"

We hurried to the source of the noise, knocking over a chair in our rush. "Hang on," Al yelled, "I'm comin'!"

Getting to the door, we looked out the window and saw cars lining up along the boardwalk. Al yanked open the door, expecting it to be resistant to her effort. It flung open, knocking her into a table beside me.

Al struggled to right herself as Her Majesty the "ice cube queen" sashayed into the room, immediately surveying all before her.

Carrying a red glittery bag, she wore white gloves, a white summer dress and white high heels. My eyes instantly fixed to the bag and followed her every overstated gesture around the room as she described the quaint location to her large gaggle of noisy friends — each one a near replica of the original.

An air of unease permeated the room. Judging by the way her twenty friends grimaced at our country décor, I suspected each had been apprised of the ice cube incident.

Completely unclear about the content of Her Majesty's speech and registering only the buttery tones accentuated by an occasionally shrill punctuation, I tried to focus on her bag. When that was discarded, I affixed to her hair since it seemed to reflect, like a lighthouse, the sunny rays bouncing through the window and was the only object capable of competing with the flashing sea of glittering jewels pulsing randomly throughout the room.

A few of the ladies seated themselves among a scattering of tables and all began chattering in a manner which suggested Al and I had walked into a field overrun with chirping crickets. Her Majesty, however, and those inspired by her, stood by their tables waiting to be seated.

Al had closed the front door and was making her way to the kitchen.

I still stood dazed and staring at the woman's hair, my blank expression prompting her to utter a forced, "*Ahem.*" She nodded slightly toward her chair, with her hands folded neatly before her and the corners of her mouth upturned as she surveyed the ladies who stood, themselves, awaiting the attentions of either Al or myself.

I continued to stare, and Al came to stand beside me, so that four eyes were now fixed upon her without any particular reason or sign of comprehension.

"For heaven's sake, are you or are you *not* going to pull out my chair?"

A round of tittering floated about the room, and Al and I glanced at one another. I figured Al's brain was functioning much like my own, and, despite the woman's probable meaning, I took her quite literally.

Her eyes followed me to her table then she fixed them straight ahead, as if waiting to be dressed or groomed.

I walked behind her and fulfilled her command, pulling out her chair — and carrying it away to a spot near the door.

Continuing to stare straight ahead and smiling to her friends, she tucked under the hem of her dress, assumed a sitting position and flailed backward.

Grabbing for the table cloth and inviting most of the table's contents crashing down upon her, she sat splayed and screaming, with dishes on her lap and bits of daisy in her hair, "Well, I never! I *NEVER!*"

A swarm of helping hands descended upon her and boosted her to her feet while brushing away stray flower petals, offering sympathetic condolences and glaring at me and even Al, who had been implicated by proximity.

Smoothing her dress and kicking a glass under the table, the woman stalked to another table and sat down with those who had been waiting with her.

"I need a *new* setting and a *new* glass of water — *IF* you think you can manage *that!*"

It had not yet occurred to Al or me that neither Willy nor Gert were present to orchestrate the unfolding affair, nor did it occur to either of us to call, which would not have mattered since they didn't have a phone. Did it occur to either of us to go for help in the form of any responsible adult? Apparently not.

We robotically reset Her Majesty's table. Since she appeared to be capable of and willing to direct our slow-to-engage brains, we lingered momentarily near the beast, though far enough away to avoid harm should she suddenly decide to impale one of us with a shrimp fork.

Disoriented and without benefit of past experience, Al and I suspected we should, next, deliver the appetizers.

A pointed look from our nemesis sent us wandering in the direction of the kitchen.

In the strangely numb universe of an alcohol-induced

stupor, the only objective became to execute each task wordlessly, carefully and in a systematic order. Such an attitude was particularly well-suited to this crowd who hired domestic help based precisely upon a preference for such tendencies.

Stoically, Al and I made our way to the kitchen where we located plates of appetizers, unwrapped them, and carried them one-by-one to the ladies in waiting. Slowly, we wound ourselves among the high heeled tips of long waxed legs and high hair-dos, randomly depositing saucers of tiny quiches.

In the fog of perfume, I strained to keep my eyes and head in focus, consciously commanding myself to run the trail between tables and kitchen.

Al and I banged into one another, swaying and grasping for handholds as we each made for the entry to the kitchen. We eyed one another, backed up and made for the entry again only to squeeze ourselves together like two mice wedged in a knothole. Al began to snigger and, suddenly, our inability to discover the mechanics of courtesy seemed overwhelmingly hilarious.

Our giggles quickly escalated to laughter interrupted only by the screeching summons of the High Ruler herself.

"*AHEM.* My hors d'oeuvre?"

Al looked at me with a glimmer in her eye. "I'll get it," she quietly insisted.

Meanwhile, back at Willy and Gert's cabin, the two had awoken from their inadvertently extended napping only moments earlier. Willy, barely without injury, escaped Gertrude as she buffeted him with a shoe and shoved him out the door and down the road. Confident that Willy could take things well in hand, she remained behind to properly dress and wrangle her new brassiere.

Hurrying down the road, Willy skittered along on bare feet and struggled against the wind to shove an arm into his flapping shirt sleeve.

Back at the café, Al strode purposefully to the kitchen counter where she began madly launching wads of plastic wrap over her head in search of additional plates of appetizers. Finally honing in on the remaining plate of quiches, she placed one on a saucer and shot me the look of someone about to undertake unspeakably wicked retribution.

I watched, mesmerized, as Al worked her way through the expressively on-looking ladies quietly munching their petite fare.

Al lowered the plate before the Her Majesty and smiled sweetly.

Glances quickly exchanged around the room, as if to say: I've seen that look before from our kitchen staff. I wouldn't eat that if I were her.

Her Majesty was on the spot with all eyes turned upon her. She met Al's gaze with a supreme glare, pressed her fork into the spongy form and slowly lifted it to her glossy, red lips.

I couldn't believe Al was holding her stare and knew there was more to this story about to unfold.

They gripped one another in a steely gaze, Al silently pressing Her Majesty to comment.

It was like watching two wild animals face off in the forest — each vying for territorial supremacy, and this woman could not know of Al's long and decorated history of survival in the same household as Skidmark. Al knew animal instinct, and this woman had no idea who she was dealing with.

Slowly, Her Majesty chewed then glanced at her water, breaking eye contact with Al. This was Her Majesty's opportunity to detract from the challenge at hand and make some biting reference to improperly prepared ice, which Al and I had failed to provide altogether.

Her Majesty swallowed, demonstrating some difficulty, then raised her flaming eyes to once again meet Al's. "This quiche... it's a bit... *dry,* isn't it?" She glanced around at her cohorts, seeking mass affirmation.

Al seized the moment she had been waiting for. Smiling demurely, she leaned toward the woman and whispered loudly enough that the women at the surrounding tables could hear, "That's because it's not *quiche.* It's maggot loaf."

Excited murmurs erupted among the women, followed by distressed faces scanning the walls.

Like an unseen contagion, loudly announced words like *"bat livers"* and *"yak eye delight"* spread terror among the throng, which instantly erupted in a crescendo of riotous screaming.

Panic yielded to pandemonium, and, like a great, bleached-blonde tsunami, the women rose, seized their handbags and rushed the door.

It appeared the entire dining room was coming undone in a be-jeweled maelstrom as one satin-clad woman viciously clawed her way upon another in an effort to reach the exit first.

Such a pulling of hair, tearing of dresses and beating of handbags upon heads I was surprised to witness among so sophisticated a set.

At that moment, on the other side of the café door, Willy stood reaching for the knob with one hand while still tucking in his shirt with the other.

Without warning, the door flew open, and the shrieking wave hit Willy head-on sending him careening against an upright support beam and grappling backward over the railing into the parking lot.

One overwrought woman looked upon Willy's wild, startled eyes and instinctively began flailing him with her purse.

Another woman leapt over the two of them like a track and field hurdler, seized her startled driver by his lapels and scaled him to the top of her vehicle's ski rack where she crouched screeching like a pterodactyl.

Cars flew from the parking lot, spinning tires and spewing gravel for a quarter mile. Within three minutes, all was calm.

Willy entered the café, knees quaking. His vibrating hand gathered back his long hair as he glanced cautiously around the room.

It had been a category-five catastrophe. Shreds of crepe paper garland hung from the wall and lie draped across tables overturned with chairs sharing floor space with spilled saucers of half-eaten quiche. Silverware, flower stems, three odd earrings and a shoe littered the floor. Lip gloss and eye shadow smeared the door facing, and the closed sign lie trampled to oblivion, perforated by forty-nine stampeding spike heels.

"What... in the hell... *happened* here?" Willy stammered.

At first, Willy was plenty steamed that we had single-handedly ruined his and Gert's chances for fame and fortune. But then we told the story — as best we knew it, with Willy providing valuable context once the gallon jug of apple jack was found overturned on the floor. In fact, picking a leftover shred of garland off a chair and glancing up at the menu, Willy actually grinned. He took two twenties out of the register and handed one to each of us.

"Tell you what," he said, "you two clean up this pit before Gert gets here, and I'll give you both an extra twenty. Take anything you want from the fridge."

Al and I dug into the fray with great gusto, clearing the last letters off the board as Gert walked through the door.

Her first and only words regarding the entire affair followed: "Where's Willy?"

She should have guessed our response.

"Out in the tree."

Amy Wilson's Pool Party

Al and I watched bitterly as small pink envelopes with red-heart stickers were passed around Mrs. Rotbottom's eighth grade math class.

With great ceremony and attention to the doorway — lest the decrepit Mrs. Rotbottom return sooner than anticipated — each envelope was hand delivered to its carefully considered recipient.

First came the round of secretive giggles then the canvassing glance to make sure on-lookers had acknowledged the privileged exchange.

We knew without receiving one that inside each envelope was a perfectly scripted invitation to Amy Wilson's thirteenth birthday party.

Al and I looked sourly at one another. It wasn't that we wanted to attend such an overblown affair, but the display of exclusivity sickened us to our very souls. Which is why our mouths hung open and we salivated on the envelope when two were finally chucked our way, landing on our desks as Amy flew down the aisle to her seat a split-second ahead of Mrs. Rotbottom's entrance.

Mrs. Rotbottom's quick, dark eyes scanned the surface of our desks and honed in on the objects of our sudden attention.

Hands on hips, she pronounced, "Well, what have we

here? Passing notes?" She held out her hand, expectantly. "Hand them over."

We obligingly passed the pink envelopes forward where they were snatched from the fingers of their hander-overers with no special consideration given whatsoever to the threat of paper cuts.

The small, fierce woman read the first little card silently then, looking at Amy, asked, "Invitations to a party, Miss. Wilson? I may assume then, the entire class is invited?" She was one of those teachers who relished diminishing anyone's slightest private enjoyment by exposing and parsing it amongst the masses for rapid dispatch.

"Yes, Mrs. Rotbottom," Amy smiled sweetly, "the whole class is invited."

Stunned, I gaped at Al who, like me, had assumed the whole casting of envelopes was nothing more than an error in trajectory. After all, Amy considered herself the sole occupant at the pinnacle of middle-school hierarchy. An untouchable, elevated far above even the half-dozen disciples she hand selected as ankle-fobs on a casually rotating basis.

Neither Al nor I were among such a lot — the predictable and happy result of mutual disdain.

Amy never failed to flaunt her family's wealth, amassed through the pain of dental surgery and braces. Her selective offers of parties, favors and fun bought her unashamed loyalty among the majority of kids in a community of ranchers, farmers and coal miners.

Constantly recruiting new loyalists and punishing those who strayed, Amy lived to humiliate those outside the realm of her worship. Invitations to her parties were always darkened with ulterior motive. The tales were infamous.

Gifts brought to an Amy Wilson birthday party were openly appraised and compared to others. Those that failed to measure up always found their way to the thrift store where they would become the topic of surprised conversation. On particular occasions, Amy was known to reserve and later present an unwanted gift to the giver at their *own* birthday party.

Amy's parties, even when conducted among her closest fobs, became opportunities to discriminate and reinforce the circumstances of her and others' social status. She was always designing a means to financially frustrate or exclude those she invited, such as hosting a masquerade ball then requiring a prohibitively expensive costume.

Those who chose to decline an invitation were presumed too poor to afford a gift or other contribution worthy of comparison.

All in all, 'Amy Events' were carefully constructed manipulations; an invitation to one was both blessing and bane. I briefly entertained the idea of attending, considering the benefits against the risks. The cake was likely to be tasty.

As I quietly pondered, Amy announced to the room, as if on cue, "It's a *pool party!*"

Thoughts of creamy frosting and tiny edible roses hit the brakes. A *pool* party. Good grief. What could *that* be? It sounded formal. Another of Amy's complicated maneuvers. It obviously involved a pool. Hopefully a swimming pool, which was the only kind I knew of. But, what would I wear? Neither Al nor I owned what one might consider a fashionable swim suit. Neither of us considered any particular outfit essential to flotation, and, if anything, such a prerequisite frustrated the joyous impulse of jumping into Quartz Creek wearing whatever we happened to have on at the time.

Fishhooks, snags and rock shards made tennis shoes much more vital to our ensemble than some swim 'suit' bought at the local discount store. So, an Amy pool party would mean we'd probably have to buy flip flops, too. Then there was the gift. Cripes. Amy was shrewd.

Inviting the entire eighth-grade was her latest and most inventive means of emphasizing her family's social and financial status while seeking to humiliate even more of us outlanders at the same time. Mass humiliation among those culled by economic fortune. She had reached a new height.

That night at the dinner table, Al snorted her disdain for Amy's latest ruse, "What she won't do. I mean, on the one hand, it's great to get an invitation. On the other... man."

"Who?" Dad asked, lifting his eyes from buttering a biscuit. "An invitation to what?"

Cripes. Al and I had decided on the bus to skip the party, but Al was unaware that no comment could be made at our dinner table without great paternal scrutiny. Dad would want all the details. The who, the what, the where, the when, the why and the how. Cursed investigator. Not only did he automatically assume we might be up to or hiding something, but he also believed he needed to air his opinion on the affair and that his opinion should hold sway.

Thirteen years across the ketchup bottle from Dad had taught me that casual table topics had to be pre-screened. But,

Al didn't know.

"Oh, it's just some dumb party," I said, reaching for a biscuit and intentionally knocking the serving spoon out of the peas as a hoped-for distraction.

"Damn it, Lisa," Dad said, picking a pea out of his iced tea. "What kind of party?"

"Just a thing this girl is having in Granite," I offered, reluctantly.

"What girl? What kind of party?"

Sigh. I ducked my head and rolled my eyes back in their sockets, muttering, "Just a birthday party she's having."

"Who else is invited?"

Al chimed in, "The whole class."

Dad nodded in the affirmative, "Well, that might be nice."

"I guess," I said. "But, she's a huge pain in the butt."

"Why do you say that?" Here came the inquisition. Here is where conversation shifted to debate and Dad labored to draw out every argument in order to defend whomever he thought I was falsely accusing.

"She's spoiled and mean and she's always trying to embarrass people," I blurted with minimal forethought.

"Her dad's an orthodontist," Al noted without emphasis while referring indirectly to the source of Amy's wealth.

Nooo, I thought, miserably. Al just gave him ammunition.

"Well, you can't blame someone for their profession, girls. Sometimes people end up in careers they never even planned for. There's nothing wrong with being an orthodontist."

"Yeah, but she's always parading her money in front of everyone," I quickly added.

"Well, maybe she's just trying to be your friend. Did you ever think of that? Maybe inside, she's a very lonely person."

Sigh... I stared at the floor, unable to force my eyeballs any further backward.

"You know, you shouldn't judge someone until you've walked a mile in their moccasins."

I hung my head over my plate. Doomed. Here it came...

Dad looked at Mother, "I think it's nice the girls were invited to a party, don't you, honey?"

"Mm hmm."

Sigh...

"I think it might do you girls some good to spend some time with other kids your age. There aren't that many opportunities for you to do that kind of stuff around here."

And we liked it that way. There were *no* Amy Wilsons for thirty miles in any direction. "Dad," I began, "we don't even have swim suits."

"We'll take care of that. What else do you need?"

"Presents."

"Okay, we'll take care of that. What do you think she would like?"

Our heads on stakes, I thought. "I don't know. A diary? A stuffed animal, maybe?" A machete, I thought miserably.

"When is this party?" Dad asked.

"Saturday. Which is, like, one of the busiest days for the inn, so driving all the way to Granite will be a pain," I grasped at my one possible escape hatch.

"Saturday is fine. The summer season's over. And, I think your mother has to run in for something anyway. You girls can go shopping, and she can drop you off at the party." He smiled, truly believing he was doing us a favor. "You can have a girl's day."

Drat, a girl's day. A rare day of fun goofing off in Granite, and it had to be tainted with an Amy Event all because of Dad's attempt to integrate us into Granite's social scene.

On Saturday afternoon Mother dropped us off at the circular entrance to Amy's house and headed off to the health-food store. Al and I quickly surveyed the layout.

Striding through the massive gate pillars and stately landscaping, we found ourselves quickly shown around the rear of the house by a uniformed usher. There, we wandered among the many guests and tables of food and beverage.

We stowed our backpacks behind a potted tree and wedged our gifts with others piled high on a vast table draped with pink fabric. Immediately, we cast about for a plate and indulged our refined tastes by scarfing only those foods we were familiar with... olives, tiny pickles, chips, dip and intricate crackers stacked with all manner of cheese and colorful, shaved vegetables. Sated, we turned our interests toward inspecting the facilities.

The rumors had been true, Amy Wilson owned a swimming pool — an utterly foreign notion to those of us who partook of creek waters for fun and frivolity. And not just *one*. Amy Wilson also owned a miniature version of the big pool. Not a little inflatable two-ringer, either. It was a round, concrete-lined hole in the ground about four feet deep and ten feet across. A 'splashing' pool, she called it.

A few girls, including Amy, were playing with their Barbie dolls in the splashing pool, so Al and I cannon-balled into the depths as well. Once the initial tidal wave of water and squealing protests had subsided, I scoured the recesses of my wandering mind for something that would measure up to luring crawdads to the shore of Muskrat Lake with our bare feet then thrashing madly for shore before they had a chance to pinch our toes.

Swimming pool etiquette, not entirely new to me, ranked low on my list of social indulgences. Back in Texas, my Aunt Gigi would occasionally tote me along with her to the country club where she would sun herself poolside and encourage me to make constructive use of time in the pool by engaging in practice kicks or some other inane thing.

Often, however, to my glee and her embarrassment, I'd choose to make use of the pool as a vast medium for experimentation. A particularly favorite pastime involved swirling my hand around just below the surface, creating little whirlpools. I imagined myself as some unseen oceanic force awaiting an imaginary and unsuspecting tanker. I worked to perfect my technique and got pretty good at it too. By gyrating my whole arm under water, I once developed a twirling monster capable of sucking in a beach ball from four feet away.

I cast a glance at Amy.

Her doll was busy holding another doll underwater until its handler conceded to braid Amy's hair after the party. Amy was fiercely competitive, so I guessed what might happen should I suggest a simple contest.

"Hey, you want to have some fun?" I asked.

Al shot me a dubious look and blasted out of the water like a torpedo. "I'm getting some lemonade," she said, without even looking back.

"Have fun doing what?" Amy asked.

"Just a contest," I replied.

"What kind of contest?" Amy asked, smirking.

"Just a race around the pool a couple times to see who wins."

Her glittering eyes betrayed a demure façade, and she smiled with anticipation, probably at holding my head under water.

Now, I must tell you, running a race in a swimming pool is a tough thing to get started. And I wouldn't recommend anyone trying it, especially since doing it might result in a court summons or worse.

Racing in water up to your chest is no easy feat. You'd make better time chugging through quicksand while pulling a pallet of cinder blocks.

But since water is so dense, once you get it moving at an appreciable speed in one direction, momentum quickly aids in your struggle to advance.

Having several friends humping through the current with you further hastens the process, rapidly creating an effect not unlike a riptide.

If you got reasonably good grades in science class or studied physics in swimming pools or hot chocolate mugs, like I have, you would probably guess that a tide generated within the confines of a small container will merely travel in circles. You might also guess that as the current quickens, centrifugal force pushes the water higher and higher against the edges of its confinement until it finally sloshes over the rim.

Just as I had predicted, as the half dozen or so of us began to move in a unified, accelerated manner around the pool's outer flanks, the water began to respond.

Gaining in speed, we excitedly slapped our hands on the wet decking like harbor seals.

As a rippling, twisted vortex began forming in the center of the pool, the water, forced increasingly to the outer edges, acted like a column of wet cement seizing everyone within it and carrying us forward at a quickening pace.

It was exhilarating, and the intense thrill of manufacturing a giant whirlpool short-circuited my usual call to alarm.

I heard my own voice respond by yelling, "Faster! Faster!"

As a monumental wave of water raced around the pool's circumference, we sprinted along on our tip-toes, every now and then lifted off our feet as we struggled to stay in step with our fellow racers.

We were now fairly speeding around the pool, and the deafening roar of the water was pierced only by brief shrieks rising from a few of the girls unsure of how to react to the sensation of hurling weightlessly into an unknown fate.

I calmed everyone by reminding them that the only way to keep from being sucked into the vortex, which was now widening to expose the pool's concrete lining, was to keep running. Of course, I wasn't entirely sure this was the right action to take, it only seemed instinctively accurate.

Whoooo hooo! Mach-1!

Too terrorized to stop in the furious current but too weak to continue, one feeble girl grabbed onto the ladder as she whirled past. Her legs flapped out behind her like ribbons, which not only created a thoughtless hazard for the other racers but also encouraged some of the panicky-type girls to grab hold of them.

Of course, as the human chain grew to more than three girls linked together by gripping one another's ankles, inertia merely disassembled them, sending each one reeling and screaming into the vortex.

Legs bobbed upside down in the current, and at one point I thought I saw one streak by on its own.

"My dolls! Stop it! Stop!" Amy shrieked, her voice trailing around the pool. "It's tearing them apart!"

Well, even if I had wanted to stop, anybody could have guessed it takes a while for water traveling at such a velocity to settle down. So, it must have been another few minutes before the current subsided sufficiently to begin extracting party guests and doll body parts.

"Cripes, Amy," I reassured her. "Stop crying. Good grief, look, the heads go right back on…"

"I *HATE* you!" Amy thrashed to the side of the pool.

The herd of rancorous girls clamored out of the pool and stormed across the lawn toward the house. A pitiful few, unable to shake the effects of inertia, tipped over and skidded head-long into the grass or ran sideways into the bushes.

Two of them made it through the patio doors where we heard them ranting to Amy's mother who was, by that time, possibly making a call to the local police station.

Al snatched up our backpacks, and it was only with a pall of guilt and amazing agility that I was able to tear loose a sizeable chunk of birthday cake as Al shoved us toward the street.

Fortunately, upon our arrival at Amy's party, Al had possessed the forethought to leave the front gate unlatched, which was the only thing that gave us the necessary two-block lead on our adversaries as we beat feet for the Mort Mart.

It's awfully difficult to outrun an angry mob when you're loaded down with backpacks and hopping along trying to untangle your toes from a twisted flip flop… which, by the way and just as I had suspected, were wasted investments proving totally useless as defense missiles.

Peevil's Revenge

With the kinds of mental peculiarities incubated by Hardrock's isolation, bus drivers came and went about as often as snow flakes in winter. Folks didn't exactly line up with a burning desire to drive us kids to Granite every morning. The roads were hellish, the weather was often the same, and we were regarded similarly.

Fall, ordinarily one of my favorite seasons, was also unfortunately associated with obligations of the academic variety, and now that it had widely edged out summer, Al and I were once again deeply mired in the lingering doom of compulsory attendance at Clive J. Wigmore's middle school.

Standing on the county road near the mailbox, Al and I shuffled around in the late fall chill, cursing Wes who had just motored by in the Green Rag. Waving with a wide grin, he and Al's sister, Georgia, were off to Granite High.

"I still don't see why he can't give us a ride into school," I grimaced after the trail of exhaust.

"Because, then he and Georgia couldn't make out in the parking lot before school," Al stated the obvious, too familiar with her sister's romantic tendencies.

"If she were squeezed any closer to him," I muttered to Al, "she'd be a wart."

Al's sniggers were silenced by the school bus roaring up to our stop and squealing to a rumbling crawl.

Usually, the bus came to a full stop before the driver-of-the-week pulled open the doors and patiently awaited our ascent or the occasional dropped book or snagged coat hem.

Anticipating this predictable pattern, I numbly followed the tires and waited for the bus to stop. When it continued rolling by, I looked up to find the door already open and a surprise behind the wheel.

Al let out a small gasp.

Our endless torment of last year's half-dozen or so applicants had left the school district little alternative than to harvest one of our own for the new school year.

Peevil.

Esmeralda Peevil.

Hunched menacingly behind the wheel, this was to be the first day of her long reign.

Peevil lived on the outskirts of Hardrock, down by the river. A startling looking woman of vague shape in nervous motion, her general fluidity was amplified by the swishing hem of a mu-mu cloaked, even in summer, beneath a long, dark, woolen overcoat.

A crocheted orange hat only partly subdued her bristling tangle of long hair. Huge, lime-rimmed sunglasses weakly concealed her constantly roving eyes which operated independently of one another and enabled her to survey her offspring as they ricocheted in opposite directions.

This physical attribute made her uniquely qualified to drive us kids to school, since keeping one eye on the overhead mirror and one eye on the road surely elevated her above ordinary candidates.

She probably would have smoked but shook too violently to steady a cigarette. Instead, she reduced large wads of chewing gum to small pellets through relentless hours of fierce maceration: *Chompchomp Chompchompsmack. Pop Smackchompchomp.*

She was only in her thirties but looked on the high side of fifty.

Prior to her position as bus driver, I'd only seen her twice — both times trekking the riverbank behind the inn. Far from home, she had been stooped and lurching with a brown paper grocery bag used, according to Al, to collect her two sons' clothing on wash day.

Peevil's husband had gone for a dump truck part two years previous, never to return. While Peevil was purported to have hatched a third child some years earlier, only scattered accounts of his whereabouts persisted. Some claimed he had reverted to an early hominid state and now ran the high ridges of Pickanaxe Peak.

A lot of us kids from Hardrock were considered unsavory by folks better associated with the civility of pastoral, small-town life such as Granite represented. Yet, to consider Peevil's two young boys merely unsavory was a stretch. In fact, that was the tall one... Stretch. The short one was called Stomp. Al and I had few occasions to associate with either of them, for which we were grateful.

Only a few days before Peevil made her appearance behind the wheel of our bus, a car-load of leaf-peeping tourists pulled up to the inn for a look around the high country at the brilliant yellow leaves which shimmered in thick groves of aspen along the river and mountain slopes during fall.

Though many of the leaves had already past their peak and we were down to mostly weekend operations at the inn, the half dozen out-of-towners decided to hike through part of the old mill site along Quartz Creek.

Stopping by the trading post to load up on munchies, they asked if Al and I could show them around the area. A reasonable excuse to delay homework, we were quick to oblige.

Gingerly, we led the group down to Quartz Creek and showed them the ruins of the old silver smelter and stone finishing mill as well as huge alabaster and marble blocks abandoned from Hardrock's mining days.

As Stretch and Stomp unexpectedly rounded a bend in the river and came into view, I was nearly run down by one of the tourists dashing for their car. "Oh my..." they gasped, scrambling by me in an effort to hurry away undetected.

One unfamiliar with the pair of lads might look upon them and say, "Why, they're just a couple of little boys." And, from a distance, that might indeed appear so, particularly to one who is near-sighted. But, as the two neared, bringing specific features into focus, I, too, often felt a sudden, almost instinctual urge to flee.

Stretch, possessing a rather pointy head with an equally pointy shock of hair on top, lurched and bobbed nearly a foot above his fraternal twin brother who was always by his side. Stretch's eyes seemed set apart wider than most, giving him the look of an iguana, particularly when he held them wide open and aimed one directly at you.

The more compact, Stomp, moved gorilla-like side to

side, his fists curled into tight white gnarls. His black eyes, set narrowly above his nose, were furrowed in a perpetual squint. Arguably the meanest and toughest of the two, Stomp rarely spoke and communicated only in grunts and growls.

Short of potential victims, the two often engaged one another. Once, I'd seen Stomp punch his brother in the stomach suddenly and without provocation. This led to a fierce, retaliatory onslaught, glimpses of which could be seen through what looked like a small dust devil spinning along the ground.

Back and forth they had raged, punching, pinching, slapping and scratching, oblivious and caught up in the ritualistic barrage. Neither relenting, the battle lasted ten minutes until both combatants lie completely exhausted and unable to hurl a blow. Even then, as they lie rumpled and writhing weakly in the dirt, Stomp flung a rock at Stretch's head which ushered a round of wrestling and biting.

As Mother had discovered earlier in the summer, contact with a Peevil boy was always accompanied by the threat of physical danger. Even with the kindest intention of helping Stomp avoid the barb of a fishhook, Mother had to secure Stomp's belt-loop with a rake handle in order to extract him from the fishing rod display in the trading post, all while buffering her leg with a piece of firewood to avoid a vicious bite.

Even Esmeralda Peevil was covered in scars from close encounters with her own spawn.

Long before parenting or family conflict resolution workshops were popularized, the Peevils helped inspire the movement a decade earlier. A catastrophe of dysfunction, anyone familiar with the trio could have foreseen the disastrous eruption of that fateful morning which Al and I would later commemorate as "Peevil's Revenge".

"Get in... chompchompchomp..." Peevil yelled through the door, which we assumed had been left open to shave minutes off the hour-long run into Granite.

Leading the bus by a couple of feet, I gauged my jump for the door. Barely making the landing, I felt the bus pick up speed.

"C'mon Hubert, *get in,"* Peevil rasped at Al. "I ain't got all day."

I glanced behind me and saw Al lunge for the doorway, grasping either side of its frame and leaping aboard just as the bus pressed into acceleration.

"Cripes," Al breathed.

Finding a seat near the mid-section, Al and I brought the total number of riders to seven, counting both two-time sixth-graders, Stretch and Stomp.

Stretch was made to sit directly behind his mother whose darting eyes continually scanned the overhead mirror for sudden movement or perhaps smoke in the back of the bus.

Stomp lumbered toward the doorway and took a position on the top step. There, he alternately watched the edge of the road blur by and fiddled with knobs under the dash. Peevil swatted him with a rolled-up newspaper, *"Knock it off!"*

Scowling, Stomp returned his brooding gaze to the whizzing scenery.

Al and I looked at one another as the bus sped into the next turn.

As we decelerated for the next stop, Stomp grabbed the steel railing next to the stairs and rolled with the wave of momentum like a trained chimp.

The bus crawled on as two more kids prepared to leap aboard. Stomp scrambled out of the way and assumed a temporary position on the edge of the unoccupied front seat.

With the passengers aboard, Peevil signaled for Stomp to reclaim his seat on the stairs and instructed him to maintain a firm grip on the bar, apparently concerned for his safety as she rolled down the county road with the doors open.

In such situations, thirteen-year-olds tend to defer judgment to adults, and Al and I were no exception. The mere fact that a kid was riding on the steps suggested it was a part of normal operations no other bus driver had exercised. After all, none of us wore seatbelts, and Stomp seemed to have already mastered the maneuvers necessary to help ensure his own safety.

Since it appeared likely that Stomp had been relegated to the stairs because of his tendency to randomly attack Stretch or perhaps any of the rest of us, we accepted the arrangement as functional.

But, "functional" is one of those words surrounded by all sorts of circumstances... circumstances which can be frustrated and perturbed.

And no one had considered how Stretch might come to frustrate and perturb things.

For the first thirty minutes of our ride, Stretch observed his brother and calculated the attention Stomp had been receiving from their mother. Even if it was only irritated glances, curt directives and whacks with a rolled up newspaper, it was attention. And Stretch was being left out.

Stretch unfurled a comic book, found a page on which an interesting illustration must have appeared and, while the bus was in the midst of a four-mile dry run, showed it to his brother then quickly jerked it away.

Everyone knew Stomp operated on a hair trigger, so it was no surprise that the *hav-er* flaunting the empty-handedness of the *have-not* created a mild commotion which quickly escalated into flailing arms and excited growling.

Fearing mutiny during her distraction, Peevil's eyes instantly roamed across the overhead mirror as she attempted to restrain Stomp with blind, erratic lunges.

Anticipating her reaction, Stomp retreated to the second step then lurched spring-like onto Stretch's seat. The bus swerved, and Peevil yanked it back across the center line. We grabbed the backs of the seats in front of us and stared on, eyes wide.

Stomp growled ferociously and, backing Stretch against the wall, lunged for and successfully commandeered the comic. Stretch then launched into a riotous counter-assault replete with vivid profanity.

A noisy blur of bodies rolled from the seat into the aisle. Continuously, the bus swerved from lane to lane as Peevil attempted her backstroke style of discipline. Peering over the rim of her sunglasses, crazed eyes lingered on the overhead mirror.

Suddenly, Peevil hit the brakes and the bus lurched forward, rolling the knot of Peevils into the welded plate at the front of the bus. *Eeeeeeeeee..TCHHHHH*, the bus fishtailed to a halt as Peevil rose and, with murderous rage, snatched each boy by the collar and lifted them into the air like rabbits. They hung motionless, facing one another with grim determination glinting in their eyes.

She dropped them into the seat behind her, ripped the tattered comic away from Stomp and cuffed him with it. Stomp flashed dark eyes from beneath the protection of his left elbow and growled ominously.

Finally, Peevil calmly, deliberately, returned the book to Stretch, leveled a threatening look at both boys and slowly reclaimed the forward position.

No sooner had Peevil taken her seat and wrested the bus back onto the highway than Stomp attacked her from the rear. With a primal wail, he clawed her coat away and bit her on the shoulder. The bus swerved to the right and hit the ditch as Stomp pounded her back and bit her neck. Everyone lurched forward as the wheels spun out of the gravel and back onto the road, but we were too riveted to the situation to pay attention to our own relatively minor injuries.

The bus slammed to a halt as Peevil shot from her seat and whirled around, her flaming eyes sweeping across every rider on the bus.

At that moment, I wondered if perhaps Peevil lacked the capacity to distinguish her antagonists from anyone else who may happen to fit the shape or size of her two offspring.

Now, in a situation in which your life may be in jeopardy, you have but three choices: freeze, fight or flight. Ordinarily, the brain will weigh options and potential consequences of any contemplated action, and the rest of the body will comply with whatever the brain decides.

But, apparently, my brain prefers an unhurried schedule within which to study options and gather opinion before action. So, in sudden survival situations it's my adrenal gland that exercises authority based upon whatever the eyeballs think they've seen. My feet then interpret the chemical flush of adrenaline, ideally carrying all of us to wherever the danger is not.

The sequence of events usually goes something like this:

Eyeballs: FREAKY THING HAPPENING!! FREAKY THING HAPPENING!!

Adrenal gland: SQUEEZE! – PUMP! – SQUEEZE! – PUMP!

Feet: POUND, POUND, POUND!

Hence, flight is my typical mode of dealing with bodily threats.

This day, my adrenal gland had no way of knowing that Peevil was merely stopping the bus to call what has, these days, evolved into a time-out. But, my eyeballs were very sure they saw a freaky thing in Peevil and instructed the adrenal thusly.

Before the bus even had a moment to drift back from its forward heave, my feet had determined that the open door presented the nearest route to where the danger was not. I rushed, quite without thought, to the front of the bus, thwarted by Stomp who had been overtaken by a similar impulse. Crouching to the aisle floor, he dove between Peevil's knees and made for the door.

But Peevil was quick, and she wrenched the door

handle, pinching Stomp tight between the rubber gaskets.

Eyeballs: FREAKIER THING!! KID TRAPPED IN DOOR!!

Confusion seized my feet, inspiring my brain to offer a surprising alternate solution: BACK DOOR! BACK DOOR!

The feet reversed course and off they went scuffling backpacks and hurdling over tens of knees crowding the aisle.

Stomp, meanwhile, was busy prying the doors apart, assisted by his brother who now sought to capitalize on the chaos as a means of escape, himself.

Peevil screeched some unrecognizable order as my hand gripped the handle and flung open the rear emergency escape hatch on the bus. She may have been yelling at me or perhaps Stretch or Stomp. No matter. Her words were indiscernible, as my thoughts were preoccupied with the forest offering sanctuary mere yards distant.

You would expect an emergency door to be outfitted with all accouterments necessary to the task of disembarking in a rushed manner. But no. The back of the bus was sheared smooth, leaving the imperiled to jump to whatever conditions awaited three feet below.

This is how I came to skin my forearm from wrist to elbow.

But in the fever of adrenal overload, blood means nothing. It was the tree-line or bust.

I looked back to check that Peevil was a safe distance behind and saw Stomp light in the ditch, recover, hit Quartz Creek and clamor downstream, vaulting over boulders and catching the current where he could. Stretch was right behind him.

Aiming for the forest, I was overtaken by Al who grabbed my arm and hauled me toward the woods. Several other kids were screaming off in different directions or crashing into one another as they rushed hither and yon. One crawled under the bus.

It's funny how panic can infect people.

It can also be quite alarming.

Peevil was a fearsome sight, launching off the bus like a mad super-villain, her dark coat billowing behind her like a cape. She rushed fore and aft of the bus, waving her arms and shrieking at kids now scattering in all directions.

Turns out she was trying to round us up and prevent some from running into oncoming traffic.

We were nearly two hours late getting to school that day, and it took the enlistment of a mail truck to retrieve Stretch and Stomp, both of whom had expertly made five miles in twenty minutes.

The following day, on the hour-long bus ride into Granite, Stretch began goading Stomp over a quartz rock he had found along the river and brought to trade for a dried-up, one-legged frog. But, intentionally or otherwise, Evil Peevil had now become infamous; her legendary stature established the day before. Now, even her sons thought twice before pushing her beyond the sketchy threshold of self-control, particularly now that Peevil had gained the tandem advantages of containment and mobility.

Familiar and, we presumed basically functional, everyone soon adjusted to the daily routine — Stomp on the stairs, Stretch behind Peevil, the predictable squabble or three on the way to school and again on the way home.

Over the course of the school year, Peevil began to behave almost normally, and Stretch and Stomp finally worked out a way to share a seat while inducing only moderate mayhem.

Eventually, Peevil even began driving with the doors closed, occasionally leaving them open as a sign someone had irritated her. Of course, we were left to contemplate who, until, grinning and popping her gum, she pinched one of us in their rubber grip while entering or exiting her domain.

Peevil wasn't the best bus driver we'd ever had, but she was the most interesting. And, she was, after all, one of our own. We were pretty sure no other driver would have allowed us a half-hour to play in the creek at Grogan Flats on Friday afternoons following that fateful morning, or any other time she felt like stopping and swinging her feet from a boulder on a sunny day… which, we were happy to discover, turned out to be often.

Bear Feet and Bare Ass

I poured another cup of coffee for Lloyd, the game warden, who sat talking with Dad at their regular table in the café Saturday morning. It was late September, and the two were discussing the success of bow hunting season and preparations for the upcoming rifle season. Nearly all the tourists had gone for the year, in fact, Al and I were scheduled to take the last trail ride up on Pickanaxe mountain later that morning.

I delivered two steaming cinnamon rolls straight from the oven — each three inches thick, the size of saucers and draped with a gooey topping of caramel-pecan sauce. Dad and Lloyd both dug in heartily.

"Yeah," Lloyd continued the interrupted conversation, "had a bear sighted in town, up at Snapbinder's place. Enis said it'd been rummaging around by his bird pens. Thought it was after his peafowl. More than likely, the bear was after the corn feed." He looked into the steam swirling out of his cup and shook his head, "I don't know how he keeps those birds alive through the winter."

Lloyd leaned in toward Dad, "I told him he'd better make sure the feral garden guinea didn't get into his pens and mate with his hens."

Dad raised an eyebrow, "Garden guinea?"

"Yeah, I told him he'd end up with garden peas!" Lloyd snorted over his cinnamon roll. "I don't think he got the joke.

When I looked back, he was checking the locks on his pens."

Dad chuckled and looked out the window, "Snapbinder's an interesting bird, himself. I imagine with the late spring freeze taking out this year's berries, the bears are going to get pretty bold. Damn, I hate to see that. They're just trying to fill their bellies."

"Bold? If this is the same bear that's been making the rounds up and down the county road, she's already broken into three houses along the river. Looks like she's making her way up into higher country."

"Broken in?"

"Yep, she's learned what a refrigerator is. Once she's inside the house, she'll raid the fridge, take a crap in the living room and crawl off to a bed or a couch and sleep off her dinner. She's up and out of there before dawn and hasn't been caught yet. Same M.O. every time. Enis said he heard this bear the other night and fired off a shot, which scared her away... for now. The campers down at the lake just don't get it. No matter how many damn signs you post, they leave wrappers and food all over the place and then wonder why a bear wanders in." He got a serious look in his eyes, "Then they call me. And you know what that means."

Dad nodded, equally serious, "Yup." He sipped his coffee. "Too bad it's the bear that gets the short end of that stick."

Lloyd looked down. "Well... I just wanted to let you all know, so you can keep a lookout."

"Yeah, I'll get a log chain and a lock for the dumpster this afternoon and remind everyone to be careful. We already police the grounds pretty good, so that ought to take care of any potential problems."

"I appreciate that, Ike." The warden fished out his wallet, but put it back when Dad waved it away.

"On me, Lloyd. Thanks for the heads-up. We'll keep our eyes open." Dad looked over at me as I cleared the plates, "Listen, you heard the warden, you girls be careful up on the Heelantoe. You see a bear, get the hell out of there. Make sure you have the .357 with you, just in case. And remember, a horse'll spook around bears. Just the scent, even."

Because of his former work in law enforcement, Dad had taught me firearm safety and how to shoot when I was seven, with the very weapon he had suggested I carry with me. Of course I'd never had any cause to pull it out of my saddlebag, let alone use it, other than for target practice, but leading a passel of tourists up into desolate wilderness, I had to admit I felt a little more comfortable knowing it was there.

Ty busted through the front door and nodded to the warden on his way out. "Ike. Hey, Lisa, grab me a cup of coffee and one of them rolls will ya, I'm freezin' my beets off!"

I rolled my eyes and went for the coffee as Ty hit the seat.

"Why are you so cold?" Dad asked Ty. "You have heat in your apartment — it's working, right?"

"Yeah, but it's expensive to run."

"Well, Ty, why don't you put in thermal solar? You install the damn systems for a living."

"Who has time? Between runnin' the horses this summer and scrounging up business, I haven't had time to do my own thing."

Dad nodded, "Physician heal thy self... that's how it is sometimes. You two making ends meet all right, speaking of business?"

"Well, you know. They say the first couple years are pretty tough. Coal, oil, gas — the big guys get all the breaks. So, it's a little tough competing for customers. We still have most of our money tied up in equipment." Ty paused as I brought his roll to the table.

Wolfing down a huge forkful and washing it back with a belt of coffee, Ty wiped his mouth with the back of his hand and refocused on the roll. "I had to spend a couple hundred on a telescoping ladder last week. But, it's really cool." Thumbing toward the apartment, he added, "And, since I'm always runnin' into town, Abbey wants her own car. But I'm going to *have* to put some more money into the truck. Suspension and brakes are about shot, plus I think it needs new engine mounts. Man, I'm still payin' the loan on Slew and that new saddle. Stallions ain't cheap."

"So you're basically broke."

"Yeah. And cold."

"That's about right."

"Abbey won't turn up the heat, so I freeze to death all night. Well, most nights — which reminds me... it's our anniversary today," Ty reported with twinkling eyes.

"And...?" Dad looked dubious.

"I can't wait till Abbey sees what I bought her."

"What?"

"It's out back of the inn, by the corrals."

"What is it?"

"A two-horse trailer. I got a great deal on it. It's a little rusty in a couple places and the back door falls off, but I can fix the hinge and hasp on that. I was going to work on it this afternoon. Think she'll like it?"

"Nope."

"No? Why not? It's a great trailer!"

"For you." Dad looked at Ty over the top of his cup and leaned back in his chair. "You think you're cold now?"

Ty thought a minute, "Hmm. Yeah… well, it's too late now. She'll perk up when I make dinner for her tonight."

"What are you making?"

"I bought a venison roast off Willy. I threw it in the slow cooker before I headed over here. Sucker was hard as a rock. I about never got it chiseled out of the freezer."

"What, you mean it's frozen?"

"Yeah… so?"

"You put it in the slow cooker frozen?"

"Yeah."

"Ty, the word is s..l..o..w cooker. You'd better find a way to thaw it out. Even if it's thawed, it's going to take all…"

Abbey interrupted their discussion when she came through the door and leaned over to kiss Ty on his cheek, singing, *"Good morning!"*

Ty returned his affection with a pat on her behind.

"Ty," Abbey began, "I thought we could go into Granite tonight and celebrate…"

Ty broke in, "Can't do it, hon."

"Why not?" Abbey was crestfallen.

"I was going to work on the trail.. er, uh, I have dinner already planned!"

"Really?" she brightened, surprised by his thoughtfulness.

"Yep."

"What is it?"

"It's a surprise!"

"Oh, Ty, you are so adorable." Abbey threw her arms around Ty's neck. "I'm going to help Jessie with some inventory stuff, but I'll be off at three, and then we can celebrate. I'm so excited!" She bounded off for the saloon, looking back to blow a kiss.

Dad looked at Ty. "Better get that roast thawed."

"Yeah, I'll get to it. I need to run out and check the tires on the trailer though. I think one's losin' air. C'mon out back, I want to show it to you, she's *fine!*" Ty snatched the remainder of his roll off the plate, choked it back and muffled on his way out the door to put it on his tab.

As they left, Dad filled Ty in on the bear doings, "She's definitely looking for grub. Keep that basket you hang off the window sill inside the apartment."

"Yeah, yeah, I mmfffm, hear you... we don't put, mmmfff, anything out there till winter anyway."

Later that morning, Al and I led five tourists through Hardrock. We were headed seven miles up the Heelantoe Trail toward Quartz City and the Lost Horse Station, one of the most photographed sites in the state. Built in 1892 on an outcrop over a cascade of dramatic water falls on Quartz Creek, the charming little wooden generating station was hugely popular with visitors.

"Joe, look!" Al yelled back to me over the undulating line of bobbing heads and horse ears. "Enis' peacock pens…"

A quick look revealed peacock feathers strewn about and a gaping hole torn into the fenced run.

"Cripes," I shouted back, "the bear must've come back and got one!"

"Bear?" a lady swiveled in her saddle with an alarmed look.

Suddenly, from high in a spruce, an ungodly wail descended upon us, as if something were wrenched in mortal agony crying out its last breath. This, of course, is the sound a peafowl makes while simply resting high in a spruce, but their horrible cries produce an instant heart-stopping effect upon people as well as notoriously unaware trail horses accustomed to plodding along, eyes closed, merely following the scent of the rump three paces ahead.

The horses jolted a couple of feet sideways before once again settling into their rocking, plodding rhythm. The white-faced tourists, however, suggested they would not be so easily calmed and may even require a return trip to the trading post for hygiene supplies.

Later that afternoon, back at the inn, Al and I unsaddled, brushed and fed the horses then hit the café for something savory. We ordered Willy and Gert's swiss-bacon-mushroom burgers with a high pile of home fries and carried our plates over to the saloon where we planned to share the story of the bear's raid on Enis' pens with Dad.

Dad sat with Ty and Abbey at a table — Abbey on Ty's

knee.

Marveling at a huge, hairy pelt draped across an adjacent table, Ty ran his hands over the fur. "This is friggin' amazing!"

"What *is* that?" I asked, munching a fry.

Abbey took on a look of forced enthusiasm. "Remember that buffalo robe from your living room wall? Your dad gave it to Ty to use on the bed this winter."

"Check it out!" Ty jumped up and hoisted the fifty-pound monstrosity which Dad had bought at an auction the winter previous. Hefting it over his head and around his shoulders, he peeked out at Abbey. "Ha! This mother'll keep us warm all night, huh baby?"

"Uh huh," Abbey muttered. "Can it be washed?"

"Nah, it's natural, Abbey, you don't wash something like this, you'll ruin the natural character of it."

"Uh huh." Abbey walked over to the bar and topped off her soda from the tap.

"No sign on the trail?" Dad asked, after we'd related the story of the bear break-in at Enis'.

"Nope," I said. "None obvious anyway."

"And you say the bird was still up in the tree?"

"Definitely," Al nodded.

Dad looked at Ty. "That tells me she came back looking around for more than just scratch. Maybe some chicken dinner, too. Surprising, since Snapbinder scared her off just last night. Must be pretty hungry. Well, listen," Dad said, hooking two fingers in the handle of his coffee cup, "everyone just be on your toes."

"Ha," Ty chortled, "I ain't a-feared of no bear!" Still hunkered under the weight of the huge buffalo robe, he growled low and hobbled over to Abbey, pretending to paw at her. He snuffled her hair and engulfed her in the black hairy mass.

A moment later Abbey erupted from beneath it, either blushing violently or flaming from the intense heat of its sweltering bulk — "*Aaa-CHOO!* Ty, knock it off, and get that filthy, horrible thing off me!"

"Aw, c'mon hon, *hee hee,*" Ty lumbered along behind her as she stormed to the café, "it ain't filthy... I just got cleaned up a couple hours ago..."

Eyes still twinkling, Ty flung the robe over the table and flopped back down in his chair. A flurry of tiny dust motes rose off the robe into the air where Al and I promptly waved them away from our burgers.

Ty reclined on the back legs of his chair, eyeing the robe. "This is great, man, thanks. She may complain now, but tonight, when it gets cold, she'll be glad you gave it to us."

"Did you give her your present yet?" Now, Dad's eyes twinkled.

"No, I forgot! Hey, Abbey, hon," Ty yelled through the pool room into the café, "c'mere, baby, I got something to show you."

Her voice floated back, "I've seen it before, and it's not worth the trip."

"Oh, c'mon, hon! It's your present! You want to go look at it?"

Abbey peeked around the door frame. "You got me something?"

"Well sure, darlin', what do you think I'm some kind of ass?"

Dad, Al and I exchanged looks of common appraisal.

Recovering her usual demeanor, Abbey beamed and walked back into the saloon. "Where is it?"

"Out back. C'mon I'll show ya!"

As the two hurried out the saloon door, Abbey stopped Ty. "Hang on a second. I want to get your present!"

Because we'd seen it three weeks prior, Al and I knew Abbey had bought Ty a sheep skin-lined leather jacket which she'd found over the summer at the Flashy Trash Second Hand Emporium in Granite. Camel colored suede and in perfect condition, it was a not-too-surprising find, since a lot of brand-new merchandise discarded by the Diamond Hills set often found its way to the Emporium. Al and I ditched classes and outfitted ourselves with their lavish inventory every chance we got.

Five minutes later and in a furious tirade, Abbey stomped down the boardwalk. Expressively, she launched her arms skyward as she stormed by the saloon. "I cannot *believe* you spent eight-hundred dollars on that piece of *junk!* That was our entire savings! Are you out of your mind?" she yelled, rattling the plate glass windows. "Yes, you are OUT OF YOUR MIND! How are we going to afford it, Ty?"

Ty followed close behind in his new jacket. "But, baby doll, we need it for the horses."

"You rent one, Ty, you RENT one! *Arrggg!*"

"But, it's a write-off!"

"ONLY if you have INCOME!" Abbey's voice trailed

farther down the boardwalk until we heard the door to their apartment slam.

Moments later, Ty wandered back into the saloon, his expression as sheepish as the liner in his jacket. "Well," he said, "so much for that. Look at my new jacket, though, nice huh?" He looked at Al and I poised in mid-chew. Our expressions must have accurately communicated our thoughts. "Hey, she'll get over it," he continued. "I've still got a couple tricks up the old sleeve. Man, this is some nice stitching on this jacket."

Ty grabbed a bottle of Abbey's favorite blended whiskey from behind the bar and asked Dad to put it on his tab. Then, he headed toward his and Abbey's place for what Al and I knew, from seeing it before, would be some serious begging outside the door.

Of course, we also knew Abbey would let him in. She always did.

Later that evening, Al and I ran down to the saloon to fetch some papers for Mother and saw Abbey sipping an iced tea at the bar.

"How goes the anniversary?" Al asked.

"Better. But I am still not over the horse trailer." She paused and sipped her iced tea. "In a few minutes we're going down to our place for dinner. Ty said he had something special planned."

Ty came out of the men's room, walked over and polished off the last of his beer. Gathering Abbey around her waist, he whispered in her ear, winking at Al and me, "Let's go have dinner…"

She smiled at us, and we mocked Ty with an

exaggerated wink as the two headed back to their apartment.

Minutes later, as we were waiting for Dad to ferret the paperwork out from behind the bar, Abbey burst through the door, tears in her eyes, asking for a shot of whiskey.

"What's going on?" we asked, having seen Abbey plenty mad, but never teary.

She sat staring at the bar, "Ty was supposed to fix dinner, and he put a frozen piece of meat in the slow cooker, and it still isn't cooked, and now we can't even have dinner, and that stupid trailer cost eight-hundred dollars, and I just... I just wanted..."

Al and I both knew it wasn't about the roast, or even the trailer.

"It's our first anniversary..." her voice quavered.

That's what it was about.

"He can just be such a jerk." She looked up, cheeks flushed, anger replacing hurt. "You'd think today would be a little more special to him."

Al and I searched for something comforting to say, but we officially sided with her jerk analysis.

"Well, Abbey," I offered, looking at Al who appeared ready to back me up, "some guys just don't..."

"Well's ass! If he thinks he's sleeping in my bed tonight, he has another thing coming!" She stood up and stalked out.

We grabbed the papers for Mother and headed to the house. That was the last we saw of Abbey till one o'clock that morning when she knocked on the door.

This was not an uncommon occurrence. Between bouts

of marital discord, Mother and Dad regularly punched the coffee on and held late night counseling sessions for the managers of the inn — who happened to also be married to their co-managers.

Abbey sat in her pink robe, sipping coffee at the kitchen table with Mother who had been waiting up for Dad to close the saloon at two o'clock that morning.

"I just can't deal with him tonight. I can't lay there under that awful buffalo hide and stare at his rotten face. I made a whole quart of margaritas to have with dinner, and he just sat in the apartment swilling it down. Half an hour later, he's totally looped, no dinner, no nothing." She looked up, eyes flashing, drawing her thumb and forefinger close together, "I swear I came this close to putting him out of my misery."

During the course of their hour-long discussion, Mother made up the couch, barely convincing Abbey she had not, after all, made a mistake marrying Ty.

Meanwhile, the door to Abbey's apartment, left ajar in her hasty departure, swung open and someone disheveled, drunk and sated peered up toward the illuminated kitchen windows of our home, hesitated a moment then retreated back inside.

Trouble was… it wasn't Ty.

Ty was burrowed against the chilly night, deep beneath the buffalo robe where he snored the snore of the blissfully unaware. As the black robe rose and fell — Ty sealed within the strata of sheets and blankets beneath its weight — Hardrock's pillaging bear quietly looted his kitchen cupboards, polishing off two boxes of stroganoff and a package of instant pudding.

The slow cooker was next. Crashing to the floor, the crock slipped from its sleeve and cracked in two, spilling a half-thawed roast onto the floor where it was consumed in one bite.

Turning her snout to the sweet, fruity aroma of margaritas, the bear uplifted the quart jar and poured its remaining contents down her gullet. She smiled the way only happy bears can, wiping her face with the back of her huge, black paw.

Ambling to the refrigerator, she opened the door, sat on the floor and munched a bag of grapes, a half pound of bacon and a bowl of leftover macaroni and cheese.

Groaning and rubbing her vast, hairy belly, she wandered into the living room where she lingered long enough to leave a deposit before scuffling off to the bedroom.

One paw on the bed, she snuffled her nose deep into the robe. *"Achpppbbbbththooo!"* she sneezed, blowing a fine mist. She shook her head and snorted, finally lifting her hind leg onto the bed followed by the rest of her bulk.

Grunting, she happily nodded off, sleeping the sleep of the blissfully unaware.

And together they dreamed their separate dreams.

Ty dreamed of his new trailer, sparkling and shiny white, trundling along the highway bearing a load of two fine horses — one, his stallion, Slew, the other a spirited, pregnant mare.

The bear, she dreamed of berry patches thick with clusters of fat, ripened fruit glittering like jewels in the dappled afternoon sunshine.

And, on they dreamed as the early morning sun climbed

the back side of Absolution Mountain and gradually cast a dim blue light over the valley.

The bear began to feel stirrings of the dawn while Ty, sobering from overindulgence, struggled to find a pocket of fresh air beneath the heavy robe. The bear shifted, rolling slightly in Ty's direction.

"Mmfff, ugggh, baby, you're gettin' fat..." Ty mumbled from deep beneath the covers, "but that's just more for me to cuddle... mmfft... c'mere sugar... gimme some lovin'..."

The bear grumbled and moved away a little.

"You still mad at me darlin', c'mon, *yawn*... let me make it up to you..."

Snuffle grumble, *scootch scootch*...

Ty squeezed his fingers out from under the robe and pushed back the long buffalo hair that engulfed his face as he stretched to free his head from its oppressive confines.

Choosing that moment to seek a more comfortable position, the bear stretched and rolled over facing Ty where she sighed long, deep and hot, followed by a sudden and violent eruption of fermented belly gas, *BBBLLLLAAAPPTTphssss*...

It took a half-second for the rolling tide of putrid odor to reach Ty's nostrils. "Godallmighty!" He struggled to rise from beneath the mass of robe, pinned by the weight of the bear. "What the hell did you eat, woman?" He freed his head and looked for Abbey's face. All he could see was more black hair. He reached over and tried to pull the wooly buffalo hair away from her face, but tugged, instead, at the forehead of the bear. Two beady eyes popped open. And, then the bear's did too.

"Aaaiiieeeee!" Ty scrambled backward, trapped in the

folds of his blankets and immobilized by the robe. "BEAR! BEAR!"

The bear backed off the bed and stood beside it, rising to her full height and roaring across the small expanse at Ty who had fallen off the opposite side.

Clamoring to right himself, Ty backed toward the living room, hoping that the half-open front door was within running distance.

The bear rotated her massive head and curled her upper lip, revealing glistening, long, white incisors.

Ty and the bear locked eyes. A moment later, the bear dropped to all fours and Ty broke for the door.

Dad, Mother, Al and I were sitting at the kitchen table with Abbey, sipping coffee, orange juice and working our way through a stack of Mother's waffles, when the commotion just over the berm in the driveway got our attention.

In the dim light of dawn, Ty streaked (and I do mean streaked) silently across the parking lot, heading toward the trading post. His legs, pumping like pistons, outpaced the rest of his body by several feet. Ten feet behind him galloped the bear, her teeth chomping at Ty's gleaming behind, as if it were a reflector beaming her in.

The two disappeared around the side of the inn as Dad bolted from the table, grabbed his holstered .44 off a peg on the wall and sprinted across the parking lot, buckling on the fly.

Abbey glanced at Mother then through the window as her hands fluttered to her mouth, "Oh my God! He's going to be eaten!" She wrangled with her robe, hurrying to free herself from the bench seat at the table.

"Stay, stay…" Mother urged, reaching for Abbey.

"Dad'll take care of it," I added, just as a shot rang out into the still, morning calm. Al and I exchanged horrified looks. "Cripes! I hope he didn't have to shoot the bear!"

"Me too!" Al said, worried.

Wes popped through the hall doorway with a towel around his waist, his wet, soapy hair raining on the kitchen floor. "What the hell?"

"Bear!" Al and I offered, together.

"Cool! Where's Ike?"

"Went after Ty... and the bear," Mother added.

Wes ran for the rifle Dad kept by his and Mother's bedroom door.

"Hold it right there, Tonto," Mother gestured. "He's already got one naked guy out there. He doesn't need a naked gunman on the loose, too."

"Man…" Wes slouched back to the table and snagged a waffle.

Our eyes remained trained in the direction of the trading post, waiting anxiously for the two to emerge. Meanwhile, Dad and Ty had walked behind the inn to Abbey and Ty's apartment, where Ty had quickly dressed and was now heading with Dad back up to the house.

As the two came over the berm and through the front door, Dad was laughing loudly.

"Shut up," Ty said, his eyes still wide from coursing adrenaline.

"Oh, thank God you're okay!" Abbey sighed. Waiting by the door, she wrapped her arms around Ty and randomly kissed his face.

"Yeah, he's okay," Dad reassured everyone, "and so is the bear. Fired a shot and spooked her into the woods. She took off across the creek and up into the brush on Dark Mountain."

"I had her licked!" Ty said, reaching for a waffle off the stack on the table.

Dad chuckled, "Looked to me like she about had you licked. And et, and spit out. It was bear feet and bare ass all the way across the parking lot."

"Yeah, but then I had her licked."

"When? When you were trying to hold the door on the trailer or when she was rocking it back and forth?" Dad poured a cup of coffee.

"Shut up," Ty said, washing a wad of waffle down with Abbey's coffee.

Abbey turned to Ty, picking a piece of wayward buffalo or perhaps bear hair from his beard. "Darling, do you really want to do something special for our anniversary?"

"Like what?"

"That buffalo robe."

"Already *gone*, baby!"

Abbey put her arm around Ty as the two made their way out the door.

"And the trailer? Maybe you could trade it back in?"

"Can't now, the bear tore it up. We wouldn't get half the money."

"Oh," pause, "well, maybe we could go out later this afternoon and have a nice lunch in Granite…"

"Can't. We have to round up the horses. They jumped

the corral when the bear came around back."

Abbey sighed, "Well then let's go to dinner later tonight… after the horses…"

"Okay. We can do that. Which reminds me, you need a new slow cooker."

"I do?"

"And, there's a big mess in the kitchen. Oh, and a pile in the living room, so you want to watch where you step when you get in there."

"What?"

By the time the two of them got back to their apartment, Abbey was tightening her robe and kicking at Ty as she hurried to close the door ahead of him.

He looked up at the house and shrugged, but we knew sooner or later she'd open the door.

She always did.

Turkey Run

"Get your coat," Mother said, grabbing a stack of tattered coupons off the kitchen table as I stirred two inches of chocolate syrup into a glass of milk. "Abbey and I are heading to Granite."

Ordinarily, Al and I would jump at the chance, any chance, for a ride into Granite on anything other than a school bus. Had Mother said, "To hunt wild boar, armed only with toothpicks" we would have gleefully grabbed a handful of weaponry and ran her down on the way to the old pickup truck Dad had bought over the summer for hauling supplies.

One of the reasons we so loved a spontaneous ride to town, apart from an opportunity to observe and chastise local wildlife — that is, more civilized social beings — was that we also enjoyed our infrequent loot and pillage of the Granite Tote-n'-Bloat. Begging black licorice, chips, soda, and a comic book from Dad or Mother, we'd scurry back to the truck with our loot, vault over the tailgate and resume our positions in the truck bed while they finished gassing up. Soaking beneath the glow of the twenty foot neon sign, we then scarfed ourselves into sugar-induced oblivion.

Smearing our teeth with macerated licorice, we laughed ourselves silly waving and smiling broadly to passersby who, shocked by our assertive manner and apparent disregard for dental hygiene, quickly hurried by. Yes, we were pathetic, but we were also young, carefree and unconcerned with pretense. Our enthusiastic expressions also made us resemble those in need of institutionalization.

To most, a simple stop at a convenience store held little potential for euphoria, but Al and I savored, perhaps too easily, life's simple joys. Cackling manically and loudly singing unpoetic verses made up to commemorate the rare occasion, we celebrated our reprieve from the familiar and reveled in the joy of the moment. I expect it is because of this behavior that our forays into town were so few.

But, probably the best part of any such excursion was the opportunity to ride vertically in the truck bed, clinging madly to the rim at the top of the cab while doing fifty down winding mountain highways. Engaged in this reckless pursuit, we were held fast by only the fickle play of gravity and uncertain traction of rubber-soled tennis shoes against matted debris comprised of pine needles, hay, motor oil and mud.

Swaying with the motion of a loosely hinged truck bed, hyper-excited from the internal combustion of sugar and carbonation, we reveled in the onslaught of what amounted to horizontal skydiving. Had we known about wind tunnel experimentation, we would have volunteered our bodies on the spot.

Screaming ourselves hoarse for the driver to go faster… *faster*, tears streamed back and curled around our ears. Our lower lips bulged with the rush of wind as our long, tangled hair lashed at our squinting eyes. This type of activity is illegal now, and for good reason. Mishaps can and did occur. But it was the 70's, and I digress.

Not surprisingly, Mother often made the run into Granite without us, so her motive to bring us along raised suspicion.

Viewing Mother's handful of tattered coupons gave me pause. The kind of pause where, eyes wide, I found myself seized by a dread that instantly rooted me to the spot and curdled my glass of chocolate milk. I barely had time to ask "Why…", let alone finish my question or engage my ordinarily reliable and well-honed fleeing mechanism.

"Because we're making a Turkey Run." And she was out the door.

A Turkey Run.

In Hardrock, we made all sorts of 'Runs'. There was the 'Parts Run', the 'Dump Run' the 'Supply Run'. If something, say oatmeal, was accidentally omitted from the 'Supply Run' there would be an 'Oatmeal Run'. Everything we went for was in bulk and on the fly.

This would be a 'Turkey Run'. Even to this day, the hollow ring of those dread words causes a debilitating chill to creep into my limbs.

Thanks to Mother, we never went hungry — and that's saying a lot living in a place like Hardrock where half the town regularly showed up on our doorstep for free eats. Of course, Dad was instrumental in keeping food within reach, but this corresponded to a large fur-bearer, dressed out, chain-sawed into quarters and stashed in a snowbank through winter. But, Mother… Mother could do wonderful things with flour.

And not just flour. She also worked masterfully in sugar and baking powder. From soft dumplings and fluffy biscuits to fat pancakes and gooey cinnamon rolls, Mother could craft magic out of what she referred to simply as "the basics".

Women of today load their shopping carts with frozen waffles, cakes and pastries, paying a high price for the convenience. Colorful labels, dressed-up products, even promises of vitamin fortification meant nothing to my mother. Advertising agencies could never extol flour's simple virtue in a way Mother wasn't already privy to.

"Just give me the basics," she would say in her no-nonsense way, stuffing the mailbag she called a purse full of coupons. She excelled at an art lost today. But, it was not without casualties, mayhem and psychological erosion.

She stuck her head back in the door. "Well, get a move on! We need you kids to hold the turkeys down."

"*Al!*" I bellowed down the hall, sloshing milk as I galloped toward the back of the house where she and I had been, only moments earlier, blissfully planning a happy day inventing board games. Al was already hunched over a piece of poster-board with marker in hand.

"Criminey, what?" she asked, staggering with a look of surprised horror to her feet. "What? Is there a spider? *What?*"

"Mom's making a Turkey Run," I said breathlessly. There was no time for forewarning. I just blurted it out.

Al froze, just as I had, eyes wide and wanting to seek an exit but immobilized by the impending doom. I felt terrible about it. She had been implicated.

"Thank God I don't have to do this alone," I said, prying her fingers off the door frame on our way out to the driveway.

We sat stupefied in the bed of the truck, our usual

exuberance stymied by the thought of what, in the span of sixty minutes, would befall our pitiful and helpless lives. Lamenting our plight as voiceless minors, we sat aimlessly prying gunk out of the truck bed and wondering how we could disguise ourselves, lest we be recognized in Granite, of all uncool things, running turkeys.

"It's almost Thanksgiving," Al said, morosely jabbing at a chip of gunk and sending it sailing over the edge of the truck bed as we rolled down the highway. "How could we not have seen this coming?"

"At least we don't have to listen to her talk about the sale," I said, trying to cheer Al with a forced smile.

"That's true..." Al said, her eyes glazing as she slouched into a stupor of remembrance. It was a cruel trick, but I had to get her mind off contemplation of the Turkey Run. As Mother gained in proficiency and technical skill, each annual event would prove more harrowing than the one previous.

Al fitfully dozed, twitching with the stick still in her hand, as I visualized how this year's event might unfold.

My mother is a force of nature which, evolutionarily speaking, has found a unique niche among the grocery aisles of the local supermarket.

Mother pursued colossal bags of rice, flour, sugar, beans and potatoes, each weighing in at fifty to one-hundred pounds and all of which were customarily stocked on bottom shelves. Mother is nearly exclusively a bottom shelf shopper, which I am pretty sure explains her slight stature.

In the aisles of the Mort Mart, Al and I bore frequent dramatic witness to her evolutionary advantages in action.

In the ageless pursuit of species hierarchy, my mother and grocers continually faced off. Shelf stockers, cashiers, the butcher, the produce manager... none could match wits with Mother as she relentlessly stalked a bargain.

Armed with only a coupon or sale flyer in hand, I have seen her dress down the bakery lady, run ragged a cart boy as he shuffled case lots back and forth across the parking lot, and mercilessly reduce a cashier to tears over interpretation of the immortal words "limit of four".

In the struggle for dominance in the grocery world, my mother reigns supreme and will be challenged by none other than store managers, who often find themselves so intimidated by the public's perception of poor customer service that they will relent to her many and nefarious demands only encouraging her boldness that much more.

Upon entering her domain, my mother's instincts take command. Seizing one cart in the normal fashion and another by its face of wire mesh, she pushes one ahead and drags a second behind. Wobbling to and fro as furiously as the wheels beneath her carts, her short legs propel her at speeds in excess of thirty miles an hour, creating a noisy and dangerously unstable spectacle.

Startled shoppers leap aside, as beneath the pallid glow of fluorescent lighting her pupils widen like a cat stalking its prey. Quick eyes darting, she can sense a 'two-for-one' three aisles away and smell the acrid fume of label adhesive from a hundred yards, inspiring terror in anyone ever to mark down a can of corn.

Al and I shlump along behind, mere pawns in her

carefully planned campaign. Instantly, she transforms from the generally amenable albeit nervous human being to which we are accustomed, to an afflicted creature whose sole purpose in life is to outwit the store manager. We stand at the ready as she barks familiar commands:

"Get me that box way up there. See how they've tried to put the good stuff way up there."

"Guard my purse. I have to go talk to the manager about this."

"Put some muscle behind that cart, these things can handle *way* more than eight-hundred pounds."

"Balance that case on your head, while I climb up your back and get that extra can of black-eyed peas."

"Use those orangutan arms to reach back in there and get the fresh stuff."

…and, once in the truck, "Stop complaining, I know you can balance at least three or four more egg cartons on your arms. And don't let that bag of oranges slip off your feet. I paid sixty-eight cents a pound for those darned things. You'd think they were made of gold."

It is usually after such a grisly and demoralizing ordeal when, fervent from battle and with bloodlust still flashing in her eyes, she forces us, weakened and captive within the truck cab, to endure the detailed and oft recounted nuances of her unholy victory.

Recalling price comparisons from 1964 at so-an-so-mart, when what's-it was still produced in 400-ounce cans or some such thing, she would drone on and on until, at last, my molars would fall asleep and stimulate the nerve attached to my left eyelid to twitch involuntarily.

This was the stupor to which Al had fallen prey. Slumped and drooling on my shoulder, she slept off the effects of contemplating such a torture.

So it is, every year around the first week in November, grocers up and down the valley attempt to lure holiday shoppers into greater purchases with the promise of a turkey sale.

It is not wise to lure someone like my mother.

This event, intended by store managers to generate broader profits by sacrificing what they called a loss leader, was viewed by my mother as an annual opportunity to secure a year's worth of meat for around twenty bucks. Putting the words "turkey sale" in a flyer bound to darken my mother's palms is like floating the Mississippi Delta in an inner tube, trolling for alligators with a cupcake. Best avoided all around.

Every year she shows up and lays waste to their best defenses. And every year grocery store managers try to impress upon their marketing people the need to better convey the *exact* meaning of the word "qualifies".

This is how it would be this year. But this time, Abbey was accompanying her — driven by empty larders and long, dark, sub-freezing nights with nothing more to keep her warm than a skinny husband in tattered long underwear. Abbey had been briefed and warned to stay out of the way while Mother took care of the serious business of collecting the turkeys.

"We'll hit every grocery store within a hundred miles..." Mother said with an edge to her voice which I knew meant we were in for a long afternoon. "With your coupons and mine, plus what I scrounged out of that stack of newspapers by the courthouse, we ought to be able to get fourteen turkeys apiece. Plus, if I spend another thirty-four dollars and buy two cases of pickled cauliflower up at Milner's General, it'll qualify me for another four turkeys there."

"I'd like to get three or four more turkeys, but I don't have room to put them in the freezer," Abbey said.

"You can rent the snowbank up at our place. I'll only charge you one turkey a month."

Poor Abbey. She was a novice.

Two empty carts at the ready, Mother hit the frozen turkey chest at the Mort Mart. Positioning a cart on either side of the open chest she effectively blocked access, forcing other shoppers to gather at the fringes.

Fervently, she began sorting through hundreds of pounds of frozen turkeys, rolling aside the smaller birds in favor of anything over thirty pounds.

"Abbey, get over here," she directed with all the sensitivity of a defensive football coach. "See how they put all the big ones in the bottom? You have to get in here and dig for the big ones."

Abbey reached into the chest.

"Not *now!*" Mother admonished, rolling a turkey from Abbey's grasp. "You don't know what you're doing and you'll only cost us time. You have to know how to handle this stuff. You turn your back on frozen turkeys stacked three-feet high against the walls of this thing and you're asking for a mashed finger. You're not ready. Just pay attention and maybe you can dig for turkeys next time."

Given that Mother on a Turkey Run created a spectacle

hard not to stare at, she had drawn the attention of several shoppers who had gathered around as attentively as if they might have stumbled upon a Turkey Run workshop. You could see many of them were intrigued not only by this small woman's hand-to-hand assault upon the turkey freezer, but some also seemed intent on studying the nuances of her unique shopping style, for Mother was nothing if not efficient.

Once she had sorted forty-some turkeys according to their categorical size, she began retrieving them in earnest from the bottom of the freezer, implementing her signature hand-off.

An expert turkey chucker, Mother squatted low, cradling a thirty-five pounder and swinging it between her knees.

Launching it toward me on the up-swing, I caught it in my mid-section, lobbed it into the cart, denting the bottom, and quickly prepared to receive another one.

Abbey looked on, absorbing technique, as Mother launched another bird a third of her weight. "How do you do that?" Abbey asked.

"It's all in the knees…" Mother retorted as one shopper scribbled notes on her shopping list.

Mother and I were five turkeys deep in the cart which had formed a thick frost rivaling that which had overtaken my hands. She now leaned so far into the freezer, only her legs were sticking out. "How're your hands?" she grunted, restacking the wall of small turkeys which had given way and once again littered the bottom of the chest.

"I can't feel them," I marveled.

"That's why God gave you armpits. Al, you're up."

Al rushed into position as Mother struggled to back out

of the freezer, anchored by another thirty-pounder.

"Grab my feet, people!" Mother echoed from the frosty depths, sending up thick clouds of vapor.

My numb hands useless, I clamped Mother's foot to my side with my elbow as Abbey and Al grabbed Mother's other foot. Together, we hove both her and a fiercely clutched turkey out of the freezer.

"Al!" Hunched with the turkey on the down-swing, Mother blew through the vapor looking for her receiver who was rushing around the chest in order to make the catch.

"Here!"

A turkey sailed through the mist and Al intercepted — "Umph!" — thudding it into her cart.

"Let's get a move on, people," Mother directed, "we've got eight stores to go! These turkeys don't load themselves!"

Six and a half hours later, we were rumbling toward home with darkness rapidly descending.

Al and I sat amid thirty-six frozen turkeys jostling beneath our weight as we alternated buttocks in order to avoid frostbite. It was a record which had left our arms aching and one store manager crouched and consuming small white pills under a customer service counter.

Now and then, on taking a sharp corner, Al and I would topple from a turkey perch and be thrust up against the bed wall, buried and bruised among ever shifting mounds of frozen turkey flesh.

Abbey was driving now, as Mother had taken on the task of rear observer. Grim faced, with a smoldering cigarette clinched tightly between her fingers, Mother banged on the rear window glass which separated us.

"I told you kids to quit playing around with those turkeys! Now hang on to em'."

We swerved to the right again, and I suspected that poor Abbey was succumbing to the effects of molar-numbness.

I could see that the old two-by-ten pine boards Dad had bolted to the rear of the truck and liberally referred to as a tailgate were beginning to surrender to the unrelenting tide of turkeys undulating against their already weakened constitutions. The boards groaned and creaked ominously.

"Do you hear that groaning?" I asked Al.

"It's just me," she said, "trying to keep from...*arrghhh...*" She went under again.

Suddenly Abbey engaged the accelerator, as was her irrational habit when approaching towering cliffs with boulders that looked as if they might, without warning, decide to come aboard as unwelcome passengers.

The tailgate began splintering as the sound of turkeys dully but incessantly thudded against it — like pecking to death an injured comrade. The boards finally relented in a last gasp of protest as they cracked in half and ushered a surge of streaming turkeys out onto the highway.

Al and I, already clinging to the edges of the truck bed, were able to resist the pull of gravity but were subsequently pummeled by the reversing tide of a half-dozen turkeys when Abbey screeched to a stop.

Hovering above her seat, Mother fluttered about inside the cab in an effort to wrench open the back window. "Oh my God! Get the turkeys! Get the turkeys!" she cried, moving her lips like some animated cartoon as she climbed over Abbey, through the window and into the truck bed.

In a flash, she was scurrying around the darkened highway visible only by the wobbling, tiny red glow from her cigarette which slowly diminished as she fumbled into the distance. Al and I stared at one another then at Abbey who sat agape watching Mother.

Illuminated by the brake lights, here she came, stooped and clamoring toward the truck, with a turkey under each arm. "Hurry up, people!" she ordered, flushing us from our dazed lull. "No one's bleeding, get those turkeys before they roll down into the river!"

All four of us managed to secure and re-load most of the birds before our frantic foraging was halted by a noisy display of rotating red lights.

We froze in our tracks along the roadside as we silently observed a county deputy pull in behind us and inspect the bed of the truck with his flashlight. The headlights from his car shone onto a glimmering turkey nestled off the road in some weeds. Suddenly, Mother darted around the officer's car and expertly seized the turkey in the ditch. As he was inspecting the empty cab, she slipped it over the side into the truck bed.

"Hello, officer," she greeted him as if this type of occurrence were routine.

"Lady…" he nodded in affirmation as he attempted to catch her moving within the halo of his flashlight.

She quickly whispered from the corner of her mouth for me to begin loading the turkeys into the cab. With a nod toward Abbey, Mother directed her to aid in our mission.

Suddenly, Mother appeared by the officer's side. "Can I help you?" she asked.

"There are thirty-four turkeys in the bed of this truck. And one in my car," he gestured to his vehicle with the beam of light. "I found it about a quarter mile back."

One must've slipped through undetected, I thought. A lump formed in my throat, which could have rivaled the huge bird I was stuffing through the passenger widow. We must look like criminals, I thought. I had never considered that. How strange it must have seemed to the officer — these two haggard women and two battered looking juveniles, all of us wild-eyed and racing down the highway at night with thirty-five turkeys in the back of a beater pickup.

"You know it's illegal to transport something that creates a road hazard?" he asked Mother as she stood casually drawing on the last of her cigarette.

Al and I loaded the remaining turkeys then ourselves quietly into the cab where we tried to assume a posture akin to the debris in the bed. "I don't want to go to jail..." Abbey whimpered.

"Don't worry," I consoled, "she'll think of something." I'd seen Mother shake down a delivery man over the wholesale purchase of a case of frozen pizzas straight off his truck in the parking lot of a restaurant she didn't even own.

Regardless of the evidence in his car, I put my money squarely on Mother, knowing she wasn't about to let the long arm of the law put in jeopardy her hard-won spoils.

Then it happened.

Of course he couldn't have known, but it was almost

pitiful the way he fell into her trap.

"Where'd you get all these turkeys?" he asked incredulously, pulling out his pad and pen, preparing to write down the license plate information.

She was quick on the draw, and he never even saw it coming.

"Well, four of them came from the Mountain Market where we would've qualified for six, but they ran short so we had to get a rain-check which took forty-five minutes on account of everyone in line, and then we went to pick up those remaining two from the Get n' Go out in Larsville, which was okay, because they were running a special on boneless pork chops and had a deal where if you bought seven packs at a dollar ninety-eight you could get…"

As his eyes began to take on the familiar glaze, Mother slid into the driver's seat and whispered to all of us still hunkering near the floorboards, "Keep your heads down."

Leaving a turkey behind in the officer's vehicle, she slipped the truck into gear and called back, "Y'all have a nice evening, and you and your family enjoy Thanksgiving dinner on us, okay?"

I glanced out the rear window to see him standing there, appearing lost. His left eyelid twitched. Poor man, I thought. He was a novice.

A Tale of Two Deer

It was chilly in the empty saloon, and the warm light of a late autumn afternoon shone brightly in my eyes as I stood near the pool table, cleaning one of the pool room's large windows with vast crumples of newsprint and Mother's homemade window cleaner. It was a tediously boring task which encouraged my squinting eyes to wander across the parking lot.

I was unaccustomed to wretchedly boring Saturdays, but winter preparations were underway and Al and I had been summoned for seasonal chores — I to clean windows, Al to sort and fold washcloths and hand towels in the motel storage room.

Heavy sigh... *spray, swipe, swipe.*

Dad was cleaning the fireplace in the adjacent room, so shirking wasn't exactly an advisable activity. Ho hum... *spray, swipe, swipe.*

What's that? A deer walking down the road? I could make out its huge antlers over the brush that lined the county road into Hardrock. It bobbed along toward the entrance to the inn then must have slipped and fallen backward. I stopped in mid-swipe to watch it regain, or *attempt* to regain, its footing.

Huh, I thought. The county road wasn't icy or even wet. Why would a deer slip on a dry road? Maybe it's wounded, I thought to myself. The buck rose once again, teetered and fell over to the side. Good grief!

"Dad!" I shouted into the other room, "I think there's a wounded buck up on the road!"

"What?" came the retort from inside the fireplace where Dad had crawled to loosen creosote from the chimney.

"A deer, I think there's a deer up on the road that's been…" I trailed off, watching the animal wander into the brush as it navigated toward the inn's driveway.

Vigorously shaking its head and staggering under its own weight, it finally fell into the tall grass and bushes along the road. Cripes!

"Dad! Dad! It *is* a deer! It fell into the bushes! It must have been hit by a car! I'm going up to check it out!" I flung open the door amid its moans of agony drifting into the saloon.

Cleaning implements clattered from the hearth as Dad bellowed, "Get back here, Lisa, you don't mess around with a wounded animal. Just a damn minute. Go up and get my .44, and I'll meet you outside."

I glanced up to the deer as I rushed to get Dad's revolver. The poor beast was writhing in pain. I knew Dad's intent was to put it out of its misery in the event it was too far gone to do more than suffer a slow and miserable death.

Pistol in hand, I hurried up the driveway toward Dad where, having followed its pitiful cries, he had located the animal and was already kneeling by its side.

As I neared, I could see Dad struggling to pull at its antlers. My hand flew to my mouth. Cripes, he's trying to make it stand!

As I drew closer, however, my brain and my eyes grappled with the image before me. What was I seeing? A downed deer, right? And Dad struggling to get it on its feet. Right? But where did the other two human legs and arms come from? What was I seeing? How was this real? Was someone trapped underneath?

"Damn it, Jake, what the hell were you thinking, cramming your head inside this mount?" As Dad tugged and twisted at the antlers, muffled shouts came from inside the deer head.

It was Crazy Jake.

With a deer hide tied around his body, Jake's head was buried inside the head of a mounted deer.

"Lisa, come over here. You hold this down while I lift up on the back. Watch those damned antlers. Jake hold still, for God's sake."

"Mmm rrphing ooo," came the muffled reply.

Dad pressed his knee into Jake's shoulder, prying up on the back of the deer's neck while I pinned its nose down. With the expected cursing and grunting from all parties, Dad finally wrenched Jake free.

The deer's head popped off as Jake flung onto his back and, eyes wild, gasped for air.

Dad and I crouched in disbelief as the absurdity of the situation slowly dawned on us.

His eyes rolling back, Jake looked as ragged as any wounded deer inhaling great gulps of sweet air.

Dad shook his head sadly, "I still may have to shoot it."

The three of us walked back to the saloon, Jake with the deer hide roped around him and dragging the head by its antlers.

Once inside, Jake untied the hide and set the head on the

bar. He swiveled on his bar stool to talk to Dad's legs, again protruding from the fireplace.

I sprayed more vinegar onto the window and listened raptly as Jake explained his latest catastrophe.

"It just needs a little fine tuning, that's all. This get-up ought to bring a herd right by the house when they move down out of the high country here in a couple weeks. Then, *heh heh*, I'll just help one of 'em on into my house where he can stay for dinner."

"Jake, first of all, that'd be poaching. Second of all, you damn fool, you try that again and you may not make it to the inn before you suffocate."

"I got that covered. My big mistake was not cuttin' out any eye holes or a breathin' hole."

Dad ducked down from up in the chimney. "Your big mistake was coming up with the idea in the first place. How'd you get your head in there anyway?"

"Whittled out the plaster. I only had my head in the neck part." Jake looked reflective. "Man, I didn't think it'd get stuck like that, though. Damn, I almost couldn't breath! And I tell you what, that son of a gun was *heavy!*"

Dad continued scraping the inside of the chimney as creosote tinkled down.

Jake stroked his long gotee, his eyes pinched in deep thought. "Huh… yep, I think I need to cut a couple eye holes and a breathin' hole in the neck, then I'd be all right."

"Jake, you aren't going to look like a deer, smell like a deer or act like a deer in that weird-ass ghillie suit."

"*I* thought he was a deer," I piped in.

"See? *She* thought I was a deer." Jake gave me an affirmative nod.

"*She* isn't a deer, either. A real deer is going to know the difference."

"Well, I got me some old deer scent I plan on rubbin' on the hide, here." Jake patted the old hide, raising a ruckus of dust. "I'm telling you, Ike, them deer are dumb. They'll sure enough believe I'm just a regular old buck. I get to scuffling around in the grass and weeds, and them does will come runnin'."

"Jake, you're going to get yourself killed. You're either going to suffocate yourself, break your neck or lure in a bear. Somehow, though, I have no doubt you'll find a way to kill yourself with this dumb idea."

Jake sat quietly then looked over at me and winked. "Yeah... you're probably right. I better get all this stuff back to the house. Well, thanks for gettin' it off my head. I'll see ya around, Ike."

Jake draped the stiff hide over his arm, snatched the deer head off the bar and gave me a tip of his hat on his way outside.

"Do you think Jake will listen to you?" I asked the general darkness around the corner of the saloon.

"Nope," came the certain reply.

Throughout the following week, Hardrock buzzed with activity as its handful of winter residents split and stacked wood, checked antifreeze and stapled plastic onto window frames. Enis Snapbinder, Hardrock's mayor pro-tem and founder of the historical society, had just finished winterizing the cages of his peafowl. His mother and aunt were out visiting from Denver, and he had decided to take them on a jaunt down to Quartz Creek to view the ruins of the old rock finishing mill.

On their way back up from the creek, Enis reluctantly followed his mother and aunt into the trading post where Al and I were busily cleaning the ice cream freezer — a project delayed until after summer's demands.

"It is so charming, dear." Mother Snapbinder pointed to the road-kill beaver pelt on the wall, traded by Jake for part of his tab. Admiring the antique woodstove with its brass accents, her eyes followed the floor to the vast, braided rug which rested beneath two heavy wooden chairs and a spruce-planked table. She studied the front of the counters comprised of pine slabs, rough with curling bark.

"I suppose," Enis muttered, habitually disgruntled by our efforts to revitalize Hardrock's commercial district.

"Delightfully rustic…" she continued musing, fixing her gaze on the deer head which we'd found in the motel storeroom and Dad had mounted on the wall behind the antique register. She looked into the mount's dark, vacant eyes and shuddered, "My, those animals are large, aren't they, Enis? Heavens. Don't you worry about them milling around your home?" She unsnapped her tiny coin purse and placed a dime and a photo postcard of the old Lost Horse Station on the counter. I rang up her purchase and shut the register drawer, eyeing Enis.

"There are a lot worse things milling around out in these woods, Mother," he said, eyeing me back. "Unholy, evil things."

Mother Snapbinder daintily tugged the hem of her hair scarf over her forehead and tightened the knot under her chin.

"Well, I certainly hope we don't encounter some of them on our way back into town." Looking concerned, she twined her arm in the crook of her son's elbow.

Between the two low aisles where she had been browsing a locally written hiking guide, Enis' aunt loudly announced, "Well, if we do, I'll be ready!" She then withdrew a 110 instamatic camera from her handbag, snapped a photo of the trading post's interior and advanced the film.

"Oh, Phyllis! You always *were* the reckless one," Mother Snapbinder tittered at her sister's pluckiness.

Phyllis brought the book and five postcards selected from the rack over to the counter. "Ring me up a couple of boxes of film for the road, too." She pointed at the film kept on the wall behind me as she plumbed her purse.

"Come along now, Mother, I've prepared a surprise for dinner." Enis hurried his mother and aunt out of the trading post and back along the driveway toward town.

As the trio made their way slowly along the county road into Hardrock, Phyllis paused every few feet to snap a photo of one subject or another. A bare-branched aspen grove, here. A sweeping vista of Pickanaxe and Kodiak, there. Dappled sunlight on mossy stones, here. A buck ambling through the forest, there.

"*Shhh*, everyone, I think I can get close enough to capture it," she said, spotting a massive buck some seventy yards distant walking through the aspen, sniffing at the breeze.

"Be careful, Phyllis!" Enis admonished. "This is rutting season, and they can charge."

Mother Snapbinder pressed closer to her son, shielding

her eyes and visually sweeping the area. "Oh, good heavens, everyone! *Another* deer! There, just off the road in that yard near that old abandoned house…"

Everyone paused and searched the vicinity.

"Look," Enis observed of the deer in Jake's yard, "it isn't aware of the other buck over there in the trees. It appears to be distracted by something on the ground."

"Oh, this is ever so thrilling! It's like a real life episode of *Wild Kingdom!*" Mother Snapbinder squealed in delight.

The buck in the forest grunted and pawed the ground.

"Look," Enis whispered, "the buck in the yard sees the one in the trees! Maybe they'll fight."

"Fight?"

"Yes, bucks always fight over which one will mate with the does in a herd."

"Why is that buck in the yard looking around behind it?" Mother Snapbinder asked.

"I'm not sure," Enis replied.

"Why is it jumping up and down? Is that part of the ritual?" Aunt Phyllis observed, aiming her camera toward the unfolding action. "Oh, it's fallen! That one by the house doesn't seem to be very manly."

"Oh, Oh!" Mother Snapbinder pointed, excitedly. "The first buck is charging! It's charging the other one that's fallen down!"

"*Shhhh,*" Enis crossed his legs in a panicked crouch, "everyone be still. Be still and be quiet or it might charge us too!"

Aunt Phyllis could scarcely believe their fortune to

witness one of nature's most dramatic scenes first hand. "Oh, that poor frightened buck. It looks puny compared to that first buck, doesn't it? Oh, look, it's gotten up and it's running. It's running up onto the porch, and it's, it's... why, it looks like it's trying to open the door!"

"Well, for heaven's sake..." Mother Snapbinder stood agape. "It's gotten its antlers caught in the doorway!"

"It's trying to paw at that other buck following it..." Aunt Phyllis observed, adding with a startled gasp, "Did you *hear* that?!" She searched the faces of her companions.

"Hear what?" Enis crowed.

"I thought I heard — *yes!* It's yelling at that first buck! It said '*Go Back! Get away!*'"

Enis looked stunned. "What?"

"It *did!* I just heard it, too!" Mother Snapbinder cried. "It's a demon deer! It's *possessed! Run!*"

Wide-eyed, Enis led the charge several yards ahead of his Mother who though frail-seeming was certainly spry for her age. Phyllis, plump and unaccustomed to the altitude, brought up the rear.

Screaming and dashing for the inn, the trio was soon overtaken by a panicked buck, itself surprised by the human vocalizations of what it had falsely identified as a normal competitor in need of vanquishing. Streaking aside Enis, his mother and Phyllis, the real buck cut suddenly into the forest, leaving his costumed nemesis to wrestle his antlers through the door of his house.

Bursting into the trading post, Enis, Mother Snapbinder and Phyllis stood heaving and patting cool water to their faces, brought by Al and myself as we listened to their harrowing tale of a close encounter with demon wildlife.

Al and I could hardly contain our sniggers.

Dad walked in with an armload of firewood and took in the disturbing scene. "What's going on?"

I assumed a grave tone, "Remember that deer that stumbled into the parking lot last week?"

"Y..e..s..." He looked around as if expecting a wall to be missing.

"Well, it's taken to terrorizing tourists."

As Enis sat in a stupor, the two ladies broke in with a flurry of excited observations followed by a long, expectant pause.

Dad nodded beneath his cowboy hat, hiding a knowing grin. Shaking his head, he finally cleared his throat, "Well, we knew last week that one wasn't right in the head. Hopefully, it's learned its lesson and we won't have to shoot it."

A Hardrock Thanksgiving

"We're coming up for Thanksgiving!" came the amplified, sing-song voice on the other end of the line. This was followed by a short pause, sputter and prolonged hacking fit which I was fairly certain belonged to my Aunt Gigi and had been caused by the inadvertent snorting of wine into her sinuses. "Isn't that — *hack* — wonderful?" Without giving me a full second to respond, she quickly followed with, "Hello? Hello?" then a far-away echo, as if she had turned from the phone... *"Ray? Are you sure they have phones up there?"*

"Mommm..." I called into the pantry, "Uncle Raymond and Aunt Gigi are coming up..."

CRASH! A case of canned goods assailed the pantry floor as Mother popped around the corner, eyes wide. *"What?"* she asked with a dramatic look of concern.

"Aunt Gigi says they're driving up for Thanksgiving," I said, pulling apart the hopelessly tangled thirty-foot phone cord and stretching the phone toward Mother.

Reaching for the phone, Mother emitted her signature 'Oh, God, why me?' groan. "Hi, Gigi. What? No, I just dropped a case of corn on my... oh. Uh huh. Well, how are... yes, Lisa told... mmm hmm..."

I looked at Al, who sat across from me at the kitchen table. We were deep into a contentious game of liar's Scrabble and the sixth night of a two-day sleep-over. "You watch," I began, "she'll be in the pantry for three minutes, and I bet she won't even get one whole sentence out. We'll just hear a bunch of, 'uh huhs, 'mmmm hmmmms' and 'oh, reallys'."

"Your aunt and uncle are coming up for Thanksgiving?" Al asked, placing the word *jorkyd* on the board.

"Looks like it," I said. "Okay, what's *jorkyd*?" I asked in accordance with the rules Al and I had invented for our twist on the classic game.

"Jorkyd," Al began, affecting the required look of complete confidence, "you know, it's an ancient style of... what was it, oh yeah... Norwegian ship painting."

I gave a look of disbelief. What a blatant lie. Which, of course, was the point.

She went on, "Don't you remember reading about it in that one unit from history class on, uh, Norway?"

I shook my head in the negative, preparing to shout "Liar!" thusly terminating Al's turn.

"*You* know," Al stressed, "it was really popular between the 11th and 12th centuries... oh, and it was made with a special paint from boiled squid ink."

"Ooo, that's good," I said. "Okay, I believe you. My turn."

"Yay! I got to use my 'J' plus the 'K' and the 'Y'!" Al dug new letters out of the letter bag. "So, where are your aunt and uncle from?"

"Texas," I said, placing *nitpins* on the board. "Nitpins. Those are the tiny nails used to nail strips of fabric to the outside of those same ships to show from a distance whether the crew had run into any trouble out at sea. You know, red for enemy encounter, blue for a good catch, green for, uh… storm damage."

"Hmm… okay, cool," Al nodded, duly impressed.

"Texas is a long way. I hope the weather doesn't turn bad." She glanced out the window at the overcast sky.

CRASH — the phone cord had coiled around itself causing Mother to pull the phone base off its mooring on the wall.

Grumbling, Mother hurried out of the pantry, accidentally kicking over the broom. Placing her hand over the phone speaker and reaching to retrieve the base swinging on the wall, she muttered, "They're bringing a boat."

"A *boat?*" Al and I asked in unison, excited by the shared image.

"Raymond bought a new ski boat and RV. They're bringing both. I can't believe he's bringing a thirty-foot RV and a sixteen-foot boat up here. In *November!*" She hung up the phone, pausing a second. "Maybe the weather will turn bad."

"Wow! A boat!" Al and I squealed.

"Plus," I interjected, "I bet it's *totally* decked out — they have more money than God!" I didn't actually know how much money God had, if God dealt in money at all, but I'd always heard my mother use the phrase, often interchangeably with 'more money than brains', so I figured it must be gazillions or at least way more than we had.

"People," Mother sighed, looking at us as if she were observing two alien life forms, "the lake will probably be frozen. I don't know what he's thinking."

"Did you tell them that?" I asked.

"When have you ever known your Uncle Raymond to listen to anyone? Of course I told Gigi, and she said she'd already tried to convince Ray. Ray said he needs a vacation and there's nothing in these mountains that could keep him from bringing the boat and RV."

"Is Roach coming too?" I asked

Al stopped rearranging her letters and glanced up, "Who's Roach, your cousin?"

"Their dog," I said. "Her real name is Cookie, but then Uncle Raymond started calling her Cucaracha and then Roach, and that's what finally stuck. Aunt Gigi *hates* it when he calls her that, so, naturally, he does it all the time."

"Naturally," Mother echoed.

"What kind of dog is it?" Al asked.

"Some kind of pompom... raisin."

"Pomeranian," Mother said, leaning wearily against the counter, "which is Latin for *spoiled horror*." She rolled her eyes and buried her head in her hands, shaking it slowly side to side, "Why, why, *why?*"

"Is it a big dog?" Al asked.

"Nah, teeny. She'd be cute if she didn't bite all the time."

"Bite?"

I leaned in. "This dog is so spoiled, you would not believe. Aunt Gigi thinks she's her *kid*. She has her own room, her own living room chair with a big blue satin pillow and a blanket, and even a high-chair at the table next to Aunt Gigi. She even has clothes!"

"No way," Al said, disbelieving.

"*Way.* A little dresser full of outfits. Doesn't she, Mom?"

"Sadly, yes." Mother answered.

Mother continued leaning against the cupboard contemplating as I continued expounding on the interesting relationship between Aunt Gigi and Roach, "Aunt Gigi is always like, 'she's so *petite...*' and 'she has to be on a *special diet* because of her *sensitive system...*'" I emulated Aunt Gigi's serious inflections.

Mother interjected, "Special diet, my foot. I've seen that dog tear into a bag of chips, rip up the mail and drag out the bathroom trash eating every bit of all of it."

"Yeah," I picked up the thread again, "she's a total pain, and if you're holding something she wants, she'll bite your ankles if you don't give it to her fast enough. She's always biting ankles."

"Cripes, I hope your aunt keeps her locked up in the RV." Al said, looking a little concerned.

"She carries her around under her arm all the time."

Dad came in through the front door, dragging a huge hunk of split cow hide, "Hon, have you seen my lacing needle?"

Mother went off like a cork from one of Aunt Gigi's champagne bottles, "Do I *look* like I have your lacing needle? You probably left it with the rest of your junk out in the shop, which is a disaster, and you never find anything in it because you never put anything back, because you always have *me* around to go find it..." By this time, her voice had trailed off as she tromped through the kitchen and hurled off the porch, leaving behind a sandal flung off in her haste.

"What's the matter with your mother?" Dad asked, looking around bemused.

"Aunt Gigi and Uncle Raymond are coming up for Thanksgiving," I said.

"Really?" Dad asked. "I thought he just got transferred to Dallas."

"Aunt Gigi says he needs a vacation. They're bringing a boat and RV."

"Huh. Okay, well, have you seen my lacing needle?"

The doings of the younger Uncle Raymond were of mild interest to Dad. By contrast, Uncle Raymond considered every doing an opportunity for brotherly competition.

Uncle Raymond's personal evolution had taken him from the university straight into the boardroom where he devoted the next twelve years of his life climbing the same corporate ladder from which Dad had just leapt. Uncle Raymond had clawed and sacrificed his way into upper level management only to grow resentful of defining his worth, goals and experience by others' judgments and allowances. In some ways, Uncle Raymond had lost respect for his own decision to work toward retirement, sacrificing nearly everything for that hoped-for dream. But somehow his and Aunt Gigi's lives had become crowded with interlocking activities that served only to support that questioned goal. It kept his blood pressure high and his patience low.

Dad's evolution had been a diverse chronology of seized-upon impulse relished without reservation. Dad had left home in his early teens to become a dozen interesting things over the next twenty years, among them, a mountain man and maker of moccasins, looking for lost lacing. He'd found the family institutional legacy of finance, law and medicine stifling and rejected it in favor of adventure. He didn't measure life's opportunities according to risk... only potential, which was why he'd been tapped to oversee regional operations with the burgeoning phone company.

Uncle Raymond thoroughly failed to appreciate what could have motivated Dad to leave corporate culture. To walk away from what appeared to be a secure executive position was stunning enough, but to walk away into the mountains with no predictable future or pension plan was far beyond anything Uncle Raymond could fathom.

Both brothers could work an expense account. But Dad could also start a fire from a wet pine tree in a snowstorm.

In a continual effort to justify his subscription to corporate advancement, Uncle Raymond nursed an aggravated desire to out-wit, out-maneuver, out-earn, out-and-out out-do everything his older brother ever did or might consider, failing utterly to recognize that the two of them simply measured their lives by very different yard sticks.

A few days before we left Houston for Colorado, Uncle Raymond had been mired in a renewed fit of discontentment. He and Dad stood in his drive where Uncle Raymond raised the electric garage door and proudly unveiled his newest acquisition. It was a brand new Ford Bronco with leather interior and loaded with every convenience money and technology could provide.

Uncle Raymond beamed at his latest effort to demonstrate the value of a high salary.

Dad looked at it and nodded, "That's a nice vehicle, Ray. Got a good engine. Nice cargo area. Good chassis. Yep, that's real nice."

Uncle Ray glanced disdainfully at our used Land Cruiser sitting in the drive. Before he could launch into commentary, Dad continued, "It's a good vehicle, Ray, but damn, between car payments and keeping the gas tank full, that thing ought to do everything including wipe your ass. It'll sure enough keep you locked into the system working overtime."

Uncle Raymond's ears flushed.

While it was true Dad had a compelling, every-guy's appreciation for fun toys like boats and all, he enjoyed building or rebuilding them in a discounted effort to acquire even more of them, which he'd later trade for others. I'd seen him scrape puckered paint off a scuttle, fish in it for a month, trade it for a used Austin-Healey, restore its interior, drive it a month then sell it to set up a photography studio which endured six months before Dad was into lapidary and knife making. Such diversions irritated Uncle Raymond all the more, because while the know-how was attainable, his time was already sold.

Uncle Raymond spent every waking moment at the office, around the office, on the way to the office or flying to some other office. Meanwhile, Aunt Gigi ran with the country club set and spent long lonely evenings browsing European vacation brochures, redecorating the house, feeding Roach bits of liver pate' and popping corks on expensive imported wine.

For Uncle Raymond, it seemed the true and fine point of his rivalries turned on justifying the on-going investment in his lifestyle. And, while both men were competent in their different worlds, only Dad was truly comfortable in his.

Discontentment was the fine grist which kept Uncle Raymond's temper razor-thin and sharp, evidenced one Friday afternoon a year earlier when he came home from the office with a pounding headache, downed a palm-full of pills and left strict instructions not to wake him until dinner. I was over at their house, helping Aunt Gigi assemble gift baskets for a fundraiser. Though much of the incident was a blur, it began when a slight, unsuspecting encyclopedia salesman approached the door and rang the doorbell.

Roach streaked to the door and began jumping at the knob, *boing boing boing* — her whole body, tensing and boinging like popped corn. BARK! BARK! BARK! She stopped just long enough to snarl and chew on the already destroyed bottom corner of the door. BARK! BARK! BARK!

Before Aunt Gigi could pull the little pieces of tape off her fingers to answer the door, the man rang the bell four more times in rapid succession, elevating Roach's excitement to that of a dozen BBs shaken vigorously around the inside of an empty coffee can. She spun in circles, clawed at the door and fired bark after bark like a machine gun, *BARK! BARK! BARK! BARK!*

Uncle Raymond emerged from their master suite, slammed the door and stormed down the hall, his wild hair scarcely more startling than his wide, red-rimmed eyes. Wearing a satin robe twisted unevenly around him and fastened with a hasty knot under one armpit, his slippers flapped madly and sparked on the carpet as he alternately stomped and scuffed to the door. Roach saw his approach and streaked back to the kitchen where she, Aunt Gigi and I sat transfixed, staring at the looming catastrophe about to unfold before us.

In a single lightening-fast motion, Uncle Raymond tore open the door, grabbed the little man by his ankles and yanked him upside down, threatening to put him head-first down the garbage disposal. I'm not sure what happened after that, since the view from under the dining room table was obscured by a dozen chair legs.

That evening Aunt Gigi suggested a vacation to Spain. But, Uncle Raymond's idea of a vacation was a corporate-sponsored evening featuring the fun and frivolity of a 'most productive division' awards banquet.

We never expected the two of them to leave Texas and visit us in Colorado, let alone venture high into the remote recesses of the Continental Divide. But, Uncle Raymond was on a competitive mission that had taken the shape of a brand new boat and RV.

We awaited their arrival with an unsettling combination of excitement and apprehension.

On Tuesday evening at 7:28, they rolled off the county road and into the drive, or at least attempted to.

"They're here!" I shouted to no one in particular, hearing the rumble of the engine from my bedroom floor where Al and I sat sorting through my rock collection.

Al and I banged into one another scattering stones and scrambling for the bedroom door. Wes met us head-on from across the hall then thwarted our advance by sweeping us behind him as I grappled for his belt loops.

"Dibs on the boat!" Wes and I yelled in unison,

neither of us knowing what we were claiming but figuring we ought to stake out any potential territory ahead of rivals.

Mother gaped out the living room window, frantically brushing her fogged-on breath from the pane with her sleeve. "Good grief, what is he *doing?*"

Headlights sliced the darkness, and the mercury light in the parking lot barely hinted at the behemoth slowly rumbling and snaking its way down the drive.

Dad, having finally found his lacing needle and still stitching the sole of a moccasin, glanced out the window from his recliner. "Looks like he's trying to get around the corner."

The night boomed with the hair-raising sound of metal scraping and grinding against metal mixed with the sound of a big engine idling down then revving. *Vrooom... screeeee...* CLANG! *VROOOOM...*

"Oh, my God! I think he hit the dumpster!" Mother ran to another window for a better view.

Al, Wes and I, electing a more direct route, jammed on our boots and pounded out into the November night.

"Stay out of his way," Dad shouted after us, realizing we probably hadn't heard him. "Damn it. I guess I'm going to have to go out there."

"I think you'd *better* before he tears the front off the inn!" Mother was near hysteria, yet reluctant to confront temperatures below forty degrees.

Al, Wes and I arrived on scene to discover the back of the RV had been bashed in by the dumpster which, in turn, had an amorous grasp on the boat trailer.

Aunt Gigi was standing outside at the front, passenger

corner of the RV, clutching Roach who was writhing and barking madly, her dark eyes bulging. Aunt Gigi gestured wildly with one hand and yelled to be heard over Roach and the RV motor, "I *SAID* to the right, TO THE *RIGHT!*"

Uncle Raymond leaned out of the driver's window. "I *went* right, damn it! Where the hell is the back of the rig? What am I up against? What's back there?"

"I *told* you I don't know! Just go RIGHT! Oh, wait, that's *MY* RIGHT! GO LEFT! GO LEFT! And, don't snipe at me Raymond. You know I didn't even want to…"

BARK! BARK! BARK! Inspired by Aunt Gigi's distress, Roach launched her own verbal assault. Aunt Gigi walked over and kicked the RV with her low-heeled designer footwear then hurried back twenty feet.

Uncle Raymond began banging his forehead on the steering wheel then suddenly jerked his head up, eyes wide and dilated. Jamming the RV into gear, he gunned the gas and lurched the whole rig forward, bucking and humping with the dumpster in tow. *Vvvvrroooooommmm… screeeeeeeee… guhhn-guhhn-guhhn…*

"Oh my God. He's dragging something behind him!" Aunt Gigi noticed us kids standing nearby and waved, "Hi Lisa… oh dear… Ray? Ray? I think there's a… stop, Raymond! *Stop!*"

BARK! BARK! BARK!

"*Sssshhh* now, Cookie, I won't let Daddy yell at you, no I won't." Aunt Gigi attempted to cover Roach's eyes, but the little dog, determined to see, ducked and dodged every pass.

Uncle Raymond inadvertently sounded the horn in one

long, loud blow while leaning over the steering wheel and straining to see out the front window. His wide eyes and gritted teeth reflected the light of the mercury lamp contrasting in the darkness of the cab. "Gigi? *GIGI?*"

A string of muttered curses followed his dark eyes across the parking lot as he craned his neck farther over the dash in an effort to locate his ground crew.

"Cripes…" Al uttered involuntarily when his gaze swept across us, unseeing.

Aunt Gigi yelled to Uncle Raymond over the sound of the engine, "I am *not* talking to you when you are like this!" Putting her hand on her hip, she turned and delivered an exasperated look to us kids. "When you stop yelling and…."

Uncle Raymond shot his head out of the driver's side window and wrenched his neck around in an effort to see behind him.

Eeeeeee, BANG, the sound of twisting metal rose up into the night ending with what sounded like a large object crashing onto its side.

"What the hell *now?*" Uncle Raymond kicked open the RV door and clamored down off the rig. He stomped around back to survey the damage as Al and I scurried to the top of the small sloping ridge onto which Uncle Raymond had just deposited the trailer.

The boat and trailer were listing twenty degrees, twisting the hitch but stopping short of full capsize with the aid of the attached dumpster, now precariously tilting over backward. Uncle Raymond stood surveying the situation, "Well, it's parked. I'll get it leveled tomorrow."

Dad intercepted Uncle Raymond in the driveway. "You need any help?" he asked.

"*Hell no.* Got 'er lined out. I'll finesse everything in the morning. Right now, though," Uncle Raymond cleared his throat, lightly hitched his waistband and nodded appraisingly at the mountains, as if he could see anything beyond the dark parking lot, "I could use a stiff drink."

"Come on down to the saloon and we'll get a scotch."

"Bring me the bottle," Uncle Raymond jested. He always jested when he was under great stress.

Within half an hour of their arrival, everyone was pulling up chairs around two tables pushed together in the saloon and Abbey was bringing a tray of drinks from behind the bar. Al, Mother and I had iced tea, Wes had a soda, and Aunt Gigi ordered a glass of white wine. Dad poured two glasses of scotch, passing Uncle Raymond the bottle.

Uncle Raymond, his eyes bloodshot and baggy, curled his fingers around the bottle's contoured neck and grinned, winking at us girls. "You don't want to straighten out your fingers too fast after a record twenty-two hour drive."

Aunt Gigi rolled her eyes.

Conversation around the saloon flurried like the snowflakes outside.

Meanwhile, the RV, lightly perfumed with the scent of Cookie's spilled kibble, had captured the attentions of a masked, rotund visitor and her many well-trained children.

A large raccoon padded up the small steps and, with nimble fingers, hooked the edge of the door which had been knocked slightly ajar by the evening's activities. Ordering the troops to duck low, she whipped open the door and ambled inside with her brood close behind. *Pad, pad, pad, pad* went the raccoon and her five excited offspring. "Look, Mama," one of the youngest said, observing the fully stocked opened cupboards, "a store!"

Back at the tavern, Aunt Gigi complained to Mother, "I can't believe that man. He drove straight through like some crazed animal. Wouldn't even stop for Cookie to go tink, did he Cookie? We had to go tink-tink in the new shower, didn't we?" Aunt Gigi glared at Uncle Raymond as she absently stroked Cookie's silky head. Roach snuggled deep in Aunt Gigi's cashmere sweater, dozing with one eye cracked to the table.

Uncle Raymond took a sip of scotch. "That's why you travel by RV, Gigi, so you don't *have* to stop. Everything is right there behind the captain's chair. Refrigerator, bathroom, bed, TV." He picked up a piece of popcorn, "Hey, Roach," and lobbed it at the little dog. She reared like a striking cobra, snatched the popcorn out of the air then quickly snuggled back down into Aunt Gigi's arms.

"Ray! I told you not to feed her those things. It gives her gas." Aunt Gigi looked at Mother. "Sometimes I could just pinch his head off. Have you ever tried to make coffee doing seventy down interstate? The stupid boat trailer was swaying so much I could barely stand up at the counter." She sipped her wine with some efficiency then asked for another. "So, where is the mall?"

Meanwhile, back at the RV... having packed off in her children's capable paws many delectables from Aunt Gigi and Uncle Raymond's cupboards, the raccoon tired of her foray and nodded goodnight to a black bear stopping by for a late night snack. "Fridge is open," she trilled. "Nice couple of steaks in there... I ate the shrimp tray though, sorry." And the bear tromped in... *tromp, tromp, tromp*...

Back at the tavern... "Well, I just can't believe the beautiful scenery up here," Aunt Gigi commented to Mother.

"Yes, it is beau..."

"But, it is primitive, isn't it?" she interrupted.

"Well, yes, it's a little re..."

"I just don't think I could go a *day* without shopping. You know, if I don't show up at the mall every day, the girls at my favorite shops call the house to make sure I'm feeling all right."

"Mmm hmm..."

"I can't believe you don't have a mall out here. You have running water, don't you?"

Uncle Raymond refilled his glass.

Meanwhile back at the RV... the bear ate the steaks, bit the tops off two cans of soup, devoured Uncle Raymond's peanuts and Aunt Gigi's French mints then commenced ransacking the quarters, searching for more chocolate. Tearing into a package of snack cakes, he finally bored of his foraging and readied to leave. He thoughtfully left a half eaten bag of chips on the floor for the family of skunks he past at the door on his way outside.

"Why, thank you for leaving us a half bag of potato chips, Mr. Bear." And in tripped the skunk family, *trip, trip, trippty trip*... "Oh look, children, a brie."

Back at the saloon... Aunt Gigi was gazing fondly at

Roach and stroking her silken ears, "Well, little Cookie looks ready for bed, aren't you, little… *[pppfffftt]* Oh my! *RAY!* I *told* you not to feed her those things. Now she's going to have vapors all night. Poor thing." Roach still had one eye cracked to the table.

After a long evening of story-telling and laughter amid a few 'mmm hmms', 'uh huhs' and 'oh reallys', we finally collectively trouped across the parking lot for a grand tour of the RV.

The dark night, with its freezing temperatures and lightly swirling flurries, concealed the destruction at the back end of the RV but enhanced the faint and familiar odor drifting across our nostrils as we neared the rig.

Hearing our approach, a low set of eyes glittered from the upper step and quickly descended to the parking lot. I didn't think much of it at the time. At any given location on any November night in Hardrock, one could always find several low sets of eyes in nearby bushes, on the roof, by the dumpster.

Roach, nestled deep in Aunt Gigi's arms and sated with a bowl of lobbed popcorn, buried her snout and fluffed her long golden locks against the frigid night.

"There, thar, Cookie," Aunt Gigi swayed slightly, soothing her dog, "Mommy'll get yer sweater… *hiccup*… once we get… inside."

With a stagger in his step, Uncle Raymond shouted behind him, "Wait'll you snee innide. She's a real booty. Thirty-five thou worthfer comfort an high-class travel, *heh heh*… she'll tame th' willerness!" He whirled around, eyes wide and swimming for a couple of seconds as he searched for Dad's familiar face to lock onto. Unsuccessful, he whirled back around, leaning off-course but continuing his narration, "She's th' bess damn land ship money can buy, right, hon?"

Aunt Gigi neglected to answer, easily mesmerized by spiraling snow flakes.

As they mounted the small set of stairs leading to the door, Uncle Raymond grasped either side of Aunt Gigi's behind and the two of them, like a couple of mal-aligned, loosely drifting locomotive cars, lumbered aboard the precariously unstable steps of the RV.

Uncle Raymond noticed the door standing open, yet was slow to process any implications. *"Huh,"* he exhaled.

Aunt Gigi stopped at the top stair and swooned in the doorway.

Trippity trip trip... a little skunk scurried down the stairs, unnoticed by all except Roach who, alerted to the pillage of her kibble closet, sounded the alarm. *BARK! BARK! BARK!*

Roach's sudden and unique modulation coupled with the quantity of liquor Uncle Raymond had consumed combined to produce a peculiar effect, and Uncle Raymond appeared at once cross-eyed and flinching, as if his head were being pounded between two large cooking pots. Unable to identify the cause of his distress, he reacted by simply swiping at his face and ears much like a bear set upon by a hive of angry bees.

Aunt Gigi was just formulating a full-on shriek when Roach launched off her chest and began her defensive. Like a trained cow dog, she cut left then right, running the skunks out from behind cupboards and into one another, inducing stupefying mayhem.

Recovering from the surprise attack, three of the skunks aligned in military fashion and offered a full salute. Three tails — *psssttt* — sprayed in unison then humped frantically toward the door with Roach in furious pursuit shaking her head vigorously and snapping at the air.

A cluster of panicked skunks unraveled around Aunt Gigi and Uncle Raymond's legs, while Roach, consumed in blind hysteria, slammed into their shins knocking them backward into the parking lot. She scrabbled up the length of Uncle Raymond and turbo-toenailed off the top of his head as he lie stunned on the ground.

BARK! BARK! bark! bark… Cookie's insatiable racket faded into the forest, only now and then drifting above the pines.

Prevailing upon Aunt Gigi and Uncle Raymond to recognize and rise from their horizontal positions, Dad directed us kids vaguely toward the end of the parking lot, "Go get the damn dog. Take the pistol and fire three shots in the air if you get in a bind. Don't go any more than a couple hundred yards out."

Rushing to the house and grabbing a flashlight, we set off calling into the dark night for the little city dog with no knowledge of wilderness dangers. We followed in the direction of two faint barks till all had fallen silent.

For thirty minutes, we called and called to no avail. "What if something ate her?" I wondered aloud to Al and Wes.

"Nothing ate her," Wes replied. "She's too mean. Plus, all that long fur."

"Dad said he saw a horse eat sausage, once," I pointed

out as we circled back around into the parking lot.

"Shut up," Wes said in his customarily comforting fashion.

As we rounded the back of the inn near the dumpster, we came upon the RV. "Cripes, this place reeks like skunk!" Al commented, pinching her nose.

We found Roach sitting on the top step, demolishing a cellophane wrapper. She looked up.

"It's not just this *place*," I added, holding the skunk-juiced Roach at arm's length as we chugged back to the warmth of the house, our breath vaporizing in little puffs as we went.

Upon seeing the wayward Roach held out for her, Aunt Gigi gathered the little dog in her arms and covered her in kisses, *smootch smootch*..."Oh, my little darling Cook.. *pllth, pllth, blech! Oh,* you smell *horrid!"* She placed the little dog on the floor and put her hands on her hips, still harboring a slight sway. "What to do with you, stinky little miss?"

"I'll go get some tomato juice from the bar," Dad began.

"Well, I hardly think now is the time for a bloody mary, Ike," Aunt Gigi frowned.

"For the dog," Dad clarified.

"Don't be silly," Aunt Gigi dismissed the notion, "she doesn't even drink."

He looked at Mother then back at Gigi. "A *bath* for the dog."

"Oh."

Uncle Raymond, crowned with eight red traction marks near his hairline, sat at the kitchen table staring at the vacant spot where Roach had been sitting before she rushed over to paw at Aunt Gigi's pant leg.

"No, Ike," continued Aunt Gigi, "I'm not going to bathe Cookie in *tomato juice*, like some common piece of celery."

Mother sighed, leaning against the sink. It was the 'Why me, God, *why?*' sigh.

"Fine," Dad said, "you take care of the dog any way you want. Ray, I'll go out and set up a smoker for the RV to knock out some of that stink."

"I'LL DO IT!" Uncle Raymond jolted to life. *"I'LL* SMOKE IT OUT!"

Earlier, Dad had suggested smoking green aspen logs to help remove the skunk odor from the RV. It was the same successful technique used to deodorize the house before we moved in.

"I know how to smoke a place out!" shouted Uncle Raymond, jumping up and knocking over the bench where he'd been sitting. He snatched the phone book off the table and rushed out the door leaving it standing open. Once on the front step, he paused and muttered to an invisible helper, "Hand me the shovel... whooze got th' shovel?"

Dad looked at Mother, then me. "C'mon," he gestured to Al, Wes and I, "let's go help him."

It was a fight to the finish, with Uncle Raymond bodily intervening in any attempt Dad made at constructing an appropriate smoking vessel.

"Look dumb ass," Dad grabbed the bedspread from Uncle Raymond as he hurried to stuff it under the green logs, "you don't know what the hell you're doing. You're going to burn the damn place down."

"Ge-awwwway. I GOT thinzzzz unner conrol."

"You can't even see straight. Now give me the damn matches."

Uncle Raymond whirled around and tore the cover off the pack. Hunched over, he ripped off a half dozen matches and scraped them furiously across the striker band in an effort to light them all at once.

"Give me the matches!" Dad reached for the pack as Uncle Raymond hoisted them over his head.

"Yooooou alwayzz get to do it... I'munna DO IT!"

WHHOOM! The matches caught overhead.

Dad reached for the now flaming ball of tinder which Uncle Raymond still waved over his head.

Slowly, the scorching inferno caught Uncle Raymond's attention, but not before hot embers fell on his head and caught his hair on fire.

"Damn it, Ray. Get the hell out of here." Dad grabbed the bedspread and proceeded to smother the flames dancing lightly on top of Uncle Raymond's head.

Uncle Raymond perceived this as an attack, dropped the matches and took a wide swing at Dad, tangling them both in the bedspread which had developed a relationship with the flaming matches.

Wes jumped onto Uncle Raymond's back while Al and I yanked the bedspread away from everyone and threw it outside, managing to prevent the flickering payload from spreading beyond the drapes.

"Everyone out!" Dad yelled, By now the RV shoving us and Uncle Raymond out the door. had taken on a soft pulsating glow

and smoke was trailing out the open door.

Dad stood on the ground in front of the doorway, shouting, "Get the hose hooked up and run it down here, go — GO!"

Wes nearly plowed over Al and I who, in the spirit of cooperation, decided to give his spindly, churning legs the lead.

While Wes hooked up one end of the garden hose and Al straightened the kinks, I grabbed anywhere I could find a handhold and ran full-bore down to the RV. Yanked backward several feet from the doorway, I was relieved the extra ten feet of hose I carried aloft was sufficient to extend all the way inside the trailer.

Dad always looked for opportunities to educate us kids. Fond of saying, "I may not always be here, and you'd damn well better know what to do," he waved Wes down to the rig and handed him the hose, giving him, Al and me each a turn at 'fogging' the fire.

With a little regulated thumb pressure and strategic handling, we were able to douse enough flame that Dad re-entered the rig and smothered any remaining embers with his jacket. Uncle Raymond, meanwhile, was still staggering around the parking lot in animated circles attempting to stomp out the smoldering bedspread.

Within fifteen minutes, we all stood in the RV's kitchen assessing the damage. "Well," Dad pointed out to Uncle Raymond, "the back end is burnt-out pretty good, and the front of the refrigerator and carpeting are history. I think the door to the bathroom is shot, but the rest of this... the walls, cabinets, even the couch here looks pretty superficial. Just smoke damage. You can rebuild the interior and scrub out the soot. Be like new."

Uncle Raymond stared blankly at Dad and appeared only to be watching his lips move. Slowly, he turned his head and gazed toward the back of the RV, muttering, "duhz anyone smell smoke?"

As we entered the house, gasps were exchanged all around. The top of Uncle Raymond's head was singed so it looked like it had been capped with a random flurry of crinkled wires.

Dad's jacket had a couple of smoking holes near the lapel and elbow, which he'd now and then take a swipe at.

Roach sat on the kitchen table, shaved bare in patches of assorted length and arrangement. Her eyebrows and snout were the only aspects of her body still in original condition. *Yarp,* she muffled, wriggling under the blue sweater Aunt Gigi was fitting over her head.

"Be still, now," instructed Aunt Gigi, "at least you didn't have to have a bath in tomato juice. I know it's not a fashionable cut, but at least it will grow back."

Mother sat at the table covered in long locks of golden fur. She held the clippers loosely in one hand and her head in the other.

Dad shouted down the hall to Uncle Raymond and Aunt Gigi who were wandering toward my bedroom to settle in for the night, "Get some sleep and we'll get everything squared away in the morning." He looked at Mother and shook his head then winked at me, Al and Wes, "You kids did a great job handling that fire. You learn anything?"

A safety discussion ensued, followed by Dad's affirming nod and declaration, "I'm hitting the shower."

"Right behind you…" Mother sighed.

Gradually, the house quieted for the night.

Exuding the scent of Aunt Gigi's pawpaw paradise shampoo and only a hint of parfum d'skunk, Roach seemed eager to enjoy the comparatively calm company Al and I provided. Well, that plus we were making cups of hot cocoa.

Yap! Roach asked for a marshmallow.

"*Shhhhhh*," Al gently admonished, lifting the whipped cream can which Mother had craftily concealed at the back of the fridge for Thanksgiving dessert, "you'll get us in trouble."

While many prefer the taste and consistency of homemade whipped cream, Al and I favored the kind that was compressed in a can and made a great *SSSQUWWAAAAW* sound when the nozzle dispensed fluffy streamers of the sweet confection. For us, this was high, high living, since we only saw the can, like eggnog — and, thankfully, green-cherry filled fruit cake — once or twice a year.

"*hee hee,*" we giggled, as I poured two mugs of cocoa and sprinkled in a heap of miniature marshmallows. Al sprayed swirls of whipped cream higher and higher.

Yap! Boing! went Roach. Woe to anyone who ignores Roach's delicate requests.

Al tilted her head back and filled her mouth with a pile of whipped cream. *Snap*, she closed her mouth, cheeks bulging, eyes glittering.

I grabbed the can, checking first the doorway into the hall then the one behind me, leading to the living room. Back went my head. *SSSQUWWAAAAW...* I sprayed a pile so high I couldn't even close my mouth. This of course, produced a spurt of riotous giggles, inducing Roach to take drastic action.

CHOMP! went Roach.

"Cripthes!" I stammered, spewing the precious delicacy and hopping around on my good foot. *"Here!"* I sprayed a small mound in my palm and fed it to the dog. She snapped it off my hand and opened her mouth for more, boinging up and down with a happy-sounding growl.

"Look! She likes it!" Al sniggered. "Give her some more! See if she'll eat it like we do."

"Yeah!" I held the nozzle toward Roach who stopped hopping and opened her mouth, growling the whole time. *SSSQUWWAAAAAW* She snapped her mouth shut and whipped cream blasted out covering her face in tiny globs. She licked frantically then, like us, demanded more.

Back and forth we three shot ourselves full of whipped cream. We stood giggling, growling, snapping and snorting as we savored our ill-gotten plunder. Just then, I noticed Aunt Gigi standing in the doorway to the hall. I could see from her stricken expression she was stunned by our guilty display and clearly saw what was going on.

"Rabies! Oh my God... *RAY!* They've gotten rabies from the skunks! I *knew* we never should have come here!" her voice trailed into the hall as she bolted toward my bedroom. *"RAAAAAY!"*

Al and I, like two burglars caught with the loot, frantically looked for a place to stash the whipped cream can before Dad or, *worse,* Uncle Raymond came to investigate. Al didn't have the same image I had of Uncle Raymond coming to investigate a nuisance which had ruefully disturbed his sleep.

Uncle Raymond staggered in under a cloud of alcohol as I quickly tossed the can behind me into the living room and Al wiped the evidence from her face. As Uncle Raymond entered from the hallway with Aunt Gigi following close at his shoulder, we three innocents stood smiling.

"Zere's nothin' wrong with thozze people. You're crazzz, *urp*, crazy," he slurred with one eye half open.

"No, Raymond, look! There's foam coming out of Cookie's mouth!"

I glanced at Roach who sported small globs of whipped cream on either side of her mouth and one atop her snout, centered between her eyes. *"Cripes,"* I breathed.

"Thasss not *rabies*, thas *snow*. We're in th' *mountains*, dummy. Now, les get some sleep, okay? Tomorrowzz a big day." *Bang* — Uncle Raymond crashed into the door frame as he turned to leave. "Tomorrow, we're gonna take out th' boat."

"Don't call me 'dummy', Ray," Aunt Gigi glared at Uncle Raymond as she helped him totter down the hall.

"Whew! That was close!" I muttered to Al who had turned and was busy staring at something in the doorway behind me. I turned to see what it was.

Mother stood in the darkness of the living room, her slight stature framed by the dim reach of the kitchen light. In her hand she held the empty whipped cream can.

Cripes.

The next morning at sunrise, Dad and Uncle Raymond were out at the rig straightening the boat trailer and hammering out the hitch.

BANG, BANG, BANG, Dad hammered. When Dad hammered or nailed or twisted a wrench, he always wore a particular expression. In was comprised of widely exposed gritted teeth, an offset jaw and squinting eyes. Certain circumstances were capable of enhancing the effect. A snapped bolt or spilt board could easily produce pulsing jaw muscles and a knitted brow. Certain other circumstances could produce a rapid succession of profanity or sometimes only one well-chosen word. Much of his facial contortions and vocal outbursts seemed also to depend upon his mood, of which I often inquired.

The simple addition of my presence — frequently accompanied by a thoughtful question about the condition of a part, a tool of choice or whether writhing in the snow under the truck had made his hair wet — was known to produce heavy sighing and even a flung implement.

BANG, BANG, BANG... Al and I watched Dad and Uncle Raymond focus on their work.

"That sledge hammer sure looks heavy," I observed. Just that comment, right there, was enough to make Dad's jaw pulse.

"Every time you hit it, you knock more paint off the hitch," I helpfully pointed out, guessing he had missed that particular effect, concentrating hard as he was on pounding the steel frame.

Heavy sigh.

Uncle Raymond, who was holding the hitch, had a different look. He held his left eye wide open while squinting his right eye so tightly, his eyebrow appeared to rest directly on his cheekbone. I nudged Al and whispered, "Doesn't Uncle Raymond look like Popeye?"

"Hey," Al whispered back, "I bet that's how Popeye got his name. Look how his eye looks like it's about to pop out..."

A family trait, Uncle Raymond also gritted his teeth, but every time Dad banged the hitch, Uncle Raymond's whole body flinched and both eyes squinted shut, bringing his eyebrows to stand almost vertically over his nose. "Do you have to hammer so damn loud?" he muttered to Dad through clenched teeth.

"I do, if you want this hitch straightened out," Dad replied through his own clenched teeth, a subtle grin escaping his facial contortion. BANG, BANG, BANG...

Al and I handed them the coffee Mother had sent us to deliver. "So when can we go out on the boat?" I asked over the banging.

Both of them rotated a large eyeball my way, which seemed to suggest it would be a while.

Al and I wandered back toward the house, loitering long enough to gape at the charred RV entrance.

Aunt Gigi and Roach, both in matching sweaters, stepped off the front porch and wandered our way. "Jessie shooed us from the kitchen," Aunt Gigi announced.

"How come?" I asked.

"She said she didn't need any help fixing dinner and said I should come outside to check on the boys, but I think it had something to do with the turkey."

"What do you mean?" I asked, looking up to see Mother leaning through the kitchen doorway and shaking her head, *'noooo'.*

"Well," Aunt Gigi continued, "I thought 'wash' meant to wash it like dishes, with soap and everything."

"Oh," I said, ever ready to collect useful culinary tips, "and that's not right?"

"Apparently not. And I guess you're not supposed to leave the little envelope of parts inside either. I thought the package was meant to keep everything tidy inside the turkey." Aunt Gigi looked exasperated. "Ray and I usually go out to dinner on Thanksgiving. It looks like a lot of work fixing such a big dinner. Maybe you girls should go in and help."

"I'm not allowed in the kitchen either," I offered. "We got run out last year after putting on a little play with two gnarly-eyed potatoes."

"Plus, the brownies," Al added.

"That, too," I seconded.

"Well, let's see if the skunk smell is out of the RV yet." Aunt Gigi stepped up into the RV. "Pee-yew," she said, once inside, "I can still smell it, can you?"

Al and I nodded in agreement.

"Well, this is horrible," Aunt Gigi sighed, toeing at the cheese wrapper on the floor. She leaned out the doorway to shout around the RV, "Ray," she paused to survey the littered contents of the refrigerator, "Ray? It still smells like skunk and smoke in here. It's just awful... and did you see that something ate the brie?"

BANG, BANG, BANG... came the reply.

"Well, darn, Cookie..." Aunt Gigi stroked Roach's shaved head, looking forlorn. "What will we do?"

"Hey," I began, "do you want to take a walk along the old mill site? There are all kinds of neat ruins and lots of little pieces of alabaster and marble all along the trail."

"Yeah," encouraged Al, "maybe you can find some pieces to take home as souvenirs. The tourists always do."

"That does sound interesting. Marble is lovely. And I've never really seen uncut alabaster. They say it looks similar to crystal, especially once it's polished," Aunt Gigi reflected information from a brochure we'd given her the night before in the saloon, which had described some of the national shrines and monuments sculpted from Hardrock's acclaimed local stone. After reading it, she was surprised that so much marble and alabaster remained littered along the trail and even the banks of Quartz Creek in chunks, slabs and shards both large and small. "This place *is* practically famous…" she announced.

"We know!" Al and I chimed in unison.

"Well, let's go, girls!"

So off we went with backpacks in tow, or, at least Al and I did. Aunt Gigi picked her way among ruts and dirt humps in a pair of flats, silk Capri pants, three or four long gold necklaces and a contented Roach tucked under one arm.

Al shared her knowledge of local lore as we traipsed along the trail, "The little quarry train that ran the rock and silver into Granite, back in the twenties, would tip off the tracks along the creek now and then, especially during mud slides and snow storms. Big blocks of rock would fall into the creek, so that's why you see it all along the bank, here."

Al told the unpublicized story of Whittletake's marble and alabaster staircase residing in the creepy unoccupied mansion on the hill overlooking Muskrat Lake. Whittletake had been the quarry's founder, and the marble, alabaster and silver taken from his Red Garter Quarry adorned many features of his once grand, occasionally occupied and reputedly haunted home where a servant had been blamed for his death decades before.

The spooky story always added intriguing dimension to the already variegated stones.

Aunt Gigi reached for a small, flat piece of alabaster and examined it closely, "Such depth and occlusion." Aunt Gigi knew her rocks. Probably from browsing diamonds at the jewelry counter at the mall.

"Wait till you see this!" Al ran the stone to the creek and swirled it in the icy, clear water then brought it back.

Aunt Gigi took the stone and marveled at its depth and spidery white veins. Holding it up to the sunshine, she admired its translucence sparkling like delicate pastel lace. "Oh my word, it's *gorgeous!*"

Harboring an urge commonly afflicting the female gender, Al and I shared Aunt Gigi's enthusiasm for rocks, shiny or otherwise. I confess I cannot go anywhere without examining and perhaps stooping to collect some kind of interesting rock.

Once, on the way home from a family vacation, we stopped at a hotel and, as Mother sunned poolside, I spent an hour under the bushes picking through the rocks which filled the shrub beds surrounding the establishment. Later, at a gas station, my trove had been discovered and jettisoned whereupon I was chastised for collecting what Dad referred to as "two *friggin'* tons of gravel". In the midst of a national gas crises I had to listen to three-hundred miles of, "No damn *wonder* we were getting such rotten gas mileage."

That experience had done nothing to dampen my enthusiasm for rocks, but it did teach me to better conceal my addiction, which led to an awkward explanation of lumpy socks and pockets as I unknowingly trailed a second payload through a Mexican restaurant later that same week.

Aunt Gigi held up a stone as I shared my vacation story.

"You know what girls?" her face beamed. "These would be *beautiful* in my flower beds along the front walk."

We were delighted to share the discarded bounty with such an appreciative collector, so happily obliged Aunt Gigi's zeal. Soon, however, we realized Aunt Gigi had more in mind than a few accent pieces and, like myself, knew no restraint. Al and I were too enamored with treasure hunting ourselves to protest her intended possession of ten tons lying in wait of our approach.

"Look at that one!" Aunt Gigi pronounced. "Let's get that one!" This statement was followed by Aunt Gigi, Al or I picking up the targeted stone and putting it in our backpack, jacket or pants pocket.

"Look!" she said, moments later. "This one is really smooth. Let's keep it."

"Look!" Al said. "That one is shaped like a frog. Let's keep it."

"Look!" I said. "This one is really flat. Let's keep it." And so on.

Two thirds of a mile along the trail, my and Al's pants pockets were so full of rocks our jeans were slipping, our backpacks so loaded we were struggling to stay upright.

Worse, our mania for small stones had somehow escalated toward those of ever increasing size and weight.

Carrying a small boulder the size of a basketball, I groaned under the collective load.

Al clutched both sides of her jeans, inwardly dragging her feet with each slow step, the sleeve seams of her jacket slowly unraveling.

Aunt Gigi teetered along the rugged trail and, with great admiration, picked up another small specimen and examined it against the bright morning sunlight. "Not a flaw in it!" She passed it to Al, who took it and toppled over.

Aunt Gigi assessed my situation. I could not, however, return the gaze. Yoked by the formidable weight on either side of my laden jacket, I was condemned to stare at my feet. As we awaited Aunt Gigi's directive, my right knee buckled and down I went.

"Okay, let's go back and put these..." she paused looking perplexed, "hmmm... I wonder where I can put these."

"Why not in the RV?" I groaned.

"Well, Uncle Raymond said we should be careful about putting too much weight in there."

Al and I struggled slowly up the slope toward the RV as Aunt Gigi thoughtfully pondered her dilemma.

Upon our approach, it became evident Dad and Uncle Raymond had relocated themselves and their tools to the RV and were in the process of removing perhaps the refrigerator or bathroom door. BANG, BANG, BANG...

"The boys are in the RV," Aunt Gigi observed. "Let's put the rocks in the boat. I remember seeing some little cubbies in there."

Grasping the aluminum ladder at the back of the boat, first Al then I labored to climb it. My grip weakening, I concentrated on Al's ankles which were beginning to tremble.

In an effort to relieve some of the weight, Al worked to free the load on her back, made more difficult by the straps of her backpack burrowing grooves into her shoulders. Finally wrenching it free, gravity immediately brought the pack downward where it would have landed on top of my head, had my forehead not been pressed in desperation against the ladder. As it were, her freight glanced off my own pack, slammed to the ground and scattered its contents on impact.

A person un-afflicted with rock-collector's dementia might have viewed our predicament and suggested collecting the rocks in smaller multiple loads, but to do so would have demonstrated an unsavory greed. And, even though our foray would end with four more trips to the mill site that day, we didn't think of ourselves as greedy or afflicted or unreasonable — only greatly more appreciative of rocks than other people.

CRUNCH, went Al's pack for the fifth time that morning.

"Cripes, Al, watch it! You about knocked me off the boat again!"

"Sorry," Al whisper-shouted as if suspecting our activity were anything less than completely allowable.

Al struggled to clear the boat's railing with her leg. "I can't get my stupid leg up. There are too many rocks in my pockets..." She swung again, hooking her foot on the railing but losing her grip on one side of the ladder.

Suddenly, the RV steps creaked with the unmistakable downward pressure of Dad and Uncle Raymond's footsteps. With some quick thinking and fear-inspired super-human strength, I shoved Al into the boat.

THUD!

"Auughh! My foot!" she groaned.

"Sorry! Here, help me in!" I whispered, stretching out my hand.

Al wrenched me in and we scuttled to the front of the boat with all the speed and grace a hundred and fifty pounds of rocks on our hips and backs would allow.

Coming around beside the boat, Dad and Uncle Raymond discussed plans to take it out on the lake that afternoon. Aunt Gigi rushed around to meet them, hand fluttering. "Let's see what you boys have been up to!"

Soon, sounds of clanging resumed within the RV, and aunt Gigi came aboard to help us locate yet another suitable hiding — er, storage place for her rocks.

"Let's take this out," Aunt Gigi said, lifting a large, yellow rubber wad from one of the cubbies. "We don't need a lot of this extra stuff back here." She stood back and checked under the lid of yet another cubby, "One more load, and I think I'll have enough to landscape all the beds in the front yard." She stood back absently petting Roach and admiring the compartment shimmering with jagged stones. "I'll be the only one in the subdivision with alabaster and marble beds."

Finishing her excavation, she exclaimed, "Okay girls, let's go get some more!"

And off we went. Our progress, however, was halted

mid-stride when Mother called everyone from the front porch of the house, "Hey everyone, dinner is ready except for the turkey, and the picnic is ready for the lake. Are we ready to go?"

"Yeah!" Al and I shouted then rushed to round up Wes, who had been down at the café learning the chords to *Long Haired Country Boy* from Willy while he and Gert prepared a second turkey, tray of rolls and another pot of mashed potatoes for the big Thanksgiving feast that evening.

The plan for the afternoon was to go out to the lake and pretend it was summer.

Dad, Mother, Wes, Al and I piled into Big Red and led the way through Hardrock. Uncle Raymond, Aunt Gigi and Roach followed in the RV, towing the boat and trailer. Willy and Gert grabbed a couple of poles and two lawn chairs and fell in with their Fairlane behind the RV.

Since all the tourists had gone for the season, the sight of a thirty-foot RV towing a sixteen-foot ski boat at ten miles an hour through Hardrock drew more than a little attention. Dad waved to Crazy Jake who, observing through the knothole, kicked open his outhouse door in order to take in the full scene. Enis looked up from feeding his peafowl and immediately ran into his house to phone Millie Swampnettle, owner of the Muskrat Lake campground.

Before long, two-thirds of the town's residents had been inspired to a bout of November fishing, and it actually began to feel summer-like despite the forty-five degree chill and anglers blowing on their hands in order to thread bait.

Uncle Raymond, Aunt Gigi, Roach, Al, Wes and I grabbed hasty stations in the boat as Dad backed the trailer into the lake.

Mother sat on the shore, bearing no trace of her previously weary countenance. Appearing amused, she perhaps had some premonition of what was to come.

Mother, like many wives who have co-owned and operated water vessels with their husbands, knew that it is usually sometime during the first outing that marital relationships come under intense pressure. The strains and stresses of negotiating an expensive land ship, later ransacked by wildlife, into the distant mountains could expose the cracks in a relationship's armor, but the launching and loading of a new boat could lay it asunder. The much anticipated launch of the *Pristina* would not only vindicate Mother's tribulations of the pervious day, but provide entertaining diversion as well.

As Dad backed the RV and trailer into position, a few of the onlookers cheered. Uncle Raymond beamed at the attention and took on a truly unbecoming demeanor, adjusting his captain's hat and shouting random orders as if we were lost at sea and deep in the midst of a raging hurricane. "Ready the moor line! Lisa, you move to starboard — your friend there can take port! *Wes*, you'll be in the navigator's seat and, *Gigi*, you'll take aft." Since none of us knew to which part of the boat he was referring, we banged around into one another with exaggerated gestures and expressive commentary which erupted like a chicken house under siege.

Wes didn't need knowledge of nautical terminology to shout "Shotgun!" and lob over the windshield into the passenger seat.

Uncle Raymond caught the bowline from Dad and

charged to the captain's seat, scattering us girls in various directions. "Stand aside seamen — I'll command the helm!"

Finally, we floated free from the boat trailer as sniggers arose from the shore-bound.

Uncle Raymond fired up the engine with a roar then a rumble and shouted over his shoulder, "This here beauty's outfitted with a hundred and seventy-five horse power inboard that'll blow your socks off! In fact, you can barefoot ski with this sweet baby!" He patted and lovingly stroked the instrument panel, lingering over the speedometer. He leaned in and murmured something as Aunt Gigi watched jealously from behind shaded eyes. "Fasten your life jackets, crew!" he shouted. "I'm about to put *Pristina* through her paces!"

"Wait a minute, Raymond! You know it takes me a few minutes to get Cookie's jacket on!" Aunt Gigi pulled a little neon-green vest over Roach's sweater and strained to buckle the strap across her back. The sweater added considerably more bulk than fur, so Aunt Gigi was still struggling with the buckle when Uncle Raymond pushed the throttle forward revving the powerful engine.

"*Raymond!*" Aunt Gigi shouted, "You stop this boat this minute, until I can get Cookie's life vest on."

"It's a *craft,* Gigi, how many times do I have to tell you it's a water *craft!*" he shouted back over the rumbling motor which significantly distorted the gist of conversation.

"Don't you call her a water rat, you ass!"

"*Fast?* You want to go *FAST?* All right, then, let's open 'er up and see what she's got!" Uncle Raymond's eyes shone with wild anticipation.

He pushed the throttle all the way forward, but the boat only lurched and fell back on the lake like a water-logged goose scrabbling to break the surface.

"What th'?" He looked over the side, as if expecting to see the *Pristina* held fast in the suctioned tentacles of a Muskrat Lake monster. Taking his cue from the captain, Wes looked over his side of the boat.

"Throttle must be stuck." Uncle Raymond pulled the throttle toward him then pushed it away again, gently. The boat revved and made a great noisy effort as it lumbered forward under what seemed like immense strain.

We chugged around the lake in a couple of wide circles raising a two inch wake.

Dad yelled from shore, "What's the matter?"

"Boat won't plane out," Uncle Raymond hollered back from the boat. "I can't get her to level in the water. It's like she's dragging or something."

Al, I and Aunt Gigi exchanged anxious looks. Uncle Raymond kept driving the boat in circles, looking over the side.

"Um, Raymond?" Aunt Gigi ventured.

I shot her a look that said 'Are you, *crazy?*' and subtly shook my head side to side, keeping an eye on Wes who occasionally glanced back over his shoulder but mostly continued to concentrate on the water on his side of the boat.

Aunt Gigi looked concerned, "Ray?"

"Not now, Gigi, I'm trying to figure out what the hell's wrong with this damn boat. Ten-thousand-dollar damn boat and she moves like she's dropped a thousand pound load in her drawers."

"Ray!" Aunt Gigi, clutching Roach, stood up and knelt on her seat.

"What is it? What is so damned important?"

"The boat is sinking."

"What?" Uncle Raymond cut the engine and quickly wormed his way to the back of the boat where he saw water streaming in through a one inch hole. *"Son of a...!* Where's the plug?"

"I don't know. What plug?" Aunt Gigi asked.

"The plug you were supposed to put in the boat when we left the house!"

"Oh, that plug."

"Oh, *that* plug," he mocked her loudly, throwing his arms in the air.

Sniggers drifted across the lake from shore.

Her eyes narrowed. "I put it in, Ray."

"Well, did you put it in *right?"*

"How should I know, Ray, I've never *had* a boat before!" she yelled. "You're the captain! Why didn't you put in your *own* plug?"

With great animation, Uncle Raymond smacked his forehead with the palm of his hand then drew his face downwardly so hard the entire lower part of his bloodshot eyeballs were revealed. I new this was not a good sign as I'd recently seen it precede a poor decision to power forward.

Wes expounded the extent of his nautical knowledge, "Um, the water's getting deeper."

"Damn!" Uncle Raymond shouted, throwing himself into his seat and turning the key. The engine whirred and

whined. Uncle Raymond grasped the throttle and slammed it against the bulkhead, instantly killing the engine and enveloping everyone in gas fumes. I stifled a gag as water continued pouring in, dropping the boat deeper into the lake.

Uncle Raymond careened around behind him and appeared surprised to not find something. "Where are the oars?" he asked Aunt Gigi.

"You broke one when you ran over the dumpster, remember. The other one you broke in half this morning using it as a pry bar."

"*Rrrggg.*" He ripped off his captain's hat and scrubbed the charred hairs on top of his head, breaking them off. "Get the raft out, just in case."

"I put it in the RV," Aunt Gigi said.

I felt my stomach and twenty-four feet of intestinal track bunch up into a great knot.

"Why the *hell* did you put the raft in the *RV?*" Uncle Raymond shouted loudly to the sky.

"To make room for the rocks," Aunt Gigi said.

"*What?*" He acted as if he had not heard her correctly, as if such an utterance were something completely unexpected. "Did you say *rocks?*"

"*Yes,* Ray, *rocks.* I put some rocks in the bin, so I could take them home and landscape with them."

"How *big* are they?" he asked, with an expression suggesting he was still trying to process the incoming information.

"They're little. Mostly."

"Where are they? Are they in the raft compartment?"

"Some of them."

"*Some* of them?"

"Ray, don't yell at me. You told me not to put a lot of weight in the RV, so I put them in the boat."

"If I didn't want you to put them in the RV, what in the *hell* makes you think I would want you to put them in the boat?"

"Because boats use ballast, Ray!"

Uncle Raymond appeared stunned. "You know about *ballast*, but you don't know how to put a plug in the bottom of a boat?"

Aunt Gigi silently fumed.

Uncle Raymond stormed over to the raft compartment and flung it open. *"Rocks!"* He went over to another compartment and flung it open. *"Rocks!"* He grabbed a handful of smaller stones and flung them into the lake.

Aunt Gigi yelled from the seat she was kneeling on, "Don't throw my rocks in the lake!" Roach, quietly observing, suddenly went off, wriggling to get loose and closer to the action, *BARK BARK BARK!*

"Shut that damn dog up!" *Plop, plip, SPLASH* — more rocks went overboard.

"I will *not* tell Cookie to shut up! You're being an ass, Ray!"

Uncle Raymond waved us away from our side of the boat and lifted the seat where Al and I had been sitting. Of course, that compartment, too, was full of rocks. He slowly turned and looked at Aunt Gigi.

With both hands, he shoveled a mound of rocks out of

the bin and heaved them into the lake.

Aunt Gigi still fumed.

Seeing Uncle Raymond flinging lids open and tossing handfuls of rocks into the lake, Dad yelled from shore, "What's the matter, now?"

Uncle Ray turned around to face the shore, shouting much more loudly than necessary given the engine had died, *"ROCKS!* SHE FILLED THE BOAT WITH *ROCKS* AND NOW WE'RE SINKING!"

At this pronouncement, the chuckling band of spectators on the shoreline erupted like a flock of rioting seagulls in peals of laughter. Uncle Raymond's face turned red and I'm pretty sure the tips of his ears sparked.

"Start the motor and bring her in," Dad suggested, himself breaking into a single irrepressible guffaw.

"HE CAN'T. HE *FLOODED IT!*" Aunt Gigi yelled back in an informative fashion.

Dad snorted as the rest of the shoreline exploded in laughter, now lined with people in various stages of hysteria. Dad stood, arms folded, chortling. Mother smiled demurely, sipping her coffee.

At that moment Uncle Raymond's temper seized control of his physical faculties. With nowhere to rampage, he savagely clawed into a compartment full of rocks and, like backward rotating propellers, began whipping rocks overhead, nary a thought as to who might be standing behind him. An endless stream of profanity accompanied the excavation, interrupted only by particularly high-pitched protests from Aunt Gigi as he dug even deeper handfuls out of another compartment.

Al and I gripped one another in the back of the boat, the tops of our heads now and then set upon by a fiercely rotating set of claws as Roach tried to free herself from aunt Gigi's clutches a foot or so above us. *BARK! BARK! BARK!*

Wes turned around in his seat and, resting an elbow on the captain's chair, observed with the same kind of mild interest I'd seen him exhibit at the movies.

Uncle Raymond finally noticed the icy water mid-way up his calf and splashed over to the wheel. He turned the key, which enlisted a low rumble from the engine. Brows deeply furrowed, he wordlessly steered the boat to shore. Aunt Gigi, grim faced, was still kneeling in the rear.

Judging from his emotional state, Uncle Raymond no longer appeared interested in a fun-filled afternoon on the lake with his new boat and, instead, prepared to load it back onto the trailer.

Interestingly, even with a quarter of the cargo jettisoned in the lake, there was enough combined rock and water weight to keep the boat low in the water — so low in fact, Uncle Raymond couldn't seem to guide it onto the trailer.

"Bring it on back!" he directed Dad, who was backing up the RV. "Keep it coming!"

Dad leaned out the driver's side window, "Ray, this isn't a boat ramp. It's a muddy shoreline. I'm going to bury this thing if I go back any more."

Uncle Raymond waved him back impatiently as gathered spectators looked on.

The RV eased back under the influence of Uncle Raymond's dramatic gesturing. Then a little farther. More gesturing. The bumper of the RV was in the water.

"Ray, why don't you just let me help you guide her onto the trailer," Dad offered. "I'm not bringing this rig back any farther."

"I don't *need* anyone's help. *Gigi,* get over here and take the wheel."

Aunt Gigi was beyond words and simply responded, as if on auto pilot, to his commands. She would seek retribution later, out of public view... perhaps in the office of a divorce lawyer or, I could see her thinking, maybe before dinner one night. She handed Roach to Al.

Leaping out of the boat into waist-deep frigid water, Uncle Raymond sloshed to the RV, seeming to barely notice the icy cold.

Dad began, "Ray, if you want to...."

Uncle Raymond waved him off and, with considerable effort to control his mounting rage, continued, "Nah, nah, I've been looking at it, and I think I can take it back a few more feet."

Dad grinned and stepped out of the rig, shaking his head. "Okay..." he said, with a perky lilt at the end, "we're already serving one turkey on a platter tonight."

Ignoring Dad's comment, Uncle Raymond vaulted into the driver's seat. A half-second later he was gunning the accelerator and exhibiting an increasingly frustrated expression. He humped forward and back in his seat and flailed the steering wheel twice with his cap. "Why the hell won't this thing move?!" he shouted to no one in particular.

"Brake's on," Dad said, standing nearby, packing

tobacco into his pipe.

With a pop followed by a loud clang, the RV rolled a bit backward. We could see Uncle Raymond's reflection in the side mirror of the RV — at least the part with the clenched teeth and roving eyeball.

Al nudged my shoulder, gesturing toward shore.

"Right!" I said, and over we went. Wes leapt fifteen feet off the front of the boat and chugged a couple of feet to shore.

Aunt Gigi seemed distant. Contemplative. She, too, was watching the roving eye.

Now it was just Uncle Raymond and Aunt Gigi. And about sixteen spectators.

Uncle Raymond floored the gas pedal and drove the trailer back so far even the RV's tail lights were a foot underwater.

Jumping down from the RV, he slogged thigh-deep to the trailer where he climbed onto the frame and yanked at the winch, throwing it in the water when it failed to fully extend.

He stood facing the boat defiantly with his hands on his hips. *"Just bring her in!"* he shouted to Aunt Gigi.

Now... from this point, the moving parts of this story come to a very fine and highly orchestrated focus. All the mechanics distill to an unspoken explosive essence when you get down to the intimate and subtle play between a husband and wife under stressful and embarrassing public situations.

Grinding almost to a halt, the interactive nuances are so intensely coiled that a series of only two or three seemingly insignificant exchanges can trigger an eruption of horrendous magnitude.

Though there may be little narrative, the deeply wounded, quiet determination on the face of the wife, contrasted with the highly pressurized frustrated rage etched on the face of the husband speak volumes to anyone who has ever been a party to or simply witnessed such an occasion.

These are the defining moments which, if the parties remain married, will cluster and fuse, clogging their differing memories and contributing even greater combustibility to the next inevitable marital crises.

So, here we were. The lake was so quiet you could hear dry leaves rustle in the breeze thirty yards away. All eyes, even Roach's, shifted between Uncle Raymond standing on the trailer in thigh-deep water and Aunt Gigi at the wheel of the *Pristina.*

"Now take her back, line her up and bring her in!" Uncle Raymond shouted.

Aunt Gigi reversed the boat, lined it up and waited.

"No, no, no, move her to the right!"

Aunt Gigi steered to the right.

"Go *more* to the right!"

She went more to the right.

"That's too far. Go left more!"

She went left.

"*Son of a...* I'm freezing my ass out here! *Go LEFT!"*

"I *am* going left, Raymond, and the water's a little cold *in* the boat, too, you know!"

"*Stop!* Stop right there. Now give her some throttle — *NOT A LOT!* Just give her a little and bring her in!"

Aunt Gigi 'gave her some throttle'.

Uncle Raymond began to shiver.

"What the hell are you w-waiting for? Give her some *th-th-throttle!*"

Aunt Gigi 'gave her some throttle'. The boat groaned forward. Aunt Gigi began shivering.

"Give her some damn *th-throttle!*"

"I *d-did*, Raymond!"

"Well, damn it, giver her some *friggin' m-m-mo...*"

The engine, systematically pushed to full throttle, roared suddenly across the valley.

"*Auuggghh!*" Uncle Raymond dove into the lake as Aunt Gigi ran the boat up onto the trailer, over the trailer and — *CRASH* — a third of the way into the back of the RV.

The crowd went wild, standing and cheering.

It was a good thing Uncle Raymond was in the first stages of hypothermia, since it kept him from advancing too quickly on Aunt Gigi and gave her the opportunity to outrun him. He staggered out of the water, arms akimbo, fingers splayed like a hunchback gun slinger. He twitched violently, flinging water with every involuntary convulsion. "Wh-what th' h-h-h-hell were you th-think-think…"

Roach dashed over and attacked Uncle Raymond's frozen leg. She gnawed on one ankle then ran over and gnawed on the other. Oblivious, he kept walking and convulsing toward Aunt Gigi who was now standing beside Al and me. He stopped short at the trailer and leaned into the rear of the boat, petting it as gracefully as possible between bouts of intense shuddering, "It's-s-s all right girl… I'll f-f-fix you up…"

Aunt Gigi ran over to Al and snatched Roach up in her

arms, yelling at Uncle Raymond, "I *knew* you loved that stupid boat more than me! Well, you can *have* it. *All* of it!" She kicked the boat trailer and stormed off toward the inn.

A change of clothes and three hours of struggle later, we freed the RV from the mud. Roping the boat in place, Dad insightfully commandeered its anchor.

Back at the saloon, among many of the locals mirthfully recounting the day's events, Uncle Raymond was deep in discussion with Dad over his boat and RV insurance policy which had been sealed in the glove compartment and thereby saved from flames the night before.

"Ray," Dad shook his head sadly, "it says *acts of God*... your wife sinking the boat with rocks and ramming it into the back of the RV is not an act of God."

"I didn't kill her though. That was an act of God, which alone should qualify everything for compensation."

"That goes both ways, Raymond," Aunt Gigi said, looking evenly at him. Sipping her iced tea, she murmured to Roach, "And he's not out of these woods yet, is he Cookie, no he's not..."

"It says here fire can be an act of God," Uncle Raymond studied a line on his policy.

"*You* set the fire, dumb ass. Now, wildlife, that's another story. Of course if you hadn't backed into the dumpster and damn near torn the door off, you wouldn't have had to worry about animals *or* the fire."

Uncle Raymond sighed and shouted above the chattering locals to Abbey behind the bar, "Bring me a scotch!"

Someone from the crowd hollered, "And *hold* the

rocks!" causing the place to erupt in laughter.

After a cold, exhausting day un-sticking the RV, calming frayed nerves and mending trampled feelings, the mere image of a holiday feast manifesting that moment in the café next door was enough to soothe even Uncle Raymond's savage temper. The penetrating aroma of roasted turkeys, savory stuffing, hot yeasty rolls and sweet corn had all of us longing to sit at the table.

At nine o'clock that night, Dad closed the saloon and we finally sat down to a spectacular Thanksgiving dinner with Willy, Gert, Ty, Abbey and Crazy Jake.

A solid night's sleep found Uncle Raymond, Aunt Gigi and Roach pulling out of the drive at seven the next morning.

The burnt-out shell of an RV groaned under the weight of an embedded nautical suppository dropping small rocks in her sad wake. A tail light flickered to life. The sound of Aunt Gigi shouting at Roach and swatting her away from the bag of turkey sandwiches floated down the drive as Uncle Raymond — sandwich in hand — waved out the window.

Mother and Dad stood with their arms around one another watching the rig pull away.

"That could have been us," Mother said.

"It once was, wasn't it?"

Mother sighed, "Till we came to our senses."

"I bet I know where we can get a cheap boat and RV…"

You know those looks that are interpretable only between couples? Dad got one.

Tic's Addiction

They called him Tic because every now and then he'd jerk his head to the left which reflexively yanked his right hand out of the pocket he kept filled with twitching fingers. Al and I noticed the habit right off as he and his large, clownish wife entered the saloon early one Saturday afternoon.

With a white, weepy-eyed toy poodle tucked under her fleshy arm, the woman shouldered her small-framed husband aside, shot him a stern look and stepped in front of him.

"I..." his speech was severed, clipped off his tongue where the rest of his sentence wilted and dropped to the wooden floor.

"Need a job," she finished for him, rolling her eyes. "He needs a job, and we heard you people might need a bartender." She paused, sucking greasy red lipstick off her teeth and flashing a dime-store smile likely perfected in the rear-view mirror. Deeply inhaling from a skinny brown cigar, she offered more details, "Heard about it in Bituminous. We just moved into the area and Tic, here, needs work. Heard you might even have a place to rent." She surveyed the dark interior of the saloon as one who intended to make it her permanent residence. Another drag.

I looked at Mother, who had just finished straightening the seven stools lining the bar. She faced the towering mass of woman, now occupied with adjusting a decorative comb overburdened with five pounds of heavily processed yellow hair. Mother studied Tic, who seemed to look away without actually looking away.

Smoothing a wayward strand of hair from her forehead, Mother flung a bar towel over her shoulder and breathlessly concluded, "What the hell, when can you start?"

"This minute! Right this *vewy* minute!" The woman kissed her little dog's head, leaving a tint of lipstick which she smeared onto the inside wrist of the cigar hand. "Mummy wuvs Wucky, does Wucky wuv mummy?" An ash fell on the dog's head. Absently, the woman blew it onto the floor.

Tic twitched.

"Tic, tell her why we call him Lucky." Pausing a half-second, the woman thrust out her right hip, rolled her eyes and took a short drag. "It's because Tic dropped a case of longnecks on his head, and after dousing him in the tap, he came to. Can you believe it?" Another drag. "He's mummy's wittle Wucky *dog*," her voice lilted under heavy brown breath.

The little dog, its front paws tucked firmly between the woman's plump fingers, simply stared ahead with fixed, bulging eyes, its fuzzy head vibrating with tiny tremors.

This was the beginning of a bold new era for the saloon. Afflicted, we could only presume, with a multitude of psychological disorders, Lucinda and Tic introduced deeper instability to the already volatile atmosphere.

Sad as it may seem to some, in Hardrock, one person's psychosis is another's entertainment. Al and I, particularly in want of recreation, closely observed the pair's odd behaviors.

A few days after Tic and Lucinda's arrival, Al and I

were delighted to see something as equally compelling come through the door of the saloon.

Cosmic Commando! It was the very first sit-down, full-color, interactive video game machine ever to grace the humble interior of our familiar little tavern. It was the first, in fact, to be placed in any Colorado establishment our side of Denver. Others eventually followed in Granite until arcades full of the blinking, buzzing, whining machines became a world-wide craze a few years later. We all took great pride in Hardrock being a leader in the industry.

But, no one took more pride, more personal interest in the electronic marvel than Tic.

At its first introduction, Tic found tireless fascination in its technological gadgetry and colorful, interactive graphics. Soon, however, fascination led to obsession.

Any hour, day or night, Tic could be found seated at the dark box hammering his thumbs at its round, yellow buttons. His hair had become permanently disheveled, face ashen, eyes glazed. He breathed only out of physical habit, and even then, he'd sometimes gape like a fish out of water, having momentarily abandoned instinct. No one knew when he went to the bathroom, and we soon realized he resented time away from his beloved machine even to bathe.

Lucinda became an elusive presence seen once or twice a week trundling past the café window toward the saloon. Poodle in tow, she'd secure a couple bottles of liquor behind the bar then trundle back down the boardwalk to her and Tic's apartment, beside Ty and Abbey's place.

Increasingly, Tic dragged himself from the machine to

tend bar only with Dad's firm persistence.

It was fast becoming a situation.

Regulars then began complaining that Tic refused to lend red quarters for the pool table.

Red quarters were 'house money', that is, regular quarters painted red on one side and given to customers to encourage a game or two. They replaced jammed or lost quarters and were often used to bribe Al and I into fifteen minutes of silence as we dusted our pool cues and worked on our bank shots. When the video game and pool table coin boxes were emptied every few days, the red quarters were always separated and added back to the register.

At least, that was the theory.

A couple of weeks after the game arrived, Mother sent Al down to the saloon to find the push broom. Instead of the broom, Al had found Tic hunched over the end of the bar with a pile of quarters from the register. There he stood, trembling and stabbing at each one with the tiny brush of Lucinda's red 'Luscious Lover' nail polish.

Not surprisingly, one afternoon the coin slot on the video game jammed, refusing any more quarters.

Al and I had just gotten off the school bus and stood raiding the bubble gum jar at the trading post when Tic burst through the door.

Eyes wildly roving across the interior, he zeroed in on Mother's keys hanging from a brass clip on her belt loop.

He rushed to her side and reached for the keys, fingers still curled to the contours of the video game's button panel.

"Hey!" Mother backed him off. "What the hell is the

matter with you, Tic?"

Staring at the keys, Tic drew his elbows close to his side and, with obvious effort, tried to remember the mechanics of language, "Box! I... uh... errr umm... *empty the box!*"

"It's full already?" Mother asked, surprised. "I just emptied it yesterday."

"*Kids!*" he blurted.

Al and I exchanged knowing looks.

Tic led a charge of one down the boardwalk to the saloon. Mother followed some distance behind jangling a handful of keys for the one that would open the lock box to the video machine.

When the box was at last pried open, ten pounds of red quarters spilled onto the floor.

"Tic," Mother began, "the kids haven't even been here. They've been in school. And where did all these red quarters come from?"

Tic dropped silently to his knees and scraped together spilled coins like a poker player raking in winnings.

"*Tic!*" Mother stood with her hands on her hips watching a desperate man. "I said, where did all these red quarters come from?"

Legs splayed and flailing behind him, Tic was now humping around under the machine, reaching for elusive coins that had rolled up against the baseboard. Now and then, he'd bang his elbows as he attempted to shove quarters, undetected, into his pockets. "I have to test the machine, don't I?" he muttered, scraping a quarter along the floor and frantically cramming it into his pocket, causing the machine to buck. "I need more red quarters, man. *Red* ones. For the customers."

He wriggled out from under the machine, rose and pivoted on his knees shoving a few more red quarters into his pockets before clutching Mother's legs, "C'mon, man, don't cut me off, I gotta beat 10,000!"

Al and I had to turn away. It was too pathetic even for us, and we could be pretty pathetic.

"Okay, Tic," Mother scolded, "thirty red quarters. Twenty for the customers and ten for you. Once you've used up the ten for yourself, you can't play again unless you use your own quarters. And, I don't want to see you on that darned machine until after hours, understood?"

"Yeah, right, right, understood. Gimme the quarters."

Tic spirited the bag of change away to the bar and pretended to busy himself with glasses and bottles until Mother finally left.

Al and I stayed in the saloon and observed, appearing as though to scrape ashes out of the huge fireplace, for which we were each to be paid $3.00. But, our attention had shifted to Tic who had quickly reclaimed intimacy with the temptress by the wall in the pool room.

Beep, beep, blink, buzzzzzz, blink, buzzzzzz.... "Ah!" he snorted, periodically. *Poom, poom, blip, blip, buzzzzzz.* Within half an hour, he had run out of quarters.

At first, he just sat there staring at the still-animated screen. *Blip, blip, buzzzzzz.* It enacted a little sample game, as if mocking his craving for action. *Blip, blip, blink, buzzzzzz... Game Over*, it flashed, taunting him.

Tic grasped both sides of the machine and shook it

ferociously, staring into its colorful depths. *"Arrgggg!"* He kicked it with his foot. He kicked it again. In grim silence he sat, elbows on the table, gripping his head. Al and I looked at one another, silently suggesting a rapid exit.

Willing ourselves invisible, we quickly tiptoed toward the door, but Tic's eyes had been trained through repetitive motion on the hypnotic screen to detect sudden movement. He leapt from his chair — knees and elbows bent, hands crimped and trembling. His head jerked violently to the left, flailing his right arm as he scrambled nearer. We froze like condemned prey near the tavern door.

"You been paid?" he asked, squinting into the afternoon sun slanting through the window behind us.

"Uh....no," we half-whispered, inching closer together. I was ready with my hand on a chair should he make a move on us.

He grunted and spun, clamoring mechanically toward the bar. Opening the register, he began rooting wildly for change. Al and I took the opportunity to evacuate outside, where we could observe safely through a window. He was a mad man, and we vowed to steer clear of the tavern, spying only from the exterior until either he or the machine fried their wiring.

A week or so later, heavy winter snow moved in as the last of the hunters began straggling down out of the mountains. Tic had been forced into a weaning period from the machine when Dad finally unplugged it and removed it to a locked closet. For a short while, Tic had been restored to his original discord, assuring Dad his addiction was well under control.

At the reintroduction of the machine, however, Tic resumed his old ways. Fastening himself to its side with an even greater intensity than before, it had become increasingly difficult for Tic to indulge his habit apart from Dad's prying eyes.

One afternoon, after building a fire ahead of the evening crowd, Dad finished splitting and stacking a large pile of firewood just outside the saloon door.

"Damn cold out there. Looks like winter's here to stay," Dad blew warm air into his cupped hands and stomped snow off his boots as he walked into the saloon. "Damn cold, Tic," he said again, looking over at Tic who stood alone behind the bar in the dim tavern, staring morosely into the varnished pine.

Walking through the pool room into the café, Dad shouted back to Tic, "There's a fire in the fireplace, Tic, don't let it go out. I split a stack of wood by the door." He waited for a reply, but was met with only the hollow echoes of popping sap and reflected flickers of dancing flame on the distant wall.

"Tic!"

"Yeah! Fire..."

Thusly, Tic was presumed to fill winter's lonely days occupying himself with the fire, inventory, and cleaning and filling the glasses of regulars. Helplessly though, drawn like a moth, he was lured by the blinking machine.

Blink, blink, beep, buzzzzzz. Poom, poom, poom, beep, buzzzzzzz. The machine constantly blipped and beeped next to the wall, enacting pre-programmed games, flashing mock scores.

Later that evening, four hunters entered the saloon

which had grown cold hours earlier. Above the machine, an electric-blue, pulsating glow reflected off the wall and lent a cold, eerie feel to the barely discernable traps and snow-shoes hanging there.

The men glanced around while removing their hats and gloves.

"I don't know," one of the men continued their conversation from the boardwalk, "sign's off. Lights aren't on."

"Yeah," said another, "but the door's open."

One of the men spotted Tic slouched over the flashing screen in the pool room. "Is this place open?" he wondered aloud. "Hey," he said more loudly, "is this place open?"

The soft humming and beeping echoed throughout the empty saloon. The hunters shrugged at one another, assuming Tic deaf. Nearing him, one of the men tapped his shoulder, "Excuse me..."

"*Getaway..arrrgh, ack!*" Tic growled through the dryness of his parched throat.

The hunter jumped backward, falling into a companion as Tic continued staring fiercely into the machine, twitching, jerking, pounding buttons.

"Take it easy, man, we just want a drink, okay. Can we get a drink?"

"*Inthebar... Getit! Getit! Getit!*" Tic yanked at the squat machine, deftly jamming at the buttons with his thumbs.

The men walked behind the bar and filled four glasses from a bottle of whiskey. Walking quietly around the far side of the pool table, they eased past Tic and toward the light spilling under the door connecting the saloon and café.

"Man," one of the men said to another as he opened the door and entered the café, "that guy in there is gonzo."

Dad looked up from the cup of coffee he had only just poured, "What do you mean, *gonzo?*"

The men sat at Dad's table as melting snow began forming small puddles around their boots. "He's a *wild* man," one of them laughed. "Hunched over some machine. Totally gone."

"We went ahead and got our own whiskey," another chuckled. "Hope that's okay."

Dad nodded affirmatively.

"Hell," said the third, "it's too damn cold to sit in the bar, so we came over here."

With a heavy sigh, Dad pulled himself from the table and started for the darkened bar. A thick chill slammed him as he opened the door.

Tic sat, eyes bulging… pale and drooling over the machine.

Expressing his customary patience, Dad stalked silently to the wall and yanked the plug.

"*Arrgrgggg!* That was my *high score*, man!" Tic rose to attack, but found himself hanging limp from Dad's fist now curled around the front of Tic's shirt and lifting him onto his toes.

"Listen, you piss-ant. You know what I'm going to do with that high score?" Dad pressed his hot breath against Tic's gaunt face. Tic hung like a dead fish. "Get your ass over to the bar and turn on the lights. Then, you get your ass over to the window and turn on the "open" sign. Then you get your ass over to the fireplace and get a fire started. If I come back over here in twenty minutes and this place doesn't toast the balls off a fruit fly, you're hittin' the road, pal. You read me this time, meteor man?"

Tic muttered something under his breath and, once lowered to the floor, shuffled off behind the bar. He waited for the door to the café to creak open then latch shut. Muffled chuckles filtered through. Late evening had settled into the valley and a ten-degree wind chill had begun to frost the windows.

Cursing maniacally under his breath, Tic suddenly flared in rage and threw open the tavern door, "You want a *fire?* I'll give you a sombitchin' fire." He grabbed the kindling hatchet out of a stump and reentered the bar, leaving the door to creak and bang in the freezing wind.

Seizing a bar stool, he flung it to the floor, hacked off its legs and threw them into the fireplace. He grabbed another then another, filling the fireplace with legs from the stools. Then he turned to the chairs and hacked off each of their legs, also. A man of intense singular focus, when the fireplace could hold no more, Tic littered the floor, hurling sticks of wood into the corner of the room.

Finally, Tic stuffed a giant wad of newspapers under the pile of chair legs in the fireplace and lit it. Fire roared as flames licked out from the mounting inferno. A gust of wind slammed the tavern door shut and, within twenty minutes, the inside temperature had grown to ninety degrees.

Sweat dripped off Tic's nose as he sat staring at the flickering screen. *Beep, blip, Poom, poom, blip, buzzzzz...*

The next day the machine was gone, forever.

But, within a week, Tic had developed a new interest.
In darts.

Christmas Eve Miracle at the
Church of Hardrock

Dad sat with Wes, Ty and Crazy Jake at a table in the saloon discussing the unusual lights that had moved in over Kodiak Mountain for the second winter in a row.

"It's aliens," concluded Jake.

"It ain't aliens." Ty rolled his eyes.

Dad sipped his coffee. "It's damn strange, I'll give you that."

Upon hearing the discussion turn to outer space visitors, Al and I became interested in the conversation and wandered over from the pool room where we had been loudly battling one another over a game of foosball.

"All right then," Jake looked at Ty, "how do you explain those three separate lights hoverin' over the peak? How do you explain them flyin' in from different directions and gatherin' in a triangle formation right over the mountain, hangin' there for a few hours at night and then takin' off. And, how come it's only from Thanksgiving through Christmas, huh? That's alien stuff, right there."

"It's probably military maneuvers." Ty looked at Dad for affirmation. "That's what I think it is."

Wes followed Ty's eyes, offering, "I don't know, it *could* be aliens. I mean, who's to say we're the only intelligent life in the universe, let alone the only ones who could develop flying saucers? The German's had that technology in World War II."

"And it was the German *military*, wasn't it?" Ty goaded Jake.

Jake piped in, "Yeah? Well, why would all the lights be different colors? Red, blue, green..." Jake leaned in and raised his rangy eye brows. "Why wouldn't they all be the same?"

"I don't know," Ty mused. "The military is always coming up with weird stuff."

"Too easy." Jake leaned back and sipped his beer. "Anytime something weird happens, everyone just says, 'military'. Them Martians are havin' a convention is what it is." Jake nodded at Al and me. "It ain't no military."

"Well, that's the logical damn thing, Jake." Ty countered. "Hell, you think everything is paranormal. Ghosts in your house. The girls, here, even have you believing in sasquatches."

Wes snorted.

"There ARE ghosts in my house!" Jake banged his beer bottle on the table, causing a rush of foam to escape up the neck. "Upstairs! Before I sealed 'em off and moved downstairs, they'd gather around my bed at night and try to get me to get up and dance with 'em. Crazy damn ghosts."

"Well, at least they know how to party," Ty chortled into his beer.

Dad drained his coffee cup and looked at Al and me, his eyes twinkling. "Speaking of *party*, it's about time to shut down the saloon and get up to the house. It's Christmas Eve, and you know what that means..."

Al and I squealed in delight. We were *ridden* with Christmas fleas, a condition that prompted a great deal of itching, twitching and general jumpiness ahead of Christmas morning. There'd be no sleeping tonight, and not just because aliens had invaded the valley.

Crazy Jake collected a couple of empty beer bottles between his fingers and deposited them on the bar as Tic switched off the neon "open" sign. Minutes later, Al and I were zooming past Wes who had pitifully attempted to thwart our missile-accurate trajectory to the house.

Bursting through the kitchen door, we saw Mother's feast of yummy treats prepared on the kitchen table which she had draped with an antique, lace table cloth.

Each end of the table was anchored with two large, freeform, sandcast candles Dad and Mother had made years ago when we lived in Oklahoma. Mother brought them out during the holidays because of their warm, cinnamon scent. They cast a soft light over the table filled with three kinds of crackers and a plate arranged with slices of baby swiss, smoked gouda, brie and even Dad's favorite, limburger.

A little pot of stone-ground, brown mustard sat with a tiny silver spoon tucked inside. Braunschweiger, each thick slice cut into four triangles, rested point-up on another plate. A small, glass tray brought from Mother's childhood farm contained compartments of black and green olives, sweet pickles and smoked oysters. An array of raw veggies and apple wedges circled a small bowl of dip.

In the living room, the lights were off, a fire crackled in the fireplace and a gargantuan Christmas tree, consuming a quarter of the living room, sparkled with tinsel, ornaments and hundreds of twinkling lights. John Denver, Kermit and the rest of the Muppet gang sang a rowdy chorus of *Little Saint Nick* on the stereo turntable.

Evening turned to night as we four loitered between the living room and kitchen with saucers of delectables and spontaneous sing alongs. Wes brought out his guitar and strummed along competing to drown out Al's and my enthusiastic vocals.

Around ten, Dad reclined in his robe and slippers, soaking in the glow of the tree while sipping laced eggnog and smoking his pipe. At his feet, Al and I had turned our efforts to relentless begging.

"Just one present, before bedtime," Al urged shamelessly.

"Nope…" Dad said, grinning around the pipe stem clamped between his teeth, "you have to wait until Christmas morning."

"*Pleeeeease!*" Al and I pleaded together.

"Other people do it!" I chimed in.

"Nope." Dad blew a vast smoke ring and began tamping the tobacco in the bowl of his pipe. "Why don't you two addle-brains pipe down so your mother can read Uncle Raymond and Aunt Gigi's Christmas card?"

We temporarily silenced our cajoling and the Muppets long enough for Mother to open the card which had arrived the afternoon previous.

She passed around two enclosed photos. One was a picture of Uncle Raymond holding up a blue marlin on the deck of a yacht. The other picture looked like a close-up of a flowery curtain, but it was actually Aunt Gigi's sarong-draped behind bending over as she fetched something out of her bag on the beach. We seriously doubted Aunt Gigi knew about the second photo.

Mother unfolded and read the note inside:

Raymond has FINALLY decided to take a two-week vacation and spend Christmas in Bermuda, which is where we are as I write this. I am, this minute, lounging in a cabana and wondering if I should consider snorkeling. A very handsome instructor has offered to teach me. The weather here is fabulous and the ocean views are spectacular. Since I'll be hosting this year's charity drive at our new country club, I've decided to go with a beach theme! Won't that be fun! Cookie's fur is still short, but, that's okay since she comes back to the hotel covered in sand every evening. You would think, though, that a bath every night would keep sand out of the sheets. Raymond has been out fishing every day and caught a trophy fish which he is very proud of. Because of all the fishing, he is too sunburned to sleep in the bed. We spent all night last night fighting over sand in the sheets. You know Ray... he tore the bed apart three times, determined to find a single grain of sand. He finally fell asleep on a chair at three this morning. Of course, because of all the fishing, his arms are too sore for dancing, which is disappointing because the island music is very lively. There goes the instructor, again. They say the snorkeling here is world class. I think I'll try it! I hope you all have a wonderful Christmas. We miss you all and your beautiful mountains! Love, Ray, Gigi and Cookie.

Mother grinned at Dad as she tacked the card to the wall beside the fireplace.

Dad got up and, skirting the tree, walked over to the window overlooking the county road where cars from Granite and Bituminous had begun streaming toward town.

"There go the folks for midnight Mass. Looks like it's getting on toward midnight, girls," Dad turned to eyeball us with an animated expression.

As we inhaled for a prolonged last-minute appeal that any special unwrapping ought to take place before midnight, we were cut short when Dad frowned, stomped his foot and growled, *"Getouttahere!"*

Al and I jolted, fearing we'd pushed our petition too far, but when Pedo shot from the lower branches of the tree, we realized his directive had been pointed at the cat. Dad grimaced in the direction of the hall.

"How come Wes gets to stay up?" I asked.

"Because, I don't *believe* in Santa Claus," Wes said in a mocking tone.

"Fool!" Al and I pronounced in unison then burst into giggles.

Al quickly added, "You don't believe in Santa Claus, but you believe in aliens?"

I chimed in, "Yeah! You've never seen either one, but aliens don't bring you p..r..e..s..e..n..t..s!"

We galloped off behind the cat, the three of us giddy with fleas.

"You know, girls, Christmas is about more than presents," Dad reminded us as we heard him drop the needle onto a philharmonic orchestral rendition of *The Little Drummer Boy*.

Yes, yes, we knew that. But our addled brains certainly considered it more fun to think about presents.

Another car passing the house honked twice in appreciation of the mammoth tree in the window then continued along the road to the tiny chapel, a quarter mile or so from Crazy Jake's place.

Enis and the historical society had, years earlier, deemed the small wooden, white-washed church erected in 1898 of historical significance. Consequently, it remained boarded up most of the year. On Christmas Eve, however, the society opened the doors for a non-denominational evening of worship and fellowship kindled by the trucking in of a visiting chaplain, thirty gallons of spiked cider and a half dozen rum-soaked fruit cakes. A quart sized jar, marked 'donations', sat on a table by the door.

As the devout revelers gathered to honor the religious significance of the season, two other nearby revelers were out foraging for an armload of firewood.

Given the doctrinal differences among the gathered faithful, the significance of events that occurred on that fateful night of December 24th is rigorously disputed, still.

Arriving around ten-thirty that evening, the church guests had gotten the fruitcake social well underway by the time Crazy Jake and Boris wandered out into the nearby woods to scout firewood for Jake's house.

It was Jake's habit to scout wood on an as-needed basis, since, he argued, no one could be certain when, exactly, the winter weather would break.

At any given time, Jake kept no more than six logs in his house. Three of the logs were scouted and chopped around noon every day through winter where they would be stacked on the left side of his stove. There, they would thaw from heat generated by burning the other three logs, scouted and chopped from the day previously and which rested, dry and ready to burn, on the right side of his stove.

Christmas Eve arrived clear and bitterly cold, and Jake was upset to discover that two of his right-side logs were rotted. Burning to a soft pile of ash within twenty minutes, they scarcely heated even the lower floor of his house which had been separated from the upstairs by blankets hanging in the stairwell.

The warm, amber lights and happy voices floating from the church were lost on the two men as Jake trundled about the forest behind his house, peering with a kerosene lantern under low hanging spruce branches.

Boris stood nearby, staring at Hardrock's sole street light across the road from Jake's house.

Rearing from the dry depths near the base of a spruce, Jake bumped into something large and soft. "A coon!" he shouted to Boris. "Hurry up and grab my rifle!" Jake was not only cautious of raccoons but seized any opportunity to fill his skillet.

Boris grunted, not especially interested in hurrying anywhere.

Jake lifted the light. "Wow, man, look at that…"

It wasn't a coon. Jake had accidently discovered a

gigantic hornet's nest measuring two and a half feet across. "Dang, that's somethin'! C'mere and look at this thing…" Jake called to Boris.

Boris stomped through the snow and grunted as Jake stood admiring the round, gray, papery structure reflecting in the halo of his lantern.

Lifting the bottle of vodka perpetually clenched in his paw of a fist and downing a sizeable swallow, Boris walked over to the tree, broke off a long branch and smacked the hive with it.

Nothing happened.

Jake stroked his gnarly gotee, "Looks like they've migrated south. Hey! Let's cut it down and hang it in the house. It'll be Christmassy!"

Boris grunted and scratched his back against the tree.

Jake climbed the spruce and, balancing one foot on Boris's shoulder, chopped at the branch from above, careful not to damage the hive.

"Hold still, dang it," Jake mumbled to Boris, "you make me tear up this hive and I'll stomp your head."

Boris acknowledged with a slight raising of his eyebrows.

Once inside his house, Jake wired the hive to a long, horizontal run of stovepipe which he had long ago suspended across his ceiling with bailing wire.

"Lookit there." He stood back admiring his work. "That's some hive! I bet no one else's got one of them hanging around their house."

"You gonna deal or what?" Boris asked, frowning from

his seat at the nearby card table.

"You know what?" Jake frowned back at his friend and neighbor. "You got about as much appreciation for art as an owl turd. This here is an aesthetical contribution to my interior design."

Boris grimaced at Jake, "You been reading them old *Home Journal* magazines again?"

"Maybe." Jake swiped at something near his ear then turned to admire the nest again. "You got to branch out some. Be hip."

"Deal the cards."

Crazy Jake stoked the fire with the damp logs he'd collected under the spruce then took a swig from Boris's vodka bottle. Sitting down to the small table beside the fire, he shuffled an old deck of cards and dealt out a hand of crazy eights which Al and I had taught him the week previous.

Boris eyed his hand, "Hit me."

"You don't get 'hit' in crazy eights," Jake admonished. "I told you this ain't black jack. And it ain't poker. You have to put down the same suit I put down or match the number, and then you can change it. If you don't have that number, but you have an 'eight', you can throw that down and change it to whatever you want. Pay attention, dang it."

Jake furrowed his brow and continued under his breath, "It's like tryin' to teach a danged orangutan how to play cards."

"What'd you say?" Boris eyeballed Jake from under a heavy mane of thick, black hair.

"I said, I'm bettin' two beers and a bottle of vodka on this hand." Jake threw down a three of hearts.

"Huh…" Boris turned his hand sideways and squinted at it. After a minute, he threw down two jacks, three fours, an ace and two sevens. "Call."

Jake ground his hat against his head.

Twenty minutes eased by. Cards were drawn and played. As Boris began to get the drift, the stakes grew higher and the game more tense.

"Dang you, Boris, you cheatin' S.O.B., I said *spades.*"

"Like hell, that was a club, you lyin' bastard. You cook dinner all next week."

"Hearts then..." Jake said, throwing down a fifth eight in a move that surprised even him.

Boris reached for his knife and felt a slap on his face. He twitched and reached again, but felt Jake slap him on his arm then again on his ear.

Jake was backing away from Boris, thinking he had just been slapped on his back and again on his right arm. "What the… did you just hit me?" Jake squinted hard at Boris.

"No, but you better knock off hittin' me!" Boris raised his voice over the steady drone not yet consciously detected.

"I didn't hit you," Jake said, staring at Boris, "I swear it."

"Ow! There it is again!" Boris eyeballed Jake, "How you doin' that? You sure you ain't ... OW! ... hittin' me?"

"Hell fire!" Jake's eyes grew wide in alarm. "It's them dang ghosts...OW! They're attackin' us!" Jake grabbed his rifle and waved it through the air, crashing the barrel against the hornets' nest.

Hundreds of thawed hornets began pouring from the

hive, angry and looking to sink their stingers.

Jake sat awed, "H..o..l..y cripes, look at all them hornets..." Overwhelmed by the odd spectacle of the thick, descending fog of insects, he was unable to comprehend the impending doom.

Rising from his seat, Boris swatted the air with the butt of his bottle and grabbed Jake by the shirt collar. Dragging Jake outside and slamming the door behind them, Boris revived his friend by sloshing a few ounces of liquor into Jake's face.

"Huh," Jake looked back at his house where the sound of muffled buzzing hummed thirty feet away, "I don't guess they migrate. Well... what are we gonna do now?" Jake asked. "We can't go back in there."

"Drink!" Boris raised the bottle skyward. "And then sleep."

Jake squinted into the freezing night. "I can't sleep out here. The danged light's shinin' in my eyes."

"Let's shoot it out," Boris suggested.

"You couldn't hit that danged thing if it was as big as a house."

"You saying I can't shoot?" Boris growled.

"You ain't even got a gun, 'member? You lost it last year in the woods after that stupid poker game with Wes. So, what are you gonna do, throw your huntin' knife at it?"

"Why, you scrawny wuss, I can out-shoot you with my eyes closed." Boris leaned in, his eyes uncharacteristically large and lending him a truly fearsome quality.

Jake reared back. "You'll *have* to shoot with 'em closed, 'cause I'm about to punch 'em out. Now, get back." Jake shoved Boris with his boot.

"You afraid you can't shoot the little light?" Boris mocked Jake.

"Dang it," Jake furrowed his brows, "you just ain't gonna quit, till I prove I'm a better shot than you."

Boris snorted as he swigged from his bottle, "Wuss."

"All right, you. I'm gonna show you once and for all who's the better shot," Jake stormed toward his outhouse where he stored several boxes of shells then whirled around pointing a long, gnarled finger, "but, loser cooks and brings in wood for a week."

"You better get your sissy apron tied on." Boris slumped back in the snow and belched.

BLAM! The first shot rang out through the clear night, retorting around the valley and halting the party underway in the church.

The street light burned on as people crowded around the church's windows for a better view and others ventured onto the porch.

BLAM! A second shot followed, but the light burned on. Violent bickering erupted as Jake and Boris fought over how close the shot had been.

Ducking deeper into the chapel, the worshipers speculated why someone would be shooting in the vicinity of the church on Christmas Eve, but when the next shot ricocheted off the steeple, they grew certain they were being fired upon by spiteful, Godless heathens.

It was eleven-thirty, and folks began to worry they would be confined to the tiny sanctuary until the shooters relented.

"There they are!" shouted one woman, peering through a portion of stained glass window. "There are two of them... under the street light!" Her husband escorted her to the front pews out of any potential line of fire.

BLAM!

The pastor rushed out onto the porch and shouted into the night, "You savages! I won't have my congregation held hostage on the Lord's night!" Then he quickly closed the shutters and rushed inside, slamming and bolting the door. Once inside, he roused the pianist and mandolin pickers to kick up an up-tempo rendition of *We Shall Overcome.*

Oblivious to the goings on inside the church, Jake and Boris swilled liquor and took increasingly poor aim as they traded the rifle back and forth, slowly expending Jake's munitions stores.

BLAM! BLAM! More bullets whizzed by the church, narrowly missing a high window.

But the light. The light burned on.

As the hour neared midnight, the inhabitants within the small building naturally began to pray.

All the different worshipers summoned all their forms of God from on high to bring forth a miracle that might end what was perceived as a scurrilous persecution of the devout.

A few forgot their charity and prayed for lightening to strike the heathen pair, perched in the snow, drinking, cursing, and otherwise forsaking the sanctity of the holy night.

Others prayed for the numbing cold to seize Jake and Boris' pickled bodies, disabling their trigger fingers.

But, most hoped they would simply pass out and stop shooting long enough for the procession to observe Mass then wind its way through town, homeward.

Gradually the drama of the situation lessened as fewer and fewer bullets were heard firing from beneath the street light that still blazed, haloed, illuminating the drunken heap beneath it.

A shot rang out.

Minutes ticked by. Another shot, but the light... the light burned on.

The pastor lifted his hand and said, "Let us prepare to receive our Lord."

Two more shots.

The congregation prepared for Mass, a simple interpretation whereupon those gathered lit candles then carried their small flames into the dark night, offering prayers and thanks to the enduring promise of the Christmas Star.

People began to filter outside.

Another shot. Someone ducked.

The faces of the onlookers were fierce and resentful, but hopeful all the same in their faith that God would provide.

And God did.

As quoted in the Christmas Day Commemorative Edition of the Granite Tablet: *"Then, at the stroke of midnight, suddenly, from out of the sky there came a light. Sent down from heaven in answer to our collective prayer for deliverance, a flaming star, directed at the evil-doers which held hostage all forty-six faithful worshipers in the Church of Hardrock on Christmas Eve. Although there is spirited debate over which of the sects is responsible and which of the worshipers received the favor, all agree that a miracle occurred and none question the spiritual significance of the holy event."*

Crazy Jake and Boris saw it differently. Well, Boris didn't see it at all.

With the frigid night needling him out of a drunken stupor, Jake sat slumped in the snow beside Boris, vaguely contemplating the trio of colorful lights hovering over Kodiak Mountain.

Suddenly, a bright white light caught his eye as it streaked into his field of vision. "Holy... man, what the hell is that?" Jake nudged Boris with his elbow.

"Mmm," Boris mumbled, his head hanging onto his bared chest, the bottle of vodka dangling from his limp fist.

"Wake up, man, somethin's happenin'!" Jake urged as he watched the light grow larger and brighter.

Unbeknownst to Jake, Boris or the congregation, a meteorite was, at that moment, hurdling toward Hardrock at a hundred-and-twenty-four-thousand miles per hour.

Boris twitched, jerking his bottle of vodka out of the snow.

Jake stopped shoving his friend and watched spellbound as the meteorite hit the atmosphere amid a shower of colorful flames erupting in a fury of blue, orange, yellow and green light.

Closer and closer, the searing object neared.

"Gol-dang-allmighty!" shouted Jake, shaking Boris vigorously. "It's one of them UFOs! Git up, Git up! They're comin' for us, man! They're comin' for us!"

Boris groaned while Jake slammed a shell into his rifle and fired at the speeding shape.

The congregation gasped and stared. A few smiled as the pastor led them into a vibrant delivery of *O' Holy Night.*

On his knees and wild-eyed, Jake scrambled to drag his two-hundred-forty pound friend through the snow and into the relative safety of the outhouse, "Git up, man! Git up!"

The meteorite neared, its fiery light blazing toward Jake's house. Larger and larger, brighter and brighter it grew.

The congregation joined hands singing louder and louder as the object vaporized a trail a thousand feet overhead.

A moment later and with a great electric fizzle, the meteorite — now reduced to a tiny, white-hot fragment — hit the street light, completely disintegrating the lamp and evaporating without a trace.

Candles were lifted skyward and righteous voices filled the valley.

Jake stared as the procession of worshipers wound past his house and gathered beneath the darkened pole. There, amid their grateful, jubilant voices someone smiled and helped Jake to his feet, patting his back and offering thanks on high, fearless in their mission. Delivered.

Jake wasn't inspired to get religious after that, but he did give up drinking for a day.

And the light? The light never burned again.

Sadie Hawkin's Dance

Cabin fever.

Fourteen consecutive days of relentless snow had obliterated all but the dimmest hint of sunlight and most of our rational faculties.

It had crept into the valley and seized every last one of us.

Its tenacious vise upon the valley, gripped tighter by the most abundant snowfall in a decade, would endure until May, ushering a months-long psychological sentence upon the valley's few, year-round human inhabitants, all of whom craved desperate reprieve through the alluring temptations of diversional drink provided by the social setting of the Quartz Creek Inn saloon.

Most of the regulars were sitting in the tavern one night in early February, comforted by the quintessential country stylings of Hank Williams on the 8-track stereo. *Your Cheatin' Heart* layered softly upon the smoky air and punctuated every sip of cocktail and warm whiskey among friends and enemies alike.

In the unyielding darkness and thick, white landscape of a mid-winter deep-freeze, the café and trading post were opened only on weekends or by special request or, sometimes, just because someone happened upon someone else inside doing maintenance. Among us locals, most folks were never too busy to welcome a spontaneous cup of strong, hot coffee and relaxed conversation regardless of circumstance.

The saloon, open evenings, seven days a week, became a dangerously familiar focal point for most of Hardrock's residents and a few out-of-towners. Even Al and I spent many a winter's eve in the saloon's adjacent pool room playing through extended backgammon tournaments, chucking darts, swilling non-alcoholic cocktails and making short work of grill-popped popcorn — the little chewy kernels, shriveled dense with butter.

We were always eager to get in on the nightly doings, at least those which surfaced within our field of vision before ten o'clock, which was our 'back-to-the-house' hour. We figured anything that went on after ten and before the 2:00am closing time had to be really good, since we weren't allowed to see it.

Wes, four years our senior, was given a two-hour extension and usually entertained himself at the pool table or played a few impromptu and often self-designed off-color tunes on his guitar for a captive and occasionally appreciative audience.

Willy played a furious fiddle, and Abbey never minded offering vocal accompaniment onstage which rewarded us light—warmth—oxygen—cash—entertainment-starved locals the singular joy of spontaneous, live musical respite.

Such respite was fortuitous given that cabin fever affected some of us more than others. Tic, for instance, had developed the unhealthy habit of continually pulling at his eyelashes. Once his eyelids were bald, he went after his eyebrows. By mid-January his eyes were red and swollen, his brows bristled with random hairs in various stages of re-growth and on weeknights Lucinda was making him wear a homemade dog-cone around his neck.

This night, Crazy Jake and Boris sat at the bar with Big John, a fifty-something, soft-spoken coal miner from Bituminus. Beside Big John, sat his secret sweetheart Miss Dixie, an elegant silver-haired belle who ran a bake shop in Granite. Her oblivious, drunken husband, Buster, sat beside her.

The rarely seen, Luce (short for Lucy), sat at the end of the bar looking like she had pulled a double shift in the coal mine. And she had. She walked, talked, fought and even looked a lot like John Wayne. She had gone to work in the Mightyslag coal mine ten years previous when her husband went to town for a new snow shovel and never returned. Her four boys were now long out of the nest and spent most nights in the Granite jail.

Ty and Abbey sat at a table by the fireplace exchanging desirous looks over his whiskey and her Long Island iced tea. Willy and Gert, working out their sixteenth draft of next summer's menu, occupied another table. Dad and Mother manned the bar while Tic recovered from the flu, presumably looked after by his attentive wife, Lucinda.

Al and I watched Skeeter and Grody, two twenty-something coal miners from Bituminous, battle one another over the pool table, each betting rounds of beer until neither could balance a cue stick on their thumbs and their best bank-shots began ricocheting off walls.

While Al and I had been enlisted by the pair as official scorekeepers, our unofficial jobs were to shuttle bowls of Dad's hot, homemade chili or turkey and dumplings to the hungry horde.

Making ten gallons of one or the other every night, most everyone enjoyed a bowl or two. Skeeter and Grody were usually good for a couple gallons. Big John, Luce and Wes polished off the rest.

Those were the regulars and, other than Luce, each one was in the saloon most nights. So regular, in fact, Big John kept a pillow and a blanket under the bar and greeted more than one early morning from the top of the pool table.

Every now and then, a few of Hardrock's town folk would stop in. These included the uneasy unions of Ray and Jill Tippits and their neighbors, Sol and Dot Goldstein. There simmered an obviously amorous connection between the four, but not necessarily between designated spouses and certainly not formally acknowledged by any of the participants in the romantic ruse. This arrangement resulted in frequent double dates, where both couples could enjoy the company of their neighbor's spouse without the trouble of filing for divorce, which they assumed best served the interests of both their sons, Dudley and Bucky, respectively, each a year or so younger than Al and I.

During the dark winter months, when daylight — on clear days, only extended between the hours of ten in the morning and two in the afternoon, Elvira and Doorite engaged in the excavation of their basement and capitalized on the lack of sunshine to conceal their shovel and bucket operation from the county assessor. It was clear, however, they had devised no means of cloaking the ever-growing pile of soil and stone that began in the forest and now terminated only twenty yards from their cabin. They too, from time to time, would take a break from their excavation and loiter about the saloon, soaking up the artificial illumination of a 40-watt bulb.

Other occasional saloon visitors included Al's parents, and among those who visited the saloon on even farther flung occasions were Enis Snapbinder and Millie Swampnettle. Striving to shroud their poorly concealed romantic liaison and believing anyone actually cared, Enis and Millie never arrived nor departed any establishment at the same time. Reliably, each led or followed the other within a neatly spaced five-minute interval.

There were also nights when an intrepid few craved a change of venue so desperately as to brave the twisting, icy county road all the way from Granite.

Just such a someone blew through the door that February night. Sub-zero wind whipped in as the stranger opened the door. He stood there, neatly bedecked in expensive outerwear, momentarily eyeing the interior and its occupants. No one paid much attention except for Al and me, because we were ever alert to the potential for any new action, and Dad, probably because he had been professionally trained to watch for the same. We three studied the stranger, but could not have anticipated the shocking thing that happened next.

"Is Hank Williams all you've got in this bar?" the stranger shouted over the steel guitar as he shut the door behind him and removed his gloves.

Of course, Hank Williams wasn't *all* we had behind the bar. We had over sixty different 8-tracks. We had Neil Young, John Denver, the Eagles, Rolling Stones, The Doobie Brothers and Joplin. We had Lynyrd Skynyrd, The Allman Brothers

Band, Haggard, Cash, Waylon, Willy and Bobbie Gentry. The thing was, Hank was all anyone ever *listened* to in the saloon. But, not just *any* Hank tape. We only listened to *Hank's Greatest Hits*. Over and over.

And, well... over.

You know how in the movies a stranger walks into a bar and somehow insults the folks inside and everyone turns around, and suddenly this stranger knows he ought to be moving on? It was like that. It was a movie moment. After this guy's comment, everyone stopped talking and turned around to see what kind of misfit out-of-towner didn't want to hear Hank on the stereo. All us locals knew Hank ruled the night, unless there was live music including the occasional local's jug band with Gert on the juice harp, Crazy Jake on the wash tub base and us kids on spoons. Everyone not only accepted this, we liked it. Counted on it.

Was *Hank* all we got. What more would you want?

As we regulars sat quietly eyeballing the surprised stranger, Hank blasted the awkward silence with an eerie peal of *"Kaw-Liiiiigaaaa"*. The note lingered as everyone continued staring. The saloon must have seemed too crowded because the visitor slowly backed out the door, shut it softly, and everything resumed its usual tone.

It's kind of odd how it takes a stranger to expose your own weirdness like that. That's why we never anticipated such a remark. None of us thought that continuously listening to Hank was weird. At least not until the stranger brought it up. And, even then, no one felt compelled to make any uncomfortable adjustments.

We considered Hank a regular, the repetition comforting. He helped define what made the saloon like an old warm coat on a chilly, desolate evening. His was a predictable and integral part of the space itself... the darkened interior; the warm, crackling fire; the conversation and collective vibe... night after night, month upon month, until the tape finally broke. For a while after that, everyone kind of fumbled along in a state of mild anxiety. Finally, Mother bought another tape and all went back to normal.

But the night the stranger walked in, he must've gotten Dad to thinking, because just afterward Dad suggested we shake things up a little and throw a mid-winter dance.

"YEAH!" the regulars roared, raising their glasses and embracing the idea with almost frightening enthusiasm.

"Let's do a Valentine's dance," Abbey suggested. Glances exchanged, some shoulders shrugged, but when Gert mentioned and explained her idea of a Sadie Hawkin's dance, the place buzzed like a live wire on the side of a tin barn.

Her initial explanation centered around the tradition inspired by Al Cap's *Lil' Abner* cartoon strip, which described an event where a man's ugly daughter had an opportunity to catch a marriage prospect in a footrace.

This explanation only seemed to stir confusion, but Gert's exasperated, *"The girls ask the guys!"* was met with vigorous approval including Ty's grappling of Abbey's ample frontal region, which always elicited a semi-violent response. Miss Dixie and Big John exchanged suggestive glances and Willy's gaze drifted beyond Gert into the unknown.

Because everything in Hardrock was up for local

interpretation, all the regulars pushed a few tables together and gathered to discuss the details of the upcoming event. Miss Dixie suggested everyone dress in old-fashioned outfits, which was quickly dismissed, since no one wanted to bother with costume and everyone wanted to get on with thinking about who they might ask or be asked by and figuring out if there would be a band.

Willy suggested we kick off the evening with a footrace in the snow, providing the women a chance to catch their man while giving the men a perhaps better chance at escape. This was pondered briefly then heartily agreed to by those laboring too greatly under the fog of alcohol to consider the consequences of such an idea. Ten o'clock came and went, but Dad let Al and I stay in the saloon until all the details were worked out, somewhere to our delight around 11:30.

The dance was set for the following Saturday night, and excitement engulfed the valley like spring run-off.

Al and I spent the next week along with the rest of the locals in crazed anticipation of the big event.

Friday afternoon, on the way home from school, Al and I reviewed our weekend homework assignments with thorough disgust. Cripes. We had all this fun to look forward to and both of us would have to write a science essay on "the physical and chemical reactions of matter". We scowled at the words on the top of the mimeographed paper which was followed by three quarters of a page of blank space beckoning our thoughtful response.

I sniffed the paper. The scent was gone. All sniffed out from second period. Such was the effect of cabin fever on me.

Peevil stopped the bus at the top of our driveway and Al and I crammed our papers into our backpacks, forgotten. We wouldn't see them again until 7:30 Monday morning. Good riddance, we thought, and shot toward the saloon to see if anyone had decided who they'd chase down at the dance.

Saturday morning broke with a gloriously clear sky full of sunny promise. We could hardly contain our excitement as Al and I jumped on the foot of Wes' bed to watch him tune his guitar.

"So, are you going to the dance with *Georrrr..gia?*" I sang, hiding his pick.

"Yep."

"*Duh...*" Al glanced at me, rolling her eyes.

"Give me my pick, punk." *strum, strum*

I flipped it in the sound hole, unable to channel any constructive energy. "What're you going to play? Are you and Willy going to play tonight? Is Abbey going to sing?"

"Cripes, you're a pain in the butt. Get out of my room." Wes shook the pick out of his guitar and resumed tuning.

"We're *bored!*" I leaned in and grabbed his tuning fork. He snatched it back and put in on his nightstand.

"Rejects are what you are. Yeah, we're playing a little tonight. Probably *Bumper Sticker Fandango*".

"I *hate* that song." Another of Wes' penned atrocities, unworthy of further explanation.

"I know. That's why I'm playing it." *strum... strum...*

"Play *Dancing in the Moonlight*," I suggested hopefully. He knew it was one of my top twenty favorites.

"I will, if you'll get out of my room."

"Play *Bobby McGee* for me!" Al bargained.

"Oh! Do *Freebird!*" Another for me.

"Fine."

"And *Bad Moon Risin'!*" Al tossed in another. "We should make a list!" she suggested.

"Yeah!"

"Oh! Don't forget," I bounced on the bed, singing, "Jeremiah was a bullfrog! I love that song!"

"Me too!" Al bounced with me. "And *Bojangles.*" She looked suddenly solemn.

"Whalebones and Crosses!" I added.

"Desperado."

"Get OUT!" Wes shoved us to the door.

"What's the point of living with a musician if you can't get him to play songs you like?" I asked Al as we galloped down the hall.

"He'll probably play *Dancing Queen!*" Al imitated her sister Georgia's come-hither expression every time Wes dedicated the song to her.

We fled the house in a fit of giggles and charged down to the inn to see if we could help Mother with dance preparations.

Since "decorations" consisted of four balloons and a few streamers left over from the Diamond Hills affair, Gert and Abbey had already stapled everything over the mirror behind the stage in the saloon, leaving little to do.

Late morning brought snowy skies, so Al and I headed out to build a snow fort and wasted the rest of the afternoon on fifteen or so flea-ridden games of darts.

By the time the first few regulars began showing up around six o'clock, three inches of snow had amassed and more was coming down fast.

Even though Dad had said he would open the bar at seven, judging by the early turn-out, the regulars must've been as anxious as us kids to get the party going.

Cigarette smoke and easy conversation curled down the darkened boardwalk as Dad unlocked the door at 6:20pm. He wore a leather vest, pressed jeans and shined boots. A cigar dangled from his lip, a .44 from his hip.

Abbey walked in wearing a red dress and an alligator-clipped red feather fluff in her hair. Ty escorted her ahead of him, removed his hat and hung it on the hook by the door.

Wow. The formality of the atmosphere was thick, and Al and I, awed by the specter, drank it in.

Ty unbuckled his gun belt and handed it to Dad. Boris came in next and took out his 14-inch Bowie knife, laying it on the bar where Dad took it and added it to the lockbox behind the counter. Crazy Jake, sitting next to Boris, slid his pocket knife across the bar next to the bottle of beer Mother brought up from the cooler.

Checking weapons was a nightly and necessary custom, particularly given the volatility of the crowd about to partake of the evening's festivities. Though it was a practice which gave a lot of out-of-towners and tourists pause, half the residents in and around Hardrock carried hardware and, frequently, a shadowed history. Within minutes, the lock-box was full of revolvers and knives.

Al and I had heard but, to our disappointment, failed to

witness Skeeter and Grody ripping the sink off the men's room wall and brawling their way through the door only two weeks earlier. Dad's philosophy held that cue sticks, darts and glass bottles added sufficient emphasis to nightly conversations among the regular crowd; and, only one person would carry the *big* stick — him.

Those that brought them leaned their snow shoes against the outside saloon wall and hurried inside before the race began at seven.

Because there was no keeping kids away from an event like the Sadie Hawkin's Dance, Dad and Willy had outfitted the café for the younger set.

The top of the partition door which connected the café to the pool room had been opened while the bottom remained latched shut. A huge pot of hot chocolate sat lidded in the kitchen, and two tables of munchies and drinks were set up along a wall in the café.

From left to right, an ice-filled washtub sat loaded with cans of soda pop, then came a huge pitcher of summershine, the non-alcoholic version of a cocktail Dad had created to break the blues of cabin fever. Bowls of pretzels, chips and chewy popcorn came next beside stacks of board games and decks of cards. We kids welcomed the chance to goof-off, play games, listen to music and scarf munchies into the late night hours while our adult counterparts tore up the wooden floor next door.

By seven o'clock, a varied assortment of regulars and not-so regulars had accumulated inside the saloon. Skeeter and Grody had taken up residence at the pool table with three imported ladies from Bituminous. Crazy Jake and Boris predictably slumped over the bar. Peevil, a sack of nerves, also stood near the pool table, keeping one eye rotated toward the café for signs of chaos instigated by Stretch or Stomp.

Ray, Jill, Sol and Dot sat together at a table, while Doorite and Elvira took up another table near the fireplace.

Although I recognized most of the patrons, there were two I hadn't seen before. Al informed me that the big woman with tiny, quick eyes and long dark hair was Treehouse Bulla. She was accompanied by Kodiak Hud, a tall, quiet man who, despite his scant thirty years, was engulfed by a head and face full of silver fur. He lived back in Obsidian Basin and had found Bulla several months before, living in a tree house along the highway a few miles outside of Granite. They now shared his cabin up in the wilderness on Kodiak Mountain. His hatchet also rested in the lockbox.

Miss Dixie and her husband sat at the bar while Big John stared into his bourbon two stools down.

Georgia flounced in wearing Wes and an emerald-green satin dress with a plunging neckline revealing most of her upper assets. They sat in the corner smoldering at one another while Wes, once again, tuned his guitar. I failed to see how Wes would be able to play *any* kind of song with drool all over his guitar strings.

Willy was tuning his fiddle and appreciating Georgia's choice of apparel while Gert subtly eyed the men-folk, casting suggestive glances toward a certain Crazy Jake who, looking around, had taken on a sudden sallow hue.

Enis came into the saloon five minutes ahead of Milly and took a seat by the fireplace. Strategically placing his fedora, scarf and wool overcoat in the seat beside him, he quickly affixed an apprehensive eye on Boris's back, inadvertently knocking over his cocktail when Mother placed it on a napkin beside him.

Tic was lining up cassettes behind the bar to play when the band took a break. Lucinda, smiling seductively and taking a long drag off her skinny, brown cigar, lifted a bottle of vodka off the liquor shelves for Boris.

Drinks continued to pass around the dim interior along with friendly slaps on the back and occasional streams of hearty belly laughs and feminine giggles. Hank Williams' mournful brays shot through the low-roaring crowd as Willy climbed onto a table, rang the dinner 'triangle' from the café wall and sounded the call, "Any ladies lookin' for a date or wantin' to trade up, git outside and git ready to grab you a pardner! *Yeeeeehawww!*"

Everyone rushed the door, and, once outside, wild eyes flashed in the glow of the illuminating mercury light. Us kids, jacked-up on sugary drinks, cut up like a herd of hyenas and quickly assembled along the boardwalk to take in the exhibition. With no one in our age range to pursue, Al and I casually lingered near the edge of the parking lot, poised to drag Skeeter or Grody through the railing should one of them stumble near enough.

All along the boardwalk in front of the saloon the crowd was getting rowdy. Snow now blanketed the ground in a dense mantle, and the night air, still swirling with falling snow, thrummed with the tenor of animated expectation.

A few of the men were strapping on snowshoes. Gert

and Bulla each hoisted a booted foot onto the railing and warmed up by performing lunges. Suddenly, everyone stopped and looked up the driveway.

A beat-up, green pickup was pulling in off the county road — oddly enough, from the direction of Hardrock. Strange, because I thought all the locals had been accounted for. I heard a few low exchanges and saw Dad nod to Crazy Jake, move his feet apart and rest his thumbs in his gun belt as he leaned against the hitching rail out in front of the saloon.

"Who's that?" I asked Al, standing beside me.

"Can't tell. I think it's Pickanaxe Pete."

"Who's he?"

"Bad dude. My dad said he killed some guy up in Wyoming, but he never went to jail."

We watched as the truck pulled into the drive, drifted a little sideways and slid to a stop just shy of the snowbank which had been plowed up against the railing.

A tall, long-haired man stumbled out of the cab with an unsightly appendage he half-heartedly attempted to help from the vehicle. A rail-thin woman with fierce features clung to his left arm and cursed a blue streak when the high-heel of her boot tangled between the seat and gear shift. Kicking the gear shift, she knocked the old truck into neutral and sent it bumping lightly into the snowbank. Pete furiously shook her off his arm as she completed her ungainly descent into the snow. Staggering, he nodded to Boris, who nodded back.

Dad stepped forward, stopping Pete before he entered the saloon.

"You'll need to check any weapons before you go in,"

he said in an ominous tone I had only heard associated with conversations between him and frozen water pipes — just before pounding them into submission with a sledge hammer. This strongly suggested his margin for patience was already running into negative numbers.

"What th' hell?" Pete looked at Boris, who cast a sideways glance seeming to suggest he'd be a potential ally should Pete decide to offer a challenge.

Pete looked at Dad, who continued to stare at him. I could almost hear Sergio Leone cueing up the soundtrack to *The Good, The Bad and The Ugly*.

Pete's hag sidled up to Dad, hanging off his shoulder. She looked at Pete, taunting him, "You gonna give *the man* your *gun?*"

Ignoring her, Dad stood perfectly still as tense seconds passed. In fact, I think time itself might have stood still. Eyeballs were the only thing that moved across the whole parking lot.

Slowly, Pete unbuckled his gun belt and handed it over to Dad.

"Boot knife, too," Dad said with one thumb crooked in his own gun belt while keeping his left hand extended to receive the knife.

Pete threw a leg up onto the rail and pulled out a five inch blade. Their eyes locked again, and Pete flipped the handle toward Dad, laying the knife in his palm.

Dad walked into the bar to lock up the weapons as the hag staggered back over to Pete. Hanging on his shoulder, she whispered something under a mass of hair. He shoved her away, and she staggered right back like a magnet.

Willy rescued the mood with a resounding shout, "All you men line up in the parking lot. Gals, get a toe hold, 'cause we're about to let 'er rip!"

The tension was immediately forgotten as Skeeter, Grody, Crazy Jake, Boris, Doorite, Sol, Hud, Willy, Enis, Ray, Tic and Big John waffled over the deepening snow and took up their positions in the parking lot.

Dad and Mother returned to the saloon and moved a few tables against the walls to make room for the dance. Skeeter, Grody, Wes and Ty had previously moved the pool table over against the wall in the pool room.

Buster stayed inside the bar, but didn't seem to mind that Miss Dixie had plans to run down a date in the parking lot. Pickanaxe Pete also lingered inside the bar, looking out the window while his hag disappeared into the ladies' room.

Ty and Wes stood outside, leaning on the railing, content with their dates and goading Crazy Jake who shrank behind the crowd when Gert hiked up her heavy skirt and stuffed it into her long underwear. "Look out, Red," she cried. "You kin *ruuuun*... but you *cain't hide!*"

Everyone cheered, and Willy — catching a glimpse of a hungry-eyed Peevil — shouted, *"RUN!"*

Snow churned three feet in the air as men scattered in all directions, peeling out as best they could in the calf-deep snow. Any advantage of height was lost in the drifts, and most of the women, treading lighter in the snow than many of their male targets, were almost immediately upon them.

The only exception was Bulla who had picked up a long

piece of firewood stacked by the saloon door and made up for a lack of momentum by sweeping it in wide arcs. Unaware of her rear assault, Boris got nailed behind the knees which sent him reeling backward grabbing anything for stability. He seized Enis and dragged him down with him. Bulla immediately pinned both men, lying over top of them like a heavy-weight wrestler. "I got my two!" she bellowed to no one in particular.

Lucinda, fire in her eyes, dropped her head like a raging bull and leapt on Bulla's back, driving both men deeper into the snow. Bulla spun around and grabbed Lucinda by her hair, pile-driving a fist into her eye.

Milly stood on the sidelines looking aghast while her intended, Enis, made desperate muffled sounds face-down in the snow and flailed helplessly beneath a collective eight-hundred pounds top-side.

Skeeter stood still and welcomed the enthusiastic attack of two of his imports while Grody desperately tried to escape Elvira who had changed her aim in mid-stride, forsaking Doorite for a man nearly half his age.

As expected, Dot immediately secured Ray. Jill had Sol in hand within half a minute.

Big John waded a few feet out into the parking lot and waited for Miss Dixie to approach where, smiling, she reached out to take his hand saying, "Tag, you're it." He then escorted her back onto the boardwalk where they watched the remaining racers shooting back and forth across the parking lot.

Amid the chaos, Peevil backed Willy against the dumpster on the far side of the parking lot. In his attempt to escape, he ran right into the arms of Milly dashing around the other side and looking for an Enis substitute. After a brief scuffle, Milly and Peevil reluctantly agreed to share their catch.

Elvira was still in blazing pursuit of Grody who was undulating madly across the field of unplowed snow, his huge snow shoes flapping wildly as he sprinted across the parking lot. The two wooden splints in the back of the shoes crossed one another, and down he splatted. Elvira sprang like a panther, driving him deeper into the snow and securing her win. She sat on his back, stroking his long damp hair. "I got *mine!*" But, her triumph was quickly replaced by jealously when she saw Doorite parade out of the crowd on the boardwalk holding up the hand of young import number three. "Look what *I* got... er, got *me!*" he grinned.

Poor Tic. Even without his cone, he was the only one without a pursuer and walked with great dejection back into the bar.

The racers had begun to settle down and seriously consider their recent pairings along with any potential benefits or disadvantages when everyone turned toward a weird, strangled cry coming from deep in the darkened woods. The cry was immediately followed by a faint but hearty, *"I got him... YeahHOOOOOOO!"*

It was Gert, and it took a full five minutes before she led Crazy Jake, haggard from chugging waist-deep through snow, out of the woods by the sleeve of his jacket.

As the racers gathered in the saloon, Dad took Mother's hand and led her away from stoking the fireplace and onto the dance floor. "I'm dedicating this first song to this beautiful woman who let *me* catch *her* fifteen years ago, saved my life and makes it worth living every day." Mother blushed to wild applause as Dad shouted, *"Good Hearted Woman!"*

Willy broke into a wide grin, slammed his bow against the fiddle's strings three times and opened the first note with gusto.

As Dad twirled Mother across the dance floor, her long, blue Gunne Sax dress whirling, Ty seconded the sentiment by whooping and raising his beer in a toast to Abbey singing with Wes on stage.

The party was already in full swing by the time Big John and Miss Dixie came through the door. Buster was nodding off in the corner by the fireplace when the two stepped onto the dance floor and cuddled close for *Carefree Highway*, the first slow dance of the evening.

After the song, someone from the crowd shouted, *"Whiskey River!"* Abbey leaned over to Ty for a quick smooch and he sneaked a pat on her behind before heading to the bar to freshen her drink. At the café next door, we kids were settling in for an entertaining evening of our own.

Bucky and Dudley, were laboring over the construction of a village built entirely of objects like sugar and jelly packs, mustard bottles and toothpicks borrowed from table tops. Stretch, Stomp and Skidmark were hunkered in the corner of the café like a troupe of chimps, every now and then jumping back only to lumber again into the corner in some bizarre undertaking involving wisps of smoke and the stench of burning hair.

Perched on the backs of our chairs for optimal view, Al and I peered easily over the café's split door. Sipping iced summershines and air-lobbing popcorn, we enjoyed the best seats in the house. If the saloon failed to produce sporting diversion, we were reasonably sure that, sooner or later, the three dufuses in the corner would pull something worthy of watching.

About half an hour had passed, and Al and I noted a series of tense glances cast among the crowd paired for the second slow dance of the night.

Sol dancing with Jill, and Ray dancing with Dot produced a kind of atmospheric circuitry, as vehemently accusing stares exchanged like arcing electricity between the two couples dancing next to one another.

A look of gleeful conquest beamed from Gert's face, contrasted by a blend of terror and remorse in the eyes of Crazy Jake as the couple gracelessly moved into the next turn.

Peevil, shunned by Willy, stood near the bar, violently gnashing her gum, her determination intensifying. Willy's face suggested a concern that engaging Peevil at this point could prove injurious if not fatal. Nervously, he avoided direct eye contact observing her, instead, within his peripheral vision. Milly sat just off-stage thoroughly entranced by the captive Willy and awaiting the band's break to seize a dance.

Boris, refusing to dance with Bulla, chose instead to sit with his back to the bar, nursing his bottle of vodka and intently observing Georgia, who listened to Wes but expressed flattery and strong interest in Boris' amorous gaze.

Bulla, nearly a foot taller than Enis and outweighing him by a hundred-and-twenty pounds engulfed him in her flannel-shirted bosom, his feet occasionally lifting from the dance floor as she swaddled him in sweeping circles around the room. Surfacing for air every two minutes or so, Enis' face was a landscape of frustration and fear.

Hud, cut from the coupled mix along with Buster and Tic, eyed Enis from the bar with a look neither angry nor jealous. In fact, his steady gaze toward Enis was surprisingly neutral, yet somehow hinted of concealed intent.

Doorite appeared elated with his dancing partner, which further distracted Elvira from enjoying her hard-landed catch. Neither Elvira nor Doorite seemed to notice the communication between Grody and young import number three, which indicated plans were being made to soon unite.

Pete and his hag, seated at a table by the saloon door, were engaged in what I could only assume were familiar stirrings. She had moved mostly onto his lap and divided her efforts between pawing under his shirt, intercepting his cigarette and drinking his beer. His attentions, however, seemed to be concentrated around the vicinity of the stage.

Wes had just begun picking out the riff to *Witchy Woman,* when Dad walked around the bar to bring in more firewood from outside. Suddenly, Hag leapt from Pete's lap and cut Dad off from the door. Hooking her finger in the front of his gun belt, she pulled herself closer like a slithering eel. Looking up at Dad, who was in the process of pushing her away, she then cast a suggestive glance at Pete.

From out of nowhere, with fierceness flashing in her eyes, Mother appeared beside Hag and offered a few words which seemed to encourage Hag to reclaim her station on Pete's lap. Dad continued outside, and Mother headed back to the bar.

As the song ended, Pete applauded, stood up and knocked Hag to the floor. He wandered over to the stage where the band was about to take a break. Hag lie on the floor a minute before dragging herself up onto the chair where she immediately began looking around for Pete. When she found him, he was over by the fireplace talking to Abbey. Ty had gone over to the bar to get Abbey a glass of water, and as a song began to play on the stereo, Al's and my jaw dropped at what happened next.

Pete put his arm around Abbey and rested his hand someplace *much* more conspicuous than her shoulder, not only lingering but aggressively exploring. Abbey backed away and, to our amazement, took a full-fisted swing at her unwanted suitor. *POW!* Pete went flying over a chair and onto the raised hearth of the screened fireplace. There, he quickly recovered and grabbed the poker.

In that instant, all the tensions of that long, dark, snowy winter, all the frustrations of that mismatched, expectant night came unwound in one un-orchestrated, tremendous release of energy.

Ty tossed Abbey's water glass on the floor and knocked over two standing microphones on his way to Pete. At the same time, Hag went airborne, leaping over tables and coming to rest, like a skinny bird of prey, on Ty's back.

Ty grabbed the poker out of Pete's hand and threw a punch, while Hag clawed at Ty's face from behind. Pete ducked and jumped a chair in an evasive move, while Abbey jumped on Hag and grappled to break her grip on Ty.

"C'mere you coward, bastard!*"* Ty choked, fighting to

free himself of the two women sparring on his back.

By now, the rest of the crowd realized what was going on and took it as an invitation to commence on a little of their own free-wheeling frivolity. Sol took a shot at Ray, while Jill and Dot clawed at one another, grabbing each other's hair and brawling between tables. Peevil flew from her perch at the bar and lit into Willy, slapping his face and screaming like a wild banshee.

Gert came sprinting toward the café, where we kids were now gathered around the door taking in the spectacle. Oblivious to our presence, she reached around the door frame and grabbed a ten-inch cast iron skillet hanging on the wall then turned and raced back for the bar, her long, heavy skirt flapping in the wind. She tripped over Enis, who was diving under the pool table in an effort to escape both Bulla and Hud. Gert sailed into a far wall as the skillet went skidding in the opposite direction across the floor.

"Get out of there, you little wimp!" Bulla grabbed hold of Enis's feet just before he disappeared under the pool table. Heaving him out like a wet sheet twisted in a washing machine, the more she grunted the more he clung to the far leg of the table now lurching and scraping across the floor.

"*Aaaaiiieeee!*" his screeching crescendo rose like a top note accentuating the generally riotous yelling permeating all three rooms.

Lucinda raced over from her post behind the bar with Tic and hoisted her leg, intending to drive her three-inch boot heel into Bulla's back. Hud intercepted Lucinda from behind around her middle then lifted and rolled with her onto the pool table where he came to rest straddled over top. Lucinda shrieked then stopped. Suddenly, she grabbed both sides of his beard and yanked him close for a hard kiss.

Tic, blinded by rage, shot from behind the bar and headed straight for the pool table.

Dad had reentered the bar by this time and was in the process of dividing Doorite and Elvira, who had nearly knocked him over coming to blows near the door.

Skeeter and Grody were punching each other out, over their standard 'no apparent reason', while the three imports cheered them on.

Through the mass of flying hair, swinging fists and crashing bar stools, Al saw Hag run around behind the bar and grab the lock-box. She was trying to break off the lock by beating on it with a piece of firewood. Hag rose, cursing at Mother, who was leaning across the bar yelling for her to drop the box and get out from behind the counter.

Next thing we saw, Mother stood on the bar's brass foot-rail and reached across the counter, grabbing Hag half by her hair and half by her shirt. She dragged Hag across the bar and clubbed her cold with Boris's vodka bottle then calmly walked around behind the bar and bent to examine the lock-box.

Boris, meanwhile, grabbed Georgia who was standing on top of a table cheering on one of the revelers. He threw her, screaming, over his shoulder and lumbered toward the door like a sasquatch. Wes headed him off and swung a chair across his iron belly. The chair bounced off, and Boris, unfazed, kept on walking with Georgia wriggling, kicking and slapping his back.

CLANG! Gert nailed Peevil with the skillet! Peevil

staggered and grabbed Gert, head-butting her before the two busted through the door of the ladies' room. Stretch and Stomp, crowding the café doorway with the rest of us wide-eyed spectators, were over the partition like two rabid wolverines zeroed in on a target.

Pete found the poker and held it high, ready to skewer Ty when Dad grabbed Pete from behind in a full-nelson, wrenching them both around and running Pete through the crowd, *"Make a hole — I'm comin' through!"* The two ran toward the door, scattering people and chairs. Dad rammed the door open and drove Pete's head into the snowbank in front of his truck.

BANG! Mother fired a shot from behind the bar, right through the roof of the saloon.

Holy cripes.

The whole place froze, and Al and I looked at each other in disbelief. Georgia bit Boris on his shoulder and managed to flail loose of his grip. He grunted, grabbed the only standing beer bottle in the place and guzzled down its contents.

Mother stood on the bar, tiny but ferocious. "Everybody just *SETTLE THE HELL DOWN! Now...* I'm going to put Hank on the stereo and everybody is going to help clean this place up. Everybody's *cut off* until we're done. *Is that clear?"*

Everyone nodded, even Boris.

Dad stood in the doorway watching Pete. "Get your head back in that snowbank, asswipe. I said you can take it out when you cool off."

Like a pack of wild animals, thirty-three savage beasts were instantly calmed by the familiar melodious strains of *Your*

Cheatin' Heart.

When Pete's head came out of the snow, Dad sent him and Hag back up to Pickanaxe Peak — barred from the saloon indefinitely. Pete vowed, in villainous fashion, that none of us had seen the last of him, which would naturally prove to be true.

Once the saloon was put back in order, the band kicked off with *So Into You.* Instead of dancing with the one they caught, everyone decided to dance with the one they brought; and, as sprinkles of snow filtered down from the hole in the roof, all was once again right with our world.

Monday morning, on the hour-long bus ride into school, I pondered the question on my crumpled science homework assignment which read: *"Conduct an experiment, and describe the chemical and/or physical reactions of matter when subjected to a catalyst in a closed environment."*

Since I derived great satisfaction in drawing academic abstractions into my own personal frame of reference, correlating the two in ways which I found if not educational, at least entertaining, I wrote:

Introducing thirty-some intimately familiar, unstable persons to a closed environment — that is, a saloon snowed-in on a Saturday night in February;

...and adding the agitating element of alcohol

...and adding the catalyzing element of an instigating creep copping a feel off the band's singer

...produced the predictable result of a skillet-banging, pool-table-clinging, fist and bar stool-swinging, table-vaulting and pistol-shooting full-on riot.

Once the catalyst, who went by the name of Pickanaxe Pete, was recovered and removed from the mix, however,

...and the stabilizing element of Hank Williams was introduced,

...this experiment showed that the physical matter returned to a semi-neutral state.

Al read my report, cracked up at remembering the melee, threw her blank paper away, and we added both our names to the top of the page.

We giggled all the way to school, recounting the detailed and stunning events of Saturday night and doubting seriously that our scientific explanation of the "mid-winter dance experiment" could be fully appreciated by anyone who didn't already have an unnatural affinity for the late, great Hank.

Winter Hazards

Among mountain folk, the mere mention of *winter hazards* conjures images of hunkering around the weather radio and listening to crackling reports like, "Tonight through Thursday, an arctic air mass moves through the region. Expect eighteen to twenty-five inches of new snow accumulation accompanied by thirty to forty mile per hour wind gusts, blowing and drifting snow with wind chills to five below zero. By midday today, roads will become icy and snow-packed, and all mountain passes above 7,000 feet, if open, will require chains."

These reports, while projecting some certain sense of doom, made the otherwise wickedly consequential whims of mother nature, from November through March, somewhat predictable.

Hearing the NOAA weather man's calm and authoritative voice (now, unfortunately mechanized) drone daily from the kitchen table brought feelings of reassurance and familiarity, and definitely inspired our adult counterparts to check and recheck food stocks, wood supplies and snow chains.

For me, Al, and the thousands of other kids scattered up and down the Rocky Mountain chain, winter hazards did not represent our concern for freezing temperatures, deep snow nor treacherous ice upon the highways. Instead, winter inspired our feeble faculties to weigh these physical hazards against their potential for fun.

The first pristine snow flakes, delivered suddenly from a foggy white sky in winter's extraordinary climatic shift, fluttered lightly, almost gaily, through the cold, thin air sometime in early November only to gently poof upon the frozen ground and find themselves pounced upon by the waxed runners of every sled-owning kid from New Mexico to Montana.

Comprised of only edges and inclined planes (or sledding slopes, as Al and I thought of them) the Rockies offer uniquely exhilarating recreational opportunities.

Valleys are merely inverted edges, serving to funnel you and snow melt toward yet another inverted edge or inclined plane. Given the surface area of slopes to edges, you are statistically much more likely to find yourself on a slope of some sort, which is why snow boots, tire chains and other traction-enabling devices are such an important part of winter gear.

Once you begin a sledding excursion, without a strong traction and breaking device, you might slip into a valley and continue funneling through the mountains until you reach the plains of Kansas, Mexico or Nevada.

Given that our house, the inn, the county road and Hardrock, itself, were all hewn from the same slope surrounded by even more slopes rising and falling at all angles and altitudes, Al and I relished the annual glazing of every surface suitable for sled-running.

There are few objects that cannot be pressed into service as a sledding device. The finest, most efficient and, more importantly, cheapest device is one which is readily available at most hardware stores sometime after September: The deceptively simple yet versatile sheet of thick plastic.

In the mountains, it is common winter practice to cover the windows of one's home with thick plastic sheeting. When stapled to window frames, the tough plastic becomes an effective barrier against winter's chill.

Referred to simply as "4 mil.", one will often hear the phrase worked into winter conversations. An example: "Where the hell's the 4 mil.? Where are Lisa and Al? Is that them sliding down the driveway on the 4 mil.?"

4 mil. was favored by us kids as a sledding device for another very important reason: supreme portability.

When traversing edges and slopes, walking can prove difficult as well as inconvenient. Pulling a 4x4 sheet of plastic from your pocket and seizing opportunities for frictionless mobility could easily shave twenty minutes off a twenty-five minute walk to Al's house or the lake.

Of course, no gift from the gods of winter is ever without its counter-measures intended to prevent its abuse. The lack of anything resembling a steering or breaking device could not only add those twenty minutes back onto your travel time, but even more should you lose control and launch off a cliff somewhere beyond your plotted route. This design flaw in the 4 mil. could easily contribute another hour or so to your estimated arrival time by requiring you to dig out of a snowbank and scratch your way back to your point of departure.

For this reason, coats were sometimes substituted as sleds. Nylon coats were best, providing if not durability then much greater velocity than wool. Further, Al and I discovered that by placing our coats under our rear ends and wedging our feet snuggly against the armpit seams, we could navigate steeper inclines while employing the sleeves as a relatively effective steering apparatus. Unfortunately, inferior stitching reduced the life-span of these types of sleds and led to the accumulation of vests in the coat closet — a phenomenon Mother quickly put an end to.

Since coats were poorly designed to absorb the sometimes enthusiastic maneuvering which accompanied our make-shift snow ships, we kids would often relent to the cumbersome transport and maintenance of the conventional sled.

Certain geographic areas of the world favor certain sled designs for various practical and cultural reasons.

The most desirable feature of a sled, however, is that it possess a framework capable of bearing weight while sliding upon an icy or snow-packed surface.

Breaking and steering are often considered luxury appointments, unnecessary to the intent of the basic design, which is why inner tubes, toboggans and disk sleds are perennial favorites among children.

For a while, Al and I benefited from a standard wooden, steel-runner sled we found stashed in the recesses of our barn over the summer. And for a while, it served us dutifully as we subjected it to all sorts of experimental activities for which it was never really intended.

For example, the classic wooden-planked, steel-runner sled is primarily designed to be sat upon in a normal fashion and ridden in an upright manner with one's feet pressed upon the forward steering device which acts as rudder and brake. This type of sled, however, falsely assumes that one will not attempt a sled run over inappropriate terrain.

Al and I, craving a bit more thrill from our sled-riding experience, considered *only* those slopes which seemed inappropriate.

To enhance our sense of excitement, Al and I often rode double, exercising an array of convenient positions. On the steel-runner, I nearly always commanded the steering, which necessitated riding one of two ways: 1) belly-down on the bottom in a double-decker fashion, or 2) in the sitting, forward position. Al, assuming the top or the rear position, navigated obstacles or commanded our unique, third-stage rope-braking device.

Occasionally, I would assume the belly-down, bottom position, and Al would assume the sitting rear position, riding astride the backs of my thighs and wedging her boots into my armpits. This was a useful solution for unique situations that called for both vertical and horizontal stability in the form of weight distribution.

In any position on the steel-runner, our first-stage braking device consisted of the on-board deployment of the "quad-groover", which was as much a technique as a physical device. In our version of a method first popularized by *The Flintstones*, the quad-groover involved both our sets of feet thrust downward, gouging four deep grooves into the snow simultaneously.

One desirable benefit of this method (hence its first-stage position) was that the actual braking devices themselves (that is, our feet) were more readily available in an on-demand situation and less likely to snap off in the midst of a challenging one.

In a configuration of me on my stomach and Al sitting on the backs of my thighs, here was how the quad-groover worked: Approximately 1.4 seconds before a potentially fatal impact, I shouted the command, "BRAKE!" at which time Al's lower extremities almost instantaneously shot out from behind my armpits and slammed into the icy ground on either side. Near to or at this very moment, I would release the lock on my knees, formerly employed to hold my feet aloft, and drive my toes into the ground while wrenching at the wooden steering device in an effort to skid into an effective stop.

While this method was superior when effective, it was often unreliable. Coordinating the steering while simultaneously deploying my portion of the quad-groover could be challenging, given that I often had a hundred and ten pounds of highly engaged passenger flailing about on my back and pulling on my ears as if they were some kind of reins.

The quad-groover was also plagued with a couple of engineering problems. Because of Al's higher position on the sled, her view of the course was significantly different than mine. This led to Al's occasional tendency to over-anticipate my "BRAKE!" command and throw our steering into a premature spin as she impulsively sought to gain braking control. Worse yet, in her constant preoccupation with the course ahead, Al would sometimes fail to recall my placement on the sled beneath her; consequently, she would forget the proper deployment of braking procedure and simply drive the heels of her moon boots into the back of my head.

Probably the best solution for this problem would have been for Al to give the "BRAKE!" command, but her tolerance for risk was less enough than mine, that to do so would have rendered our rides far less thrilling.

After ten or so runs down the hill, the quad-groover became an unstable method altogether, as its successful deployment left great trenches crisscrossing the run. While this lent an exhilarating aspect to ramping over frozen wakes, the great ruts bounced our feet, negating our braking system and further tended to seize the sled runners, confounding our steering. This led to the activation of our second-stage braking device.

Our secondary breaking device was a simple, voice-activated system whereby I or Al would inform the other of us to "Roll! Roll! Roll!"

When time was of the essence, however, the second-stage breaking device was often deemed inadequate or cumbersome, leading to the third, emergency breaking device consisting of a three-and-a-half-foot rope tied to either side of the steering rudders.

Activation of the third breaking system required that Al and I act in tandem to bring our knees forward along the sides of the sled and rear dramatically upward with Al maintaining strict tension on the rope sufficient to lift the sled into the air resulting in a forced dismount while dislodging and flipping the sled over our heads behind us. Naturally, Al had to coordinate this complicated maneuver while under great duress, tremendous speed, and less than comfortable physical circumstances. Although this third device was reliably deployed even without voice command, it was indeed difficult. So, sometimes, Al and I considered it easier to, for instance, squish down in the manner of mice and thread the fence at the end of our favorite sled run.

In the pursuit of greater thrills and new challenges, we eventually traded our old runner sled for a new trailer-type sled Dad built for transporting hay bales and other supplies. It was made of sandwiched sheets of 4x8 plywood attached to a buttressed 2x4 frame riding on four, full-length downhill skis scrounged from a dumpster in Granite. It weighed three-hundred-fifty pounds, but this particular design finally allowed Al and me to ride upright or horizontally side by side.

An obvious drawback of this design, however, was its weight. In order to launch the monstrosity from a necessary level position, a great deal of thrust was needed in the form of two kids, scuffing, scootching and grunting forward with all their pitiful strength. Most of the time, our efforts failed to produce the initial power needed to urge the sled forward, which, of course, forced us to search for ever steeper hillsides. Locating a suitable and nearby slope was difficult, but once located, we would teeter the bulk upon the rim, simultaneously leap aboard and continue our exhilarating descent.

Its tremendous weight and altogether absence of brakes or steering added new dimensions to our sense of excitement, but, unfortunately, also forced us into a week of indentured servitude repairing a quarter mile of damaged fencing.

Considering our inability to properly weigh the risks certain winter hazards might hold for us, Mother constantly reminded Al and me of the consequences we could face should we ignore her many grave warnings.

She was always telling us, "Don't eat that, you'll ruin your dinner."; "Don't hold it that way, you'll cut off your thumb."; "Leave that alone or you'll be grounded." Some mothers warn their kids every winter: "Get in this house or you'll catch your death." Mother always preferred: "You'd better get back in this house or you'll lower your resistance." Some might assume she meant resistance to catching a cold. We always figured she meant lower our resistance to temptation, since our winter activities held all sorts of delicious perils outside the realm of what most mothers could imagine.

Periodically, our Maker must, too, remind us of our mortality. For us kids, this reminder generally came once every season or so. In the spring, while tempting the newly accessible waters of Quartz Creek, we would forget how fast and deep icy, murky snow-melt could rush down from Pickanaxe Peak. In the summer, we would forget on-coming traffic as we barreled our bikes full-bore down Deadman's Hill. In the fall, we forgot how cold and deep an early snow could settle over a tent in the yard. And, in the winter, well… winter was a time of unique stupidity.

Dad, Al and I were walking up from the back of the inn where we had just finished hauling stacks of old newspapers into the crawlspace. The papers made good fire starter, but they were also useful for winterizing water pipes — a debatable function, given Dad's perpetual struggle against frozen water lines under the inn.

Al scooped some snow with her inky hands and packed it into a fat, black snow ball.

"Look how cool!" she said.

Dad grinned, "It's the dreaded black pearl snowball..." He scooped a wad of snow and zinged it at us. His speed and aim, once employed by the Navy football team, was wickedly accurate. Snow blasted off my left shoulder and exploded across my face.

I glanced at Al, "Are my teeth black?" then shouted after Dad who had taken off at a trot for the house, "You'd *better* run, you weed! And you better hope I don't fix your oatmeal anytime soon!"

POW! A snowball ricocheted off Al's thigh. We looked up to see Dad peeking across Big Red's hood.

Al double-packed her black pearl and whizzed it across the parking lot, missing her target by two feet.

Dad sprung up behind Red, "HA! *Missed!*" He zinged another that detonated against my midsection.

"Oh, that is IT!"

Al and I rushed the hill, securing our position behind a boulder and firing four shots in rapid succession.

Dad shot out from behind Big Red, roaring, "*RAAARARRGG!*" Like some crazed animal with gritted teeth and wild eyes, he charged our nest with a barrage of saved up ammunition.

"*Eeeeeee!!*" we screamed for the woods where we quickly exhausted ourselves churning through thigh-deep snow.

"Hee hee," Al sniggered, flopping over backward once we heard the front door close and knew Dad was safely in the kitchen pursuing coffee. "What do you want to do now?" she asked.

I ruffled ice crystals out of my hair, "I don't know."

"Hey, I know," Al spoke slowly, deliberately puffing small vapor clouds, "let's go in and get some hot chocolate and then go sledding."

"Nah," I replied, "there's no where good to sled."

"Yeah, that's true," Al pondered, waving her fingers through the fog of her breath.

"Hey, I know!" I brightened, "Let's build a chute!"

Chute was the original name for the luge, just like *idiot* was the original name for winter athlete.

Long before luge sledding ever became a professional sport, Al and I invented it and broke the world land speed record on that optimistically bright March day of our pitifully ignorant youth.

"Okay," Al said, and we were off.

We searched for suitably inappropriate slopes around the house, finally favoring the twenty-percent grade which descended fifty yards or so off the north end of the inn.

"Wait! I got it!" I said, *"Dark Mountain!"*

"No *way*," Al said.

"WAY! When we build the chute, we can build a huge ramp at the bottom and jump the creek!"

"No *WAY*," said Al.

"C'mon, if we're gonna build it, we might as well do it right." Wasn't Dad always haranguing us with that very notion? "It'll be so cool!"

"Okay," said Al, and we were off.

Unbeknownst to any of our parents, we trudged up the slippery slope of Dark Mountain which was so steep it clung to a blanket of snow only long enough to monthly disrobe in a torrent of ice and rock.

"Hang on to that limb, there," I nodded in the direction of the tiny tree, offering Al a hand-hold as we practically lie vertically against the surface of the precipice sixty feet above the creek, "it looks pretty strong."

Al lunged for the tree and worked her booted foot between two boulders. "I'm not going any higher on this stupid mountain. This is it."

"Yeah," I said, looking down at the trickle of ice blue water far below, "this ought to do it. Let's start here and work our way down."

As Al and I snaked and scooted our way toward the bottom of the mountain, we shoved snow and packed it along the sides creating a smooth, narrow chute flanked by three foot high walls of snow. On curves we ramped it even higher. "I tell you, Al... Al?"

"I'm over here — grab my foot in case I slide past you..."

"Right — anyway, this is going to be great! We're gonna get some serious speed up on this monster! Whooeee it's — whoops, here, wedge yourself sideways between the sidewalls, like me — anyway, man, we should have thought to bring the sled."

"Whatever," Al said. "I just want to get this thing built so we can get off this mountain."

"Not till we go *down* it, right?"

"*No.* I mean when we're done *building* this stupid thing. We can come back tomorrow and try it out."

"Are you crazy? We can't come back tomorrow after all this work! An avalanche will probably take it out by then."

"All right," Al conceded. "One run. Then we go home."

"Great! See, we're already pretty far back down. Here's where we'll start building the ramp."

While the chute only took thirty minutes to scoop from the vertical field, Al and I labored for three more hours gathering and packing enough snow to create a gargantuan ramp at the base of our run.

Our ramp began twenty feet or so up from the creek. We worked from the bottom up off of a huge boulder, five feet across, figuring it would give us the best launch to clear the creek which, this time of year, was only about twelve feet across and a couple feet deep.

Finally, the run was complete, and Al and I trudged back across the creek to admire our masterpiece from afar.

"Hmmm, it looks pretty puny from here," I said.

"Yeah, I know," Agreed Al, disappointed.

"Still afraid to go down it?"

"Nah, not really. I thought it'd be bigger than that."

"Oh well. It'll still be fun. Let's do it!"

"Okay," said Al, and off we went, picking our way back up the frozen, rocky face, careful not to mar the perfect finish on the chute.

Once at the top of the run, it again looked massive, long and steep.

"I don't know," said Al, suddenly aware of our mortality

and how it seemed to be inextricably influenced by poor judgment when we collectively embarked upon activities to occupy our roving intellects.

"It just *looks* scary from up here," I reassured her. "Remember how pathetically small it looked from down by the creek? In fact, it's too bad we don't have any 4 mil. Let's slide down on our coats to get up more speed. I think we're going to need it to clear the creek."

Reluctantly, Al removed her coat and layered the bottom half of it over the top half of mine, creating a slicker sliding surface which was presumed to greatly reduce any drag.

As was our custom, Al took up the rear, so, should anything horrible befall me, she would either have a moment to abandon the effort or benefit from the cushion of my limp body.

We braced ourselves by pressing our outstretched feet against the sidewalls of the chute. I glanced over my shoulder at Al. "We'd better wrap our coats around us and tie the arms in a knot."

"Don't talk about arms tied in knots, Joe."

"Okay, ready?"

"No."

"C'mon. Ready?"

"*Rrreeeaddyyy...*" her voice trailed off into a high crescendo, and I could tell from past experience she was speaking with fiercely squinted eyes.

"Okay go, go, go!" I shouted, scooting us forward for maximum thrust and pulling in my feet. I hadn't accounted for the inertia an object is capable of possessing even prior to descending a steep slope, and before I could retract both feet, the friction from my left foot spun both Al and I into an ungainly tumble — something wisely disallowed by current sporting rules.

"*Aaaiiee!*" Al screeched, grabbing my eyebrows and clawing her way over my chin and around to my backside. I rolled under her and we spun down the slope two and half turns before regaining our original position, though reversed, with Al now assuming the lead.

"*Lay back, lay back!!*" I bellowed, grabbing Al's shirt collar with both hands and pulling her toward me, as if I were reigning in a run-away horse. This poorly considered action, however, only served to speed our now aerodynamic and relentless drop.

"*Aaaackckkk I 'ant vreave! Aaaiieeeeee et o, et o! aaiieeee*"

I gripped her collar harder as Al's hair whipped my face and we sailed into the first turn. "*Whhhaaaaaaaaeeeeeeee!*" I shrieked, contributing to Al's wailing chorus.

Al clawed her fingernails along the sidewall and we pumped our quad-groovers in a useless effort to gain traction and slow our frenzied plummet in altitude.

Al's screeching, and perhaps mine, seemed to dislodge a few of the lesser stable rocks and shrubs, since a few of them rushed past us and one or two managed to hitch a brief ride in my lap. It was hard to discern any avalanche activity given our riotous verbal assault on the still, winter atmosphere.

Spitting out pine needles and rounding another curve, we rose along the outside edge, cresting the top of the chute which slowed us to approximately a hundred-twenty miles an hour before we ricocheted toward a straight-away, quickly regaining any lost velocity.

Al had become quite reflective, only emitting tiny squeaks as we briefly slammed into each subsequent embankment.

The world streaked by as the mountain became a blur of white. With a grip on Al like an anaconda, we sailed curve after curve like melting butter around the inside of a hot skillet, faster and faster then... we *rose* in a rapid and wholly unexpected way which seemed to meld our heads directly to our shoulders.

It occurred to me that I should scream, if nothing else than to break the monotony of terror, but my tongue, previously frozen and hanging out of my mouth, was now solidly cemented between my teeth. Al was mashed down too, so I could clearly see over her head some distance beyond, but, strangely, there didn't seem to be any recognizable landmarks.

It was then that time seemed to slow, and Al and I appeared to be suspended in space. Al's hair took on the graceful plumery of a mermaid underwater. We did it, I thought, though without any great feelings of accomplishment. We've broken the speed of sound. I looked down in this uniquely animated and suspended condition to see the tops of trees passing stoically beneath us. Then the creek... then more trees... I looked up.

Al and I had separated, and she was embracing the sky while appearing to scale a huge invisible ladder.

I decided I ought to climb too, given I was unclear on the circumstances surrounding how we came to be airborne and figured Al knew the proper thing to do.

Suddenly, the ground came into broader view, quickly filling more and more of my field of vision until I found myself plunged face first into a six-foot snowbank.

I heard Al plop into the bank next to me, sounding rather like a cue ball dropped from some height into a bowl of peanut butter.

All might have been lost were it not for the divine and fortunate arrangement which left two-thirds of our bodies protruding from the snow, useful in leveraging backward exertion.

I rested vacuum sealed in the snowbank, contemplating all the sensory excitement encasement in cement had to offer, then instinctively began seeking air and light at the surface. When my efforts met with grass under my fingernails, I wrenched my elbows free and began digging in the other direction. Finally, gasping for air, Al and I surfaced nearly simultaneously.

Wordlessly, we turned and took in the view across the creek. No evidence of our perilous journey. What had once been a magnificent chute, now rested silently beneath twenty feet of compacted snow and ice forming a tidy dam across Quartz Creek and ending some fifty yards behind us.

We slowly pulled Al's coat out of the rubble and listlessly dragged mine from the lower branches of a spruce.

Al and I walked the long but sweet trek back up to the house, visions of hot cocoa and miniature marshmallows drifting in and out of our minds intermixed with harrowing flashbacks of blurred tree tops, tumbling boulders and clawed snow chutes.

Al jerked involuntarily and wobbled into a snowbank.

I walked to within a few feet of the house then suddenly went limp, crawling the rest of the way up the steps and through the front door.

"Good grief," Mother said, taking the opportunity to swat a tree branch out of my hair with a dishtowel on her way to the pantry. "Where have you two been? It's thirty degrees out there. If you don't watch it, you're going to lower your resistance."

Though I mindlessly mumbled my agreement with her observation, I knew Al and I were now uniquely able to resist the lure of winter hazards well beyond this season and at least part-way into the next.

Hardrock Summershine

(For one 12-ounce goblet.)

In my humble opinion, this is the best cabin fever blues-busting drink ever invented with or without the vodka...

Begin with a large goblet style glass. To this, add:
Enough finely cracked or crushed ice to firmly pack the goblet (about 20 medium cubes).
Remove the ice to a shaker.
Note: Use only cold liquids if possible.
To the shaker, add 1 ounce of simple syrup (1 part real sugar + 1 part water heated to dissolve then cooled)
1 ounce filtered water (or seltzer water)
2 TBS lemon juice (fresh squeezed lemons are best)
1 ounce premium vodka (this can be left out for the non-alcoholic version, with the balance made up of filtered plain or seltzer water)
Shake vigorously in shaker for 10-15 seconds.
Fill goblet with cocktail.
Add a small drizzle (1/4 tsp) of maraschino cherry juice in the center of the drink and garnish with a small sprig of spearmint (lightly pressed to release slight fragrance), a stemmed maraschino cherry and a lemon twist.
Serve with a smile and a toast to the forthcoming summer.
Please be of legal age when consuming alcohol and enjoy responsibly.

Wes' Windmill Card Trick

Note: this trick is complicated, so you may want to read through it a couple of times before walking through it step by step.

Shuffle a complete deck — discarding the jokers.

STEP ONE
Create three vertical rows of seven cards each — placing the cards face-up from the top of the row to the bottom of the row, slightly overlapping as you go. Discard the remainder.

Have someone secretly choose a card from one of the rows, pointing to the row the card is in (but keeping the card itself a secret). Instruct them to keep the same card throughout the trick. *(You may wish to have the person secretly note what card they selected on a small piece of paper, folded securely and placed on the table as confirmation.)*

Collect the cards row by row, face-up and in order, making sure the row that contains the selected card is in the middle. *(Note, It doesn't seem to matter how you layer each row in your hand, as long as the selected row falls in the middle. However, if you have trouble executing this trick, you may try collecting the rows systematically either clockwise or counter-clockwise... again, being careful to keep the chosen row in the middle.)*

STEP TWO

Keeping the cards face-up, redistribute the cards into three vertical rows of seven cards apiece. This time, however, you will place each card left to right across all three rows until you complete three vertical rows of seven cards each.

Have the person find their card and point only to the row it is in.

Again, collect each row, face-up and in order, being careful to keep the selected row in the middle.

STEP THREE

Keeping the cards face-up, redistribute the cards into three vertical rows of seven cards apiece. Once again, you will place each card left to right across all three rows until you complete three vertical rows of seven cards each.

Have the person find their card and point only to the row it is in.

Again, collect each row, face-up and in order, being careful to keep the selected row in the middle.

STEP FOUR

Turn the cards over.

Distribute the cards face-down into windmill configurations comprised of four cards each. Count your cards as you distribute. The eleventh card will be the selected card. Remember the placement of this card.

You should have enough cards to create 5 windmills, with an extra card left over. Discard the extra card.

STEP FIVE

Do you recall which card is the 11th card? I hope so. The idea from here forward is to manipulate the person you are playing with into eliminating all the cards from the 21 cards presented except for the one they have selected.

Begin by having the person select 3 windmills. If they choose a windmill containing their chosen card, discard the other two windmills. If they choose three windmills — none of which contain their chosen card, then discard those three.

Continue in this fashion, having the person choose first windmills, then two cards at a time, until they have gotten down to choosing between two remaining cards.

Depending upon which final card they choose, you know that one will be the card they selected. Have them choose a final card and either discard it or, if it is the 11th card, reveal it.

Though I have no idea how this trick works, I've never known it to fail when performed correctly. Seemingly impossible, it continues to surprise me.

Note: Windmill configurations are optional. You could just count out and reveal the eleventh card. However, because you control the elimination process, the windmill aspect adds another layer of mystery to this already amazing trick.